BY MICHAEL J. SULLIVAN

THE LEGENDS OF THE FIRST EMPIRE

Age of Myth · Age of Swords · Age of War
Forthcoming: *Age of Legend · Age of Death · Age of Empyre*

THE RIYRIA REVELATIONS

Theft of Swords (contains *The Crown Conspiracy* and *Avempartha*)
Rise of Empire (contains *Nyphron Rising* and *The Emerald Storm*)
Heir of Novron (contains *Wintertide* and *Percepliquis*)

THE RIYRIA CHRONICLES

The Crown Tower
The Rose and the Thorn
The Death of Dulgath
The Disappearance of Winter's Daughter

STANDALONE NOVEL

Hollow World

ANTHOLOGIES

Unfettered: "The Jester" (Fantasy: The Riyria Chronicles)
Blackguards: "Professional Integrity" (Fantasy: The Riyria Chronicles)
Unbound: "The Game" (Fantasy: Contemporary)
Unfettered II: "Little Wren and the Big Forest" (Fantasy: The First Empire)
The End: Visions of the Apocalypse: "Burning Alexandria"
(Dystopian Science Fiction)
Triumph over Tragedy: "Traditions" (Fantasy: Tales from Elan)
The Fantasy Faction Anthology: "Autumn Mists" (Fantasy: Contemporary)
Help Fund My Robot Army: "Be Careful What You Wish For" (Fantasy)

Age of War

Age of War

BOOK THREE OF
The Legends of the First Empire

MICHAEL J. SULLIVAN

DEL REY
NEW YORK

Copyright © 2018 by Michael J. Sullivan
Map copyright © 2016 by David Lindroth Inc.

Published in the United States by Del Rey, an imprint of Random House, a division of Penguin Random House LLC, New York.

DEL REY and the HOUSE colophon are registered trademarks of Penguin Random House LLC.

Map by David Lindroth was originally published in *Age of Myth* by Michael J. Sullivan (New York: Del Rey, 2016).

Library of Congress Cataloging-in-Publication Data
Names: Sullivan, Michael J.- author.
Title: Age of war / Michael J. Sullivan.
Description: New York : Del Rey, [2018] | Series: The legends of the first empire ; book 3
Identifiers: LCCN 2017060618 | ISBN 9781101965399 (Hardcover) | ISBN 9781101965405 (Ebook)
Subjects: | BISAC: FICTION / Fantasy / Epic. | FICTION / Action & Adventure. | FICTION / Fantasy / Historical.
Classification: LCC PS3619.U4437 A75 2018 | DDC 813/.6—dc23
LC record available at https://lccn.loc.gov/2017060618

Printed in the United States of America on acid-free paper

randomhousebooks.com

246897531

First Edition

Designed by Christopher M. Zucker

This book is dedicated to the artist Marc Simonetti.
People are told not to judge a book by its cover, but
as long as Marc is creating them, judge away.

Contents

Author's Note

Welcome back to The Legends of the First Empire! When I started this series, I planned to write a trilogy that told the events leading up to the first conflict between men and elves. *Age of War* was slated to be the final book. As a result, you'll likely notice many plot elements and character arcs have come to fruition. There is a kind of *finale* feeling to the book. But when I finished the tale, I realized I hadn't gone far enough. If the series had ended here, I'm sure you would agree.

My problem was that this series was titled The Legends of the First Empire. Sure, I've introduced you to the characters, the Legends if you will, but the formation of the Empire was still an untold tale. If you've read The Riyria Revelations, you already know who won the war, but if I ended the series here, I wouldn't have fulfilled my mandate. Also, those who *haven't* read Riyria would be left confused, wondering what the eventual conclusion came to be.

Those who have read The Riyria Chronicles (my prequel Royce and Hadrian tales) know that I strive to do more than rehash previously mentioned events. I search for ways to make those stories fresh and worth reading. I've done this by revealing untold aspects and, in some cases, showing how what readers believed to have happened, didn't—at least not the way they thought. This is the same technique I employed to get from the end of *Age of War* to the formation of the First Empire, and I did so by doing something no one expected, including myself. I wrote three more novels to provide readers the closure they deserved. The result is two closely related trilogies under a single banner. In practical terms, what that means is that the next book, *Age of Legend*, will continue the tale but with a slightly different focus. Don't worry, it'll pick up where *Age of War* leaves off, and you'll continue to travel with the same characters, but the tale will *expand*. I'm quite proud of my solution and how I turned a potential problem into an opportunity, but that's for another day and another book's author's note.

As for *Age of War*, one of the reasons I write author's notes is to give readers a backstage pass, a behind-the-scenes look into my head. I'm not vain enough to think such a tour matters to many, but some people have found these insights interesting. I've already mentioned a lot of things regarding this book and the series as a whole, but I've not previously talked about my inspirations, so let's do that now, shall we?

The most significant influences for Legends of the First Empire are *The Wizard of Oz* and the island of misfit toys from the *Rudolf the Red-Nosed Reindeer* Christmas special. Some similarities you might already recognize. Many of the characters in my story weren't likely to be picked first in gym class. They are the castoffs, the unwanted, the useless. They are the broken toys losing hope of ever finding happiness with each passing year.

You may also have noticed that the majority of the primary characters are women. Few classic fantasy books have featured females in all the major and most powerful roles (good as well as evil) with as much success as *The Wizard of Oz*. One of the things I noted from that story (and from my own life married to an incredible businesswoman, who spent much of her early career in the male-dominated engineering field) was how women deal with conflict. Male protagonists—even my own—have a proclivity to play the hero by charging in, often alone. By contrast, Dorothy Gale of Kansas gathered a team of like-minded individuals of diverse backgrounds and unique abilities that afforded her victory. I saw value in Dorothy's approach that I sought to build on. Now that you know I've been having fun paying homage to these two classics, maybe you'll know what to look for, and I suspect you'll likely spot when I tip my hat. I hope you'll smile when that occurs.

Okay, what else should I mention? Oh, I know. If it has been awhile since you've read the other books and you want to catch up, you'll find recaps under the Bonus Material menu of The Legends of the First Empire website: firstempireseries.com/book-recaps. I should note that reading these shouldn't be necessary, because I've put in little reminders about essential facts from previous events. These are not lengthy dissertations, just little memory joggers. Also, keep in mind that each book has an extensive spoiler-free glossary of terms and names. So if you forgot who Konniger is, you could look him up in this book's glossary. What you'll find will be different than the entry in *Age of Myth,* because it'll reflect what is known up to this point in the overall story, but you'll not find anything that'll ruin *this* book. I should note that there are a few entries that will be left out of the *Age of War* glossary, for instance, the name Turin. Why? Because there just isn't any way to write a spoiler-free entry for that. However, if you look it up in a future edition of *Age of Legend,* you'll be reminded why that name is important. Bottom line, if you want further memory refreshers, go ahead and skim through the glossary.

Well, I think that's plenty for now, except to say that I've greatly appreciated receiving all the amazing emails, so please keep them coming to michael@michaelsullivan-author.com. As I've said before, it's never a bother hearing from readers—it's an honor and a privilege. So now that the preamble is over, I'd like to invite you back to an age of myths and legends, to a time when mankind was known as Rhunes and elves were believed to be gods. In this particular case, allow me to take you to the Age of War.

HENTLYN

ERIVAN

Ervanon

Estramnadon

Nidwalden

Avempartha

Harwood

Seon Hall

Swamp of Ith

North Branch

Under
the
Dragon

Mount Mador

Alon Rhist

High Spear
Valley

The Forks

River

AVRLYN

Bern

Nadak

Dureya

Gula

Urum

Rhen

Merredydd

River

RHULYN

Melen

Green Sea

Menahan

Tirre

Warric

BROKEN LANDS

Neith

BELGREIG

Blue Sea

100 Miles

Fhrey towns
Rhune towns
Dherg towns

Age of War

CHAPTER ONE

The Road to War

Life had been the same for hundreds of years. Then the war came, and nothing was ever the same again.

—THE BOOK OF BRIN

Suri the mystic talked to trees, danced to the sound of wind chimes, hated bathing, howled at the moon, and had recently leveled a mountain, wiping out centuries of dwarven culture in an instant. She had done so mostly out of grief, but partly out of anger. A dwarf had been insensitive after the death of Suri's best friend. He should have been more sympathetic, but during the days since it happened, Suri had come to realize she could have shown more restraint. Perhaps merely setting Gronbach on fire or having the earth swallow the vile wretch would have been a better choice. Neither option had occurred to her at the time, and an entire civilization had suffered. It had been a bad day for everyone.

Nearly a week later, Suri woke in a field amidst salifan, ragwort, and meadow thistle, the sun peeking over distant hills. Golden shafts made diamonds of dewdrops and revealed the labor of a thousand spiders who had cast nets between blades of grass. Having spent the night outside, Suri, too, was soaked and a bit chilled, but the sun's kiss promised to make everything better. She sat in the dew, the sun on her face, and stared at the fields surrounding the seaside dahl, listening to the faint hum of bumblebees as they began their morning's work. Then a butterfly flew across her sight and ruined everything.

Suri began to cry.

She didn't bow her head. Keeping her face to the sunlight, she let the tears roll down her cheeks, spilling onto the grass, adding to the dew. Her little body hitched and shuddered. Suri cried until she was out of tears, but the pain still tore at her heart. Eventually, she merely sat in the field, shoulders stooped, arms limp, fingers reaching out for the warm fur that wasn't there.

Since returning from across the sea, most days started this way. Mornings offered a tiny respite from the pain, but before long she remembered, and reality crashed in. Then the sky became less blue, the sun not nearly as bright, and not even the flowers could make her smile. And there was one more loss left to face. Arion was dying.

"Suri!"

She was slow to react, slow to realize it was *her* name being called. Somewhere behind her, the grass rustled and feet thumped. The rapid tempo of those footfalls indicated it could only be one person, and that meant just one thing.

"Suri!" Brin called again.

The mystic didn't bother to turn. Didn't want to see—didn't want to face—

"She's awake!" Brin shouted this time.

Suri spun.

"Her eyes are open." Brin was running, plunging through the tall grass, soaking her skirt.

Every muscle in Suri's body came alive. She sprang up like a startled deer and sprinted past Brin, racing toward the road. In no time she reached the tent Roan had built specifically for the Miralyith. When Suri burst in, Arion was still on the pallet, but her eyelids fluttered. Padera was helping her sit up to drink.

"Tiny sips," the old woman barked. "I know you want to guzzle like a drunk, but trust me, it'll come right back up on you—and me. Even if you don't care, I do."

Suri stood under the flap, staring. Part of her refused to believe what she was seeing. She was afraid it was merely a dream and worried that the moment she embraced the sight, the illusion would dissolve and the pain would rush back with twice the force. She didn't know how many more blows she could survive.

"Come in—go out—pick one!" Padera snapped. The old woman, her lips sunken over toothless gums, squinted with her one good eye against the blinding sunlight.

Suri took a step forward and let the flap fall. The lamp was out, but sunlight burned brightly through the cloth walls. Arion was resting against Padera's shoulder. The old woman helped the Fhrey hold a ceramic cup to her lips. Over its top, Arion peered back with weary eyes as she slurped loudly.

"Okay, okay, that's enough for now," Padera said. "We'll let that settle a minute. If it stays down, if you don't erupt like a geyser, I'll give you more."

The cup came away and Suri waited.

Arion's voice—Suri needed to hear it to be sure, to make it real.

The Fhrey tried to say something but couldn't. She pointed apologetically at her throat.

Suri panicked. "What's wrong with her?"

"Nothing," Padera grumbled. "Well, nothing beyond sleeping for almost a week without food or water, which made her dry as the dust she nearly became." Padera looked at the Fhrey with a small shake of her head and a confounded expression. "With as little water as she's had, she ought to be dead. Any man, woman, child, rabbit, or sheep would have passed three days ago. 'Course, she's none of those, is she?"

Once more, sunlight pierced the room, blinding everyone. Brin stood in the entryway, holding the flap. She didn't say anything, just watched from the gap.

"Come in—go out—pick one!" Suri and Padera barked in unison.

"Sorry." Brin stepped in, letting the flap fall.

All of them watched Arion. The Fhrey lifted her head slowly, focused on Suri, and smiled. Arion reached out a shaky hand. That was enough. Suri fell to her knees and discovered she still had tears left. She buried her face in the side of Arion's neck. "I tried, I tried, I tried . . ." Suri managed in between sobs. "I didn't know what I was doing. I opened a door and found a dark river. I followed it toward a light, a wonderful and yet terrible light. I . . . I . . . I tried to pull you back, to fix you, but . . . but . . ."

She felt Arion's hand patting her head.

Suri looked up.

"Not . . . tried," Arion managed to croak with a voice as coarse as gravel. She then mouthed the word *succeeded*.

Suri wiped her eyes and squinted. "What?"

With more effort, the Fhrey said, "You . . . saved . . . me."

Suri continued to stare. "You sure?"

Arion smiled. "Pretty . . . sure."

Raithe refused to sit. Something about being seated in the face of such lunacy felt too much like acceptance. The rest of the clan chieftains, who referred to themselves collectively as the Keenig's Council, sat in the familiar circle inside Dahl Tirre's courtyard. Four chairs had been added: three to accommodate the chieftains of the Gula clans and an elaborate seat with carved arms for Persephone. Gavin Killian, the prolific father of numerous sons and the new chieftan of Clan Rhen, sat in Persephone's old chair.

Nyphron wasn't seated, either; he was up and speaking. Persephone nodded when the Galantian paused.

She's not actually considering this, is she?

Besides the ten chieftains, most of the other usuals were there, except for Brin, the keenig's personal Keeper of Ways. Raithe had last seen her heading toward Padera's tent, the one they had Arion in. The Death House some called it, since the Miralyith hadn't shown any sign of life in nearly a week. The other non-chieftains in attendance included Moya, Persephone's ever-present Shield with her famous bow; the dwarf named Frost, who always stood in for Roan and reported on weaponry progress; Malcolm, who simply had a habit of showing up; and Nyphron, who represented the Fhrey. That's how Raithe saw Nyphron's role, as the voice of a small band of warriors. Given that Raithe represented only himself and Tesh, he couldn't begrudge the Galantian leader a place at the council.

At least I shouldn't, but I'm not making insane recommendations that will get everyone killed.

"We must take Alon Rhist, and we must do so immediately," Nyphron repeated. He wasn't asking or suggesting; this wasn't a bit of advice or an option being presented. The Fhrey leader was demanding agreement.

Raithe usually refrained from talking in the meetings, and he felt Nyphron should keep quiet, too, for the very same reason: They represented virtually no one. But Raithe didn't like the look on Persephone's face. Her expression indicated she was weighing Nyphron's words carefully.

None of the other chieftains possessed the courage to challenge the Fhrey leader, so Raithe had to say something. Lack of proper weapons had been the reason he'd refused to be the keenig in the first place, and Nyphron wanted to take the Rhist before they had time to prepare. Persephone had returned from Belgreig with the secret of iron, but forging enough weapons for an army would take time.

"Your recklessness demonstrates why Persephone is the keenig and you are not," Raithe said loudly to Nyphron, drawing attention. "You're Fhrey. You don't care about the lives of us Rhunes. The only thing you care about is winning. The amount of blood spilled while reaching your goal is inconsequential—because it won't be yours. Attacking Alon Rhist before we're properly trained and have adequate weapons will be suicide. Hundreds, maybe thousands, could die on those walls. And then—"

"No one is going to die," Nyphron replied in a superior tone that suggested he was speaking to an imbecile.

Raithe took a step toward him. "If we attack one of the most fortified strongholds in the world with farmers armed merely with mattocks, men *will* die. Many men." Raithe turned to the other chieftains. "You've been to Alon Rhist, right?" He pointed at Nyphron. "Isn't it filled with an army of Fhrey warriors like him? Charging those walls will be like slapping a beehive with a stick. Except these bees don't just sting. They cut off your head with very sharp bronze swords while hiding behind massive shields."

Persephone was paying attention to him, listening.

That's something, at least.

"I'm not asking for anyone from here to fight." Nyphron spoke to Persephone rather than to Raithe. "Your people won't even have to get near the Rhist. They will merely be decorative, a garnish if you will." Nyphron began to pace back and forth. "That fortress is my home. I *own* it. My father was the head of the Instarya tribe, the people who have lived in that fortress for centuries. He was the supreme commander of all the western outposts. That position typically falls to the son upon the father's death, which makes me the lord of the Rhist."

"But the fane—the leader of your people—put someone else in charge after your father challenged him, correct?" Tegan of Clan Warric asked.

Thank you, Tegan. At least one person is paying attention.

"True," Nyphron replied. "But that Fhrey isn't well-liked by my tribe, and the Instarya have been ill-treated for centuries, alienated and exiled through no fault of their own. They need a leader who understands their plight and can right their wrongs." Nyphron sighed. "Do you think this is some impetuous idea that popped into my head this morning? I've worked on this plan for quite some time. I know how to take Alon Rhist. And I can do so without the loss of a single life."

"That's not possible," Raithe said. "We need to—"

Nyphron rolled his eyes. "Allow me to explain why we must act immediately. I'll do so in short sentences with small words. Right now, the fane is preparing his own forces. He'll need to marshal his troops on the frontier to attack us. His best soldiers are the Instarya tribe—*my brethren*—and they're headquartered at Alon Rhist. The Instarya are the greatest warriors in the world; without them, the fane has no troops. I intend to steal his strength, but we have to move quickly. We can't allow Lothian to reach Alon Rhist first." Nyphron moved closer to Persephone. "I can nullify the whole Instarya tribe from Ervanon to Merredydd. Doing so will cut off the fane's arms. He'll have no army to fight for him."

"Will they fight for us?" Siegel asked.

Nyphron looked at the Gula-Rhune chieftain as if he were a child. "Of course not. Fhrey don't kill Fhrey, but if you do as I say, I can ensure that they won't kill Rhunes, either. And without his warrior tribe, the fane will need to train others. That"—he pointed at Raithe, still without looking at him—"will give us time to forge weapons. Something we can do more effectively behind the Rhist's walls." Nyphron began counting off with his fingers. "Alon Rhist has tools, facilities, shelter, and food, everything required to build the sort of fighting force needed to face the fane's inevitable assault."

"But *how* do we take it?" Tegan asked.

"Just leave that to me."

"See, that's where I have a problem," Raithe said. "You expect us to trust you?"

Nyphron dragged a hand over his face in frustration. "It doesn't matter if you have doubts. The Rhunes will be perfectly safe. I don't want any of them within a quarter mile of the Rhist. *I* and my Galantians will secure the fort. I only want you to be there."

"You're certain the Rhunes won't have to fight?" Persephone asked.

"That's correct. I want you and your people to stand across the Bern River Gorge in the high plains of Dureya. Is that too much to ask?"

Persephone looked at Raithe.

"You can't listen to him," Raithe said. "This is foolishness. He can't take an entire fortress with a party of seven. Either he's delusional or this is some kind of trap. At least wait until we have a thousand swords and shields." He turned to Frost. "How long will that take?"

The dwarf puffed air through his beard and mustache, clearing the hair out of the way in order to speak. "We've selected a dozen good men who are eager and capable of learning, but we're still struggling with the method and system.

"Although Roan carefully watched the swordsmiths produce an iron blade, she apparently missed a number of details. We are still working out the process—but we're getting there. Once we have the steps down, those twelve will take what they've learned and train a smith in every village in

Rhulyn. And those smiths will take on apprentices, expanding our numbers. When the system is perfected and people are trained, the work won't take long. But getting all that going is the problem." He rubbed his chin. "I estimate we could outfit a small army in . . . a year."

"There," Raithe said. "And in that time, we can train the men to—"

"It will be too late by then," Nyphron said. "The fane will consolidate his hold on the frontier before winter. This is a race, and we've already delayed too long. Besides, there is a fine smithy inside the fortress, and a few residents in the city have excellent forges and tools. Also"—the Fhrey looked at Persephone—"where will the people of Rhen winter? Here? Will you shelter from the icy blasts against that wall?" He looked to Lipit. "Do you have room for them inside the city's walls?"

Persephone's eyes darkened.

Raithe was losing her. Losing her to *him*, which made it worse.

"My way will ensure we can defend ourselves if things go wrong," Raithe declared. "If he fails to deliver on his outlandish promises—"

Nyphron smiled as he cut Raithe off. "And my way will win this war."

Raithe glared at Nyphron, but the Fhrey steadfastly refused to even glance his way. Nyphron continued to study Persephone.

"How soon would you want to move on Alon Rhist?" she asked.

"Immediately," Nyphron said. "We have already wasted too much time." He gestured at the dahl around him. "While we sit and talk, who knows what the fane is doing."

"I'd feel better if we had some *Artistic* support." Persephone looked Raithe's way. "In case anything goes wrong. But Arion can't be moved, and Suri won't leave her side."

"We don't need a Miralyith to take Alon Rhist, and we can't afford to wait," Nyphron said. "Arion is more likely to die than recover, and that mystic child is no Artist. Waiting for Arion's death won't change a thing."

Brin raced into the courtyard, and all heads turned. She was moving so fast she had to skid to a stop. A huge smile stretched her cheeks. "Arion's awake!"

· · ·

They weren't an army—far from it.

The course of humanity had shifted in a very real sense. Suri was certain she'd seen rainstorms with fewer drops than the number of people walking north. And while Suri wasn't an expert on such matters, she imagined that even the worst army carried weapons, unlike the crowd around her. They were shepherds, farmers, leatherworkers, hunters, woodcutters, fishermen, brewers, and traders. Most didn't own weapons. They carried bags and baskets. The rumpled host of that would-be army struggled to walk in line. They also complained about the pace, the road, and the sun—or its absence when the rain came. Most of the women had been left at home, except for those of Dahl Rhen, who didn't have a place to stay. Those without small children walked alongside their men, carrying bundles of food and clothes. The majority of the host was ahead of the wagon where Suri and Arion sat, all marching along the road that went by Dahl Rhen, the same path they'd traveled down seemingly a lifetime ago.

Arion and Suri were tucked alongside barrels, sacks, pots, and wool, rocking and bouncing with the ruts and dips. The Fhrey had declared herself fit to travel, but she wasn't up for the long walk. Padera and Gifford, who served as cooks to that migratory march and also looked after Arion, rode with them. The two won seats on the wagon by virtue of Nyphron's desire to travel quickly.

Suri didn't make a habit of riding in the wagon, but she checked on Arion frequently and sometimes napped among the sacks in the afternoon. No one questioned her right to do so. No one spoke to her much at all.

Rumors had circulated about her *incident* in the land of the dwarfs. While Suri had always received stares as an outsider and a mystic, now the expressions of curiosity and disapproval were replaced by looks of fear. Folks sped up, slowed down, or even changed directions to keep their distance. With Persephone, Moya, Roan, and the dwarfs all so busy, the only ones who spoke with Suri were Padera, Gifford, and Brin. Everyone else acted as if she were poisonous.

I've always liked being alone, she reminded herself. *I prefer it. Too many people in one place isn't natural. This is better.* But she wasn't alone. Suri was surrounded by people, yet not a part of them. She was the daisy among the daffodils, the fly in the goat's milk, the butterfly in the army.

Suri turned and saw the trees off to their left, a slope running upward, leafy boughs nudging into darker piney ridges. She knew that line, that rise of trees, that curve. Just beyond was a river and over the next hill they would see the full face of the wood—the Crescent Forest.

"We're almost back," Suri said. She checked the sun. "By midday, we'll be there. How do you feel?" she asked Arion. "We'll walk slowly. No need to rush."

Arion, who was sitting up and wrapped in a light shawl, appeared puzzled. "Are we going somewhere different than everyone else?"

"Yes, to the Hawthorn Glen. Home."

"But Persephone—I thought we were headed to Alon Rhist." Arion looked perplexed.

"That's where *she's* going; *we're* going home," Suri said. "You'll love it, Arion. The garden will be a disaster, but I'll take care of that. You won't have to do a thing except rest and get stronger. We'll go swimming!"

"Suri, there's a war starting," Arion said. Suri believed the Fhrey's voice reflected her health, and Arion's speech was still far too windy and hollow.

"Yes." She glanced at the men with hoes and mattocks on their shoulders. "And in the glen we won't even know it. We'll be safe and happy. In a way, it'll be like old times—the way it was with Tura."

Persephone had wanted Suri and Arion to go to the Fhrey fortress, but Suri didn't think war sounded very pleasant. Instead, she had come up with a better plan. The two of them would ride on the wagon back to the Crescent Forest, then hop off and walk to the Hawthorn Glen. Arion was still weak, so they would go slowly and stop often. Might take all day, but once there, Suri would show Arion the most beautiful place in the world: the little vale where the sunlight was more golden, the water sweeter, and where birds of different species sang in harmony. Suri knew Arion would love it, and in that wondrous place the Fhrey would grow strong again, and then—

"Suri?" Arion stared at her. "Are you ready to talk?"

Suri looked away, focusing on the forest as home came into view over the rise.

"Are you going to tell me what happened?" Arion asked.

"What do you mean?"

"Last thing I remember, we were trapped under a mountain. We had a deal, you and I. Since I'm here, I have to assume you didn't keep your end of the bargain. Don't you think it's time we talked about what happened?"

Padera shifted uneasily. "You should rest," the old woman said.

Arion ignored her and continued to focus on Suri.

The Crescent Forest revealed itself in its formal gown of deep summer green. By contrast, the fields that skirted it were bright gold with speckles of orange, yellow, and purple. Birds were swooping low, bees darting, and above it all, bright, white puffy clouds drifted without a care.

"Aren't you going to tell me what happened to Minna?"

At the sound of the name, Suri tore her sight from the beautiful vision but didn't look at the Fhrey or say a word.

"Suri, I'm not an idiot."

"I didn't say you were."

"Why, Suri? Why did you do it?"

Suri lowered her head, her lips bunching up in protest. She didn't want to have this conversation—not now, not with Arion, not with anyone, not ever.

"You loved her," Arion said.

"Still do." The words escaped.

A feeble, quivering hand touched Suri's wrist, long, delicate Fhrey fingers gently rubbing. "I wanted you to kill *me*, not *her*."

"I know."

"Suri . . . I can't go home with you."

Suri pulled away, folded her hands in front of her, and looked back out at the forest. The vast expanse of green filled the view to the west. As Suri watched it roll past, she thought, *It looks so strangely small. Has it always been that way?*

"You can't go, either," Arion said. "You know that, right? You're a butterfly now—in more ways than I would have ever expected. Days of eating leaves are over. The flowers need you. Your home isn't in the Hawthorn Glen, Suri; it's in the sky. You can't hide. You need to fly. You need to show everyone the beauty of those wings."

Suri frowned and climbed off the slow-moving wagon. "Right now, I think I'd rather walk."

She let the wagon roll ahead. This left her at the rear of the long column. Quiet there, less hectic, and she enjoyed the feel of her feet on familiar, albeit sadly trampled, grass. Despite bringing up the tail end of the migration, Suri discovered she wasn't alone. Raithe trudged along in the soft ruts left by the wagon wheels. He had his leigh mor folded and tied shorter and looser, in the way most men did that time of year. It exposed more of his hairy legs and arms—*furry* was the thought that came to mind. He glanced her way but didn't speak, and the two fell into a silent tandem march.

They walked side by side in silence until they came to the intersection of the trail that led to Dahl Rhen. Suri didn't think she had come at it from this direction since the morning after Grin the Brown was killed. Both she and Raithe slowed. Both looked at the nondescript trail, just a narrow path that wound through tall brown grass. Up that way stood the shattered remains of a wall, a lodge, and a well—the past that marked a turning point.

"Strange how deciding to walk one way rather than another can change your whole life." Raithe managed to put her own thoughts into words. "I probably shouldn't have gone down that road."

Part of Suri wholeheartedly agreed. If she had refrained from going to Dahl Rhen that spring, Minna would still be alive and the two of them would be enjoying another summer together. Of course, if she hadn't gone, everyone else would likely be dead.

Do bad things happen if I don't know about them?

Suri sighed and wondered if Raithe had been speaking to her, or just talking to himself. She also wasn't entirely sure who she spoke to when she said, "The worst part is that I still can't tell if it was worth it."

They looked at each other knowingly, then resumed following the wagons at a greater distance, lagging back, letting the world drift away.

"I wish I were going home." Suri kicked a loose stone into the tall grass.

"I wish I weren't," Raithe said. He glanced over. "I'm sure yours is much nicer." He pointed at the wagon ahead of them. "How's Arion?"

"Annoying." Suri expected him to show surprise and ask why. Instead, Raithe simply nodded as if he understood everything. "I wanted her to come home with me to the forest, to the glen where I used to live. I figured we could be happy there, but she insists we have to be part of this war."

"Sounds remarkably like Persephone."

"Really?"

Raithe nodded. "Won't listen to me. Listens to Nyphron, though. She hears him just fine. We're going to war against the Fhrey, and whose counsel does she take?"

"So, you don't want to go to this *Rhist* place, either?"

"I'd rather we were all in your glen." He wiped sweat from his eyes and peered up at the blazing sun, as if he and it were having a disagreement. "Can you swim there?"

Suri smiled. "In a clear lake with swans."

"Got food?"

"More than enough."

"Sounds perfect."

"It is," she said and meant it.

"Over there, right?" He pointed at the cleft in the forest.

"Yep," she replied. "Up that slope, around to the left, and then over into the valley. We could arrive before nightfall, e~ ~ No one would even know we left."

The two looked at the wagons and the long column of men snaking to the north, which kicked up a cloud of dust. No one was looking back, but if they did, Suri and Raithe would be hidden by the cloud. They could slip away unseen and vanish into obscurity forever. The war would go on, but without them.

Do bad things happen if I don't know about them?

They both stopped, standing still in the middle of the road, listening to the sounds of the wagons fade.

"What do you think?" Suri asked.

Raithe sighed, then shook his head. "We can't leave them. And it seems stupid to start being smart now."

Suri nodded. "Yes. You're absolutely right. You must be the world's wisest—" She caught herself, mortified. Everything felt so familiar that the words just came out as they always used to, just as if she were walking with . . .

Suri began to cry. She felt guilty and hated herself for betraying Minna's memory so easily.

He stood quietly, waiting beside her without judgment.

Suri embraced him then. There was no thought in it. She needed to hug something and he was there. Suri thought he might pull away, but he didn't. Instead, she felt his arms wrap around her, settling gently, holding her. Raithe never said a word, and she knew that was exactly how it should be between friends.

CHAPTER TWO

Before the Bronze Gates

Alon Rhist was just one of the seven Fhrey fortresses that dominated our borders, but it was more than the seat of the Instarya tribe and the tomb of a long-dead fane. Alon Rhist was the personification of Fhrey power and the absurdity of challenging it.

—THE BOOK OF BRIN

Raithe pulled Persephone up the last ledge. She could have climbed it on her own, and none of the chieftains had needed or been offered a hand, but she took his. Persephone felt it best to be agreeable when she had the luxury, knowing she couldn't always be so generous. That's what she told herself, but she knew that if anyone else had made the gesture, she'd have waved them off.

Raithe was brave, capable, and handsome, wearing his leigh mor with a casual indifference. The young Dureyan was a popular topic among the women, but he took no notice of their flirtations. What he wanted, she couldn't give. Persephone was still married to her dead husband in ways she couldn't put into words, or even thoughts; emotions had a language of their own that didn't always translate.

Raithe and her husband were nothing alike. Reglan, nearly thirty years her senior, had been more like a father, a teacher, a guide. With Raithe, she was the wise one, the steady hand that kept the rows straight. And yet, Raithe's hand felt good—safe, warm, strong. She was the keenig, chieftan of the ten clans, and supreme ruler of millions, but she still needed more. Power couldn't replace respect, devotion couldn't replace friendship, and nothing could replace the enveloping warmth of love. He did love her, wanted her, and while she couldn't grant his wish—at least not yet—she cherished the idea. The gift of his desire was another of those impossible-to-translate, difficult-to-corral feelings. Passion was a wild, selfish thing that didn't respect boundaries or common sense, but without it life felt pointless.

"What did you call this?" She looked around, getting a feel for the natural pillar of rock rising sixty feet above the plain.

"Misery Rock," Raithe replied.

The sheer drop on all sides of that far-too-small-for-comfort pillar produced a flutter in her stomach. She nodded. "I can see that. Sure."

Persephone walked in a tight circle, shuffling her feet, too scared to lift them. Falling was an irrational fear as long as she didn't do anything crazy. The rock was as flat as a table, but she didn't trust herself. *Stumbling isn't an option, unless flying is, too.*

Persephone had never been one for heights. As a child, she stopped climbing trees at a young age and escaped roof-thatching duties by claiming illnesses that were greatly exaggerated. Standing on Misery Rock, looking down and seeing the tops of all those walnut-sized heads that made up the Rhulyn clans, she felt dizzy. *How did I ever find the courage to jump off that waterfall in the Crescent Forest?* That incident seemed decades ago rather than just a few short months.

Wolves, she recalled. *Yes, a pack of wolves in pursuit provided the necessary incentive.*

Persephone watched in awe as Suri scampered up as if the summit were a foot off the ground. The young woman was beyond fearless; she appeared thoroughly bored.

From where they stood, Persephone could see for miles. "Did you live around here?" Persephone asked Raithe.

He pointed toward the northeast.

Most of Dureya was a dusty plateau, one great rock interrupted by jagged stone formations like the one they stood on. Looking in the direction he indicated, she spotted a black mark on the consistently blond plain.

"That was my village, Clempton," Raithe said. "Thirty-seven buildings, forty families, and almost two hundred people." He continued to stare without blinking, a hard, brutal look. She wondered what he was thinking, then imagined herself gazing on the ruins of Dahl Rhen.

Persephone put a hand on his arm. Her touch broke his stare, and he offered her a forced smile.

All the Rhulyn chieftains were with her on the summit, while the Gula leaders were with their men, strategically stationed among the dips and clefts of the Dureyan plain. Nyphron had positioned them the night before, saying he knew the places where Alon Rhist's watchtower was blind. Persephone had been forced to repeat his instructions; the Gula refused to take orders from the Fhrey. A wild and vicious people, the Gula-Rhunes were little more than a pack of rabid animals—great when you needed that sort of thing, maddening when you didn't.

Persephone forced herself to inch closer to the edge to get a better look at the world below. The northern boundary of the yellow plateau was a steep, jagged gorge that from their vantage point formed a curve resembling a frown. At the bottom of that canyon, the Bern River flowed, which historically marked the end of Rhulyn and the start of the Fhrey lands. Somewhere beneath Misery Rock, a worn path, appearing little more than a chalk mark on that open plain, ran north from Dureya to the gorge. The vague line ended at a set of white stone stairs that climbed to a bridge. For miles, the only place to safely ford the river was that span, which linked the Fhrey and human sides of the canyon like a single stitch in the gaping wound that was Grandford. On the other side was the city and fortress of Alon Rhist with its great dome and soaring watchtower, the whole of it protected by massive stone walls and a pair of impenetrable bronze gates.

Persephone had crossed that bridge of sculptured stone every year while married to Reglan. Each time had terrified her.

We had been invited, but I was still scared.

"They're at the stairs," Tegan announced. The Chieftain of Clan Warric looked like an overgrown dwarf with neat dark hair and a brushed beard. Possessed of a sarcastic wit, he had a sharp mind and had become one of Persephone's closest advisers. Tegan pointed, and everyone on Misery Rock looked toward the Grandford Bridge.

"I can't believe you agreed to this." Raithe was shaking his head while looking at the sky.

"Nyphron knows what he's doing," Persephone said, trying to sound more confident than she felt. Her hands were clenched tight. She forced them open and made a deliberate effort to relax her shoulders.

"What if he's wrong? What if they kill him?" Raithe asked.

"My people aren't prepared for this," Harkon said. "Most of Clan Melen are carrying farm tools. We can't fight."

"If that happens, we fall back. We already have a sizable lead," Persephone told them.

"And Nyphron?" Harkon asked. "If things don't go well, will he retreat?"

"I don't think Nyphron or his Galantians understand *that* concept," Tegan said. "They always assume they'll win."

"Let's hope there's good reason for that." Persephone straightened up. She kept reminding herself to stand tall. Her mother had always complained about her bad posture. *No one will respect the wife of a chieftain who hunches over like a troll.* Her mother could never have imagined that *Persephone* would be a chieftain, much less the keenig, but Persephone guessed the advice was still valid.

"There's a first time for everything," Krugen said.

"Then pray this is not that time."

True to his word, Nyphron hadn't asked a single human to cross the bridge with him. Persephone's army was barely in sight of the Fhrey forming on the far side of the Bern. The Gula were even farther away—more than a mile—having formed on the crest of the high plain. That was the way Nyphron wanted it. Persephone hoped that his plan was designed to give them ample time to scatter if something went wrong, but Tegan was correct: Galantians didn't understand defeat. She agreed that the odds of Nyphron anticipating failure were equal to his expecting a day without a sunrise.

From the vantage point of Misery Rock, Persephone could see the Galantians approach Alon Rhist. The little troop of Fhrey appeared like a line of seven ants. They reached the bridge and without hesitation began to cross.

Trying to see better, Persephone took a step forward, forgetting—if only for that instant—that she was standing near a deadly precipice. Raithe caught her by the arm, silently reminding her of the danger and his concern for her. She glanced at him, and Raithe let go, looking embarrassed.

Harkon, the Chieftain of Clan Melen, shook his head in awe. "Fearless."

"Crazy," muttered Krugen, whose only interest beyond fine clothing was sleep—something the man did a great deal of, snoring far too loudly to hide the fact.

"Why isn't anyone stopping them?" Lipit asked.

"Same reason you wait when catching rabbits," Raithe replied. "Better to be sure you have them fully in the snare before pulling it closed."

Persephone's hands resumed their fists, and much to the dismay of her dead mother, she was imitating a troll again.

"What's that?" Krugen pointed.

"Do you see it?" Harkon asked. "On the plain—on our side!"

"More Fhrey," Raithe said.

Persephone saw them as well. Two dozen bronze-armored warriors had appeared out of nowhere, cutting off Nyphron's retreat.

"Where'd they come from?" Tegan asked.

"Cracks," Raithe explained. "The rocks out there are split with fissures and fractures. You can get into them, cover yourself in a dirt-colored blanket, and an enemy will walk right by. We did it all the time."

"Shouldn't Nyphron know about that?" Krugen asked.

"And there you have it—not as smart as he thinks," Raithe concluded with a morbid, self-righteous tone. Persephone knew he was directing his frustration at Nyphron, but she felt it spilling on her. After all, she had been the one who had sanctioned this action. The callousness of his cold judgment stung because he'd been right, and she hadn't listened.

"Do you think they planned for this?" Alward of the Nadak pleaded as if those gathered on that rock could grant wishes.

"The Galantians?" Tegan said with an incredulous expression. "They don't *plan* for anything. Forethought ruins the adventure, I'm told."

Alward frowned, his mouth still partially open, his shoulders slumping.

Persephone took another step forward. Once more, Raithe grabbed her arm.

The first time was bad enough; twice was uncalled for. Persephone was about to chide him, but then she looked down and saw she was less than a foot from the edge. Sucking in a short breath, she drew back.

"Can't afford to lose both you and the Galantians in one afternoon," Raithe said.

Lose them? The idea, so impossible, coalesced for the first time. *What if they are killed or taken? What happens to them? What happens to us?*

Persephone looked down at the hundreds of her people nearby and out beyond them at the thousands. She turned to reassure herself that Suri was still there. The girl had leveled a mountain, so she ought to be able to protect them from a few hundred Fhrey. That was why she was on the rock, why Persephone had insisted she come. But Persephone had no real clue how magic worked, what Suri was really able to do. And the mystic had embraced Arion's distaste for killing. A good thing, Persephone often told herself, but just then she wasn't so certain.

She noticed the black patch on the plain, the village that had once housed forty families, and she wondered if she'd made her first and last mistake as the Keenig of the Ten Clans.

Clutching the rolled-up flag in his right hand, Nyphron led his Galantians across the Grandford Bridge toward the bronze gates. Forty feet above the entrance, the crossed-spears symbol of onetime fane Alon Rhist frowned down. It would have been damn hard to erase, but the fact that Petragar hadn't tried illustrated the difference between the current ruler of the Rhist and himself—*one* of the differences. Only Ferrol knew how long that particular list might be if anyone thought to sit and compare. Nyphron imagined that he and Petragar didn't even chew food the same way. If the situation were reversed, Nyphron's own symbol would have replaced the mark of Rhist. Nyphron didn't have a symbol yet, but he would soon—a dragon or perhaps a lion—something fierce, something powerful, something worthy. All great leaders needed to leave their mark on the world, and he would have already chiseled his on that wall.

"You shouldn't have come back," Sikar said, standing first and foremost among a brace of shields at the far end of the bridge. He wore full armor, as if he expected trouble. He also wore the red-plumed crest on his helm, an indication that the spear commander had risen in rank since the Galantians' banishment.

"Couldn't stay away." Tekchin threw out his arms and puckered kisses at Sikar. "We missed you *too* much."

Sikar frowned and shook his head. The captain of the Rhist wasn't in a joking mood. "You're an idiot, Tekchin." His gaze moved to Grygor and paused briefly on the wooden box the giant carried, then it shifted to the flag in Nyphron's hand. "Surrender or truce flag?"

Elysan, an older Fhrey who had been a close friend and adviser to Nyphron's father, stood on Sikar's right and answered first. "Truce. When have you known the Galantians to surrender?"

Sikar kept his eyes on Nyphron. "You know, it's customary to wave that *before* approaching. Not that it would do any good. The fane has declared you exiles—no longer protected by Ferrol's Law." There was a terrible gravity in his tone and enough remorse in his eyes for Nyphron to make a mental note.

Tekchin chuckled as he folded his arms across his chest. Nyphron had given orders that no one was to touch weapons, and Tekchin was likely going through withdrawal. "So this is your big chance to rid yourself of those gambling debts you owe me, isn't it?"

"This isn't a joke!" Sikar shouted. "They're going to—"

Overhead, horns blared and the gates opened.

"Quiet," Tekchin said. "Your boss is coming. Don't worry. I won't tell him anything."

Sikar didn't look irritated; he looked sad. He slowly shook his head as he sighed.

"Relax, Sikar," Nyphron told him. "I'm back now. I'll make everything right again."

"They're going to execute you—you understand that, right?"

Nyphron only smiled.

Out of the gate poured a cohort of Instarya warriors. Nyphron didn't need to look behind him to know that more would be blocking their retreat. He guessed Petragar had turned out the entire First Spear to *welcome* them. The show of force was more than a compliment, more even than evidence of Petragar's cowardice; it was exactly what Nyphron needed.

The warriors fanned out in precision to either side of the bridge, filling the landing before the gates and denying them entrance. Nyphron didn't have any intention of taking another step. He had planned this meeting down to the block of stone he stood on and, more importantly, the landing where the Instarya had gathered. After centuries, Nyphron knew every blind spot and vantage point.

Petragar was the last one out. *A brave one, he is.*

At his side waddled Vertumus, legate to the fane. A portly Gwydry, he'd somehow managed to rise in station—or fall out of favor—in order to earn his post in the wilderness of Avrlyn. Vertumus had accompanied Petragar when the latter arrived to replace Nyphron's dead father as lord of the Rhist. All Nyphron knew about the man was his complicity in the plan to send Rapnagar and the other giants to destroy Dahl Rhen and kill Nyphron, Arion, and Raithe. *The boy and his weasel make quite the pair.*

"Nyphron, son of Zephyron," Vertumus began, "you have been—"

"Shut up," Nyphron ordered. "I didn't come all this way to speak to you."

Petragar's eyes widened. "You have no—"

"Didn't come to talk to you, either, you son of the Tetlin Witch."

Petragar looked confused by the Rhunic insult, the tone of Nyphron's voice, and . . . well, everything. That was just the sort of Fhrey he was. While he looked to the others for understanding, Nyphron took in the gathered faces of his family. He knew them all.

Nyphron's father was a tyrant when it came to his son. Zephyron, lord of Alon Rhist and supreme commander of all the western outposts, granted Nyphron no privileges or special treatment. His son was forced to sleep in the barracks with the other Instarya. Nyphron was also made to take his meals in the communal dining hall. Zephyron's son marched in the same mud and fought and bled alongside the lowliest soldier. At the time, Nyphron had protested, but now, while standing on the Grandford Bridge, he mentally thanked his father. This was just the second time he'd done that; the first was when Zephyron had gotten himself killed during the Uli Vermar.

"I've come home to speak to my brothers." The moment he said this, Grygor set the box down and Nyphron stepped up. "Instarya!" he shouted from his elevated position, wielding the still-rolled flag as a baton conducting a symphony of eyes. "The lord of Alon Rhist has returned. I come as a liberator to free you from the tyranny of morons and cowards."

"How dare you!" Petragar nearly screamed, his voice a perfectly discrediting screech. "You are a—"

"For too long, we have suffered the indignities and humiliation of a fane who does not respect us, who does not appreciate us, who does not love us." Nyphron had no trouble drowning out Petragar's squeals. The Galantian leader had a good voice for speaking: loud, deep, confident.

"You're a traitor!" Petragar shouted. "And the son of a traitor!"

Without looking at him, Nyphron chose to respond to the accusation, mostly because it dovetailed neatly with his speech. He hadn't expected help, certainly not from Petragar, but Nyphron wasn't above accepting it when offered. "My father gave his life for his tribe, in service to his people, to free them from exile, from the mud and the blood that only we are forced to suffer. We fight and die while the Miralyith, Umalyn, Nilyndd, Eilywin, and Gwydry all enjoy the benefits of our sacrifice. Even the Asendwayr are allowed to return across the Nidwalden. Only the Instarya are banned from our ancestral home. Why is that?"

"Because it is the fane's decision, not yours," Petragar shouted. His voice sounded thin and reedy.

"Indeed!" Nyphron was really starting to appreciate Petragar's assistance. The weeping willow of a Fhrey possessed the unexpected virtue of making him look good, a gift Nyphron loved more than all others. "Because the fane has decreed that we—we who shoulder the greatest burden—should receive scorn and humiliation as our reward. Those of you who were in Estramnadon, those who witnessed my father's challenge, can attest to this. Were those the acts of an honorable fane who respects his people? Or did he act the tyrant, imposing his rule through terror?"

"Sikar!" Petragar yelled. "Arrest him! Get him off that box!"

Sikar hesitated.

They really hate him. This might be easier than I expected.

"Let me explain why I came." Nyphron softened his tone and said, "I am here to rescue you, all of you. Alon Rhist is the only home I've ever known, the Instarya, my family. I've come to save you."

"You're the one who needs saving," Petragar growled, pushing forward through unresponsive ranks.

"For many years, I have warned that the Rhunes are capable of combat equal to the skill of the Fhrey. Few believed." He focused on Sikar. "I was proven correct when Shegon was killed while on patrol at The Forks."

"Shegon was murdered while he lay unconscious," Sikar said.

"Doesn't matter. I personally witnessed a Rhune warrior kill Gryndal. Slaughtered him with a perfect blow to the neck, severing his head from his shoulders. You remember Gryndal, don't you?"

This drew a reaction from every face, including Sikar's. He turned, and like many others, looked at Petragar.

"Is that true?" Sikar asked.

"I—I was told that something—"

"A Rhune killed Gryndal, and you didn't tell us?"

"And Gryndal wasn't unconscious at the time," Nyphron said. "If that's not enough, then know that I myself have fought the Rhunes, and in

Rhen I was nearly killed in a one-on-one battle. Only the timely intervention of Sebek saved me." He paused and looked at Sebek, who nodded.

This brought even greater expressions of shock to those gathered.

"Then you have lost your skill," Petragar said as he shoved past the remaining shields to join Sikar. The lord of the Rhist shouted in frustration. "Draw your weapon and take them into the duryngon, or kill them where they stand. But do it now or you'll be accused of defying the fane and will be prosecuted as one of them."

Sikar recoiled from Petragar's rant. He made a miserable face, then sighed and reached for his weapon.

"You don't want to do that," Tekchin said.

"Shut up." Sikar pulled his sword as if it weighed more than Grygor. "For once, can't you just shut up?"

"I know it's hard to believe," Nyphron told Sikar. "But this time Tekchin's right. Put the sword away."

"I can't." Sikar shook his head. "You shouldn't have come back."

Sikar was a good soldier, which meant he was no free thinker. He was a strong pair of arms for whoever pulled the strings, and at that moment the puppet master was Petragar.

Time to snip those cords.

"Before you order my friends to kill us . . ." He spoke slowly, clearly, and loudly as he unrolled the ruddy-red face of the flag. "Let me show you one more thing that you might not have noticed."

"There is no need for your theatrics. We've already seen the ragged band of Rhunes you traveled with," Sikar said.

"You saw only the ones I wanted you to know about," Nyphron spoke to Sikar. "Let me introduce the ones I didn't."

Nyphron waved the flag over his head.

In the distance, horns replied.

Nyphron didn't turn, didn't need to. Everything that happened behind him was reflected in the wide-eyed faces of those before him. Even Sikar's mouth opened. Petragar appeared as if he might faint.

"Seal the gate! Seal the gate!" Petragar cried.

"Wouldn't do that, either." Tekchin grinned.

"Once more, Tekchin defies the odds by being correct." Nyphron stopped waving and lowered the flag. "What you are looking at are five thousand battle-hardened, Dherg-armed, Gula-Rhune warriors. And before you start thinking the walls of Alon Rhist will save you, consider this—we also have a Miralyith."

"Miralyith?" Sikar and Petragar said together, and like an echo in a cavern, the word was repeated throughout the crowd.

"You know her as Arion, the tutor of the prince."

"She was sent to arrest you," Petragar said.

"Changed her mind. Even she recognizes that the fane has gone mad."

"And the fane sent giants to punish her for that error in judgment."

"A giant mistake." Tekchin chuckled.

Nyphron smiled and shook his head. "Yeah, that didn't work out so well for the giants. They're dead now, and she's working with us. So closing those gates won't help. She'll blow them open or simply tear down your walls."

"You're lying," Petragar said.

Nyphron turned to the Galantians. "On your honor, speak the truth before your brethren and our Lord Ferrol. Is the Miralyith Arion, former tutor of the prince, in our company by her choice and assisting us in our endeavors?"

Together in one voice the Galantians replied, "Yes, by our honor."

"You're lying!" Petragar howled. "They're all lying."

Irritated beyond the ability to keep quiet, Elysan turned and faced him. "These are Galantians."

"And they're liars!" His voice was a shrill rattle.

"Don't say that again," Sikar said, setting his jaw so that his words were forced through his teeth.

"You don't tell Lord Petragar what to do," Vertumus spoke up. "Petragar is in command here."

"That's right," Petragar said. "I am in charge. These . . . these Galantians are wanted heretics and traitors and are to be returned to Estramnadon, or, if they resist, they will be executed. This is the will of the fane." He faced Sikar. "Do your duty."

"The war is going to begin here," Nyphron told Sikar. "I can't allow this fortress to stand if it stands against me."

"You can't ask us to kill our own. Even if the fane is a poor choice to rule, Ferrol's Law still stands."

"I'm not asking you to *do* anything." Nyphron began rolling the flag up again. "In fact, I want you to do absolutely nothing."

This was the key to the lock that Nyphron inserted and prepared to turn. He could see the surprise and, more importantly, the eager interest in Sikar's eyes. The soldier was trapped between duty and honor, desperate for a way out.

"Nothing? I don't under—"

"I said arrest or kill him!" Petragar barked, causing Elysan to roll his eyes.

"I'm the leader of the Instarya," Nyphron responded to Sikar, ignoring Petragar. "I don't ask my people to do anything I am not willing to do myself. And I am not willing to break Ferrol's Law. If I were, do you honestly think *he'd* still be alive?" Nyphron used the rolled flag to point at Petragar. "All I am asking is that you don't get in the way. Just stay out of it. If you need to, simply report to the fane that you were overwhelmed, that you had no choice but to surrender to a vastly superior force certain to slaughter every last Fhrey in Alon Rhist, which I'm afraid is the truth of the matter. That's why I brought them, why they're here. The Rhunes are here to absolve you, to expunge any concerns about tarnishing your honor."

Sikar narrowed his eyes. "What is your plan?"

"Stop listening to him!" Petragar gave Sikar a shove from behind, which anyone who knew Sikar even a little would recognize as a mistake. The captain of the guard brought his elbow around and slammed it into Petragar's jaw. The Fhrey screamed, staggered, and fell. Without looking back, Sikar addressed Nyphron again. "How do you see this working?"

"The Rhunes are in total revolt. The Gula *and* the Rhulyn. They've united and appointed a keenig."

"Yes, we know," Elysan said, looking past the Galantians toward the hills.

"The Rhunes will be the arms we shall use to make the fane understand reason," Nyphron explained. "Or the swords by which we will replace him."

"But this is . . ." Sikar looked pained. "I hate to say it, but Petragar is right. What you're doing is treason."

"And what the Miralyith have done to the Instarya is what? Right? My father tried to follow the rules. He obeyed the laws, and you saw what happened. Do you think Ferrol, who gave us the horn, intended that one tribe should be forever dominant? What's the point of the horn, then? The Miralyith will never give up power, and who can hope to succeed in single combat against one?"

Sikar and Elysan shared a look, and while it was slight, Nyphron was certain he saw Elysan nod.

"So, what do you say?" Nyphron asked. "Will you turn your back on Ferrol and learn to worship the Miralyith as your new gods? Or will you trust me, a fellow Instarya who was raised to lead this tribe by a father who gave his life to save us from these so-called gods?"

"Bas-ward! My jaw bwoke again," Petragar slurred. He had only managed to make it back up to his knees and crouched on the ground holding his face, tears in his eyes.

Sikar turned fully around but didn't even look at Petragar. He faced the gathered Instarya and said, "The fane has ordered us to apprehend or kill these Fhrey. Nyphron asks us to stay our hands. The fane is our ruler, the Galantians our family. In this, I am inclined to side with family, and I'm willing to recognize Nyphron, son of Zephyron, as the rightful lord of the Rhist."

"I concur," Elysan said. "But, as it is against the will of the fane, no one can be ordered to do likewise."

Sikar nodded and backed up, clearing the path to the bridge and the Galantians. "Any Fhrey who doesn't wish to defy the fane's orders, you are free to draw your weapon and do what you believe is your duty."

Sikar took a few more steps away from the bridge and made a show of looking and waiting for those loyal to the fane.

Petragar, still clutching his face, shifted his head, looking around. "Ooh it!" he shouted when no one moved. "Obey your fane!"

Still, no one moved.

After several minutes of stillness and a silence that was broken only by the desperate outbursts of Petragar, Sikar nodded. "So be it." Then he turned back to Nyphron. "Welcome back, my lord."

"What do you think that means?" Krugen asked when most of the Galantians and the defending Fhrey disappeared inside the gates of the fortress. Only Tekchin and Grygor walked back across the bridge.

"They didn't kill them," Lipit said. "That's got to be a good sign, yes?"

Persephone was already descending the narrow dusty trail, wondering how fast she could safely move. She wanted to be at the bottom, wanted to learn what transpired, and was wondering why she'd climbed up in the first place.

"What happened?" Moya was the first to greet her. Her big eyes loomed larger than usual. "Did they fight? Did Suri do something?"

The mystic looked at her, surprised.

"No to both questions, but we don't know *exactly* what happened." Persephone slipped on a loose stone two feet from the bottom, stumbled, but landed safely on the hardscrabble plain. She touched down within the gathering of the chieftains' Shields. They had all remained there after Raithe explained there wasn't room for everyone at the top. "Tekchin and Grygor are on their way back, I hope with good news."

"Tekchin?"

"Yes, Moya." Persephone rolled her eyes. "Your boyfriend is fine."

"Just asking, Madam Keenig," she said crisply.

"Don't call me that."

"Everyone else does."

"No, they don't."

Persephone pushed past Oz and Edger, grabbed the hem of her skirt, and trotted down the slope to the road. From there, she saw the two Galantians striding toward her. The gathered clansmen, a mixture of Rhen, Tirre, and Warric men, flowed in behind, all curious for news.

"Madam Keenig," Tekchin greeted her with a modest bow.

Persephone scowled. "What happened?"

"We're in."

"What do you mean by that?"

Tekchin made a lavish wave of his arm in the direction of Alon Rhist. "Welcome to your new fortress. I think you'll find it more suitable than East Puddle."

"*My* fortress?"

Tekchin laughed. "Madam Keenig, weren't you watching? You just conquered Alon Rhist."

CHAPTER THREE

The Rhist

We traded dirt and rough-hewn logs for marble and glass.
—THE BOOK OF BRIN

The other times Persephone had been to Alon Rhist she'd stuck close to Reglan, and neither was prone to wander. No one *wandered* inside Fhrey territory, much less in the heart of their principal stronghold, whose largest tower had come to symbolize a monolithic sentinel. During those early visits, the procession of chieftains marched across the Grandford gorge under guard. When the men were led to a meeting hall, the women—those allowed to come—waited in nearby rooms. Persephone had marveled at the lamps, windows, curtains, and furniture. She didn't dare set foot out of the little apartment; none of the women did. They weren't offered a midday meal, and all the Rhunes ate the evening meal together.

On her second visit, Persephone and Gela—who she'd assumed was Lipit's wife only to later discover that she was his mistress—dared to climb the stairs to the window level where they peered out at an unprecedented view of the great dome, the beautiful city below, and the massive tower that rose higher than she thought possible.

No one had stopped them, no one so much as looked their way, but she'd been scared to death. They only had the courage to approach the one window, but that view had stayed with her. She'd had dreams where she walked the city's paved streets, visiting the pillared shops. She was never frightened in her dreams. No one could see her, and somehow she knew this. Persephone had never once believed those dreams would come true in waking life.

The day Nyphron became lord of Alon Rhist, he spent the afternoon providing Persephone with a personal tour of the fortress that would be her new home. The outpost wasn't as large as she had thought. The majestic fortification crowned the pinnacle of the crag, appearing as the inevitable conclusion to the natural rock. The city, formed of lighter stone and some wood, spilled out below. These smaller buildings trickled down the hillside in tiers, curling around the base of the butte like the tail of a dragon around a hoard of gold.

"And that is Mirtrelyn." Nyphron pointed to a nondescript open door in a cluster of three-story buildings.

"Land of Mirth?"

Nyphron smiled in surprise. "Your Fhrey is very good." He nodded. "Mirtrelyn is . . ." He stopped walking and stood in the middle of the street, thinking. "I don't know if you have such things in Rhulyn. It's a place where people go to drink, sing songs, and tell tales."

"We do that in our lodges."

"This is less formal, a place common people can come and relax. Most enjoyable. The Galantians and I spent many a long night in there."

"Seems small. Why come down here when you have that grand dome that I imagine could accommodate the whole town?"

"The Verenthenon is our tribal chamber, our general assembly hall— a smaller version of the Airenthenon—where the leading officers of the various Spears discuss issues and advise the Rhist Commander."

Persephone smiled politely. "I see."

"You don't have a clue what I just said, do you?"

"You said that dome building is your lodge, only you don't drink there."

Nyphron laughed. "Okay, yes. I suppose that's about right."

"Wouldn't work in Rhulyn," she told him as the two began walking again. "Can't call a meeting if there isn't food and drink. No one would come."

He laughed again. *A nice laugh*, she thought, *and generous*. Persephone often saw humor and laughter—the good sort—as a gift that both the giver and receiver enjoyed equally. The humorless she viewed as misers. Most of the men she knew were far too serious, which made Nyphron a ray of sunshine through a grim canopy.

The city wasn't at all like her dreams. The real thing was far less perfect, and much more amazing. The complexity of twisting streets paved in flat stones, the pretty arched bridges, the brightly painted multistoried homes with their tall windows and dark wood trim were all things beyond her imagination. But she had been surprised to find piles of manure, broken pots, unconscious drunks sleeping on stoops, lewd graffiti, and the smell of urine, which was unmistakable on the narrower streets. But the biggest difference between dream and reality was that all the inhabitants could see her. Everyone stared. Those gathering water from the fountain forgot what they were doing. They stood frozen, watching as Nyphron and Persephone passed. Conversations halted; doors closed, and laughter died. In every face she saw fear mingled with revulsion and disbelief. One Fhrey openly cried.

Nyphron didn't appear to see any of it as he continued his tour, pointing out landmarks and curiosities in a proud, positively jaunty manner. "I won't take you up there." He pointed toward a narrow lane that ran uphill underneath a bridge that joined two three-story buildings. "But there is a wonderful bathhouse up that way."

"Bathhouse?"

"Where you go to bathe, to steam, to socialize."

"None of those words seem at all related."

Another warm laugh. Persephone was apparently the goddess of humor that day. "Trust me, it's very nice. You'll love it."

"I'm sure I will," she lied.

They had returned to the stairs and were on their way back. The tour was coming to an end, but Persephone had a few questions she needed answered before they rejoined the rest. When they reached the first landing they were alone, so she seized the opportunity. Nyphron was a warrior, and she thought he would appreciate a direct approach. "So, what happens now?"

Caught by surprise, Nyphron turned to discover he'd left her behind. "I thought I'd show you around the fortified areas. Not the Spyrok, that takes too long to climb, but I think—"

"I mean now that we've taken Alon Rhist." She toggled her index finger between them. "What happens now?"

"You're the keenig; you tell me."

"I'm not an idiot," she said. "This is a huge victory for you."

"For us."

She rolled her eyes. "This won't work if you continue to treat me like a child."

He peered at her sidelong, his mouth partly open; he licked his lips, then his tongue lingered, touching his front teeth.

"You planned this," she said.

"Of course I did. You were there when—"

"No—you planned this *before* you ever came to Rhen."

He stopped. Again, the contemplative stare.

"You've plotted this maneuver for months, maybe years, but you didn't count on me. *You* expected to be the Keenig of the Ten Clans."

Still, Nyphron didn't say anything, but his face shifted to genuine interest—perhaps for the first time in her presence. She wanted to think there was respect as well, but maybe she saw only what she wanted.

"When you came to Dahl Rhen, you said you were outlawed because you wouldn't carry out the fane's edicts and refused to destroy the Rhune dahls. You expressed outrage at the other Instarya who destroyed Dureya and Nadak, killing every villager. But I'm not buying that. Your assistance wasn't because of moral outrage over the slaughter of innocents."

He didn't try to refute her, so she went on. "I don't know. Maybe you do have a genuine aversion to butchering women and children. Or perhaps killing is a mindless habit for you, as easy to do as it is for Padera to snap the neck of a chicken. But you didn't give up your heritage . . . leave all this"—she gestured at the city—"because a few houses were burned, a few babies killed. Such an act would take far more compassion than I think you're capable of feeling. Honestly, I don't care. What I do care about is what your plans are now. How do you see this grand adventure of yours playing out?"

"How do you think I see it?"

Persephone stepped to the handrail and looked down on the roof of a home that had a flower-and-vegetable garden on top. The plants were doing well for such a hot summer. "I think this bloodless victory, the capture of a fortress that my people believed to be impregnable, establishes you as a worthy hero among the ten clans. You're gaining trust and allegiance. Another similar success and you might not need me at all. You might *already* feel I'm unnecessary." She looked behind her. "And these stairs are very steep."

"They are," he said, then surprised her by holding out his hand.

She stared at it suspiciously.

He smiled at her hesitation, lowered his hand, and began to nod. "You're smarter than I gave you credit for, but I'm probably not the only one to underestimate you. I suppose I could lie, I could insist you are wrong and reaffirm my devotion to the cause of saving the Rhunes, but I suspect you'd see through that. You're a hard woman to lie to."

"No—people have no trouble lying to me. The hard part is making me believe. So, what happens next? What are your plans . . . for me?"

Nyphron ran fingers through his hair, leaving his hand to linger on the back of his neck. "Okay, I was planning to tell you this in a more appropriate time and place." He looked around the steps and shrugged. "But since you insist . . . it was my hope to marry you."

Persephone's mouth dropped open. Conquering the premier Fhrey stronghold in a matter of minutes without the loss of a single life paled in comparison to her shock at that single sentence.

"*Marry* me?"

"You do that, right? Rhunes have marriage?"

"Yes, *we* do, but *we*"—she once more toggled her finger between them—"don't."

"Why not? Don't tell me there is a Rhune law against that, too."

She opened her mouth, but the number of possible ways to answer that question jammed in their flood to escape, leaving her speechless.

"In Fhrey society, most marriages are arrangements of convenience. They advance social status, grant access to certain circles, form needed alliances. Rarely are they romantic. This is what I'm proposing."

He's proposing!

"To win this war, we need to join forces. I need credibility in the eyes of the clans. Without it, I have no means to fight. You need the support of the Instarya, which I can obviously provide. My recognized authority will bring all the Avrlyn outposts to heel. Our marriage would bind these two otherwise antagonistic groups into an extremely effective and overwhelming force. Your numbers, my guidance and resources"—he wove his fingers together in front of him—"together we would become the knot at the confluence of two ropes, forming a line strong enough to pull up the whole world."

"Or enough rope to hang ourselves with."

"That too." He smiled. There was an amazing power about him, and his smile was warm, friendly, inviting.

But is it genuine? Well, at least he's not treating me like a child anymore.

"There's no need to give an answer now—I'd prefer if you didn't. Like I said, this wasn't the time and place of my choosing. Let's get settled in, get to know each other better. Then we can revisit the topic."

Revisit the topic? He's really pouring on the charm.

And yet, she found his practical approach appealing. She had rejected Raithe's overtures because they were based on selfish desire. He wanted her all to himself, for them to run away and live a fantasy on a hill overlooking the Urum River. She had no doubt Raithe loved her. She remembered what that looked like, how it felt. But love was for the young, the innocent, and the stupid. She couldn't see herself putting those blinders on again. She had a job to do, and that was more important than her own happiness.

She held no illusions about Nyphron, and he appeared to see her just as clearly. Persephone had little interest in being a wife again, but a partner—an equal partner—that was something else.

She looked at the Fhrey lord appraisingly. He was more than attractive; he was beautiful, godlike, and yet if he tried to kiss her, she thought she might scream. They weren't even the same race. The whole idea was absurd, and yet his logic was irrefutable.

"C'mon," he said. "We need to get back. I don't want Moya hunting me down with that giant bow of hers."

"Thank you," she told him.

He paused, puzzled.

"For telling me the truth," she explained.

He smiled again.

A nice smile.

"That's where I used to live." Malcolm pointed at a beautiful home, its door ornamented with a bronze handle and a decorative knocker in the shape of a sword striking a shield.

Raithe had never seen anything like it—aside from the countless other homes they had passed. The street was perfectly straight and paved in flat stones with such precision that no weeds could grow between the cracks. The only visible dirt to be found was packed in planters, which produced vegetables and herbs.

"You lived there?" Tesh asked.

"That's Shegon's old house. Meryl and I both worked here. He didn't need two servants after his wife left, but he kept us both on anyway."

"You lived *here*, and you *ran away*?" Tesh's eyes widened. "Is the inside a fancy torture chamber or something?"

"The inside is lovely—an artful clover motif reflected in the curved archways as well as the spring colors."

Tesh just stared at him.

Malcolm chuckled. "I wasn't there long. I used to serve in the fortress."

They both looked up toward the Spyrok; that's what Malcolm called the insanely tall watchtower linked to the Kype by a giant bridge. Upon seeing it for the first time, Gifford had described the tower as looking like Mari had been tending her garden and left her shovel jammed in the dirt. That's what the potter meant to say at least, but because of his inability to pronounce the R sound, what he said was: "Looks like Ma-we left a shovel in the ga-den."

"*That's* where they tortured you?" Tesh asked. "In the fortress?"

"No one mistreated me."

"Didn't even beat you?"

"No."

"Starved you?"

Malcolm shook his head and frowned.

"They must've done something pretty awful for you to run from this. I know families who'd sell their firstborn to live here."

Again, Tesh looked at Raithe, who supported him with a nod. Having already gone through this conversation with Malcolm, Raithe wasn't as shocked, but there was a difference between what he'd pictured and reality. Usually, Raithe's imagination outstripped the real world—not this time.

Tesh had worried eyes, as if this was the part in the dream where monsters closed in and a door to safety refused to open. He'd had that look ever since they'd crossed the Grandford Bridge. The kid was swimming in a pool of deadly snakes, waiting for the first one to bite. Raithe understood. He felt it, too. These were their enemies, the evil gods who'd butchered their people, and he and Tesh were strolling their streets as if they owned the place. They didn't. The ten clans had done nothing to earn this right. The Fhrey had invited them in. Spiders did the same to flies.

"How many families lived there with you?" Tesh asked.

"None," Malcolm replied. "Just Shegon, me, and Meryl." The ex-slave tilted his head with a puzzled look. "The plants are doing well. I wonder who lives there now?"

"What made Shegon leave the fortress?" Raithe asked him.

"Shegon was never in the fortress. He was from the Asendwayr tribe, not in the Guard. Very few non-Instarya are."

"I thought you said you were in the fortress."

"Oh, yes." Malcolm nodded. "Ah . . . I had a different master then."

"He sold you?"

"Died."

"*Died?*"

"You of all people should know Fhrey do that."

"How old was he?"

Malcolm shrugged. "Fifteen, sixteen, maybe."

"That young?"

"Hundred. Fifteen or sixteen *hundred*."

"Oh, okay—I always wondered how long they lived."

"He didn't die of old age."

"Accident?" Raithe looked up at the walkways between the massive tower and the dome. A fall from either of them would kill anyone.

"He was killed in combat."

Raithe couldn't imagine what sort of beings killed Fhrey, prior to him at least. Giants, goblins, a dragon? Likely it was something he'd never heard of. Seeing the inside of Alon Rhist made Raithe realize how limited his understanding of the world was.

The three paused at the city square near a big well with a little roof to protect those using it from sun or rain.

"How long did it take them to build all this?" Tesh asked.

Malcolm shrugged. "A thousand years or so."

"It's so beautiful."

"Where are all the people?"

"Hiding." Malcolm dipped a hand into the fountain's pool and wiped his face. "The barbarians have entered the gates. The residents have no idea what might happen. This is unprecedented, and likely terrifying."

"They're scared?" Tesh said. "The *elves* are scared . . . of us?"

"When we arrive by the thousands, and the Rhist's guards let us wander their streets, yes. These people have been told that we're wild, little more than mindless animals. I suppose they expect we're here to loot, pillage, and burn."

"So goes the planting, so comes the harvest," Raithe said. He stood up on the rim of the well and looked out. The place was fine, to be sure, but a bit too orderly. This was a home built by warriors, for warriors. It lacked the flowers and winding paths of Rhen. To the south, over the orange clay roofs, he located the river gorge. At Grandford, the Bern River flowed through a canyon. Somewhere down that way the Bern joined forces with the Urum at a place known as The Forks—the place he'd buried his father. "The Gula still might have a mind to do a bit of pillaging."

"I suspect that's why Nyphron asked them to remain camped in what's left of Dureya," Malcolm said.

"Not going to like that. Probably disappointed there was no battle. I know several who were looking forward to killing those they previously believed to be gods."

"I just can't believe the elves are scared of us," Tesh said.

"Fhrey," Raithe corrected. "These ones are on our side now. At least that's the story Nyphron is spreading."

"Not all of them are frightened," Tesh said, pointing in the direction of the house Malcolm had lived in.

Raithe recognized Meryl, Malcolm's onetime partner in servitude—the coward who'd ridden away while screaming, "Murderer, murderer." Meryl stepped out of the too-pretty-to-be-true house, and leaving the door wide, took four steps. This left him still in the front yard, still behind the little decorative wall. He glared at them from his tiny battlement.

"Meryl!" Malcolm greeted him happily and walked over.

"*Murderer!*" Meryl shouted back in Fhrey.

Malcolm stopped. "*I didn't kill—*"

Raithe didn't catch everything they said. They spoke quickly in Fhrey. All he caught were the words *bloodthirsty*, *cannibalism*, and *monsters*. He wasn't even certain of those due to Meryl's thick accent.

Malcolm was trying to calm his old roommate. Raithe didn't need to understand the words to know that, but Meryl was having none of it. He shouted his replies and grew more red-faced with each round. Before long he was slapping the top of the wall. Other doors opened. Ghostly faces materialized at windows. Fhrey couples appeared on balconies. From the third floor of what looked to be a leather shop, Raithe heard a reedy Fhrey say, "*Please come away. It's dangerous.*"

More were coming out, standing on stoops with folded arms, stiff lips, and nodding heads. "Maybe we should move on," Raithe said. "Let's head back and find Moya and Tekchin. Or maybe Roan needs a hand with the wagons."

Raithe tugged on Malcolm's sleeve.

The ex-slave waved back at him with one hand. As he did, Raithe noticed another pair of eyes looking down from the upper-story window of Meryl's house. Remembering Malcolm's question about who lived there now, Raithe tilted his head up for a better look, and the figure withdrew into the shadows. All that remained was the flutter of a curtain.

It took a full-out drag by his wrist to get Malcolm walking, but Raithe outweighed his friend by no small amount, and Malcolm soon gave in to the idea.

"Idiot," Malcolm grumbled. "He's completely forgotten who he is. He actually thinks being a slave is a privilege. A privilege! Can you believe that? And he refuses to even admit he's human—or *Rhune*, as he so derisively refers to us. The little partisan bigot—*traitor* is what he is." Malcolm marched up the street with loud slaps of his feet.

"You used to think of us as Rhunes, too."

"That's before I knew better." Malcolm jabbed his pointed finger at Raithe. "See, right there; I can be reasoned with. But not him. Oh, no, not Meryl, the little weasel. He knows—he *thinks* he knows—everything, except that he's no better than anyone else. I honestly don't know how the man manages to dress himself in the morning."

Malcolm continued to fume, but more quietly as they rounded a wall painted with crude images.

"So, did you find out who his new master is?"

"Doesn't have one," Malcolm said. "He empties chamber pots in the Kype and cleans out cells in the duryngon now. Not too happy about the change. Blames me for tarnishing his otherwise impeccable reputation. I don't know what he's complaining about. He still gets to live in one of the best houses in the city, and he has the whole place to himself."

"Then who was in there with him?"

"Meryl made it very clear he was alone, and how it was my fault he was now a pariah."

"I saw someone upstairs."

Malcolm looked at him skeptically. "Really? Why would Meryl lie about something like that?"

Raithe shrugged. "Take it up with him the next time we never come down here again, okay? Nyphron just gifted us this pretty place; might not be a good idea to get exiled before we've tasted the veal."

This made Malcolm smile. "They do have wonderful veal."

CHAPTER FOUR

Council of the Keenig

Persephone was my hero. I am proud to say she was also my friend—nearly a second mother. She was also the keenig. But that was just a word, just a title that did not mean anything until she stood beneath that dome and we heard the thunder of her voice.

—THE BOOK OF BRIN

Nyphron called the meeting.

Persephone had told him they needed to sit down and talk with representatives of Alon Rhist, as well as discuss future plans with the other chieftains. They had only ruled the Fhrey fortress for four days, and already there was talk of the coalition breaking up. Many saw the surrender of Alon Rhist as a job well done and a problem solved. She, Nyphron, and the chieftains rode a wave of goodwill, but the men were tired of standing around and wanted to get back to their farms, livestock, wives, and children. What they didn't realize, what she needed to explain, was what Nyphron had explained to her: This wasn't the end. It wasn't even the beginning. All they had done was shift position to higher ground. The first battle was still coming.

Persephone had imagined the meeting would be similar to those she held at the lodge in Dahl Rhen, where a dozen men would gather around a fire and roast a lamb. She would sit in her chair and shout over the noise of belches and the bellows for more drink. If left to her, Persephone would have ordered a fire and a spit built, and a barrel of beer rolled out in the middle of the lower courtyard, an open space between the front gate and the general barracks. But she hadn't called the meeting, Nyphron had.

The lord of the Rhist, dressed in an uncharacteristically elegant long-shirt, blue cape, and sporting gold arm- and wristbands, escorted Persephone into the Verenthenon. Tiers of seats climbed the walls like the sides of a giant bowl, granting everyone a clear view over the heads of those in front. Waiting for her were hundreds of men and Fhrey. Nyphron led her down a central aisle that descended with wide steps to the bottom. Streaming shafts of sunlight entered through strategically placed skylights, illuminating a raised dais.

That's why he was so adamant about the time of the meeting. She had wanted it at night, but he insisted on just after midday.

Realizing that Nyphron was leading her to that platform, she began to panic. This wasn't something she was used to. Persephone had experience speaking with a handful of familiar men, but this was another matter altogether. What's more—there was no chair. She'd always had a place to sit. The Chair had been the greatest symbol of her position, more important than the torc. She felt diminished without it, smaller, as she was forced to stand before all those seated at a higher elevation. She didn't feel in command, but rather like an accused criminal brought forth for questioning.

In the front rows sat all the chieftains, including the Gula, alongside several dignified-looking Fhrey she'd never seen before. Moya was there, too, bow in hand, standing just off to the side and out of the light. As the Shield to the Keenig, only she bore a weapon. Moya didn't say a word as Persephone passed, but she expressed a wide-eyed exclamation that Persephone knew would have been a slew of profanity if the two had been alone.

Nyphron walked with her as she climbed the remaining series of platforms, but then he stopped. He, too, remained in the shadows, urging her to step forward to the white-hot column of light that entered at an angle and lit the stage.

Pressing quivering hands against her sides, she took those five remaining steps. The moment she entered the light, the dome erupted in applause. The sound scared her nearly to death. She almost backed off but forced herself to take deep breaths and straighten up. *This is no time to be seen as a troll.* She waited for the turmoil to calm, then opened her mouth. "I am Persephone, the Keenig of the Ten Clans." She stopped, stunned. The sound of her voice boomed with godly volume and silenced any remaining applause. She hadn't even spoken that loudly. She looked around bewildered.

"The dome," said someone in the second row. It was Malcolm, who pointed up.

Stupidly, she looked above her, then smiled and nodded, and this time she mouthed the words, *thank you.* Hardly a sound was made as the audience awaited her next syllable. A few people coughed, but the sound was muted, as if they were in another room.

She swallowed and began again. "I am Persephone, the Keenig of the Ten Clans, and I've called this meeting to explain a few things and to hear any problems or concerns you might have." Her voice wavered slightly, and she took another breath. "The Instarya of Alon Rhist have graciously agreed to act as our hosts in our efforts to stand against the aggression of the fane. Fhrey law, bestowed by their god Ferrol, prohibits them from taking another Fhrey's life. As a result, they will not join our cause as active warriors, but they will also not seek to jeopardize or undermine it." She stared at the seven Fhrey in the front row, all of whom nodded.

She smiled and nodded back. *Step one complete.*

"Now, a number of men have spoken to me about going home. They have fields that need attention, animals that need tending, and trust me, we need you to do those things. An army is only as good as its supply of food." Nyphron had given her that line during their two-day preparation. Seeing the very serious nods of approval from both the Fhrey as well as the Gula, she understood why. Credibility. She was still earning it.

"We need you to keep farming. As much as I would like this victory to be the end of our troubles, it isn't. The first battle of this war has yet to be fought. Now that we've moved into his command fortress, the fane must act. He will send a force to dislodge us. And make no mistake, that force will be powerful and determined. It will take every last man, every sword, every ounce of will we have to weather it. But . . ." She paused, letting the thunder of her booming voice fade. "We don't know when that day will come. It could be next week, or next year, and we can't afford to let fields lie fallow. So, here is my plan. I am told that Alon Rhist already has a system of signal fires built between here and Ervanon, their outpost in the far north. I am ordering that we extend this system, building additional woodpiles in the High Spear Valley in the east and south to Tirre. In this way, many of you will be able to return home, but if scouts learn of an impending attack, I will order the signals to be lit, and this will be the sign for all able-bodied warriors to return."

There were fewer nods, but no one complained.

"Now, not everyone can go, and not everyone can stay when they get home. We need to train. Nyphron, his Galantians, and many of their fellow Instarya have volunteered to teach us how to fight."

"We already know how to fight!" one of the Gula shouted, but his voice was a mouse squeak compared to hers.

"They can make us better," she said. "And you'll become familiar with new weapons. My good friend Roan, and a network of smiths trained by her, will be working night and day to forge swords made of iron, a magical metal that is stronger than copper and bronze. She will also oversee the making of armor, shields, and helms."

"What about the bow?" someone farther back shouted. "Will we get to learn that?"

Persephone looked at Moya and smiled. "Indeed. But it will require making hundreds of bows and thousands of arrows—another reason why we need men to stay. We will work in shifts. I will send home groups of men for a month at a time; then they will return and others will leave. We'll make sure to stagger the groups so every village will always have some men able to work communal fields. And I will establish supply routes using wagons to haul food, salt, wood, and wool."

More nods, fewer folded arms.

"We need to work together to prepare. We must remain committed to the path we've started down. It's essential that we trust one another, and if we can do that, together we will survive."

That was the end of her speech, but only Nyphron knew it, so there was an awkward pause. Persephone wasn't certain what to do. In the past, she just sat back in her chair, drank from a cup, or began eating. *How does one get off this stage?*

Nyphron came to her rescue by clapping. This ignited applause in the audience. Sadly, Persephone noticed, it, too, was muted.

CHAPTER FIVE

The Giant and the Hobgoblin

*Even to this day, we do not know much about Mawyndulë, which is
unfortunate since I still cannot decide whether, in the grand scheme
of things, he was a hero or a villain.*

—THE BOOK OF BRIN

His name was Sile, and he went everywhere Fane Lothian did. Mawyndulë
couldn't remember the other one's name, the female. Not that he needed
to. Both of his father's new bodyguards were silent watchers who weren't
inclined to conversation. Sile was unusually large. Mawyndulë would go
so far as to call him grotesque, and he harbored doubts that the hulking
guard was Fhrey at all. Sile had a large head, broad and endowed with a
protruding brow that cast shadows on his eyes. His jaw was a hinged
shovel, and his ears lacked the traditional teardrop shape. Mawyndulë se-
cretly suspected Sile was a diminutive member of the Grenmorian race.
He even carried a battle-ax. Sile certainly wasn't Miralyith.

"Nanagal completed his survey of the damage this morning," Imaly
told the fane as all five of them stood on the steps of the Airenthenon.

"How long until you resume meetings?" Lothian asked.

"He's confident his people will have it back in order in a month."

"A *month?* Are you certain it wouldn't be better to have the Miralyith . . ." The fane's comment lost confidence when facing Imaly's growing frown. The curator, still sporting a cast on her leg and a sling on her arm, had a way of cowing everyone with her disapproval, even Lothian.

"I know you mean well," she told him. "But given the circumstances, I think it would be wise to follow traditional roles and allow the Eilywin to handle the restoration. I think the Airenthenon has seen enough of the Miralyith's Art for a while."

"A month," he repeated.

The stairs and the plaza continued to bear the scars of battle. Scorch marks blackened the nearby walls, and the eastern steps were still missing. The paint in the market that had looked so much like blood had been cleaned up. An ancient tree was gone from the plaza, but the remaining stump still smelled of sawdust. To one side of the gathered group, the deer in the fountain had yet to be repaired; its severed stone legs were all that remained.

Weeks had passed since the revolt. The days had flown, blurred in a smear of anxiety. Mawyndulë had lost weight. A lot of people had. Imaly looked thinner, too, and paler.

"We are Fhrey," Imaly said. "We do things slowly."

"It's just frustrating." The fane frowned. "I want it cleaned up. I want this whole episode erased and forgotten so we can move on."

The Curator of the Aquila gave him a strained smile. "I believe that is exactly what the surviving members of the Aquila, and the tribes they serve, are afraid of, my fane. These scars serve to remind the Miralyith of the need for restraint, so they don't want this particular corpse buried too soon."

Mawyndulë's father scowled but nodded just the same. "How bad is it inside?"

The fane began to climb the steps, and everyone followed, including the giant Sile and the other one—the girl whose name he still couldn't remember. She was short and ugly. Not claw-your-own-eyes-out ugly, not even Rhune-ugly, but revolting enough that Mawyndulë didn't bother remembering her name. She was supposed to be a gifted Artist. The word he kept hearing was *fast*. Apparently, Miss What's-her-name had been in the plaza the day of the attack and done something right.

"Not as bad as it could have been." Imaly allowed her sight to focus on Mawyndulë.

The fane saw it, too, and acted as if he had forgotten his son was there. "Oh, right."

Mawyndulë waited until his father looked away before frowning and shaking his head ever so slightly. Miss What's-her-name was the talk of Estramnadon, but he, Mawyndulë, who had saved the most important landmark in the city and the lives of most of the Aquila, was lauded with such lofty praise as *oh, right*.

Mawyndulë turned to discover that the girl had seen his reaction.

Tiny little hobgoblin sees everything.

"Any news from Rhulyn?" Imaly asked.

"Not yet," the fane replied, taking care to avoid a shattered step. "I'm told such things require preparation, and that the Instarya have yet to begin culling the Rhune horde." He gestured around them. "Apparently that tribe shares the same lightning-fast response to my decrees as the Eilywin."

Imaly nodded with that same stoic calm she always used when speaking to his father. Mawyndulë imagined she was making an assortment of lewd mental gestures.

"I hear there are something close to a million Rhunes," she said. "Mindless but dangerous animals, it seems. Perhaps you should have addressed their numbers centuries ago, before they took root. Now it will take years to exterminate them."

"My fane!" a voice called from behind.

Everyone turned to see Vasek frozen in mid-step at the bottom of the stairs. His mouth was open, his eyes locked. He held one hand up, a finger pointing toward the sky. Dressed all in gray, he could have been a new statue.

"Really, Synne?" Lothian said. "He's a trusted adviser."

"Which is why he's not dead, your greatness," the hobgoblin explained.

Synne! That is her name.

"Release him."

"As you wish."

Vasek stumbled, sighed, and adjusted his asica before resuming his climb up the stairs. "My fane." He gave a tentative glance at Synne. "I have news."

"What is it?"

Vasek looked at the others and hesitated. "It's not good, my fane."

Mawyndulë's father frowned. He turned to face Imaly and sighed. "See they clean this up."

With that, the fane and Vasek marched back down the stairs, followed by Sile and Synne—the giant and the hobgoblin.

Imaly turned to Mawyndulë. "What do you think it is?"

He shrugged. "Probably nothing. Vasek jumps at shadows all the time, even more often as of late."

"With good reason, don't you think?" Imaly adjusted the sling on her shoulder.

Mawyndulë couldn't be certain if this was meant to illustrate her point or if she was merely uncomfortable. Mawyndulë always had to be wary of her. Imaly often used insinuations that he didn't always understand. This was partly why he found speaking to her so interesting. Their conversations were little puzzles to work out. There were times after concluding a talk that he went home, thought about it, and realized he'd gotten the discussion all wrong.

"I don't know—maybe." Mawyndulë didn't like being too definitive. He loathed revealing a position, fearing it would be the wrong one. Somehow, he had managed to impress the Curator of the Aquila, who so often impressed everyone else, and he very much enjoyed having someone respect him. Mawyndulë feared opening his mouth and ruining everything.

"Aren't you curious?" Imaly tilted her head toward the fane, who was crossing the square, heading back toward the Talwara with Vasek whispering into his ear.

"Not really."

"Still angry at him?"

Mawyndulë didn't answer.

She continued to stare. Imaly wasn't going to let this go.

"He sided with Vidar," Mawyndulë said—not because he felt he couldn't avoid answering, but because he wanted to. He was angry and wanted to voice his outrage even if it might mean appearing petty or childish.

"Don't you think Vidar deserved some compensation? The Fhrey was nearly executed for something he didn't do."

"It's still embarrassing. I saved the whole building and everyone in it, and my reward is expulsion."

"You weren't expelled."

"Replaced—it's the same thing."

"No, it's not, and you know it. Besides, would you have wanted Vidar as your senior again? To go back to being the junior councilor?"

Mawyndulë shook his head. He hadn't thought of that. The idea sickened him.

"There you are. It wasn't a career for you, just a learning experience, and I'd say you learned a great deal. More than your father ever intended. What's more, you endeared yourself to the Aquila. They won't forget your heroism. Most owe you their lives, and when you become fane, you'll discover that goodwill to be invaluable." Imaly sat down on the steps, taking care not to bang her arm.

Sitting there wasn't unusual. Many Fhrey sat on the stairs that led to the Airenthenon, enjoying the view it afforded of the plaza and the river. Some even picnicked or taught classes there, taking advantage of the natural amphitheater it created. Mawyndulë just found it odd that *she* would sit there. The difficulty Imaly had in getting up and down more than validated his sense that such an act wasn't natural for her.

"When you think of it," Imaly said, "leaving the Aquila is the best thing that could have happened. You made friends that day, and now you won't have the opportunity to lose them."

Mawyndulë looked at her, stunned on multiple levels. First, he wasn't aware of having any friends, except perhaps Imaly herself, and he felt presumptuous for even having that thought. The day after the rebellion, Mawyndulë had hidden himself away, terrified of seeing anyone who had been in the Airenthenon that day. He was certain they hated him. After all, he had been the one who invited Makareta. Second, if he did have these phantom friends, why would he risk losing them by staying?

She must have noticed his expression because she added, "Right now, you're a hero, and everyone will remember you that way. But if you stayed a member of the Aquila, well . . . familiarity erodes pedestals. Eventually you'd be on the wrong side of an argument—we all are at some point—and your legend would diminish. This way, Mawyndulë, Savior of the Aquila, will remain frozen in everyone's minds, pristine and perfect. What more could a future fane want?"

He smiled and sat down beside her. The old lady had a way of making things seem better. He felt bad about her arm, the way she clutched it. He pointed. "I can fix that for you."

Her eyes widened and she leaned back. "No, thank you." She caught herself and took a breath. "I mean, that's very generous, but I'm, well, I'm old-fashioned. I prefer to let nature take its course."

"You're just scared."

She raised her brows, and with her good hand, Imaly indicated the devastation of the battlefield memorial around them. "Absolutely."

"I was offering to fix your arm, not challenging you to combat."

"And I wasn't rebuking you, but I'm aware of the inherent complications that can result from taking shortcuts."

They looked down at the market. Only a few of the vendors had returned. Those that were brave enough to do so had little business. People had shifted most of their shopping to stands along the Greenway. Since the battle, Florella Plaza had become a haunted place fit only for ghosts. Mawyndulë's sight was naturally pulled to a familiar spot where once stood a stand that sold outlandish paintings—melodramatic landscapes of the frontier created by those with imagination rather than firsthand knowledge.

"Did they find her?" Imaly asked.

Mawyndulë continued to stare at the empty square, at the sawdust and the rubble. "No. Not that I've heard."

"Have you looked?"

"No."

"You liked her."

"A lot of people liked her. Then she went insane and tried to kill my father. That has a tendency to change things."

"But you still want to see her."

"She's probably dead." Saying the words was harder than he would have thought, and afterward he swallowed twice.

"They never found a body?"

He looked at Imaly then. "Miralyith don't always leave bodies."

He anticipated awe or perhaps fear. Instead, Imaly appeared amused. "Such the expert in magical combat now, are we?"

"I went to Rhulyn with Gryndal, was there when he dueled Arion."

That wiped the smile from her face, but once again, she failed to respond with the awe and fear he deserved. Imaly looked concerned in a maternal sort of way, worry creasing her brow. "Was it awful?"

Mawyndulë nearly laughed. "It was amazing. Gryndal was such a master. I miss him."

Imaly didn't say anything for a moment, then asked, "So, how's the new tutor?"

"What?"

"Your father was just telling me about his desire for you to resume your studies. I thought you already had."

Mawyndulë was aghast.

"I have to go." He stood up.

"Mawyndulë." She raised a hand to stop him.

He reached down and pulled her up.

"Thank you."

Mawyndulë started to turn, but she held on to him.

"No, I mean thank you for *everything*," she said in a soft voice, and then she leaned over and kissed him on the cheek.

A month ago he would have recoiled. A month ago he would have scrubbed his face with a bristle brush. But a month ago he'd never served in the Aquila nor held up a building while a rebellion raged around him. A month ago he didn't have the respect of one of the highest-ranking officials in the city. Now, as he trotted down the steps, he smiled.

Mawyndulë stormed on to the east palace balcony where his father, Vasek, Vidar, and Taraneh were holding an impromptu meeting in the summer sun. The senior officer of the Lion Corps stood awkward and stiff, his helm under one arm, listening intently as Vasek droned on about something.

"I've just learned I'm to have a new—" This was all Mawyndulë got out before he was blown onto his back.

"Synne, that's my son!" the fane barked, without nearly enough conviction or outrage to suit Mawyndulë. "I don't think he's here to kill me."

Mawyndulë lay moaning. The floor of the Talwara was tiled in marble, and he'd landed on one hip and an elbow.

"Oh, get up, boy. She hit you with wind, not a bolt of lightning."

Mawyndulë crawled to his feet and sneered at Synne, who didn't see. She'd lost interest, dismissed him as no one of importance. If he returned the blow, she'd fly off the balcony and into the Shinara River—if she was lucky. He considered it, even chose the sounds and movements that would be required to summon a good strong gust, but his father's voice was already raised, and Mawyndulë had another, more pressing, issue. Still, he was embarrassed and more than a little angry to be knocked on his backside by a diminutive goblin-girl whom he hadn't heard of until after the Gray Cloak Revolt. He also felt the fight to be unfair. He hadn't heard the attack. Without a warning, there hadn't been any time to defend himself. Thinking about it, he hadn't heard her freeze Vasek either, and she'd been just behind Mawyndulë at the time.

She's fast. That's all there is to it. The girl is fast—and apparently silent.

"Call a general assembly of the Shahdi," his father told Vasek. "And let Kasimer know I want to see him."

"Shahdi?" Mawyndulë said, coming to the balcony on the side that was opposite Synne. "Why assemble the general army? We have the Instarya."

"Alon Rhist was taken," the fane said. "We'll need to re-form the Spider Corps. It's been too long since the Miralyith went to war."

"Alon Rhist was . . ." Mawyndulë was certain he hadn't heard correctly, or that his father had misspoken. He sometimes did. Old people had dusty minds that didn't always work right. They forgot where they put things, called people by the wrong names, and while they could remember an incident from a thousand years ago with perfect clarity, they had no idea what they had eaten for breakfast that morning. His father had once called him Treya, mixing him up with his servant, of all people.

"Clean the wax from your ears, boy," his father growled. "The Rhunes surrounded the fortress and took it."

"But that's not possible. They're just Rhunes," Mawyndulë protested.

"Rhunes led by Nyphron and Arion, I suspect." The fane looked at Vasek.

Vasek nodded. "Information is still coming in. What we know is that thousands of Rhunes, both Gula and Rhulyn, swept up from the south and surrounded Grandford. Within hours, the Instarya Guard surrendered."

"The Instarya don't surrender," Mawyndulë said. "Those people are fanatical about combat."

"You visited them once and now you're the expert, are you?" His father shook his head.

"Nyphron is the son of their tribal leader," Taraneh said. "After all those years of isolation on the frontier, it's possible the Instarya's loyalty tipped more toward one of their own and away from your father."

The door at the end of the corridor opened with a bang and immediately slammed shut again. Cries of pain were followed by unintelligible cursing.

"My fane?" Haderas called out.

"Let them in, Synne," the fane told her. An instant later, the door swung free.

Haderas and Rigarus entered. One tall and the other short, the two were almost always together, usually drinking. Neither was Miralyith, so Mawyndulë knew no more about them than their faces and names.

"You sent for us, my fane?" Haderas asked. His voice was muffled as he rubbed his cheek where the door had hit it.

"We have a problem," the fane explained. "I ordered the Instarya to invade Rhulyn and destroy the Rhunes. Instead, Nyphron has yoked them into his service. And just like he did with the Gray Cloaks, he's managed to seduce the Instarya to revolt against me. He's taken control of Alon Rhist."

Both Fhrey returned blank faces as if they had only understood every other word. Since they weren't Miralyith, Mawyndulë wasn't surprised. His father would likely need to draw pictures.

"What do you want us to do, my fane?" Haderas asked.

"The son of my challenger has stolen my army. He has my fortress, and I suspect he's bent on revenge. What do you think I want? We are going to war, you fools! I want an army of my own. Haderas, you'll raise and command the Bear Legion, Rigarus, the Wolf."

Both Fhrey looked terrified.

"Our people will be no match for the Instarya in combat," Haderas said.

"We aren't certain the Instarya have agreed to break Ferrol's Law," Vasek added.

"The Gray Cloaks had no such concerns," the fane shot back, harshly enough to surprise even Vasek.

His father's adviser nodded, conceding the point, but added, "I just mean that, as warriors, they place a high value on entering Alysin. This may be enough to deter them."

"It doesn't matter," the fane said. "I am also reinstating the Spider Corps. Kasimer Del will lead them." The fane waited for a response from Haderas and Rigarus. When none came, he added, "You and your troops will be mostly for show, support, and cleanup. The Spider Corps will do the heavy work."

They both nodded but looked even less confident than before.

"This needs to be stopped, and quickly," the fane said. "I want it over. There will be no half measures. No one is exempt. I want two thousand ready to march by spring."

"Two thousand?" Haderas looked shocked.

"By spring?" Taraneh said.

"Is that a problem?" the fane asked.

Taraneh looked to Vasek with desperate eyes. "We left the defense of Erivan to the Instarya. We only have the Lion Corps and the Shahdi on this side of the Nidwalden. Even combined, they aren't much of an army, and training new recruits takes time."

"You have until spring."

"What do we need an army for?" Mawyndulë said. "We are Miralyith."

"So, what would you do, boy? Wish them out of existence? You have that kind of power, do you?" His father was more than angry; he bordered on rage. "Can you snap your fingers and make thousands of people, people who are hundreds of miles away, vanish? Did your idol, Gryndal, teach you this miracle during your two-week jaunt to Rhulyn? The same trip where he got his head chopped off? I'm seeing a bit of a problem with your counsel!"

Mawyndulë was so shocked by his father's tone that he took two steps backward, bumping into Sile. His father had never spoken to him like that before. He rarely raised his voice, and Mawyndulë found himself frightened that Lothian might lose control and do something he wouldn't regret until later—if then.

The fane walked to the balcony and leaned on the railing. He stared down for several minutes. No one else moved or spoke. Mawyndulë imagined that even the songbirds went silent for fear of further angering the fane.

At last, Lothian turned. "Taraneh."

"My fane." The Fhrey snapped to attention.

"You will make me a new army. The members of your Lion Corps will train the new recruits for the Bear and Wolf Legions. You will inform Minister Metis regarding your needs for weapons and armor. Let her know this is now her tribe's top priority. By spring, I will have two thousand trained and equipped warriors ready to march west. Is that understood?"

"Yes, my fane," everyone replied.

"With luck, they won't be needed, but luck hasn't been on my side recently."

The others filed out quickly, eager to get to work, or just happy to get away. Mawyndulë was left alone with his father, Sile, and Synne. He wished they would leave, too, but, of course, they wouldn't. He hadn't seen the fane's double shadows leave his side since the Gray Cloak attack.

"Why are you still here? What do you want?"

Mawyndulë remembered about the news of the tutor, but it was trivial now. "I want to go," he said before even thinking.

"Go? Go where?"

"With you. When the army is ready, you'll be leading it, won't you?"

The fane narrowed his eyes and stared at his son as if Mawyndulë had changed colors or spun his head around in a complete circle. "Yes," he replied. "How did you know that?"

"Just makes sense. You sent Arion, and she failed. Sent Gryndal and me, and we failed. You sent the giants, and they failed. You want it done right this time."

His father was nodding.

"I want to go."

"Why?"

He considered explaining his desire for revenge for his idol's death but then reconsidered. His father would most likely think *he* should be his son's idol, so Mawyndulë took another tack. "The Fhrey don't go to war often. If I'm to be fane one day, I should see it, understand it. Your mother took you to the Battle of Mador when you were young. That's why you know how to deal with this. If I don't go, if I miss the chance to experience battle, how will I know how to handle my own future conflicts?"

His father studied him as if baffled by what he'd just heard. He glanced out the window, then back at his son. "Admirable. You do understand that if you were to stay here, and I were to be killed on the field of battle, you'd be fane—the youngest one ever—assuming you won against whomever blew the horn in challenge. Going with me is risky. You could die."

"I'm not afraid."

"No—I can see that. I suppose you're too young to worry about death. It's not even a possibility in your mind, or if it is, you see your end as some heroic accomplishment and you would take pleasure in cementing your place in history." Lothian rubbed his hands together, palm sliding against palm. "Getting older, Mawyndulë, is like climbing a mountain. The higher you go, the greater the view. From time to time, you look back. At such heights, you can see paths behind you: the trails you took and the ones you foolishly disregarded; the blind alleys you fortunately missed, purely out of chance rather than by some greater wisdom on your part. You also spot others following you, people making the same stupid decisions. From your elevated position, you witness their bad choices, the ones they can't see because they aren't standing where you are. You could shout down, attempt to warn them, but they rarely listen. They are too blinded by the indisputable fact that the path you followed got you where you are, to the place they want to be."

His father stared then, as if waiting for a reply, but Mawyndulë had no idea what his father had been babbling about. Maybe he wasn't saying anything, dusty-minded after all. Older people just talked sometimes. Maybe hearing their own voice was reassuring to them somehow.

"Yes, you can come," the fane said at last, sounding disappointed. "You, too, can go to war."

Mawyndulë smiled.

"But you'll be precious little use to me without an education."

The smile vanished.

"I've enrolled you at the Academy of the Art."

Thinking his father had appointed a new tutor was bad enough, but this . . . this was out of the question.

"The academy?" Mawyndulë said, stunned. "But that's for—I'm the prince. I don't belong in a public school."

"That's exactly where you belong." The fane took a step toward his son. "You need a formal education in the Art, and tutors haven't been working out well for you, or them."

"But at the academy?" Mawyndulë was horrified at being forced to practice, to take more stupid lessons, and this time in front of an audience. "How can I—your son—attend Art school? That's so . . . wrong."

"Wrong? You do know about the academy, right?"

Mawyndulë rolled his eyes. "I know it's no place for the son of the fane."

Lothian laughed. "You *are* aware of how the school came to be?"

Mawyndulë thought a moment. This was one of those things he felt he ought to know, but for some reason, he couldn't recall if he'd ever learned that particular fact. By the way his father was acting, Mawyndulë had missed something important. He gave up. "No."

His father let out a small huff that Mawyndulë couldn't translate. He didn't sound upset, but he didn't sound thrilled, either. If anything, the fane appeared mildly amused. "The school was founded by Pyridian."

Mawyndulë stared at his father, who stared back with enough expectation in his eyes to make Mawyndulë nervous.

"Oh, by the face of Ferrol, you have no idea who I'm talking about, do you?"

Mawyndulë slowly shook his head. He didn't like it that Sile and Synne were listening. Not that he cared about Sile; the giant didn't look capable of understanding which object in the sky was the sun and which was the moon. Synne was another matter. Mawyndulë didn't want to look stupid in front of her, and he felt he was doing just that. But what did it really matter if he didn't know who founded the Miralyith Art Academy?

"Mawyndulë," the fane said, "the Art is ours."

Now he felt his father was just making fun of him. "I know it's ours, but the Fhrey—"

"No!" Lothian held up a hand to stop him. "Not the Fhrey—*ours*." He pointed at himself and then at Mawyndulë. "Our family invented it. Your grandmother was the very first to use it. When she taught others, her lessons were always one on one or in small groups. The learning process was slow, random, inefficient. No one ever thought of formalizing the process until Pyridian came up with the idea. He built the academy using the Art, the same way Fenelyus created Avempartha. He taught a whole generation of Fhrey, trained them to teach, and appointed them as instructors in his school. Gryndal and Arion were both his students."

Mawyndulë couldn't care less about The Traitor, but . . . "He taught Gryndal?"

"Oh, yes."

"Ah . . . I don't recall—have I ever met Pyridian?"

The fane shook his head. "He died before you were born. In fact, you could say your very existence is due to Pyridian's death, which is why I find it so strange that you don't know about him."

Mawyndulë glanced again at Synne, feeling certain his father was purposely humiliating him.

The fane noticed and shook his head. "Trust me, this oversight is more embarrassing for me than for you. I should have mentioned him before."

"Why? Who was he?" Mawyndulë asked.

"Your brother."

CHAPTER SIX

Second Best

That winter, seeds were planted. The army learned to fight, smiths learned to forge, people learned what it felt like to live in a house rather than a dirt-floored shack, and I learned to write. Human civilization was born under a blanket of snow, sheltered by walls of stone.

—THE BOOK OF BRIN

The little window in the door at the base of the Kype slid aside, exposing just a pair of eyes and part of a nose. As always, the sentinel said, "State your business." This was repeated in Fhrey; why, Raithe had no idea.

"Back again to see Persephone."

"State your name and your business with Madam Keenig."

"You know my name."

"Refusal to answer will—"

"Raithe, and because I want to speak with her."

"About what?"

"None of your business."

The little window snapped shut, but Raithe didn't leave. He waited.

After living in Alon Rhist for eight months, Raithe felt isolated even though he resided in a city of more people than he ever thought existed. Lately, he'd been blaming it on the snow. Drifts blocked the narrow streets, sealing people inside, discouraging communal gatherings. By spring, he realized it wasn't the snow.

To make matters worse, he was always cold. For a man who grew up in a dirt house heated only by wafers of dung, the grand marbled halls of the Rhist were surprisingly chilly. *Dirt is wholesome, life giving. Stone is just cold.* It took only a single winter in the Rhist for Raithe to develop a nostalgia for his youth in Dureya. For the first time in recent memory, the weather had warmed and was downright hot. The snow was in full retreat, lingering only in deep shadows under bridges or tight alleyways. Birds were back, buds popped, flowers sprouted, and Raithe wasn't pleased with how things had been going in the Rhist. Wasn't his call; he was still just a chieftain of one—two, if he included Malcolm—which he didn't. Now that Malcolm was back in the Rhist, Raithe was less confident about the ex-slave's loyalties. There wasn't anything Malcolm said or did, but Raithe felt things had changed between them—a feeling in his gut like a cold coming on.

He started to lean against the bronze door that led to the inner sanctum of the fortress, but the sun had made it too hot to touch. He walked back across the bridge and peered over the edge. *Long way down.* He had no idea how far, but red roofs the size of cranberries spilled at his feet. Out to the east, he could see all the way to the rocky highlands beyond the High Spear Valley where his brothers had been slain. To the south, he could see The Forks where his father's body lay. While his village was much closer, the great dome blocked the view, and he couldn't see where his mother and sister had died. His village was right underfoot, but hidden from him. He was surrounded by death in every direction except one.

Returning to the door, he beat on the bronze again.

The window slid back once more. "Yes?" asked the eyes and nose.

"Still waiting."

"Did you have an appointment?"

"A what? Just tell Persephone I'm here, will you?"

"And why does that matter?"

"Because she's a friend of mine."

"And?"

"And what?" Raithe asked.

"That's what I'm asking. Madam Keenig is a very busy woman. If I can't inform her of what this meeting is pertaining to, I don't see how I can report it at all."

"It's not a meeting. I would just like to talk to her."

"That's what a meeting is, sir. Is the topic of your conversation a matter of Rhist security? Is that why you are refusing to divulge its nature? If so, I can assure you that I am quite trusted by the administration of the citadel, and you should have no concerns about revealing any information to me."

Raithe didn't understand most of the words, even though he was certain they were in Rhunic.

"Listen, I just . . . I just want to say hello."

"If that's all, I can pass that information to her. You don't need to bother the keenig."

"I also want to see how she's doing, okay?"

"So, this is a cordial call, a purely social visit?"

"Yeah, whatever."

"Please wait."

The little window slid shut again.

Raithe backed away from the heat-radiating door, wondering if the interior was roasting. That might account for the interaction. The guard's brains were baked.

Once again, he went out on the bridge, but this time he looked up. The Kype was a building of solid stone as high as the Verenthenon. It had but one entrance, and its only windows were narrow slits near the top. This made the Kype, and everything beyond it, the most secured portion of the fortress. Anyone attacking would need to cross the Grandford Bridge, break into the big gates, fight through the lower courtyard, climb the winding ramp, then battle through the narrow city streets. And that would just get them to the fortress proper, where another smaller wall and an additional set of bronze gates waited. Behind them was the upper courtyard, which housed the barracks, training fields, tannery, kitchens, smithies, and livestock pens. Above that and up a steep, narrow staircase was the domed Verenthenon. An invading force would need to climb up that deathtrap of a staircase, around the Verenthenon's series of terraces and balconies just to reach the long corbel bridge where Raithe now stood. Given that the famed Spyrok—that sky-piercing watchtower of stone and glass—was on the far side of the Kype and accessed by another bridge, it was the most isolated place in the Rhist complex. So far, after more than eight months of trying, Raithe had never made it farther than where he now stood. He hadn't been able to get inside the Kype, never made it past its bronze door.

The little window opened once more.

"Madam Keenig is not available at this time."

Before Raithe could say anything, the little window slammed shut, this time followed by a metal-on-metal snap.

In a field of grass scarred by patches of worn dirt, four dozen men beat each other with sticks. A few others used metal swords—the more advanced ones, the quick learners—but most swung hickory imitations at each other's heads. Raithe could tell the trainees were getting better, since wood-to-wood cracks outnumbered soft fleshy slaps. In addition, the curses and genuine screams were rare. That morning, rapid staccato clacks carried across the training field, punctuated by the occasional hoot of success.

"See her?" Malcolm asked, even before Raithe was completely down the stairs.

"I think she's taking a bath."

Malcolm and Suri basked in the sun at the bottom of the stairs, reclining with their legs extended on the grass. The two looked like a pair of lizards lounging in the heat. Malcolm craned his head back to squint at Raithe. "Turned away *again*? Did you tell them you're a chieftain?"

"They know that." Raithe sat in the light alongside Suri. It felt good to soak up the sun, to feel it on his face. *Never know how much you appreciate something until it's gone.*

"Are you sure?"

Raithe nodded while watching the practice field where the closest combatants were Farmer Wedon and one of the younger Gula. Pride prevented the older northern men from training with the Fhrey, but they sent their boys and young men, who likely repeated everything they learned when they returned home. Everyone wore nothing but breechclouts, their skin slick and shiny with sweat. He could tell the better fighters by the number of grass blades stuck to the backs of their opponents.

"He's doing it on purpose," Raithe said.

"He?"

"Nyphron," Suri offered. She had her eyes closed, hands folded on her chest as if she were dead.

Malcolm glanced at the girl, then back at Raithe. "Nyphron was there?"

"No—well, I can't actually say. All I ever see are eyes and a nose, so maybe, but I'm sure it's by his orders. He's trying to keep me away from her, doesn't like the competition."

"You think he's—what? You think Nyphron is romantically interested in Persephone?"

Raithe smirked. "You were the one who once told me Fhrey and humans weren't so different, remember?"

"I'm not saying it's impossible, just wondering what makes you think he's interested."

Suri answered for Raithe. "It's because Nyphron raises his fur whenever Raithe gets too close."

"Raises his fur?" Malcolm chuckled.

"Like a badger on a fresh kill. Gets all protective and tries to scare off anything that gets too close." When Malcolm chuckled again, she added, "I wouldn't go laughing at a badger. No sense of humor—none at all. Trust me on that."

"Every time I see Persephone, he's there. I can't get the woman alone. They sit together at every public meal and council meeting."

"He finishes her sentences now. Have you noticed?" Suri said, looking up at him while shielding her eyes from the sun.

Raithe hadn't, but he'd seen little of Persephone of late. Most people weren't allowed inside the Kype. Persephone's personal attendants, such as Moya, Padera, and Brin, were among the few that had access. Suri could get in because she and Arion shared a room behind the bronze door. As for Raithe, he only saw Persephone during the large, noisy, obligatory, and increasingly infrequent council meetings held in the Verenthenon. "He keeps her imprisoned in that tower like a dragon guarding its hoard."

"She's just busy," Malcolm said. "You forget, she's the Keenig of the Ten Clans. If you add the Instarya to that number, it means she's in control of the whole frontier. I've heard she has constant meetings, all day and late into the night."

"With who?"

"All kinds of people: civic leaders from here, who are still fearful of Rhunes in their midst; messengers from all the Rhune villages; and Fhrey commanders keeping her posted on developments from as far away as Ervanon."

"What's Ervanon?"

"Another fortress like this, but north of here. All the Instarya outposts now fall under her control because they recognize Nyphron as head of the Instarya and rightful lord of the Rhist, and he acknowledges her rule as the keenig."

He pointed at the Fhrey instructors moving through the combatants, holding their own little sticks and shouting instructions, encouragements, and insults. "And then there are these fellows here. Persephone has them reporting on the training process. And there are the supply train organizers and the quartermasters giving reports on growth, field rotations, and forecasted yields, not to mention the Fhrey who keep the Rhist functioning. I've heard the wells are running low. And, of course, she has to listen to grievances in the high court of the Karol."

"I have grievances," Raithe said.

Malcolm plucked a long blade of grass from near the bottom step. "But not pertaining to official business. The things I'm talking about are complaints about new regulations or unfair treatment."

"I'm being treated unfairly! She's my friend; I shouldn't need *official business*. I used to be able to just walk over and see her."

Malcolm shrugged with an apologetic smile. "Times change."

Suri sat up and addressed Raithe. "I've told you before, I can get you in."

Raithe looked at her and she smiled. Her grin was more than an offer to escort him through the door. She was hinting at greater consequences.

Suri had spoken of her trip to the land of the dwarfs. Not all of it, he could tell some parts were too raw to get near. Her reluctance was similar to Raithe's silence about his family and life in Dureya. Certain moments were avoided, hinted at but not trod upon—not from a lack of trust but due to a desire to avoid walking over old graves. She'd told him enough to know that, if so inclined, Suri could reduce the Kype to rubble or melt the bronze door to an insignificant puddle. This was what her grin had meant, and that smile was accompanied by a mischievous twinkle in her eyes that said it would be as much fun for her as it would be advantageous for him.

He smiled but shook his head. "If I really needed to get in, I could. Frost or Flood would pop the hinges off that door, or I could just ask Brin or Moya to arrange an audience."

"My way would be more fun." Suri wiggled her eyebrows.

"Arion wouldn't like it," Raithe said. "You know she wouldn't."

"I'd put it back," the mystic said.

Raithe had no idea what it was she planned to put back—the door maybe? Knowing her, and judging from the size of that grin, it might be the entire front-facing wall of the Kype.

"So, why don't you?" Malcolm asked Raithe. "Why not arrange for an audience?"

"Because I don't want an *audience* with the *keenig*. I want to *see Seph*, and . . . I don't want to see her if she doesn't want to see me." He pulled his legs up and sighed. "I've been to that door a couple dozen times over the winter. Everyone knows. I'm sure she's heard by now, but even if she hasn't, why has she never come looking for me? And don't tell me she's busy. No one is *that* busy."

The sound of cracking sticks diminished as most of the pairs stopped fighting. Everyone's attention was drawn to the center of the field where no grass grew, and two combatants faced off.

"What's going on?" Raithe asked.

"Tesh and Sebek," Malcolm replied.

"Again?"

"The kid's determined."

Raithe backed up the steps to see over the heads of the sweaty men gathering in a ring around Sebek and Tesh. The two used actual swords, no shields, and were naked to the waist like everyone else. As always, Sebek held both his swords, Nagon and Tibor. Tesh had his own pair of Roan-made iron short swords.

Over the course of eight months, Tesh had excelled at combat training. The boy, who had marked his sixteenth birthday just two months before, had thrown himself into learning everything he could about fighting. He was out before dawn and came back to his bed late each night, falling asleep as soon as his head hit the mattress. At least twice he never made it to the bed, and Raithe found him asleep on the floor or table with a half-eaten meal beside him. All the exercise and ample food had turned the onetime cadaverous whelp into a lean, muscular lad. Still lanky, still not as tall as he would likely one day be, Tesh was already well on his way toward his goal of mastering the disciplines of the Galantians.

"Up for another beating?" Sebek grinned, spinning Tibor in his grip.

Tesh didn't reply. He was crouched, blades up, concentrating, staring into Sebek's eyes.

No one fought Sebek except Tesh. The Fhrey didn't teach, he humiliated. He also injured. Everyone knew Sebek was talented enough to avoid injuring his opponents, but he was easily irritated by weak competition and showed his disappointment by drawing blood. During one match, a terrified farmer from Menahan started crying, and Sebek responded by cutting off the man's little finger. No one fought Sebek after that—no one except Tesh. The lad desperately wanted to beat the master. The desire had turned into an obsession.

The kid invited Sebek to come at him, and Sebek obliged. His two blades looked more like ten as they whirled in circles, crisscrossing their course in a weaving pattern that left only streaks. The blades themselves moved too fast to be seen. When Tesh's swords collided with Sebek's, the sound was the crash of metal waves upon a metal shore. There were sparks. Raithe never saw any other colliding blades spark. He had witnessed the Galantians sparring with each other. Vorath and Tekchin frequently held grudge matches, but their clashes didn't kick sparks. When Tesh fought Sebek, it always produced a light show.

The boy fell back. He always did. An onslaught from Sebek was a force of nature that couldn't be resisted or contained. Raithe remembered the one time he'd battled Sebek, and it had been nothing like this. The Fhrey had calculatingly probed and then disarmed Raithe with his bare hand. Tesh was genuinely trying to win. He managed to catch strokes he couldn't see, deflecting blind thrusts and ducking swipes even before they were made. Tesh looked like he was reading the Fhrey's mind. And still Sebek was way out ahead, planning three strokes in advance, knowing not only that Tesh would manage to block, but *how* he would block—Sebek formulated attacks to counter Tesh's moves *before* the lad even thought of them.

All forty-eight men stood in the field intently watching what was sure to be the most amazing display of combat any of them had ever seen. The spectators winced, gasped, and cringed, always after the fact—after disaster *almost* happened. Reactions were too slow to keep pace.

By Mari's name, the kid is really good. Raithe wondered how such a thing was possible after only a year. *No, not just a year. He's Dureyan. That kid's been fighting his whole life.* He remembered how Tesh had brandished a dagger the day they first met, and how the boy had tripped him numerous times when the two sparred on the beaches of Dahl Tirre. Raithe had thought Tesh was entertaining. He'd had no idea what the kid was capable of.

He might have been able to kill me, even back then. It was like I was playing with a lion cub, and now it outweighs me.

Raithe never saw it happen. Everything was too quick. He heard it, though, an off-note, a *clang* instead of a *ping*, and one of Tesh's swords flew from his hands.

Sebek didn't let up; he attacked with unrelenting aggression. Tesh couldn't block both of Sebek's swords with just his one. The boy caught the first, but the second came across his open side. Sebek was going to exact payment for the fight; he was going to cut Tesh across the chest, leave a mark his opponent wouldn't forget. But that didn't happen.

Tesh slapped the blade away with his bare hand.

He did it three times before Sebek stopped the fight and lowered his blades. He nodded. "Better."

The crowd of sweat-slick men erupted into cheers and shouts of jubilation. Sebek hadn't been beaten; the match wasn't even close to a draw. Disarming Tesh counted as a victory, and the kid hadn't mounted even a single offense in the whole match. But he had held his own, and for the men on that field, it was a victory beyond any of their dreams.

Sebek flipped Tesh's lost sword into the air with his foot and struck it with a sharp swing from his own blade, sending the weapon spinning at the kid. Tesh caught it by its handle, and slammed both blades into their scabbards.

"Well done, *Techylor*," Sebek said.

As if the contest had been the finale, training for that day ended when everyone rushed to clap Tesh on the back.

Raithe turned to Malcolm. "What's it mean? What Sebek called Tesh?"

"*Techylor?*" Malcolm said. "It means *swift of hand*, or just *swifthand*, I suppose."

"Great. The kid's going to be impossible to live with now," Raithe grumbled.

Malcolm nodded. "Probably, but you ought to consider yourself fortunate. Next to Nyphron, you've got the best Shield in Alon Rhist."

Raithe frowned. "Apparently, I'm second best to Nyphron in a number of things."

CHAPTER SEVEN

Dreams and Nightmares

I started writing to chase away demons and to preserve the loved ones I had lost. After all these years, none of that has changed.
—THE BOOK OF BRIN

The moist hand clamped over Brin's mouth. The other one wrapped around her waist, trapping her arms. She was hauled away, her heels dragging across stone as the raow rasped in her ear, "Relax. Don't struggle. I have you now. Just need to get you back to the pile."

Back to the pile!

Brin couldn't scream, couldn't move; she could barely breathe. She tried to kick her feet, but that did nothing to save her. As disgusting as it might be, she tried to bite the hand, but her mouth couldn't open.

The thing continued to whisper in a frighteningly reassuring tone, as if it were trying to save her. But it wasn't speaking to her—not really. "Yes, everything will be okay. We have you now. Just need to get back, back to the pile. Need to get back so I can eat and finally sleep."

She felt it lick her cheek.

"Such a sweet face."

She woke up, her heart racing. Something covered her face, making it hard to breathe.

Brin reached up and found the pillow. Ripping it away, she threw it on the floor. "Stupid thing," she whispered in the dark, shaking.

She propped herself on her elbows and took a few more breaths, calming down. The raow was long dead, and Brin was in a pretty little home on Lyonet Street, in Little Rhen. Moonlight entered the window, casting a skewed square across the floor, the wall, and over the feet of the two beds. Roan's was empty again. Downstairs, Padera was snoring.

Brin's nightshirt stuck to the sweat on her skin. She shivered, drawing the blanket around her.

Just a dream, she imagined her mother saying. *Go back to sleep.*

But Brin knew that if she tried, the raow would come again. It always did. Once the raow invaded her sleep, only daylight chased it off. She'd managed to go a whole week this time without a visit. But tonight . . . She leaned over the edge of the bed and pointed a finger at the fallen pillow. "I blame you."

Brin wasn't used to pillows, never had one before. The bag full of feathers collapsed under the weight of her head, folding in and doing its best to smother her. She sighed, frowned, and folded her arms. She wasn't going back to sleep anytime soon. She'd be exhausted in the morning, but there was no getting around it. She was up.

She started to swing her feet off the side of the bed, but pulled them back at the last second. She spun around on her stomach and carefully lowered her head to peer under the bed. Then she looked under Roan's. Nothing. Relief and embarrassment washed over her in equal parts. *How old am I?* She got up and fumbled in the dark, her hands searching for the leather satchel. She had made the carrying case herself. A single piece of goat hide was folded around her stack of parchments and bound up with straps. From the small night table, she grabbed up a handful of quills. Brin had been using reeds dipped in ink to mark on the pages but found the quills better. After employing hundreds of people to strip birds of their feathers for making arrows, Alon Rhist had piles of naked quills lying around. They, too, were hollow, and much more durable than reeds. Thanks to Moya, Brin had hundreds.

Brin carried the parchments, ink, and quills to the desk by the window and set them down. After a long winter, she had an impressive pile of vellum parchment. Part of the stack was a translation—as best she could manage—of the tablet rubbings they had saved from the Ancient One's chamber in Neith. She was still working on those, but after translating the metallurgy portion for Roan, she had jumped ahead in order to record more recent events while things were still fresh in her mind.

She did that a lot.

Brin first started writing about growing up in Dahl Rhen, focusing on her parents. Then she jumped forward to the trip Persephone led to Neith. She went to great literary effort to eviscerate Gronbach the dwarf, recording his treachery as legendary, the very definition of evil. Then, Brin jumped even further ahead and wrote about life in Alon Rhist. Fhrey and Rhunes mingled about as well as fire and ice, or Gula and Rhulyn, who also had problems coexisting. A number of outbursts had resulted in some deaths. Persephone decided to segregate the tribes before riots broke out. The cold weather helped to cool tempers, but both were warming up again.

Since sleep wasn't an option, she thought she'd do some writing, but before starting, she decided to reread the section where the Gilarabrywn ate the raow, her favorite part. The night was cold, and she grabbed a blanket from her bed and was searching for a lamp when she heard voices coming from the street below.

Who is out chatting in the middle of a chilly night?

She returned to the window and leaned closer.

Whoever it was spoke softly, and in Rhunic. "No! I forbid it. And you know better than to be out here."

"I'm hungry!" the voice said in a hoarse whisper, just like in her dream. Brin shivered.

"I'll arrange it, like I did with Jada. You have to trust me. Haven't I taken care of you in the past? You need to be patient."

"It's been a long time. I'm tired and need to sleep."

"We have an agreement! Spring is here, and the time is approaching. Until then, you need to stay hidden."

"I can smell them—all of them—so many. The wind blows south. It's—it's maddening!"

"It won't be long now. I promise. Then you can kill for me. Now, let's go back, and don't slip out again, or we'll both be killed."

With every ounce of courage she could muster, Brin pushed the window open wider and stuck her head out far enough to look down. All she saw were a pair of shadows disappearing around the corner of her building. In the dark of her room barely illuminated by the pale moonlight, she drew the blanket tighter and shivered.

Early the next morning, Brin stood in front of her adopted home, looking up at the bedroom window. The house was one of the many two-story, whitewash-and-timber buildings. This was no warrior's home. Its carved door, tile-and-stencil work, branching stair banister, and flower beds filled with perennials already beginning to bloom spoke of a place once cherished. Brin felt guilty being there, and in eight months, she hadn't so much as moved the furniture.

Persephone had insisted they weren't conquerors of Alon Rhist, but allies, what Nyphron referred to as *liberators*. A fair number of Fhrey had packed up and walked out. Persephone let them go. Huhana Hill, one of the nicer parts of the city, became the first to empty. That previous autumn when the Fhrey fled Alon Rhist, Huhana Hill became a neighborhood of abandoned houses, and Persephone filled the vacant buildings with surviving inhabitants of Dahl Rhen, creating the Rhune District. Given that most of the other clans had homes to return to, Huhana Hill became known as Little Rhen.

The house that Padera, Roan, and Brin shared was one of the finest. There were bigger and more elaborate ones, but inch for inch, this one was the most pleasant. Brin was certain that wasn't an accident. Persephone would have invited them to stay with her in the Kype, if such a thing had been practical, or desired. No one—not even Persephone—liked the stark, cold fortress filled with intimidating male Instarya. More of the Fhrey in the city were female, and while they didn't exactly welcome the Rhunes, they didn't protest, either, at least not publicly.

Over the winter, Little Rhen had begun to resemble Dahl Rhen, if it had died and gone to Alysin. The well in the center of the tree-lined square was frequented by the likes of Arlina, Viv Baker, and Autumn, whose husbands— like most of the able men—were in training and bunked at the fortress. Gifford lived in Little Rhen, too, as did Tressa, Habet, and Mathias Hagger, who was too old to walk up the Hill's steps alone. Padera was the first to call it Little Rhen, and that's how Brin—how everyone living there—had come to see it. But on that morning, looking up at her pretty new home, Brin saw that part of town as sinister.

They had stood right here.

She looked around, trying to gauge the exact spot where the two speakers had held their conversation.

They didn't sound human.

Brin imagined them as a pair of raow, but that was most certainly the result of her nightmare.

And they had spoken Rhunic, not Fhrey.

Near the corner of the block, just below her window, was a flower bed. The four delicate sprouts that had emerged with the warming weather had been crushed, pressed down in the soft dirt. She bent over to look at the depression in the soil.

"Lose something?" The voice came from directly behind her.

Heart pounding, Brin shot up and spun so fast she nearly fell. A hand grabbed her forearm, catching her. Terrified, she pulled back and nearly screamed—but it wasn't a raow that had hold of her.

"Oh—sorry, didn't mean to scare you," the young man said, letting her go the moment she was steady again.

"Shouldn't sneak up on people, then," Brin snapped. The moment she spoke, she wished she could take the words back.

This wasn't the first time Brin had seen this particular young man. She had first noticed him in the training yard, a place she'd passed each day when delivering Roan's midday meal. If left to herself, Roan would forget to eat, so Padera and Brin delivered. Would-be-warriors were always practicing in the upper courtyard in front of the smithy, and this young man was always there, even in the snow and rain. On warm days, he'd take his shirt off, and Brin was thankful he was so intent on his lessons that he didn't see her sneaking a peek his way. His body was pure lean muscle, but it was his smile that attracted her most. As he sparred, a huge grin dominated his face, like he was taking down a giant or slaying a dragon. Something wonderfully wild lay behind such a grand grin. She'd felt the same way about Raithe when he first came to Dahl Rhen. Neither of these men were farmers, shepherds, or woodcutters.

When she first noticed the young man, she thought he looked familiar. Back in Tirre, there had been a boy, a scrawny kid who lived with Raithe and Malcolm. Brin only noticed him because he was one of the few beneath the wool who was her age, and he came to the few chieftain meetings that Raithe had attended. But the young man she watched practicing in the upper yard, the same one who'd just grabbed her arm, was bigger, fuller, and taller. He sported disheveled locks, dark beautiful eyes, and patches of hair on his cheeks and chin. The boy she knew from Tirre had been covered in a torn, stained rag. This man wore a longshirt cinched tight at his waist by a sword belt holding two blades.

What had started as a chore became the most anticipated part of her day. After dropping off the food for Roan, Brin would linger in the yard outside the smithy, watching. Each day she hoped he would notice her, but he never looked her way. During the long walk back home, she daydreamed about the day they would eventually meet. Most scenarios involved him making some blunder, falling perhaps. He'd feel foolish, look awkward, but she would smile and make light of the misstep, assuring him it happened to everyone. Then he would invite her to take a walk. As they strolled through some lovely forest—not that there were any within two days' travel—she would tell him about her book. She'd talk about language, writing, and the story she had found on the tablets from Neith; the young hero would be so impressed that he would fall in love with her.

They would marry, have children, then grandchildren, and finally die in each other's arms, wrinkled and gray.

Reality was quite different.

"I wasn't sneaking. I just—"

"You certainly weren't announcing yourself from afar." Brin didn't know why she said it. She was nervous, off-balance, and the words just came out—and they came out angry.

"Well, I—ah . . ." He looked awkward, then glanced at the house. "I was looking for Roan, the metalsmith. I heard she lived around here."

"She does." Brin then eyed him suspiciously. "What do you want with *her?*"

"I want to be fitted for armor."

"Oh," Brin said stupidly. Having saved her from falling, he remained close. She could have leaned out and kissed him. The thought hovered in her mind, forming a terrible distraction. Catching herself, wondering how moronic she must look staring his way, she blinked. "Ah . . . Roan works up at the fortress in the upper courtyard. She lives here—is supposed to at least—but she spends all her time over there."

"Yeah, I know," the pair of lips, dark eyes, and open shirt said. "But I was just up there and . . ."

"And what?"

He shrugged. "I didn't see her anywhere around. So, I thought maybe she came here. And then I found you on all fours groping around the ground, so I—"

"I wasn't *on all fours!* And I most certainly wasn't *groping!*"

He held up his hands. "Honestly, I don't know what you were doing."

"If you must know, I was looking for footprints." Another sentence she wished she could take back. *This conversation is not at all like I imagined.*

His eyes narrowed. "You were . . . *what?*"

"Never mind. Roan's not here."

The young man hesitated, then finally nodded, turned, and walked away.

You're such an idiot! Brin screamed in her head. *Great impression. Maybe if I'd actually been eating the dirt, if I'd had a mouthful of soil that was spilling in clumps over my lips and was—*

"Why were you looking for footprints?" The young man had stopped. He was staring back at her.

"I heard people talking below my window last night. I—I was wondering who they were."

"And you thought you could tell that by their footprints?" He lifted his own foot and looked at the bottom. "You can do that?"

She scowled. He was making fun of her now. *He thinks I'm an idiot! Great.* "No." She felt her heart sink. "Please, just leave." She felt so awful she might cry and absolutely didn't want him to see that.

He turned to walk away again, but once more stopped. "Okay, so you have to tell me, or it will bother me all day. *Why* were you looking for footprints? How would that help you identify who these people were?"

I hate my life.

Brin didn't say anything. She didn't trust herself to talk anymore, and thought he might just leave if she remained silent. He didn't. Feeling stupid—no, she was well beyond that—she sighed.

I never had a chance with him anyway. What was I thinking? I wasn't— I was dreaming. Look at him! Gorgeous, strong, dashing, and those eyes— those eyes! And then there's me, a pale twig with no shape, an orphan who spends her days scribbling nonsense with discarded quills. He never was going to be interested in me. I might as well light the pyre under that dream and just let the whole thing burn.

"I—I was looking for footprints that *weren't* human."

"Are Fhrey feet that different?"

"Not Fhrey."

He looked at her, puzzled. "You mean . . . wait—what do you mean? A dog or something?"

She shook her head. "Dogs don't talk."

He stared at her, eyes narrowed, his head tilted slightly to one side. "Then . . . what do you think was below your window last night?"

Don't say it. Don't say it. Don't say it!

He walked back to her. His expression was exactly how she pictured he would look as she captivated him with tales of her literary prowess just before he fell in love with her. But that wasn't going to happen now. She sighed and gave up. "A raow."

You moron, Brin! I told you not to say it! Idiot! Idiot.

He'd laugh now—no, most likely he'd ask what a raow was and then not believe her when she explained. She'd face the humiliating experience of telling the tale of how she'd once nearly had her face eaten by one. Any thoughts about her being the sort of person he should stay clear of would be confirmed. He'd see her for what she really was—the real her—what she never was in her fantasies.

"Really?" he said.

Brin didn't know how to respond. She searched his eyes for evidence of sarcasm, his lips for hints of mockery. Nothing—nothing obvious, at least.

"You . . . you believe me?"

He nodded easily, shifting his weight, and resting a hand on the butt of one sword. The confident, casual act was so insanely attractive that Brin sucked in a breath.

"My mother told me about the raow. Come from bodies left unburied, people who were wronged in life—betrayed, usually. Wait, you're Brin, aren't you?"

"You—" Her throat closed on her. She swallowed hard to clear it. "You know me?"

"Well . . ." He chuckled.

"What?" Her heart hesitated mid-beat.

He pointed to the house. "I was told Roan, Padera, and Brin lived here. I've met Roan." Then he chuckled again. "I'm guessing you aren't Padera."

"Oh—" Brin laughed then, too. "No . . . no, I'm not her."

"Yeah, I heard she's like a couple hundred years old and doesn't have any teeth."

She nodded.

"I'm Tesh." He extended a hand.

Brin hadn't shaken many hands. Her mother and friends were huggers. Unsure and tentative, she reached out. He did the rest. He had rough skin that in places was polished to smooth calluses and a firm grip that tightened in stages, but he didn't squeeze. He pulled her hand toward him giving it three solid pumps before letting go.

"Nice to meet you," she replied, then immediately wondered if that was the right thing to say. She'd thought it was appropriate, but coming out of her mouth it sounded too formal and—

"Why do you think a raow was here?" he asked, looking down at the flower bed.

She shrugged. Her hand was still up from the shake, and she had to will it down to her side. She could still feel the warmth of his palm. "It's hard to explain. But what they were saying was—"

"Raow talk?"

"Yes, but maybe it wasn't two raow—maybe it was one raow, and one . . . I'm not sure. I only know for certain that one was a raow."

"How do you know?"

"The voice. It sounded—"

Tesh's eyes grew big, realization dawning. "You're *Brin*."

"We've already established that."

"I mean—*the* Brin. Roan mentioned you. Told us about how you were grabbed by a raow under a Dherg mountain. She said you almost had your face eaten off."

Thanks a lot, Roan. I should just die now.

"Is it the same one? Did it follow you?" Tesh looked around, as if the monster might jump out at them from a nearby hedge.

"No," Brin said. "The one in Neith was killed."

"So, why is this one after you? Do you think it knew the other raow?"

After me? The thought rocked her. *Is it? It was outside* my *window, wasn't it?* "I didn't until just now. Thanks. I'll never sleep again."

"Sorry." He looked guilty, which only made him more handsome. "What did it say? What did you hear?"

"The raow said it was hungry, and the other one insisted it was too dangerous, and it had to wait. Said he would bring the raow something to eat. That he would arrange it."

"Arrange it?"

"Like he did with Jada."

"What's Jada?"

"No idea."

"And they weren't both raow?"

"I don't know. Only one of them had a voice like the one I heard in Neith. But maybe not all raow sound alike."

"What did it sound like?"

"A raspy, dry whisper."

Tesh looked less convinced. "Maybe it was just an old man with a cold." She shook her head.

"I'm just saying—I mean . . ." He looked around again. "What would a raow be doing here? Raow live in remote places where they can keep their piles of bones. They need them to sleep on. At least that's what my mother told me. Raow roam the countryside looking for victims because once they wake they can't sleep again until they feed, until they add bones to their pile. So, how could such a thing live here? Where would it keep its pile? People would notice."

"Well," she said, figuring it out as she spoke, "maybe someone is hiding it."

Tesh looked skeptical. "Someone is hiding a raow?"

"It sounded that way."

"That's like saying a lamb is hiding a lion. Why wouldn't the raow just eat the person keeping it?"

"I don't know."

Tesh scratched his head and narrowed his eyes. "Unless that person was Fhrey. Maybe raow don't eat Fhrey."

Brin shook her head. "They were speaking Rhunic."

Tesh looked skeptical.

Brin shrugged. "Maybe it *was* just an old man with a cold."

Tesh looked up at the house again. "Maybe you should keep your window closed and bolted just the same, huh?"

"Yeah," she said.

An awkward silence followed. Finally, she said, "Well, when I see Roan I'll mention you were looking for her."

"Right, and I guess I'll check back at the smithy."

"Sounds like a plan," Brin said. She was torn. On the one hand, she didn't want him to go, but on the other, she didn't think she could endure more self-inflicted humiliation.

Brin watched him walk down the road and around a corner.

Tesh, she thought. *Not a bad name.* She had expected something more like Spencer or Stanton. He looked like a Stanton, or maybe a—

"Brin!"

She turned to see him coming back into sight, waving for her to join him. She trotted down and followed him around the corner. There, in another, muddier, bed of would-be flowers, Tesh pointed to two sets of footprints. One was clearly made by a pair of common sandals. The other was barefoot, and had just three toes . . . and long, sharp claws.

CHAPTER EIGHT

The Tetlin Witch

I think we accept all too readily what we are told by those we love. It is not that our friends and family lie, but that they do not know the truth.

—THE BOOK OF BRIN

Gifford sat in the corner on a small stool, his usual place when visiting Roan. She had a staff of more than twenty, and a cripple anywhere else in the workshop was a roadblock to progress. He watched her work and hoped to be on hand if she paused to eat the meals that Padera made and Brin carried up. The weather being so nice, he even dreamed of persuading her to go out to the courtyard for a picnic. He figured his chances were about the same as beating Brin in a foot race, but if there was one thing Gifford had in abundance, it was dreams.

Leaning back against the wall of the smithy, he watched Roan beat sparks out of a brilliantly glowing glob. She didn't hit very hard and had to take frequent rests, but there was a single-minded clarity of purpose behind each stroke. When beating metal, Roan was more authoritative, decisive, and sure of herself than Nyphron when he gave a speech at the general assembly. Even the three dwarfs took direction from her.

Creating iron swords turned out to be harder than anyone had thought. That included Roan. Her first attempts ended in failure. Observing the process was distinctly different from replicating it. Roan had lamented her misery, explaining the hundreds of little specifics she hadn't noticed, things she didn't even know to look for: the amount of air, when to pump the bellows, the exact time and temperature to leave a blade in the furnace, the ratio of carbon to iron, and how often to temper. They saw their first snow fall before Roan produced her first sword, and it was an awful-looking thing, heavy and dull.

Gifford expected the dwarfs to be of more help, but as it turned out, none of them had a clue about metallurgy. Still, Frost and Flood were able to build first-rate forges and workstations throughout the fortress and the city by studying the ones the Fhrey had made. This tripled the smithing capacity of Alon Rhist. They also trained members of each clan, who were charged with going back to their dahls and building their own equipment. While Frost and Flood were busy building the infrastructure of smithing, Rain spent the winter days leading teams of miners who dug for raw materials. It wasn't long before carts of iron and coal flooded into Alon Rhist. All this help was well appreciated, but it was up to Roan to figure out the magical secrets of metallurgy and the keys to sword making.

A major breakthrough occurred when Brin finished translating the entire text from their trip to Neith. Gifford had been there when she read the passages. Roan had sat in openmouthed wonder listening to what Brin said, calling the girl a genius. Brin laughed, saying she had no idea what she'd just said, but Roan understood at least some of it. Despite Brin's genius, Roan continued to struggle, and the number of failures grew into a mountain that the dwarfs routinely melted down for new attempts. But it wasn't just the method that vexed Roan. Part of the problem was her inability to physically wield a heavy hammer. That issue was largely resolved when she created a smaller, more Roan-sized tool.

The last part of the equation was Roan's belief that the formulas of the Ancient One weren't right. Maybe Brin translated incorrectly, or perhaps the prisoner in the Agave had held back some of his secrets, but she kept insisting that she could do better. Even after her first success, Roan wasn't satisfied. She was looking for something more. Under pressure from Persephone, Roan was forced to establish a method others could duplicate, even though it wasn't as good as Roan thought it could be. By midwinter, human-made iron weapons were being produced at varying degrees of quality all over Rhulyn, but Roan continued her struggle to find a secret only she seemed to know existed. Gifford could see it in her face, in the way her eyes searched in a void for answers to questions no one even knew to ask. She saw something no one else could, heard music others were deaf to, and for Roan, iron wasn't good enough.

On that spring day, Gifford sat in the corner watching Roan use her whole body when swinging her specially made hammer. Her hair, chopped to a short, practical length, still hung in front of her eyes. A drop of sweat always dangled from the tip of her nose, and in her eyes was a fire hotter than the furnace. The woman was possessed.

She's fighting her own war.

Watching, Gifford had to wonder if Roan was happy. He imagined she liked feeling useful, and he knew she loved working, but Persephone had asked for ten thousand swords, helms, and shields of the finest metal. It didn't matter that by spring hundreds of smiths all over Rhulyn were working night and day to meet the quota. Persephone's decree was, for Roan, her own personal task—her fight to win or lose. Roan was the faithful hound who would run to death for her master. Was it a tragedy when such a dog died, or was that the life and death the animal would have chosen?

Roan put down the hammer and set the glowing glob back into the fire. She wiped her forehead with the rag that was never far from her left hand.

"You hun-gee, Woan?"

Hearing her name, she looked up, her face red from the exertion and heat. She raised her brows in surprise. "When did you get here?"

"This mo-ning," Gifford replied.

"Oh," she said, considering his answer. "Didn't see you come in."

He held up the cloth sack and shook it side to side. "Bwin went to all the twouble of bwinging it to you. Seems a waste not to eat."

Roan hated waste.

"Maybe later," Roan said. "I want to get some more done before noon."

Gifford held back a laugh. "No, Woan. Be night soon."

"Night?"

Gifford nodded.

She looked out the window. "Oh. I guess so." Roan looked back at him apologetically. "And you've been here since this morning? I'm so sorry. I was so—"

He threw up a hand. "No need to explain. You be busy, I know; it's fine. All of humanity depends on the swing of that mallet—but you need to eat, yes?"

"I suppose . . ." She looked back at the crates of iron ore that would have to be smelted, then at the dwindling pile of charcoal.

A wagon pulled into the yard, another delivery. Roan rushed out. He could hear her voice outside, shouting. "Where is it from?"

The reply was a list of village names that Gifford had never heard of. Roan probably knew every one of them. In her head, she likely had a list and mentally checked off the locations. "Plenty of shields, why so few swords?" Gifford didn't hear the reply. The man's voice was low and didn't carry the way Roan's did.

She stayed out there until the weapons were unloaded and the wagon rolled out. Then she returned, wiping her hands on her apron. Immediately she picked up her hammer and headed for the forge.

"Woan, you need to eat," Gifford said.

"You still here?"

"Yes, Woan. Still am. And you still need to eat. You know . . . *food*? It's like the fuel you put in the fu-nace. If you don't keep putting some in, the fu-nace goes out and all things shut down. Don't want that, do you?"

She smirked at him.

He shook the bag once more. "Smells good. I think it's chicken."

She mopped her brow again and, wiping her hands on the leather apron, walked over.

"Let's eat outside," he said.

"Why?" She pierced him with an intent stare. Anyone unfamiliar with her would have seen it as suspicious, or accusing. Gifford saw it as the bright light of a focused mind capable of seeing beyond the shadows that confused everyone else. Roan always wanted to know the *why* of everything.

"I have this old fwend I want you to meet," Gifford replied. "You'll like him. He's quiet, but pleasant, handsome, and especially bwight."

Another smirk. "The sun?"

He grinned. "Is nice out. Pwetty, even."

With the desperate concern of a young mother asked to leave her child with an irresponsible guardian, she looked back at the ore glowing in the fire. Gifford pressed his lips together as he imagined how Roan would one day have her own children and look exactly that way. Gifford wouldn't be the father. He couldn't even be a guardian; she couldn't trust the wretched cripple to protect her baby. The thought hit hard. He felt it in his stomach like a punch, and in his throat like a hand squeezing so hard he couldn't breathe.

"What's wrong?" Roan asked, the bright light of her stare upon him again, eyes that saw far too much.

"Nothing," he managed to say.

"You look in pain. Are you feeling okay?"

He put a hand to his chest. "Nothing a little sun wouldn't fix."

As they walked out of the smithy into the sunbathed courtyard filled with the grunts, shouts, and clangs of men training to fight, Gifford mentally chided himself. *Greedy is what I am. I should appreciate that she talks to me at all. If Iver hadn't messed her up so badly, she wouldn't dream of eating a meal with me. She'd have already married one of Tope's boys and wouldn't be allowed to speak to the twisted pottery goblin.*

The thought was well intentioned, but the pain devouring his insides wasn't listening. He was going to lose her when the better man came along, which could be virtually anyone. *No, not anyone. Not me. I'm not the one man whose touch she can accept. The man who could take her in his arms, who could kiss her without her screaming.* That day would come. He knew it would. He constantly prayed each day for Mari to heal Roan, to let her live the normal life she deserved. He had faith it would happen, and when that day finally came, he would cheer for her even if that same day his heart would shatter, and happiness—as he knew it—would fly out of his world.

"How about this?" he said, finding a sunny patch of thick grass far enough outside that the sounds of crashing hammers wouldn't interfere with conversation.

"Wait," she told him and took off her apron. "Ground will be wet this time of year." She laid the thick leather out for them to sit on.

He smiled.

"What?"

He shook his head. "Nothing—just you."

"Just me, what?"

I just love you; that's all; I love you with every breath, every thought, every beat of my heart because you're more than a person, you're a world unto yourself—a rich, vibrant, exciting, fascinating universe, and I want to spend my life exploring every forest, field, and stream.

"Always thinking," he said.

Roan looked down at the leather beneath her knees and shrugged. "Just didn't want us to get muddy."

He dumped out the bag's contents.

"Chicken legs!" Roan burst out with a huge smile. "I love chicken legs. I'll have one; you have the other."

"They both fo' you."

"No! No!" She was shaking her head even as she bit into the first leg.

"This isn't my meal. I'm just going to watch you eat."

"You have some, too. It's good." She wiped grease from her chin, then grabbed up the other leg and held it out.

"I'll have a bite."

"Oh, and yellow cheese!" she said, unwrapping the cloth-covered hunk.

He watched her devour the food in precise bites, while in front of them a class of soldiers practiced moves under the barking tutelage of a Fhrey instructor. Behind them, the smithy's little chimney belched black smoke that blew east with the spring breeze. Roan forced him to eat some of the chicken before she finished it.

"Nice out, isn't it?" He lay back on his elbows. They were off the apron, and he felt the wet soak into his sleeves. "What do you say we do this ev—we day?"

Chewing, Roan looked around and nodded, but he wasn't certain which question she was answering.

"If you'd like, we could go fo' a walk," he ventured.

"Can't." She pointed at the smithy and swallowed. "Have too much work."

"I thought Pe'sephone said she was astounded by how much you'd accomplished."

"Still behind."

"Says who?"

"Me."

"But I'm only asking—"

"I can't," she told him.

Gifford was disappointed, even a little upset. He saw so little of her that he was slipping into his own depression. That was how he tried to rationalize everything afterward, but in truth he didn't know why he'd said it. It just came out. "It's like old Ivy is alive again."

Roan looked as if he'd hit her with the smithing hammer. She stared down at the food, at the sack it came in, and at the grease on her hands. "You talked to Padera, didn't you?"

Gifford had no idea what she meant. "I have talked to that old woman on many occasions."

Roan began to shake.

Gifford felt his heart sink. He'd done something terrible. He'd hurt her somehow. "What's wong, Woan?"

"Don't blame her. It wasn't . . ." Roan began to cry.

Gifford hated himself. He had no idea what he'd done, but nothing—nothing in the world—was worse than hurting Roan. He wanted to make it better, but didn't know how because he didn't know what he'd done. "Woan? What's going on?"

She got up then and ran back to the smithy, abandoning her apron, Gifford, and the warmth of the sun.

. . .

The old woman was in the kitchen cutting mushrooms into a series of neat slices while a kettle boiled over the cook fire. "What do *you* want?" she asked as Gifford let himself in.

"I just had a meal with Woan," he said with an ominous tone in his voice.

"Doubt that you *just* had a meal with Roan." Padera scraped her choppings into her palm and tossed them into the pot. "If you ate with her, it would have been in the smithy, which had to have been hours ago given your lightning-fast travel speed. Or has love given you invisible wings?"

Gifford was going to be polite. She was an old woman after all. He planned on being compassionate, easing his way to the point, but Padera was being her normal witch-self, and Gifford cut right to the dark meat. "Did you kill Ivy?"

The thought had come to him on the walk from the fortress, which was just as long as Padera described. It had also given him ample time to ponder why Roan was so upset. Guilt. She blamed herself for Iver's death because Padera had killed him on her behalf.

The old woman had her back to him as she faced the fire. Padera was just as hunched over as ever, her true form hidden beneath layers of old wool. "By Ivy, do you mean Iver the Carver?"

Gifford scowled. She knew whom he meant. "Yes."

"Why do you say that?" Her tone was controlled, even relaxed.

Why not surprise? Why not outrage? Why not laughter? Why isn't she asking if I'm making a joke?

"I told you, I just had a meal with Woan. A meal that ended with Woan weeping."

"I would imagine any meal with you would end that way."

"You did it, didn't you?" He hobbled to the table and looked at the pile of uncut mushrooms. "Was such a shock when he just died, when he went to sleep and failed to wake up. Did you poison him?"

Padera silently prodded the fire.

"How you find these mushwooms?" he asked. "We all new to this place, but you can locate mushwooms . . . and some mushwooms be poisonous."

Padera turned and peered with her one eye. "What are you saying?"

"How old is you?"

"How old *are* you," she corrected him.

"You know I can't say that."

"If you can't talk, you should keep your mouth shut."

"How old?" he persisted.

"Don't know—lost count."

"Uh-huh. You always say that when anyone asks, don't you?"

"What does my age have to do with this?"

"You oldest in Dahl Wen."

"What of it, cripple-boy?" Her voice took on an edge.

"So, maybe you not even fom Wen. Maybe you just showed up one day and have outlived all who knew that."

Padera shambled back to the table and sat down in front of her mushrooms. "And I suppose my husband, Melvin, and our sons, were imaginary?"

"Maybe—I not met Melvin, not met sons."

"Because you're a child."

"Most childwen outlive pawents."

"No, they don't." She looked almost sad, but it was hard to tell with that leathery melon face of hers. "Most people don't live as long as I have."

"I'm thinking maybe *no one* lives as long as you."

Again, she gave him the squint. "What are you saying, gimp?"

"I'm saying that maybe you don't just look and act like a witch."

He saw the change in her face. A twitch, a grimace—brief but it was there. He'd touched a nerve.

"All people say the name, use it when cussing. Just a name, not a god, so it's safe. But what if it isn't just a name? What if the witch is weal?"

Padera's malleable lips folded up into a smile. "So, you aren't just accusing me of being *a* witch, you're saying I'm *the* witch?"

"All those tales have to begin someplace."

"What stories are those?"

"That's just it. All Elan knows the name, but no one knows what it means. I think you do."

She nodded. "Yes . . . I do."

This admission surprised him. For all his bluster and certainty, he had still been guessing. He'd even been glad Brin was gone. He had wanted to speak to Padera alone. If he'd really believed his own suspicions, he wouldn't have walked into that witch's den by himself. In retrospect, that might not have been the best idea. No one knew he was there.

"So, was Ivy poisoned?" he asked.

"Yes." Padera picked up her knife. "Iver was a bad, bad man. No one knew that. No one except me . . . well, and Roan of course. He hurt her, but you already know that."

"All of Dahl Wen knows that."

"No. People suspect, but no one *knows*. Even I don't know all of it." She leaned back and fixed him with a one-eyed glare. "Did you know he killed Roan's mother?"

"Woan told me she died like mine, in childbiff."

"Assuming you mean childbirth, she tells everyone that; I think she's getting to the point where she can almost believe it."

In the past, the look Padera fixed on him had been an eccentricity, but standing before that mushroom-strewn table, Gifford now found it frightening. *Can she cast a hex with a look like that?*

"He had both of them to himself," the old woman went on. "Roan and her mother Reanna—both slaves with no recourse. Everyone saw Iver as a great man, a pillar of the community because he was also careful and kept his depravity confined to the inside of his home. I lived the closest. I heard the screams, and I didn't buy his explanations. I knew better. I'd seen his like before. Reanna tried to run. Roan was about nine, and Reanna was pregnant again. I think maybe she refused to give him another child, or perhaps Roan was starting to grow up, starting to look more like a woman, and Reanna knew what that meant. She wrapped Roan up and plotted to leave Rhen. Had no idea where to go, or how she'd live. Reanna was a slave, the only one in Rhen at the time. Iver had bought her while at an auction in Dureya. Once she had been a Gula—a war trophy."

Padera sucked on her lips a moment. "She was his property, and Iver could do what he wanted. Never crossed Reanna's mind that anyone might help. If she had come to me, things would have turned out different, but she was scared, and I was the last person she would trust. Like I said, I lived the closest, and Iver was a clever man. He told Reanna I was a witch, and that I would just as likely eat her as help her."

She gave Gifford a long accusing stare. "Iver caught up to them, and he beat Reanna to death while Roan watched. He took Roan on a trip and disposed of the body. When they got back, Iver told everyone Reanna had died in childbirth. They offered condolences, but he acted like he didn't care because she had been just a slave. Folks thought he was in denial, that it was his way of dealing with grief. It wasn't."

Gifford leaned on the table trying to remain calm. *She's just trying to get into my head.* "So you weally the witch?"

"*The* witch?"

"You know what I mean." Gifford couldn't bring himself to say the name—even though there were no R sounds in it—he couldn't say it, not standing so close.

"You're asking if I'm the *Tetlin* Witch?"

He nodded.

"What if I were? What would you do?"

He didn't say anything. He honestly didn't know.

"Would you call me out? Get the neighbors to tie me to some pile of last year's firewood and burn me to death?"

He still didn't say anything. He'd never liked Padera. She'd always been cruel to him while being kind to everyone else, which was worse than if she'd been mean to everyone. She once tried to explain it as some sort of twisted tough love that filled him with guilt over his mother's death. He'd believed her, but now he didn't know what to think. If she really was the witch, who knew what she was up to. Still, he didn't want to kill her. He didn't even want to hurt her. If he were honest with himself, which for

Gifford was usually a very painful experience, he'd have to admit he respected the old woman. He couldn't even find fault in her killing Iver. Had he known what was happening, Gifford would have tried to kill the woodcarver himself.

"That's what they do to witches, you know." Padera went back to cutting mushrooms.

With nothing else to do or say, Gifford watched as those old hands chopped with generations of experience.

"You want to know about the Tetlin Witch, so I'll tell you. There was a terrible plague, a horrible sickness," Padera said, her head down, focusing on her work. "Killed thousands. Wiped out whole communities. One woman, who had learned the art of herbs and roots from her mother, who had learned it from her mother before her, stretching all the way back to the Old Country—the one beyond the sea—discovered how to combat the illness. Only she wasn't a chieftain, or a man, or even a mother. She had no standing in the community, and no one listened. No one trusted her. The plague came and killed everyone in the village of Tetlin—everyone but her. She went to other villages and tried to tell them how to survive. They didn't listen, either, and each village she visited was wiped out by the plague shortly after her arrival. People got it into their heads that she wasn't trying to stop the sickness; that, instead, she was causing it. She was a witch, they said. They hung her in a forest where she went to hide."

She sadly shook her head. "That, boy, is the real story of the Tetlin Witch. Not as spectacular as the others you've no doubt heard over cups in the lodge. And of course, the story didn't end there because the Tetlin Witch wasn't the only woman with a mind, with knowledge and skills. Women who refused to fit in, who didn't act the way others thought they should, who embarrassed those in power with their wisdom or knowledge, they, too, were declared to be the Tetlin Witch. And we all know that the Tetlin Witch is evil. In some cases, these unfortunate women were merely driven away, but some—like that original wise woman from a little village named Tetlin—were killed. A lot of women have suffered—still suffer—for the crime of knowing what others don't, or doing what others can't.

Turns out the Tetlin Witch is everywhere, and she—in all her forms—is the real plague."

Padera finished the last of her mushrooms and, scooping them into her hand, she looked at him with both eyes. "So, yes, Gifford, I am the Tetlin Witch, and the same goes for Reanna, Roan, Moya, Brin, Persephone, and Suri. Not to mention a great many more. So call the mobs to kill me or leave me alone. I don't have time for your foolishness."

Gifford lived in Hopeless House at the end of the stone alley across the square from Roan's cottage—the one she was supposed to share with Brin and Padera, but rarely visited. The name Hopeless House came from the fact that Gifford, Habet, Mathias, and Gelston lived there. The Cripple, the Slow, the Old, and the Unlucky all tucked neatly under one roof. Gifford was the one who named it, learning from experience it was better to stay out ahead of ridicule, to choose his own insults rather than leave it to others. Not that he thought people would choose worse, but if left to the public, then the mockery became one more thing done to him. This way, they could still laugh, but it was his joke.

He found Tressa sitting on the porch steps when he came up the alley.

She was an unofficial member of Hopeless House. The only reason Tressa wasn't bunking with them was because she was a woman. Otherwise she'd fit right into their league of misery. Her unofficial Hopeless House title would have been the Hated.

"How's he doing?" Gifford asked.

Tressa had a ceramic jug on her lap, hugging it to her chest. Her hair was a mess of snarls, and the sleeves on her dress were decorated with dingy brown stains. She looked up with a pair of sour lips that seemed a bit like Padera's, only with teeth behind them.

"I don't know," she said. Her voice had become raspy, just as worn as the rest of her. "Some days he seems better, you know? The old bastard gets my hopes up, and then the next day . . ." She spat between her feet. Tressa was a good spitter, better than Gifford. It was one of the things he admired about her. Gifford made a practice of finding something to admire about everyone. Not terribly hard, since for him the ability to stand straight was a source of awe.

"I take it this is . . . *the next day?*"

She looked over the top of the jug at him with a smirk. "Old bastard didn't even know who I was. Just stared at me."

"I thought that was why you helped Gelston, what made him so appealing. *Because* he couldn't wememba you."

She nodded, but it was a slow, sad nod. "I come over here every day. I feed him, bathe him, wash his clothes, clean his backside, and we talk. We talk for hours, he and I, about stupid stuff like hats and snowflakes and why the gods hate us. Sometimes he smiles when he sees me come in, but yesterday he . . ." Tressa sucked in an abrupt breath and held it with mashed lips. She stayed that way for a second, then let it out slowly, carefully. "Yesterday he rushed right over and gave me a . . . a hug." She halted again, and swallowed twice. "A real tight, I-love-you kind of hug, you know?" She glanced at Gifford and shook her head. "Okay, so maybe you don't know, but it was nice—*real nice*. Not romantic—nothing like that— just appreciation, love. I hadn't been hugged like that in . . ." She looked up at the sky and took a few more deep breaths through her nose. "And then today—today it's like that never happened. He's a stranger again."

She hooked her thumb in the jug and tilted it up to her lips. "Want some?" Coming off the neck of the jug, her breath was an invisible cloud of fermented rye.

"No thanks."

"It helps. Trust me, it helps."

"Thank you, but no."

Tressa nodded and wiped her mouth. She also deftly wiped her eyes, trying to clear the wetness on her lashes without him seeing. He pretended not to.

"Did you manage to have your picnic?"

He nodded.

She stared. "Didn't go well, huh?"

"No."

"Any other man would have given up on her by now."

"If I was anyone else, I wouldn't have to."

Tressa laughed. "Is that what you think? You think *she's* the catch in this pairing? Roan would fit right in here at Hopeless House. I realize you love her and all, but honestly, that girl is messed up. She won't even let you touch her, will she? Won't let anyone. How's that gonna work, do you think? I mean, even if you pull off some miracle and get her to marry you, what kind of marriage will that be when you can't touch your own wife? For Mari's sake, you can't even hold hands, can you?"

"Not without Woan scweaming."

Tressa shook her head and held the jug out to him again. "You sure?"

He shook his head. "Woan has weasons."

"We all have our reasons." Tressa took another pull from the jug. "Mari knows; we all have our reasons."

CHAPTER NINE

The Pottery Man

Heroes are those who refuse to create or become victims. I failed to see it then, but I lived among many heroes. I think maybe everyone does.

—THE BOOK OF BRIN

Balancing on the railing of the Spyrok balcony with her arms opened wide, Suri imagined she was flying. Wasn't that hard. The world spread out below her, and the wind was so strong it watered her eyes. For the first time, she wished she had longer hair just so she could feel it blow.

"Having fun?" Arion asked, but Suri heard, *Are you insane? You're scaring me to death!*

That was happening a lot. Suri had always received messages from Elan, from trees, the weather, and animals. What she had believed to be a mystic talent had actually been the Art, whispering. Intuition, premonition, a sense of oneness with the world were all the result of her gift for hearing the language of creation. Most people heard its call. Moments of unexplained dread before a tragedy, inexplicable coincidences, or a sense of destiny were all faint signals sent from Elan. No one was entirely deaf, but few had the ability to understand what they were told; fewer still could hold a conversation.

While not as strong as Suri, Tura must have also had a talent for the Art. All genuine mystics and seers had at least a knack for hearing the whispers of the world. Sadly, Tura died never knowing the true nature of her power. Had she known, the old woman might have learned to focus, to train her inner ear to listen. Suri had spent the winter doing just that, and now instead of merely hearing the voice of the wind, she could hear other people's thoughts. At least it seemed that way. Arion insisted Suri merely picked up on strong emotions the same way people sensed changes in temperature. Her talent made her adept at interpreting people in the same way she was good at reading bones.

At that moment, Suri could tell, Arion was terrified.

Suri didn't care. She was too busy flying. Tilting her hands, she noticed how her cupped palms caught the wind, giving them lift. *I really should have been born a bird.*

"Can we fly?" Suri shouted against the wind.

"No." The single syllable was drenched in tension.

"I meant with the Art."

"I *know* what you meant, and *no* you can't." The last few words were hastily added, as if Arion was certain Suri was on the verge of giving it a try.

"I thought you said anything was possible."

"I said it *feels* like anything is possible. It's an illusion. You can't do anything unnatural. You can't become invisible or turn yourself into a frog. You can't create life, bring back the dead, or—"

Suri turned her head, feeling pleasantly like an owl spying a mouse. "I brought you back."

"I wasn't dead."

"Sure?"

"Pretty sure."

"And no flying?"

"No flying."

Suri sighed and jumped down off the rail, planting her feet back on solid ground. Arion's posture relaxed, and Suri could feel a wave of relief pour off the Fhrey. Arion was looking much better, healthier than ever, and the wound on her head was nothing more than a white scar, which could be clearly seen since Arion had resumed shaving her scalp.

The Miralyith had resumed a great many things.

Suri had done the unthinkable that night under the wool with Padera and Brin. She had opened a door between their world and that of the spirits—then she walked through. She'd passed through the gateway to the dark realms of Phyre, to the long river that spirits traveled to reach their final homes. In that sunless stream, she'd found Arion struggling against the current, but slowly slipping away. Everyone eventually succumbed to that flow, every living thing. But Suri still had a toe in the world of the living that acted as an anchor, a lifeline. She had reached out, grabbed hold of Arion, and pulled. In doing so, she'd done more than just restore her to the living world—Suri had fixed her. There had been a hole in the vessel that had been her body. From that side, Suri could see it plain as a tear in a blanket held up to the sun. She had sewn it shut, woven it closed, and dumped Arion inside. With Arion safe, Suri had passed out from exhaustion. Only later did she learn how close she'd come to death herself. Swimming in the river, in that dark stream of the dead, wasn't an activity for the living. Had she stayed too long, grown too tired, the current could have pulled her in and severed her lifeline. Then both of them would have been carried away into Phyre.

Even after all that, Arion still didn't wake up for days. That week was the worst of Suri's life. She had lost Minna, and even after dragging Arion out of Phyre's mouth, the Fhrey had not opened her eyes. After she did, Suri fretted over her like a mother with a new baby. As Arion grew stronger, the Miralyith discovered she wasn't merely alive. She was whole.

Arion could use the Art again.

"This is very disappointing," Suri continued. "I can't become invisible. I can't be immortal. I can't create my own animals. I can't convince flesh eaters to prefer plants. I can't rearrange the stars or add a new season, and now I can't even fly."

Arion pointed at her with the little ceramic cup she held in her hands. The Fhrey had a fondness for an awful-tasting tea she'd found in a shop in the city. Supposedly it was the same stuff she used to drink back in Estramnadon. "But you *were* able to make beautiful flashing images with fireflies."

Arion was always bringing that up.

"Really impressive," Arion said. "Never saw anything like it before. I still don't know how you made such real-looking bears and bunnies out of streaking lights."

"Flies didn't much care for it." Suri left the balcony, returning inside the tower, getting out of the wind so they could talk. "So, what's wrong? Persephone still refusing to send a message to the fane?"

Arion looked up, innocent as a thief. "What makes you think anything is wrong? Are you sensing something?"

"Don't need to. You just climbed the Spyrok—way too many steps just to tell me I couldn't fly."

Arion smiled.

"What?"

"You're just . . . maturing so quickly—thinking like a Miralyith."

"Is that a good thing?"

She nodded while rubbing the cup. "I think it is."

"So I'm right? No message-bird?"

Arion nodded. "The keenig is still siding with Nyphron. The Instarya here at Alon Rhist are just as unconvinced about the existence of a human Artist as Rapnagar was, which lends credence to my suspicion that the prince never told Lothian about you. Given that, Nyphron wants to keep your talent hidden. He believes the fane's ignorance gives us a tactical advantage. Surprise, he says, is more valuable than revealing your existence. Right now, Lothian believes he has the only Artists capable of causing harm because I won't break Ferrol's Law. Nyphron sees you as our secret weapon."

"And what do you believe?"

Arion looked into her cup. *Sadness. Embarrassment.* Suri read these as: *Old as I am, I'm still a fool.*

"I suspect I may have been too optimistic about the effect of Rhune Artists softening Lothian's attitude toward your people. And now that we've taken Alon Rhist, I fear things have gone too far. The fane can't just forgive and forget anymore."

"But you still want the bird sent?"

Arion nodded. "War is inevitable, but one day when both sides have drunk their fill of blood, the truth about you could provide the honorable excuse to end it. It's just so horrible to think people—so many people—need to die to reveal wisdom that ought to be common sense."

"So turning me into a butterfly didn't save the world after all."

Arion looked troubled. "I can't explain—maybe you could, but I can't. Your ability to interpret is better. All I know is that the Art tells me you are the key to saving both your people and mine. I thought it was by proving a link between Rhunes and Fhrey and extending Ferrol's Law to the Rhunes—that just seemed so sensible—but people aren't sensible. Still, I feel it, this little string that stretches between you and peace. When I look at you, I sense hope. You're like this light in the darkness, and you get brighter every day."

Arion thoughtfully rubbed the ceramic cup in her hands.

Suri narrowed her eyes at Arion. *That's not it. Something else brought her up here.* She couldn't read Arion's thoughts, but there was another clue. "Why did you bring that cup? Why carry it all this way? The tea must be cold by now."

Arion nodded and held the drink up. "Yes, this is actually why I came."

"Tea?"

Arion shook her head and put the cup down. "Do you know the word *Cenzlyor?*"

Suri thought a moment. "Mind swift?"

"Swift *of* mind, to be precise," Arion said. "That's what Fenelyus called me. You're swift of mind, too. The most naturally talented Artist I've ever known, and I've lived a long time. Thing is, I was given the title when I was fifteen hundred. I didn't realize until after she died that I was the only one she'd bestowed it on. I suppose she thought I was special somehow, and now I wonder if she knew that I would be the one to find you. She wanted me to be a teacher, and I am—*your* teacher. I assumed she wanted me to teach the prince, and maybe she did, but now I think that she sensed the importance of my life the way I sense the same about you—in vague pieces, some clear, and some impossible to fathom because they haven't yet happened."

Arion moved to the balcony's edge, put her hands on the railing, and looked out toward the east. With the evening sun behind them, it appeared to Suri as if they could see the whole world. The Bern River was a hairline at their feet, Mount Mador a bump on the landscape. Then came an ocean of trees—what Arion referred to as the Harwood. Beyond that stretched another river called the Nidwalden. Suri took Arion's word for this as she couldn't actually see it through the many trees. Across that river, what to Suri was a mere blue haze, was what Arion called home.

"Only a week away," Arion said so softly that Suri almost didn't hear. "A week and forever." She turned back to the mystic. "Nyphron and Persephone want us to recruit more Artists, find more swift-of-minds, more Cenzlyors. They think the fane will be sending an army of Miralyith—the Spider Corps. They are trained to weave attacks and defenses together—you know, like spiders. Get it?"

Suri rolled her eyes. "A minute ago I was swift of mind; what happened?"

"Sorry."

"So Persephone wants her own Spider Corps?"

"Something like that. Good sense would advocate more than two Artists."

"And how do we find them? Look for people really good at starting fires?"

"Unfortunately, no. Most don't manifest as readily as you, but dormant Artists can usually be identified by creativity. Miralyith often start as regular artists: painters, sculptors, or even talented craftsmen. The better the art, the more likely it is the person is a latent Artist."

Arion held up the delicate cup. "Do you know who makes these?"

By the time they found the little house at the back of the Rhune District, it was dark. For years, Suri had lived under the stars and never had any trouble seeing. Then she moved to Dahl Rhen and felt blinded by its torches and braziers. The same was true for this Fhrey city. Lamps on poles took the place of torches, and the effect was the same—they chased shadows from one place, making them gather all the more darkly elsewhere. That was the problem with people, too, Suri realized as she and Arion made their way down the narrow alleyway. Unlike all other living things, people were never content to just live in a place, to be part of it; they always wanted to change things, to make places conform. Maybe that was why the gods and spirits appeared so cruel—their way of saying, *Quit it.*

The house was a simple wooden shack placed like an afterthought at the end of the narrow alley. A large storage shed, or maybe a small servant's quarters, it bore little resemblance to the other grand homes along the street. As they approached, Suri noticed a man and woman sitting out on the stoop. The woman was the one called Tressa. No one liked her, but Suri didn't know why. No one liked spiders, either, and Suri had long since given up trying to understand the insanity of walled-in people. Beside Tressa sat Gifford, the potter. A jug rested in between.

The two had been talking but stopped at their approach.

Tressa put one hand on the jug and pulled it closer to her. "What do the likes of you two want down here?"

"That's him." Suri pointed at Gifford, whose brows jumped.

"What'd he do?" Tressa asked. "There's no need to pick on him. Gifford's a walking curse to himself as it is."

"We aren't here to *pick on* him," Arion said. "Just want to talk a while."

"Talk, eh?" Tressa peered at them suspiciously. "About what?"

Arion held up the cup. "About this." She addressed Gifford, "You made it?"

He nodded.

"What of it?" Tressa spoke with the verbal equivalent of an antagonistic shove. "You against a cripple making a living?"

Arion looked at Tressa. "Could we speak to Gifford alone, please?"

"Will that make it easier to cast some hex on him?" Tressa asked. "I have a better idea. How about the two of you just leave. Go back to your fancy stone fortress, your one-eyed newts, cauldrons, and bat wings, and leave us in peace. Will you do that, *please*?"

"I've never known any newts with only one eye," Suri said. "And I know quite a few."

"Sure, sure. I'll bet you're on a first-name basis with them, aren't you?"

Suri nodded. "Of course. Newts are ridiculously friendly."

This left Tressa looking confused. She glanced at Gifford as if at a loss.

"Gifford," Arion said, holding the cup up. "I think your workmanship is wonderful. Stunning, really. I've never seen the like. The porcelain is so thin, so delicate, you can almost see through it."

"Has a lot to do with the type of clay I use: soft, usually white; the wheel I spin it on; and the heat. You need lots of heat."

"Well, it's lovely what you do, and not just the skill, but the creativity. The way the cup is shaped, this flower-like tapering, and the gentle swirl of the handle."

"Thank you."

"Came all the way down here to compliment him on his pottery?" Tressa asked skeptically.

"Partially," Arion replied. "I also have a few questions. Gifford, do you sing?"

"Ha!" Tressa slapped her thigh. "Like a bullfrog with a cold."

Gifford frowned. "I can't speak well. Singing is even mo' difficult. My mouth doesn't act like it should. The sounds get mushed sometimes."

"Okay, maybe not singing; how about humming? Do you ever hum while working?"

Gifford thought, then nodded. "I suppose."

Arion looked at Suri with a smile.

"So the man hums, so what?" Tressa grumbled. "Is it a crime to hum? I've been known to hum on occasion myself. What of it?"

Arion ignored her. "Have you ever felt certain it was going to rain when there wasn't a cloud in the sky, and then it did? Or have you known winter would arrive early or late?"

Gifford shrugged. "I don't know. Maybe."

"Have you ever started a fire by clapping your hands?" Suri asked.

Both of them looked shocked.

"No," Gifford said.

"I think what Suri meant to ask was, have you ever wanted something to happen and then it did? Have you noticed a lot of happy coincidences, like finding someone or something when you really needed to, or having rain hold off until after you were safely inside?"

"Don't think so."

Tressa laughed. "This"—she indicated Gifford with both hands—"can hardly be mistaken for the face of *happy coincidence*. This"—she clapped him on the shoulder—"is what you get from a life of careful misjudgment and a bunch of drunk-off-their-asses gods in a bad mood." Tressa spit, wiped her chin, and shook her head. "You think he's some sort of magician because he can make nice cups?"

"It's possible," Arion said. "I want you to do me a favor, Gifford. I want you to move your hands like this." Arion made a plucking motion with her fingers while sweeping her hands back and forth. "That's right. Now look at my palms and think *hot*. Imagine my hands on fire. Imagine them melting. Imagine my hands turning black as ash. Concentrate. Close your eyes if you need to."

Gifford stared at Arion's hand, and Suri was worried the potter might succeed in setting Arion on fire. She assumed Arion knew what she was doing, but, just the same, Suri was ready to smother even the hint of a flame.

Ever since Neith, Suri no longer had any trouble tapping the Art. Over the last eight months, her work with Arion had been mostly about technique. To Suri, it was like they were back in the lodge, once more playing the string game together and learning Rhunic and Fhrey. Arion would demonstrate a standard weave, and Suri would take it and often improve the idea, making Arion smile and often laugh or shake her head and say, "Why has no one ever thought of that before?" Suri was certain she could protect Arion from anything Gifford might do; still, she was nervous.

The deaths of Tura and Minna, and the appointment of Persephone as the keenig, had left Suri not only devastated, but alone. People were all around, but her family was missing. Trapped in the cold dark of Alon Rhist in winter, Suri had suffered depression so black she couldn't eat. Raithe and Arion had pulled her out, but the losses were still fresh, and this made her protective, perhaps beyond reason.

Gifford stared long and hard at Arion's hands. His brows crawled up in a fleshy cramp above the bridge of his nose.

"Oww!" Arion jerked her hand back. "Okay, stop. Stop! STOP!"

"Did I cause you pain?" Gifford asked, stunned.

Arion rubbed her palm. "Just a little."

Suri stared at Arion's hand, confused. She hadn't sensed anything, and any use of the Art would have been obvious.

Tressa glared at the potter and inched away, pulling the jug with her.

"You actually felt pain?" Gifford asked. "I made yew hand hot—just by thinking about it?"

Arion still rubbed her hand. "Not too bad. Felt like—like I was holding a sunbaked rock."

"But I . . . I . . ." Gifford looked at Arion and then at Suri, and finally a bit guiltily at Tressa, who glared at him.

"People who are creative are usually that way because they are more attuned to the power and forces of nature. They can hear the whispers of the world, and it helps guide them in the right direction. Oftentimes we hear it as our own thoughts telling us to go left, or just a sense that going right is a bad idea. Some might call it intuition or a gut feeling, but it is the world speaking in an ancient language that you can almost understand. Animals are fluent in this language; that's how birds know to fly south in autumn, squirrels know to store nuts, and bears know to sleep late when snow falls. Trees know it, too. This is how they realize when to shed leaves and when to wake up from their deep sleep. Everyone can understand the whispers because they are spoken in our native language—the language of creation. It's how the world was made. It's how *we* were made. Rediscovering how to speak our native tongue, how to tap and use that power in meaningful ways, is what we call the Art. Not everyone is capable of making an intentional connection; fewer still are able to manipulate the power to their will."

"But you think I can?"

Arion held up her hand and rubbed it again. "Yes," she said. "I believe you can."

Suri didn't say anything as they walked back up the alley. She glanced at Arion a few times but didn't ask. Maybe it was none of her business. They were nearly out of the Rhune District when Arion stopped.

"You want to know why I lied," Arion said.

Suri wasn't the only one with the ability to read feelings. Suri didn't answer, but she waited.

"Because I think he can." She began walking again, heading toward the lantern that hung near the well. "Most of the time people just lack confidence. Doubt kills any chance they might have. People believe magic is impossible, and so it is because they refuse to try, or if they do try it's only half-hearted because they know—deep down, they *know*—they can't. Sometimes all a person of talent needs is a little encouragement and someone—sometimes anyone—believing in them. Avalanches have been caused by the tossing of a pebble, and miracles have come from wishful thinking that just happened to spill out in words."

They were alone in the square that was dominated by the common well. This was where Brin, Padera, and several others from Dahl Rhen now lived. Spring had arrived, but nights were still cold, and Suri pulled her asica tight.

"Gifford will think about what I said. He'll play with it in the back of his mind, wondering. The seed of doubt in the absolute certainty of the visible world will grow. And when no one is looking, he'll try to make something happen. He'll try to hear the whispers of the world. And because I said it worked once, he'll keep trying long after he would normally have given up. Sometimes sheer tenacity does the trick."

"Why is it so easy for me?" Suri asked.

"People are different, and maybe you suffered somehow."

"Suffered?"

Arion paused at the well and nodded. "When people are happy, they can become deaf. I don't know why that is, but I've noticed it to be true. Misery helps us hear. We notice more when we're in pain. We see beauty more clearly, hear the sufferings of others more loudly. Since you pulled me back, every sunrise is so much brighter, every breeze a delight. I think people who survive tragedy aren't so much scarred as they are cleansed. The wax comes out of their ears and the clouds leave their eyes. The barriers between them and the world are reduced."

"You think I suffered somehow?"

"Maybe."

"But I've been able to make flames since I was young."

"Then whatever it was must have happened when you were a child, which makes sense. I think the younger the pain, the stronger the influence. That's why Gifford seems a likely candidate. Looking at him, you can see he must have suffered for a long time."

Suri was left to ponder this as they continued on. She couldn't remember being unhappy as a child. All the misery in her life had started a year ago with Tura's death. Before that, her life had always been wonderful, her youth a marvelous experience—at least the parts she remembered.

When I found you, you were wailing so loud you made the trees quiver, Tura had said.

And back in Dahl Rhen, Suri remembered Persephone saying, . . . *Some children, the unwanted ones, are sometimes left in the forest, given over to the mercy of the gods.*

Even Gifford hadn't been dumped in the forest, thrown away as garbage and left to die. His father had loved him, and Gifford belonged to a village that raised him. For her, a desperate infant abandoned in nature's palm and clawing at anything to live, how thick could the veil between worlds be?

You made the trees quiver.

They were heading out of the square, rounding the corner of the quaint little house that Suri thought might be Brin and Roan's new home, when she felt abruptly cold, so cold she shivered.

Arion asked. "Feel that?"

Suri nodded. "Cold and clammy chills? Like someone dropped fish down the back of your shirt?"

Arion nodded.

"Thought it was my imagination."

"You need to recognize that your imagination is more accurate than other people's sight." Arion moved to the side of the house. She put her hand to the stone and ran her fingers along it.

"What is it?"

"I don't know," Arion replied. "A message, I suppose."

"Message?"

"A warning, like a bear urinating on a tree."

Suri smiled; usually Arion's explanations were vague or built on examples she didn't understand. This, at least, she knew.

"Something is marking their territory with the Art?"

"Maybe, or just leaving its scent in its wake. This is strong or I wouldn't notice. I'm not all that gifted in second sight. You probably are. Do you get any impressions? I just feel cold—cold and threatened."

Suri nodded. "Very cold—like death, but damp and clammy. And . . ."

"And what?"

"Hungry—starvation and exhaustion; frustration, too."

"Can you see it? Do you know what it is?"

Suri shook her head. All she had were sensations, emotions that lingered like smells. "What does it mean?"

Arion shrugged. "Maybe someone did something unpleasant here."

"I don't think so," Suri replied as she, too, touched the wall of the house.

"What are you feeling?"

"I don't think something bad *was* done, I think something bad *will* be done. And I don't think someone will do it. I think some *thing* will."

CHAPTER TEN

Lord of the Rhist

The Kype was this huge stone building filled with rooms, stairs, and corridors. It was where the rulers of Alon Rhist had lived. On the ground floor was the Karol, a small chamber where the keenig listened to grievances and passed judgments. Persephone used to call it her torture chamber: Each day there was a different torturer, but always the same victim.

—THE BOOK OF BRIN

Being the keenig, Persephone realized, was as rewarding as a punch in the face. The perks were equally as stellar, consisting of no sleep, no privacy, and excessive ridicule. Nothing she did was enough, yet every act was going too far. She'd been accused of favoritism toward people she'd never met, of knowing too little or too much, and of being insane. There were those who actually believed she was mentally unstable, suggesting the stress was driving her mad. *Women weren't built to bear such weight* was a common sentiment expressed when she made an unfavorable judgment against someone. People, Persephone realized, had very short memories, even shorter tempers, and acted like children.

This was on grand display with Erdo, Chieftain of Clan Erling, who came before her that day in the Karol to plead his case for taking his entire clan home so they could help with spring planting. She sympathized with him—the man had a point—but sacrifices had to be made. That day it was Clan Erling.

"I'm sorry," she said, looking down. She tried as hard as she could to sound compassionate, but after giving the same disappointing news hundreds of times, to hundreds of people, the sincerity was difficult to maintain. "We can't afford to lose so many men at this time."

"My people will starve!" He slapped the bronze railing that divided the room between the lower and upper half. The metal bar rang in the small chamber with a dull note.

"Erling will receive shipments of grain from the south to help them survive until—"

"We don't want charity!"

"It's not charity. Consider it payment for standing guard."

"It's putting the Gula at the mercy of Rhulyn. That's what it is! Putting a noose around our necks and calling it a leash."

Erdo had succeeded Udgar as the leader of the Erling after Moya killed the prior chieftain in the contest that made Persephone the keenig. She had expected more challenges from the northern clans, but trial by combat was seen as sacred by most and especially by the Gula, for whom combat was such a large part of their lives. The Gula so far had been honorable in their acceptance of her rule and obeyed her judgments, even if they couldn't always control their people. Over the winter there had been eight cases of murder that had come before her. The majority had been committed by Gula-Rhunes against people from Rhulyn, but the Rhulyn-Rhunes weren't innocent and had a fair number of killings on their hands. Even more deaths had been reported in the territories, where interaction between the two sides had been required. Persephone had left those issues to the local elders and hoped they would prove to be wise.

There were no reports of Fhrey killing or being killed.

Erdo, new to his post, was the loudest of the Gula-Rhune chieftains. This wasn't his first visit to the Karol. Most of the Rhune leaders aired grievances in the monthly council meetings, which made them run notoriously long. Erdo wasn't the sort to wait.

"The south is better equipped to grow food," Persephone explained.

"There's better soil and a longer season, and the fields are farther from the enemy who might otherwise be inclined to burn them. I promise you— your people will be looked after, but right now we need you here."

"Makes no sense," Erdo said. "All we do is sit. Easy for you, all warm and happy here in the city. Me and mine have to sit in the fields, in the cold, in leaky tents. No need for us to be here. Been two full seasons. The Fhrey are scared of us. All this waiting is stupid. Use us or send us home!"

Persephone looked at Nyphron, who sat to her left.

Nyphron leaned forward. "How many times did Alon Rhist launch attacks on the Gula in winter?"

The Gula-Rhune shook his head. "Don't remember."

"Then let me help you recall—never. Wars are fought in warm weather. If you look outside, you'll see the snow is off the ground. Your enemy is on the march. They will be here soon enough. And if I were you, I wouldn't be so eager for their arrival. Now, we have others to listen to."

He waved his hand in dismissal.

Persephone cringed.

Erdo glared at Nyphron, his mouth a stiff, tight line. He spun and stomped out.

"You really shouldn't do that," Persephone whispered to Nyphron.

The Fhrey leader looked at her, puzzled.

"It's not your place to dismiss—"

"Oh!" Nyphron nodded. "You're right. My apologies." He glanced across the hall as Erdo retreated out the door. "It's just . . . I don't like the way they speak to you—these Gula especially. They show no respect. No Instarya would dream of speaking to a superior in such a way."

"No?" Moya asked. Only one word, but she managed to saturate it with a sea of sarcasm. "That's not what Tekchin tells me." She smiled at Nyphron.

Moya stood to Persephone's right. There was a chair, but Moya always stood, leaning on her strung bow. She complained endlessly about the need for more than a mere bronze bar and a four-foot step separating those coming to complain to Persephone. People with grievances were angry folk. But Persephone wasn't worried. Moya had proved she could nock and launch three arrows faster than a man could jump the bar. The tale of her stunning victory over Udgar and her increasing mastery with the bow had made her a legend. Most of the clans imagined her in mythic hero terms, which was the only way most could resolve the contradiction of someone so beautiful being so deadly. Even the Fhrey extended an unusual degree of . . . perhaps not respect, but caution . . . for something they, too, did not entirely understand. While the secret of the bow had been disseminated to those interested in learning, Moya, who practiced daily, remained the master. And just the sight of her standing at the ready was better than twenty armed guards.

The doors to the Karol opened and Petragar and Vertumus were led in. Seeing them, Moya grinned. "And what do you think these two would say about the respect Instarya show their leaders?"

Nyphron smirked as the two approached the bar. "I didn't say leaders; I said *superiors.*"

The Karol was excellently suited for grievance hearing. Located in the base of the Kype, the chamber was off-limits to most of the inhabitants of Alon Rhist, and as such, it sustained an air of mystery and awe. The room was also small enough to be intimate, but divided to maintain a judicial separation. There were no windows and only the two doors, one for the petitioner and one for the judges, making the proceedings appropriately private. In some ways, the Karol reminded Persephone of the lodge in Dahl Rhen, but this was far more formal and ominous. She especially bemoaned the lack of windows. This time of year the doors of the lodge would have been thrown open to let the spring light and air in. Instead, she was trapped in a dim cave of flickering flame, listening to complaints about her leadership and being forced to disappoint nearly everyone.

"*We have spent* . . ." Petragar began in the Fhrey language, then faltered. He looked to Vertumus, who whispered in his ear. "*We have spent more than eight months incarcerated. I am a ranking member of the Fhrey, and as such, I demand our immediate release.*"

Throughout this demand Petragar never once looked at Persephone. His attention was focused on Nyphron.

And while it didn't please her, it didn't surprise Persephone when Nyphron responded on her behalf.

"You're responsible for sending a troop of Grenmorian killers to murder me," Nyphron said. *"You're lucky to be alive. Thank Ferrol you were born Fhrey."*

"A civilization's worth can be measured by its treatment of prisoners," Vertumus said to Persephone; then he, too, directed his comments to Nyphron. *"Returning us to the fane would be the first step in changing minds."*

"We don't need to change minds," Nyphron said. *"You had your chance to listen to fair debate. Now it's our turn to repay the kindness."*

"Nothing can be gained by keeping us here," Petragar said. *"If anything, we are a drain on your resources."*

"Good point." Nyphron turned to Persephone. *"I agree with Petragar. You should authorize their execution immediately. No sense wasting good porridge on the likes of them."*

The two looked at Persephone in wide-eyed horror.

She had never ordered the death of anyone before, and the idea made her nauseous. She could do it; Reglan had. But it was never easy, and rarely sensible. A clan needed all hands working together to survive. Execution was a last resort when all else failed, but there were times when it was necessary. This wasn't one of those times.

"Escort them across the Grandford Bridge," she ordered, still speaking in Fhrey. *"Give them food and water in the necessary quantity for a journey to Erivan, then let them go."*

Smiles brightened the faces of both prisoners as the guards hauled them out.

"You're being foolish," Nyphron said quietly, switching back to Rhunic, "and also weak. Weakness is no way to run a territory."

"I'm not running a territory. I'm leading a war."

"All the more reason. You need to be more decisive, less accommodating."

"You may feel comfortable kicking your feet up in your home, but I have not forgotten that I am living in the house of my enemy. They watch us. You don't notice, but the Fhrey in the city stare at us with loathing. Padera cooks my food because the Fhrey chefs refuse. Roan and her smiths are struggling to produce weapons and armor working in Alon Rhist's smithy, but your metalworkers refuse to help. They don't know how to make iron and refuse to learn from a Rhune. It's as if those Fhrey who chose to stay did it in expectation of our failure. They're waiting for us to give up and go home so they can scrub the smell of us off their floors and return to their old lives."

"What does that have to do with—"

"To date, only Shegon and Gryndal have died at the hands of Rhunes, and no Fhrey has been killed while I've been the keenig. The Fhrey are watching. If I execute two high-ranking Fhrey, if they witness two of their own being murdered by humans, their tolerance may well fade. I already have one war on order. I don't need another conflict inside the walls of my fortress."

"Power is kept with fear, not compassion. Fear of the fane united the Rhunes and made you the keenig. Fear of the keenig will keep your people and mine united when they no longer fear the fane."

"I don't want my people to fear me. They shouldn't have to fear anyone. That's the whole point."

"A fine ideal, which you should repeat in public every chance you get."

Persephone frowned. She didn't want to be sucked into the same old argument. Mostly because she was starting to think Nyphron might be right.

Initially, the gleaming Fhrey lord had terrified her, but over the last year she'd come to depend on him for so much. Unlike the clan chieftains, Nyphron, in fact all the Fhrey, hadn't showed the slightest concern with her being both a military leader and a woman. She knew that, until recently, the Fhrey had been ruled by a female fane named Fenelyus, who led them to victory against the Dherg. Nyphron in particular had been very supportive. Persephone found it odd how she felt more comfortable with, and accepted by, a member of another race than she had by her own husband, which made resisting Nyphron's counsel all the more difficult. "How many more prisoners are there?"

"You're changing the subject," Nyphron told her.

"She can do that; she's the keenig," Moya said while smiling innocently. Persephone was certain she had the only Shield capable of wielding her eyes as a deadly weapon.

"And good Shields are supposed to be silent," Nyphron replied.

A year ago, such a comment would have terrified both of them. Instead, Persephone braced herself for the inevitable reply. Moya always had a reply.

"And Fhrey are supposed to be gods." Moya shrugged. "Isn't life just full of disappointments?"

Moya's mouth! Persephone had mentally turned the phrase into a curse. The three of them had spent nearly every day of the winter together, planning and organizing. At first, Persephone was certain Moya would get them both killed. She loved the girl to death, but Moya could make difficult situations impossible. Then, by the first snows, she realized Nyphron invited attacks. He appeared to enjoy her barbs. By midwinter, the two were regularly greeting each other with scathing insults. To aid her, Moya had Tekchin teach her Fhrey profanity.

"How many more prisoners?" Persephone asked again.

Nyphron continued to look at Moya a moment longer, then shifted over. "A little more than a hundred."

"A hundred? Why so many?"

"I thought Instarya never disobeyed their superiors," Moya jabbed again.

Moya!

Thankfully, this time Nyphron ignored her. "Petragar and Vertumus are the only Fhrey down there."

"You have humans imprisoned?" Persephone asked.

"No," he replied, as if the question was ridiculous.

"Dwarfs?"

"Why would we imprison dwarfs?"

"I don't know, but what else could there be?"

"We use the duryngon as holding pens mostly. Patrols sometimes capture goblins, welos, or bankors. We even had an ariface once, and for a few years, we had a white bear that we named Alpola, after a Grenmorian legend of a snow giant."

Persephone didn't know what most of those words meant but imagined a menagerie of mystical creatures, a terrifying collection of nightmares underneath her feet.

"What do you do to them?"

"Study, mostly. We learn weaknesses and strengths, attitudes, motivations, and languages if applicable."

"Are we done here?" Moya asked. At midday, she taught the bow to a hundred would-be archers.

"Looks like it." Persephone was getting the nod from the door guard, who closed the chamber on that side.

"Then I'm off to belittle and humiliate this month's crop of manhood."

"How are they doing?" Nyphron asked as he stood up and they headed toward the judge's door.

"Very well—but don't tell them that. This is part of the same group I had back in autumn, and I'm pleased to find they've kept up with their practice."

"Any standouts?" Nyphron held open the door for the two women.

Moya nodded. "A kid named Tesh is the best. He loves challenging me."

Nyphron was nodding. "Sebek has the same problem with that boy."

"He's a natural, very athletic and driven. I've seen him practicing in weather so cold that stone cries. Made himself a pair of gloves without fingertips on his right hand so he could better feel the string. And he's the only one, besides me, who can hold five arrows in the draw hand. The rest of my trainees hold them in their bow hand, which slows them down. Tesh isn't accurate enough, and he's not thrusting the shot with his bow hand, but he can loose three arrows faster than you can say your own name."

"He's been asking for armor." Nyphron closed the door behind them. "Wants to get used to the weight and balance. They keep telling him he's not done growing, but that hasn't stopped him from asking."

"He's Dureyan, you know," Moya said as they entered the Kype's main hall, which was dominated by the huge doors and dangling chandeliers. Not a shaft of sunlight entered. The Kype was the fortress within the fortress; the only windows were four stories up and very narrow. "Explains why Raithe appointed him as his Shield. Well, that and great foresight on Raithe's part. That kid is going to be a killer one day."

Persephone insisted on climbing to the top of the Spyrok once a day. She wanted to see the world, and there was no better view than from there. She also loved leaving behind the shackles of her keenig duties. If only for an hour, she could be just one of the birds that circled the tower. Recently, Nyphron had taken to joining her. At first, she'd found it irritating. This had been her alone time. She climbed the thousand steps, which she counted on five separate occasions, to find solitude. He was an invader. Yet as intruders went, the lord of Alon Rhist had proven to be . . . *charming*? Somehow, that didn't quite fit but it was as close as she could come. How else could she describe how he matched her embarrassingly slow progress and pretended to need the occasional rest?

The two reached the top and looked east at all creation, cast in shimmering gold by a setting sun behind them. Wind blew. Wind always blew up there, and Persephone gripped the icy stone ledge and leaned into the cold gusts, which felt good after the long climb. The world appeared so beautiful; hard to believe that out of that splendor death marched toward them.

"Do you think it will be soon?" Persephone asked.

"Yes," Nyphron replied. "The fane will have built his new army over the winter, same as us. I suspect they are already on the move."

"How long, then?"

"We have time. Armies, even experienced ones, are notoriously slow. Supply lines need to be established, which will be the first thing we'll target after the initial battle. Disrupt an enemy's supplies and it's like poisoning a village well—everybody leaves."

"You've fought in many battles?"

He nodded with a smile that said he was being modest. He walked around the circle of the parapet with his arms outstretched. "These mountains, forests, rivers, and caves were my playground. I grew up exploring every crag, cleft, and shadow. And those that came with me became legends." He looked out at the purple and gold of the most distant peaks and sighed.

She thought she saw sadness in his eyes and realized he was likely remembering fallen comrades. "Have you lost many Galantians over the years?"

He appeared surprised and shook his head. "Just two."

"Medak and Stryker were the first?" She felt foolish for never having offered condolences for—

"Stryker wasn't a Galantian," he said with a little chuckle. "Stryker was a goblin. One of the many guests of the duryngon. I pulled him out of his hole thinking he might be useful."

"And Grygor? Is he a Galantian?"

Nyphron shrugged. "Sort of. We picked him up a few centuries ago in Hentlyn during a clan dispute where—"

"He's that old?"

"Grenmorians age like trees. Act like them, too. Some fall asleep for years, the bigger ones especially. Furgenrok, the ruler of the dominant Rok Clan, allegedly fell asleep for so long that dirt built up on him, grass grew, and sheep were grazing on his face. Legend holds that one little lamb tugged on an eyelash and what was known as Mount Furg—for reasons no one could by then remember—got up and turned out to be Furgenrok himself."

Persephone smiled as she imagined a mountain getting up and dusting himself off.

"My father was the leader of the Instarya tribe. That made him lord of Alon Rhist, commander of the whole frontier. This granted me certain privileges, although not too many as my father wasn't one for favoritism. But I was allowed to handpick my cohort. I chose only a few, but that was all I needed because I picked the best." He placed his hands on the balcony ledge and looked out. "And the adventures we had." He sighed again. "But I'm no longer five hundred, and there comes a time when you have to grow up, I suppose."

He turned to her, looked straight into her eyes, and asked. "Have you had time to consider the proposal I mentioned when we arrived? I don't mean to push, and I admit that I have very little knowledge of Rhune customs when it comes to marriage, so I apologize if I appear to be rushing things."

Once again, Persephone was caught by surprise. "More than half a year between comments wouldn't be considered a rush."

"Good," he said and waited.

Persephone felt flustered. "To be honest, I haven't given the idea that much consideration. We've been together nearly every day, and you've never . . . I mean . . . I guess I thought you might not have been serious, or you might have changed your mind."

"Not at all. I merely wanted to give you the necessary time to evaluate the proposal."

I was right, charming really isn't the right word.

Persephone had contemplated the proposal a great deal over the winter, so much so that she'd refused to meet privately with Raithe, even though he'd attempted to see her dozens of times. During council meetings where all the chieftains were present, she made a point of avoiding him. Persephone couldn't afford to be alone with Raithe, not even for a second.

Over several cold months of contemplation, she determined that Nyphron was right. Their union wasn't merely advantageous—it was necessary. Persephone also realized that, despite everything, she loved Raithe. *Probably since the day I met him.* Back then it wasn't an option. Reglan's death was so fresh, and they faced so many troubles. *I made excuses. He was too young; he didn't believe in me, didn't believe in fighting; his dreams were childish, selfish things.* But even though he knew he couldn't win, he would have fought the Gula champion for her. And he was still there, still training men in Alon Rhist. He hadn't seen her in months, but the man hadn't left. *I'm running out of excuses.* And she missed him more than she ever expected she would. *Strange how infrequently I thought about Raithe when he was here, but how important the man has become in his absence.* Thoughts of love had always been a luxury before, frivolous and indulgent, but now she had to think. She needed to decide, and that decision led her to a comparison. Nyphron made his argument, which, while sensible, felt cold and empty.

In his absence, Raithe couldn't defend himself; he also couldn't ruin the growing appreciation that bloomed in a rich soil of selected memories that became all the rosier in light of Nyphron's calculated arrangements. All of her mental debates, all of her reasons to choose the Fhrey, sounded foolish against the powerful backdrop of longing that, instead of diminishing as she had hoped, had grown stronger.

At first, she had been ridiculously busy. Now, she didn't dare allow herself to see Raithe, to be alone with him. The winter had made her weaker. This couldn't be a selfish decision. That was a girl's choice. She was a woman, and the keenig. Her own happiness couldn't get in the way of that.

Persephone looked back at him with a concerned frown. "Do you . . . do you even *like* me?"

Nyphron drew his head back in surprise. "I . . . is that important?"

"I think so, yes. I'm not saying you have to be in love with me. I've seen Fhrey women and guess you find me somewhere between ugly and grotesque. But for a successful marriage, I certainly think a genuine, if only general, affection of some kind is necessary."

He nodded thoughtfully. "I believe I can honestly say I have enjoyed your company this past winter."

"Oh, well, that is . . . that's wonderful. I hope you didn't strain yourself with that admission."

She turned away and crossed the parapet to the south side. Leaning on the wall once more, she stared out at the Bern and Urum River valleys without seeing either. These climbs were so much more enjoyable alone.

"You seem upset."

"Me? No. Not at all." She refused to look at him. His blank, bewildered stare was too infuriating.

Why am I so angry?

Nyphron was being forthright and honest, offering her a very sensible arrangement that would benefit nearly everyone. To her knowledge, there had never been a Fhrey-human marriage. Such a thing would go a long way toward eliminating misconceptions and establishing respect between the races. That was the real battle, the *real* war that needed winning.

So why does it hurt?

Persephone remembered the first time they scaled the Spyrok together. She recalled laughing with him when, after climbing those thousand steps, they couldn't open the door to the balcony because of the late winter snow. They'd just sat there, slumped on the top step cursing the gods. She remembered how he'd lent her his coat, putting it on her so thoughtfully, and how he'd caught her when she slipped on the ice, and held her hand as they crossed the rest of the bridge on their way to the general assembly for the midwinter address. His hand had felt warm; it had felt good; it had felt like . . .

I thought . . . I thought maybe he . . .

"Do you still need more time to decide?" he asked.

"Yes," she replied, and then, biting her lip, she sucked in an unsatisfying breath.

Spring was supposed to be a time of new beginnings or renewal, of love and the joy of rebirth. Instead, spring was just a time of waiting, and death was on its way.

CHAPTER ELEVEN

Monsters in the Dark

*He was handsome, brave, strong, and sixteen. Neither one of us
knew what we were doing. We did not care.*

—THE BOOK OF BRIN

Tesh wiped the sweat from his eyes. Sebek had beaten him again, but just
barely. Tesh had also very nearly lost a hand. The better he got, the nastier
Sebek became.

"You're still watching my blades too much, Techylor," Sebek told him.
The Fhrey wasn't sweating, not even out of breath. "The story is in my eyes."

"Your eyes lie."

Sebek grinned. "Noticed that, did you?"

"Nearly lost my hand because of it."

Sebek's mouth grinned while his eyes laughed. "Yes, you did."

Despite Tesh's success, the other trainees avoided Sebek, which was
likely his intent. With no students, he spent his days drinking in the sun
and shouting curses at the pitiful performance of the sword-fighting hope-
fuls. The insults started in Rhunic, but as he got drunk, Sebek slipped into
Fhrey. By the end of the day, he routinely threw things.

Sebek was also undeniably the best living warrior. Having trained with all the Galantians, Tesh knew this to be true. Eres had no match with a spear. Tekchin remained peerless with a thin, long blade. They all had specialties, but everyone knew that if the whole of the world fought, Sebek would be the last one standing. He was more than a pair of short blades, more than lean muscle, more than finely honed technique. Sebek was a killer. He enjoyed the sight of blood. Even the other Galantians didn't challenge him.

Tesh made a habit of it.

He relentlessly dogged Sebek. At first, the Fhrey laughed at the stupid kid with the death wish. When Tesh refused to let up, Sebek taught him a lesson. Tesh had bled, but he'd also learned. Sebek hadn't believed it when Tesh came back for more. After a few additional short-lived instructions in humiliation, Sebek became intrigued at the suicidal toddler who learned from his mistakes. When Tesh deflected an attack with a bare palm, Sebek stopped calling him *stupid*. He even stopped calling him *kid*. Tesh's new name was Techylor—swifthand. He was pretty sure Sebek never knew his real name—positive the Fhrey didn't care. Tesh didn't care, either. All he wanted was to learn what Sebek could teach. All Tesh desired was to be the best.

"He's just trying to scare you, Techylor," Eres said.

The Galantian reclined on the grass of the courtyard, his hands behind his head, his chest bare to the sun. They were all there—all except Nyphron. The Galantians found the matches between Sebek and Tesh as entertaining as the trainees did. Sebek liked the attention and usually put out the word that he'd be *teaching Techylor* again, which brought the rest running.

"He should be scared." Sebek returned his blades to their scabbards.

"Give him a break," Grygor said. He was sitting by the barracks wall, struggling to repair a tear in the sleeve of his shirt. "The kid is out here every day and most of the night."

"If we had a hundred like him," Sikar said, "we could invade Erivan and be done with it."

"He's not that good," Sebek said.

"He's the best Rhune I've ever seen," Sikar put in.

Sebek gave Sikar a dismissive glance. "I'm not interested in the best *Rhune*. What good is that?"

Sikar got up and dusted grass off his legs. "Just saying—he's practically an infant, and been training with us for less than a year, and already he's dangerous. Just imagine if he had been in Nadak or Dureya when they were burned." Sikar paused and looked at Tesh. "Oh, wait, you're Dureyan, aren't you? Thought I heard someone saying that. Where were you when the attacks came? Out hunting or something?"

Tesh didn't answer. He'd spotted Brin sitting in the grass across the courtyard. He pointed at her and smiled. "Sorry, can't talk. More important matters to attend to." He followed this with a wicked grin and trotted away.

Brin was leaning against the lamppost in front of the smithy with that same satchel in her lap. He grabbed his shirt and crossed the yard. Tesh expected Sebek to make a comment about the pitfalls of women, an insult at the very least. He didn't. The only sounds were the light-hearted taunts of the boys and men in his squad, none of which he bothered addressing.

Tesh thought Brin was the best-looking girl in Alon Rhist. An argument could be made that this wasn't such a big deal since there were little more than fifty Rhune females within a day's walk, and most of them were old or married. Still, some were worth looking at, like the archery instructor, but he didn't dare look at her. She scared him even more than Sebek.

Besides Brin, the only other girl his age was Nixie, who lived with her mother down by the goat pens. She was all right. He'd tried to speak to her once, but her mother was quick to shoo him away. "You shouldn't talk to that *Dureyan* boy," he heard her say. The mother's tone made *Dureyan* sound like a disease. Brin was better looking than Nixie, nicer, and she didn't have a mother. She didn't have a father, either. This was something they shared, and Tesh imagined it connected them in some way, or perhaps it was a sign from the gods—a big eternal hand pointing at her and whispering *this one!* Tesh had noticed Brin when he had lived under the wool with Malcolm and Raithe in Tirre. There had been more girls there, pretty ones, too, but Tirre ladies were a different breed, wearing sandals and dresses of dyed linen.

Brin wasn't a Dureyan girl—she was softer than that—but she wasn't a Tirre lady, either. Long brown hair, face as cute as a morning chipmunk, with high cheeks and smiling eyes. Since the weather had warmed, he'd seen her in the training yard, always with that satchel. Everyone else noticed her, too. Even the old men watched for Brin, and when she sat out on the grass, the trainees nudged each other and pointed—first at her and then at him. This warning gesture spread until all the other students moved away, fearful of being paired with Tesh. When Brin was there, he had a tendency to show off.

Tesh wasn't intimidated by many things, but pretending to look for Roan that day had been the most frightening thing he'd done since reaching Alon Rhist. It hadn't gone as well as he had hoped. All that talk about raow, footprints, and voices in the night didn't set the right tone. At first, he thought she might have been messing with him, but when he found the clawed footprint around the corner, he had to take that seriously. Since then, he'd made a habit of going for nightly walks down by her house. He'd circle it, then sit in the shadows by the well, waiting to see if anything was lurking around. Nothing ever was, and when he got too cold, he'd head back to the barracks. Tesh wasn't sure what he was looking for, didn't know what a raow looked like, but if anything tried to hurt Brin, he'd take his training out for a test run.

Since their first meeting, he'd spoken to her after every practice. The last four times she'd allowed him to hold her hand. This time he hoped to kiss her. The thought had his heart racing. As usual, she was making black marks on incredibly thin sheets of skin with a featherless quill. Usually, she stopped well before he reached her, but this time her brows were furrowed and her tongue stuck partway out of her mouth. According to Moya and some of the others, Tesh did the same thing when aiming a bow. *Another connection. This had to be destiny . . . Didn't it?*

"Hi again," he said when she failed to look up. None of his training had included classes in eloquence. He had learned how to curse in three languages, but somehow he didn't think calling her a whore in Grenmorian or Fhrey would impress Brin.

She looked up, and rapidly sucked in her tongue, making a little slurping sound. She opened her mouth after that, but didn't say anything. She just stared.

She's finally fed up, tired of me bothering her, probably wants me to leave. You shouldn't talk to that Dureyan boy!

Every muscle in his body contracted, and he started to sweat. He needed to say something. For the first time in a half-dozen visits, he asked, "What are you doing?"

She continued to stare for a few more seconds, then looked down at her lap as if she'd forgotten. "Oh—I, ah . . . I was writing."

"Writing?"

"Yeah, I'm the Keeper of Ways for the Rhulyn clans, and I—"

"You are?" he blurted out, hating himself. He was shocked because he thought Keepers were old, like that Padera hag. The one in Dureya had been. He just couldn't imagine a girl as young as Brin being a Keeper. Still, he should have known she wasn't just *some girl*. She was an orphan, but she was in Alon Rhist. All the other women in the Rhist were married to, or daughters of, serving soldiers. The rest stayed home in their villages to tend animals and babies. If she was at the Rhist, she had to be special.

Brin nodded. "I thought you knew."

Tesh shook his head. "I don't know much, but I guess being Keeper you know everything."

"I think you're confusing Keepers with gods. I only know the history of the clans."

"Still, that's not easy, right?" He was trying to compliment her—sort of like doing a backward parry with his off hand in a first match. He hoped this went better.

"I had to memorize the ancient stories word for word from the last Keeper, Maeve."

"How long did that take?"

"Years. I started listening when I was real young. Made my first recital, of the *Song of Estuary,* when I was five. That's when Maeve really started training me, but there were still a few things I never completely learned. That's what this is all about." She laid a hand on the stack of markings. "I'm working at making a permanent account of those stories, so anyone can know them."

Tesh knelt down on one knee and leaned in to look at all the wavy marks she'd made. "Is it magic?" He knew that the keenig had magicians working for her. He also knew all of them were women.

"No, these marks just represent sounds, the same ones we speak when talking. If you know which marks make what sounds, you can read them."

"Oh," he said, nodding confidently but not understanding. He didn't need to. He didn't care. All Tesh wanted was for her not to shout at him to go away. Every word he uttered was a gamble, and an opportunity. "So, what is it you're *writing?*"

"I used to call it *The Book Pine Markings of Brin,* but that's too long. Moya shortened it to *The Book of Brin,* and I guess that's okay. Makes less sense, but is a lot easier to say. It's going to be the story of the whole world—from how it began to the present."

"Since you're from Rhen, I suppose you'll say Mari created everything."

"Actually, no. Erebus did."

Tesh wasn't an expert on gods. In Dureya, they worshiped the Mynogan, the three gods of war, and he knew that Clan Nadak worshiped Bakrakar, the stag god of the hunt, and Rhen worshiped Mari. Each of the clans had its own god, but he had never heard of Erebus.

"Erebus is the father of all the gods. And he had four children, Ferrol, Drome, Mari, and Muriel."

"I knew Mari would get in there," Tesh said with a smile. He wasn't really interested in the gods and was ready to move to another topic, like whether she'd consider taking a walk with him. Talking to her in the open with everyone watching was horribly awkward. Humiliation hurt less in private.

"The Dherg like to call themselves Belgriclungreians, but they were originally called Dromeians."

Tesh smiled and nodded. "I was wondering if—"

"Do you see it? Do you understand?"

Tesh hadn't been paying close attention and felt he'd been caught. He made a guilty grin that he hoped might be seen as charming. Knowing he was asking for too much, he added a shake of his head.

"Ferrol sounds like Fhrey, and Drome sounds like Dromeian—even Dherg and dwarf—they are all variations of the same word. Although Dherg comes from the Fhrey for *vile mole* and *dwarf* is a Rhunic word to indicate *something small,* in our own language, and they shouldn't have anything to do with each other, but I think they might. That somehow all those words come from the same root. That would mean the Fhrey, Belgriclungreian, and our own language share a common ancestry. I have no idea how that could be possible. And then there's Mari . . ." She looked at him expectantly, inviting a response by making a hand-it-over motion with her fingers.

Tesh was at a loss. *I never should have asked what she was doing. Now she thinks I'm—*

Brin smiled at him.

I'm okay. It's like the first part of a joke; she doesn't expect me to know the answer.

"The masculine form of the word Mari is Mani—do you see now?" Thankfully she didn't even pause to give him time to answer. "Mani sounds a lot like *man,* doesn't it?"

She was excited—really excited. He could see it in her eyes, bright and wide. This was important to her, and she wanted him to respond with equal enthusiasm, but all he wanted was a kiss.

"Okay, so maybe it isn't so obvious to everyone," she went on when he failed to say anything. "Even Roan didn't make the connection, but think about it. Those words aren't similar by accident. Ferrol is the god of the Fhrey. Drome is the god of the Dromeians, and Mari is the god of Man. It says so right in the tablets I found in Neith. *Those born of Ferrol, those born of Drome, and those born of Mari moved out into the world.* You see, we are Mari born, the children of Mari, daughter of Erebus. Only . . ." She looked away, perplexed.

"Only what?"

"None of it makes sense. I mean, okay, so this Erebus had four kids, but with who? Elan? We call her the Grand Mother of All, so what does that mean? For that matter, who was Mari's husband? Or Ferrol's wife, or Drome's . . . I don't even know what Drome is—the Belgriclungreians called the peak above Neith *Dome* Mountain. Could that be a derivation? And what about Muriel? Did she have children? Maybe she made the plants and animals. I don't know, but someone had to, right? And where'd Erebus come from in the first place? Did he have parents? Wouldn't he have to? And where'd they come from?" She sighed. "I thought I had it all worked out, most of it written down: father of the gods, three kids that made humans, Fhrey, and the Dherg, but no. That's what you get from talking to Roan about anything. She keeps asking why until you want to punch her in the face."

Tesh just stared.

"You wanna go for a walk?" Brin asked.

"Huh?" He blinked. "Oh—ah, sure."

"Great," she said. Brin wrapped her pages up in the satchel and capped the ink bottle.

"Where we going?" he asked. For all his desire to go someplace quiet, Tesh hadn't put any thought into where.

"I'd love to go for a walk in a forest, but there aren't any. Have you been in the Verenthenon?"

"Not much."

Brin smiled. "I'll give you a tour."

Tesh grinned. "I'd like that." He took her hand and they set off.

The Verenthenon was beautiful, and Brin hoped he would be impressed. While not forbidden, the rotunda was reserved for *official business*, which left it empty much of the time. Brin had been there often as she attended every meeting conducted beneath the dome. She also found it a good place to write when the weather was bad.

"Here, I want to show you something." She pulled him up a flight of stairs to the platform where Persephone and Nyphron made their speeches. The sunlight shone through the skylights, but it was late in the day and the dais wasn't illuminated. She led him to its center and then whispered in his ear. "Say something."

Her heart beat quickly with the intimacy of being so close, her lips so near to him.

"Something," he said, and his eyes went wide in amazement at the tremendous volume produced. "How did you do that?" he exclaimed. Spoken louder, these words echoed. He turned, searching for the speaker who was mimicking him. Then the truth dawned, and he smiled.

Brin smiled, too.

She led him off the stage, and they circled around and went out to the tiered benches. "This is where all the important people sit when Nyphron and Persephone are addressing them."

She took Tesh's hand again and led him across the tile to a door in the back.

"I discovered a world of hallways and doors beneath this place. I tried nearly every one. Most are open but some are fastened shut. Behind a few, I've heard noises. Maybe they keep some livestock down here: goats or pigs. Haven't seen any, but it's kinda interesting. Come on, I'll show you."

They dipped their heads under an arch, descended a set of stone steps, and entered a carved-out passageway. The upper portion of the corridor was made of blocked stone, the lower section hewn from natural rock. They were entering the body of the butte, and Tesh had to admit it was a little creepy, like going into a cave. Still, he didn't care. He was alone with her and that was all he wanted.

"Did you get your armor?" Brin asked as she grabbed a torch and led him down the steps.

"No."

"You couldn't find Roan?"

"Oh, I found her. It's just—they want me to wait. I'm not sure why."

He knew exactly why. They said he would grow out of it in just a few months. He was the only one who could go toe-to-toe with Sebek. They'd sparred twelve times, but *he* was too *young* for armor. He wasn't going to tell *her* that.

"You came down here by yourself? Isn't this a little scary?"

Brin shrugged. "I've seen worse. I went with Persephone to Neith, and let me tell you, dwarfs know how to dig deep. This is nothing."

"Oh, right," Tesh said. "You fought a raow, didn't you? I suppose this is a walk in a dewy field next to that."

She waved the torch at a clot of cobwebs, burning them away. "It's a little scary, but not with you—not with Techylor who's fought Sebek twelve times and only received one scratch."

She has *been watching!*

"Speaking of scary," he said, "have you had any more visits from the raow?"

"No, just that one night."

She stopped at the bottom of a narrow corridor. Across from them, an open door revealed a small chamber with dry straw on a dirt floor. Brin stared at it as if trying to make up her mind about something.

Tesh had an idea what it was—at least he hoped he did. There were few places in the city where two people could be alone.

Tesh moved past her into the room. "It's all right. Nothing to worry about in here, see?"

She stood in the hallway, watching him with big eyes, biting her lower lip.

Tesh put his hand to the wall. "Stone is dry." He sniffed. "No mildew or mold. Not a bad little place. Nicer than my home in Dureya actually."

Brin placed the torch in a sconce outside and entered, taking unusually short steps.

As she moved toward him, Tesh found he had to take two breaths to gain the same amount of air. He placed his hands on her hips, drawing her closer. As he did, he noticed Brin was having the same issue with the air, her chest rising and falling. Tesh leaned in, pressing against her. She was trembling; he was, too. Their lips, less than a finger's width apart, drew in a common breath.

His arms slipped around her. She answered by closing her eyes. Then as his lips touched hers, Brin arched up, meeting him.

Tesh had never kissed a girl before. The moment he felt the press of her lips, he stopped thinking.

Nearly every combat instructor had stressed the need to be in the moment, to not be pondering the future or past. Such a thing wasn't as easy as it seemed. So much of everything was held in the vessel of what came before and the anticipation of what came next. Blocking out those thoughts was as hard as forgetting he existed. Tesh was certain he'd never achieved that singular state of perfection, never even knew what he was aiming for, until that kiss. In one flawless moment, Tesh forgot the rest of the world. He might have stood pressed against Brin for hours, or days, lost in the smell of her skin, the feel of her hair. His only thought: *I can't believe I'm really doing this.*

Legs weak, they slid down the wall to the dirt and straw. Some part of him wondered how he was still getting air, but it was a thought with no more substance than the cobwebs.

Then everything changed.

Brin stopped kissing. Her whole body went rigid, and he felt her muscles tighten as she pushed him away.

What's wrong? What did I do? Does she think I was pulling her to the floor? Did she think I was going to—

"I didn't—" he started to apologize, but stopped when he saw the terror on her face. It wasn't him she was upset with. She was horrified but acted as if he wasn't there.

She retreated to the door, pulled the torch free of the sconce, and brought it down toward the floor.

"Look," she said. Their movement in the cell had brushed aside a patch of straw. The flickering glow revealed a familiar three-toed footprint—one with claws.

CHAPTER TWELVE

The Witness

Alon Rhist had been the fourth fane, the first from the Instarya tribe, and the first male ruler of Erivan. He took power in the midst of the Dherg War after Fane Ghika of the Asendwayr had been killed in the initial battle. For five dark years, he had fought a losing war against the Dherg. After his death, Rhist became the only fane to be buried west of the Nidwalden River. The fortress that bore his name was also his tombstone.

—THE BOOK OF BRIN

As Suri walked, her feet gave rise to a cloud of dust. It was unlike the sickly yellow soil of Dureya, easily disturbed and slow to settle. There, the pallid grit collected on her asica, muting its color, dulling everything. Here the dirt was light, but the air was heavy. Spring breezes failed to lift the sense of suffocation. It couldn't. The stifling misery Suri felt wasn't caused by weather.

Months of working with Arion had opened countless doors that Suri had previously ignored. Hand in hand they had explored those new corridors, and with each discovery, Suri's understanding of the Art increased. With understanding came awareness. The more she learned, the more she realized how little she knew. In the past, she had overlooked so many things that had screamed for her attention. She hadn't been blind to them, just never noticed. People always did that. So devoured by their own problems, they never noticed the wildflowers in their path. That spring, she saw the world in a new way. She had learned to not merely look but to see. Not everything she saw was pleasant.

Overhead, the dark wings of seven vultures circled against a gray sky that was too big, too bare, too vacant.

"How can there be no trees?" Suri asked and let her arms clap her sides, issuing a burst of yellow dust.

"There's a tree." Raithe pointed at an ancient stump whose long-dead roots resembled the skeletal remains of a hand clutching a fistful of rocks.

"That's not a tree."

"Used to be a tree."

Suri turned her head side to side, viewing the entire tabletop plain. "Is that what happened? People cut them all down?"

Raithe shook his head. "Don't think there were many to start with."

The two had left the Rhist early that morning. No plans had been made, no rendezvous agreed to. Suri had awakened with itchy feet, the sort of irritation that could only be calmed by a good solid walk over new ground. She found Raithe at the ford, standing on the bridge and looking down into the chasm where the river rushed. She, too, had paused to take a peek. Nothing was said, no greeting, not even a wave.

When Suri moved on, Raithe fell into step alongside her. That's how it usually happened. Raithe likely felt it was coincidence, but armed with her new sight, Suri recognized more was at work. In terms of the Art—the Language of Elan—she saw it as a golden thread that connected the two of them, just as she felt linked to Arion. This heightened connection indicated a relationship of importance and the reason they so often found each other at just the right time. Suri imagined that she would have noticed a similar thread between her and Maeve had she known how to see it back then. What significance that thread indicated, Suri had no idea, but that was how the *sight*—as Arion sometimes referred to it—worked. In a way, they were puzzles, clues, bits and pieces of half-heard conversations. Suri liked mysteries, but all too often when put together these puzzles revealed unhappy pictures.

"How did you live here without—" Suri shook her head. "It's not just the lack of trees; there's so little life. No greenery, all rock."

"Now you know why we crossed the Bern. Look." Raithe pointed back west and slightly south where the land turned a lush green. "The Fhrey call it Avrlyn."

"Green hills," Suri translated.

"Yep." He gestured longingly with his hands at the sight. "In my village I woke up every day, and there it was right across the river. Look at it—paradise rising up into the clouds. We weren't allowed there. That was the land of gods." He sighed and frowned as his sight returned to the rocky world around them. "This, we were told, was our place, our divinely prescribed lot. What we deserved." Raithe scraped his boot on the face of the stone escarpment he stood on. "In a way they were right. This land suited us: dry, hard, barren, prone to extremes of hot and cold, but . . ." He looked at her. "I wonder how much of that came from living here? If we all lived where you did, would we have been different?"

"Wouldn't matter," Suri said. "Regardless where you're born, the world has a way of finding you and ruining everything."

Raithe looked surprised.

She shrugged. "Okay, not everything, and maybe not utter ruin, but nothing stays the same."

She resumed their hike along the edge of the canyon, looking for routes down. During the cold of winter, all they could comfortably handle were short explorations of the city. Sometimes Tesh or Malcolm came along, but mostly it was just her and Raithe. They had tried crossing the ford months before, but the winds and snow of Dureya were brutal. The city, with its twisting narrow streets, was sheltered but complicated. Exploring it provided just enough adventure to keep her sane. After months of darkness trapped in stone, the fortress became an uncomfortable cage, but when she and Raithe teamed up and slipped out, they were—for a short time—free. The advent of spring felt like the end of a prison sentence. They were out, the day was hot, and Suri was intent on swimming. She just needed to find a way to descend the cliff.

"There's no way down," Raithe told her.

She frowned.

"Wouldn't have been nice, anyway," he continued. "Maybe down by the Crescent in high summer it's a fine swim. Up here in spring, it's ridiculously cold, and I know that from experience."

She hadn't told him what she planned. Until she mentioned the lack of trees, the two hadn't spoken all morning. Still, he knew. Only once before had Suri experienced that degree of harmony, that sense of comfortable companionship that had no need for questions or answers. She couldn't help feeling a little guilty.

"Rivers age as they go downstream," Suri told Raithe while they looked at the disagreeable gorge. "That's what Tura once told me. They start out as tiny trickles, then in their youth and adolescence are like this, boundless energy throwing themselves heedless against unmovable rocks. Then they usually fall. Sometimes it's a series of tumbles and sometimes one great plummet, but hitting bottom usually takes the fight out of most rivers. After that, they mellow and learn to meander around the rocks they encounter, taking life slower, easier. They spread out and grow quiet until, at last, they flow into the sea, becoming one with something greater."

Raithe's eyes grew glassy, his lips squeezed shut, and a moment later he wiped away tears. For the first time she was baffled.

"Sorry," he said. "I ah . . . It's just that you remind me of my sister. She would have been about your age, and she used to talk like that." He looked at his feet. "I don't miss too many people, but I miss her. I remember laughing when she was around. She had a way of doing that, even on the cold nights when there was no food. I can't remember the last time I laughed. And in all honesty, being with you sometimes makes me feel a little guilty, like I'm betraying her memory." He waved a defensive hand. "I know that sounds stupid but—"

"Not so much," Suri replied.

"No?"

"You remind me of someone, too."

"Who?"

Suri smiled. "*My* sister."

Raithe looked at her; he was puzzled for a moment, then a smile came on his face, and he chuckled and nodded. "Must be the fur." He reached up and ran a hand through his hair. "So, what do we do now? How about another game of Stones?"

"We could get rocks and juggle. You didn't do so well last time. You could use the practice. Oh, and I've got my string! We could just bask on the ground over there, and I could show you how to do a four-handed—"

Suri had been pointing at a flat place on the plain, one of the few areas where there was grass. While she was thinking about how soft it would be to sit on, a blast of despair hit her.

"Suri?" Raithe said.

"Rocks," she replied.

"Rocks?"

"Piles of rocks."

"I don't see any," Raithe told her.

"Sadness here, terrible sadness and incredible loss."

"That's Dureya."

Suri felt the sorrow welling up until she thought she might drown. That suffocating feeling rushed back, smothering her.

"Suri!" Raithe shouted as she collapsed to her knees and began sobbing.

"There's so much anguish here," she cried.

Raithe lifted her up and began carrying her back toward the bridge. "I think you've had enough fresh air for one day."

"No, no!" Suri said. "I don't want to go back yet."

She squirmed and he let her down. Suri wiped her eyes and took a breath.

"You okay?"

"Better." Suri took a few more calculated breaths, then started walking back toward the bridge. She felt a powerful need to get farther away from that grassy place.

"What happened?"

She shook her head. "Felt something awful."

"This is an Art thing, isn't it?"

She nodded but wasn't entirely sure. Suri really didn't know what had happened. It felt a bit like the sensation of cold she and Arion had experienced in the city. But this sensation had been far more powerful, and personal. It had felt so strong that she was surprised—

"You didn't feel it?" she asked.

"Feel what?"

"Never mind. Maybe it was just my imagination."

You need to recognize that your imagination is more accurate than other people's sight.

Suri didn't like that idea, not in this case. She wanted it to be a mistake, felt it had to be, but not so much that she'd turn around to test the idea. Suri was happy to leave the question unanswered because, just as with the sensation with Arion in the city, Suri had the impression she wasn't sensing some awful event from the past. Whatever horrible thing Suri sensed had yet to happen.

Feeling a need to hide from the terrible in a bath of ordinary mindlessness, she veered off course toward the once-a-tree. "Maybe we should just sit over here for a bit."

"Sure," he said. Then she saw him glance back across the plain, and he asked, "Suri? Can you really . . ." He hesitated.

"What?"

"Can you really move mountains?"

She frowned. "Yeah, but it was sort of an accident."

"Sort of an accident?"

"I was upset at the time."

Raithe stopped abruptly. "You're upset right now." He put his arms up feigning fear. "Should I be worried?"

Suri smiled and moved her hands as if she were going to hex him. "Very."

"Ooh," he said, grinning. "Going to turn me into a frog?"

"No." She walked toward the stump. "Frogs are no fun. What would you like to be?"

"I don't know. Something that can fly, I guess."

She nodded. "Me, too."

. . .

Nyphron entered the High Hold, a large living space on the seventh floor of the Kype that most of the Instarya called the Shrine. The suite of rooms, decorated with tapestries, sculptures, mahogany chairs, and gold-rimmed chamber pots, was originally built as the living quarters for the lord of the Rhist. In reality, the seventh floor had only had one resident, and he'd used it for just a short time. Although nothing official had ever been declared, the quarters—although meticulously cleaned and maintained—had been left empty and unaltered since Fane Rhist died. That had been a few thousand years ago, before Nyphron was born. Legend held that not a thing had changed. A golden cup famously rested precariously on the stone molding near the grand open hearth, and it was believed that Rhist had placed his drink there just before rushing out to his death—his last act in that room. Nyphron had come in and looked at that cup many times, wondering what foolish little thing might be his last act that future generations of people would look back on with misplaced worship. He hoped it would be something grander than setting down a cup of wine.

"So, what is it that has you so jittery you want to speak in private?" Nyphron asked.

Sebek didn't answer. He closed the door behind them.

Nyphron folded his arms. "Oh honestly—give it up. What's this all about?"

"It's Techylor." Sebek spoke just above a whisper.

"The kid? What about him?"

Sebek proceeded to walk briskly around the Shrine, opening the doors to the side rooms and looking inside. Nyphron waited until he was done. Sebek had always been a little volatile, a little odd, but the truly talented always were a touch crazy.

Nyphron had known Sebek for a thousand years. He couldn't say they were friends, but then *friends* meant different things to different people. In all honesty, Nyphron had never had what he would call a friend—someone like him, someone he could relate to, someone who loved him and whom he could unequivocally trust. Sebek was more his opposite. Cold and detached, the Fhrey loved only his swords and cared only that he was the best at killing, which he was. Sebek liked killing. He cared nothing for power, for advancement, or wealth, just had a thing for fresh blood. Sebek wasn't an intellectual, not a thinker. Thoughts other than those associated with combat were a distraction, something to avoid. Sebek was as interesting as a dull rock, but he was a damn fine warrior.

"Well?" Nyphron asked, taking a seat on the gold-framed, red-cushioned couch as Sebek walked back to him.

"I think Techylor knows."

"Knows what?"

There was a knock on the door, and Sebek reached for his swords.

"Who is it?" Nyphron called out. Sebek's nervousness had him concerned. When the best warrior in the world was checking doors, whispering mysterious warnings, and reaching for metal at the slightest sound, only a fool would be relaxed.

"Your humble servant," came the reply.

Nyphron looked at Sebek. "Is Malcolm allowed in?"

Sebek answered by opening the door. "Anyone see you come up?"

"Maybe, but who would care?"

Malcolm walked in, still dressed in his absurd Rhune outfit of wool despite the change in weather. He also wore a confused look similar to the one on Nyphron's face. "What's going on?"

Sebek checked the hall before closing the door.

"I was hoping you knew," Nyphron admitted.

"Sebek asked me up," Malcolm said.

Sebek closed the door again. "Techylor is from Dureya."

Malcolm glanced at Nyphron with a smirk. "Yeah—we know. Is this news to you?"

"He was there."

Nyphron leaned forward. "What do you mean by *there?*"

Sebek walked away from the door, making the wooden floor boards creak with his weight. Alon Rhist had likely made the same sound. Probably he made that noise when he walked to the stone molding and set his wine cup down.

"The kid was in one of the little villages we burned. He lived there."

Nyphron shook his head. "Not possible. We checked. No one survived those raids." He pointed again at Sebek. "You—you were charged with making certain there were no witnesses."

Sebek stopped short of where the famous cup rested, gathering dust. "He must have been hiding."

"He saw you?" Malcolm said, glancing back and forth between them. "That's . . ."

"He didn't see us," Nyphron said, willing it to be so. There were times he felt he was genuinely capable of such things. During battles, or in general, sheer determination and willpower were all that was needed. If he wanted anything bad enough, he could make it happen. This was often a warning sign of Miralyith talent. As nothing could be more repugnant to him, he also willed that not to be so. "What makes you think he did?"

"Raithe and Tesh are the only surviving Dureyans," Sebek said. "Raithe lived because he was in the wilderness with Malcolm, but Techylor was a kid. Why would a kid be away from home by himself?"

"That's all you've got?"

"And when I asked him where he was, how he avoided death, he didn't answer. He ran off and wouldn't even look at me."

"Tesh would have said something by now," Nyphron said. "If he really was there, he would have seen us kill his family, his whole clan. If that were true, do you really think he'd be training with you?"

"He wants revenge," Malcolm said thoughtfully, as if thinking out loud. The skinny man sat down on one of the three fancy footstools. "When we first met him, Tesh asked to be called *Fhreyhyndia*."

Sebek's eyes widened. "That explains the dedication. He's learning to kill us." He walked the length of the room, then turned around and stared at Nyphron. "I'm guessing he'll start with you."

"This is all . . ." Nyphron shook his head. Sebek wasn't as quick with his brain as with his swords. "Has he told anyone? Has he actually said he saw us?"

"No," Sebek said.

Nyphron shifted his sight to Malcolm.

"Don't look at me. I didn't even know about this until now. If he was going to tell anyone, it would be Raithe. They're both Dureyan, and Raithe is his chieftain."

"*Did* he tell him?"

Malcolm shrugged. "It's not like we're always together. They've had plenty of opportunities to chat without me around."

"All the more reason to keep Raithe away from Persephone. If she were to hear of this . . ." Nyphron made a peak with his hands and rested his face in them, his fingertips pressing the bridge of his nose.

"Do you think she'd believe him?" Malcolm asked. "Things have come so far. You've built so much trust and credibility over the—"

"She's still a human," he snapped. "They aren't rational."

Malcolm raised both eyebrows and tilted his head slightly to one side. "Excuse me?"

"You know what I mean. Besides, you're practically Fhrey."

Malcolm smirked. "I'll choose to interpret that as a compliment."

"Even if he hasn't told anyone else, Techylor is still a threat," Sebek insisted as he continued to pace. That was another problem with Sebek; he always needed to be moving. Moving, fighting, killing. The Fhrey's nightmare must be dying and being brought back to life by the gods as a still pond. "He's only sixteen years old—sixteen. What will he be like in another ten years?"

"This kid is that good?"

Sebek raised his brows. "How good were you at sixteen years? Not sixteen hundred, not fifty—*sixteen!*"

Nyphron hadn't touched a weapon of any kind at such a young age. Like most Instarya, his first century was considered childhood, his first decade was looked on as infancy, a time for unencumbered frivolity and discovery. "It's not the same with them as with us."

"Doesn't change the fact that in one year the kid managed to master what takes most Instarya a hundred. I didn't call him Techylor to boost his confidence. Right now, he has enough skill to best most Erivan Fhrey. And he's just *sixteen.*"

Nyphron dismissed the idea. "In a practice bout perhaps, but there's a big difference between training and the real thing. The kid will hesitate. He has no experience."

"He's Dureyan," Malcolm reminded them. "Traditionally, they aren't a squeamish people."

"Even so, it's not the same." Nyphron stared at Sebek.

Sebek shook his head. "He's still a danger. If he's this good now and remains dedicated to improving, what will he be like after fighting in a war? What will he be like in ten, twenty, fifty years after he's gotten used to taking the lives of Fhrey?"

"Old," Nyphron said. "More than likely, dead. Don't forget; he's still a Rhune."

"He learns fast, too fast. He's soaked up everything we can teach him. And the bow!" Sebek rolled his eyes and threw his hands up. "Moya tried to train us. Eres should be a natural, but compared to Tesh, they're bumbling fools. That kid can do anything. Now he's asking for armor—iron armor."

"A lot of them are."

Sebek shook his head. "Don't you see? That's the last thing. When he gets that, Techylor will be ready. You nearly died fighting Raithe, do you—"

"I did not!" Nyphron scowled. "You should know better."

Sebek smiled. "I do. I fought him just to be sure. But it's still nice to hear you say it."

Nyphron glanced at Malcolm, who looked up at him from his perch on that stool with an almost whimsical expression. "Everyone had to believe a Rhune could beat a Fhrey in fair combat—even the Galantians."

"Well, guess what?" Sebek stared at him. "You don't need to pretend anymore. In five or ten years, there's a good chance Techylor could beat you in a fair fight, but something tells me Techylor isn't partial to fair fighting." Sebek walked toward the cup and gestured at it. "You want to go back to your room one night and find a full-suited Rhune with two iron swords swinging at you from out of the shadows while you're squatting on your chamber pot? Maybe that's what they'll leave standing untouched in the middle of your shrine for people to visit."

Nyphron looked at the cup on the ledge and nodded. He had too many plans to let it all fall apart because of some revenge-driven brat. Disappointing. If what Sebek said was true, Tesh might have been the first Rhune Galantian. Sounded like he'd fit right in. Maybe that was the secret of the Rhunes. They didn't last long, but while they lived they burned brighter.

"Kill him." Nyphron sighed and looked up at Sebek. "Make it look like an accident—nothing embarrassing, either. The kid deserves that much. I can't exactly hate him for wanting revenge against the people who killed his kin, now can I?"

Sebek drew his sword and looked down at it as if the blade spoke to him. "I'll do it in a practice fight. I'll kill him and say Techylor caused me to slip. That he was that good."

Nyphron nodded. "A fine epitaph. He'll be a legend after that. The Rhune that tripped up Sebek."

"He deserves it. One day he might actually have done it."

CHAPTER THIRTEEN

Avempartha

What Drumindor is to the Dherg, Avempartha is to the Fhrey. To the rest of us, it was a terrible boulder in our path.

—THE BOOK OF BRIN

Fenelyus had once referred to the tower of Avempartha as the *mill wheel of magic*. Only Fenelyus could have gotten away with calling the Art *magic*, but then Fenelyus got away with a lot of things. She grew her hair long, forgave the Dherg after a horrific war, and made a habit of crying late at night in the Garden until she was escorted back to the palace. No one had seen her drink anything stronger than apple juice, but Mawyndulë had heard there were rumors.

He'd barely known his grandmother. Mawyndulë saw the old fane only during official gatherings. By the time he was born, she was too old to do much more than drool. She lived to the ridiculous age of three thousand one hundred and twenty-seven. Some people thought she'd never die. First in that line had to be his father, who had waited forever to be fane. Mawyndulë imagined his father had gone to bed at night and dreamed of smothering the old lady with a pillow. He hadn't; instead, Lothian endured the passing of years in the shadows as the son of an icon that no one was eager to see die. Such a sentiment was understandable; the old fane was the first-ever Miralyith and the savior of the Fhrey. Mawyndulë had never been a fan. He never liked anything old, and she was beyond ancient. The fact that Arion—The Traitor—idolized Fenelyus only made him dislike the old fane more. Nevertheless, he remembered having second thoughts the first time he had seen Avempartha.

The tower was widely considered the grand pinnacle of Miralyith achievement. Not a hammer or chisel had been used. Wielding the Art, Fenelyus had managed what no builder could have. At the edge of the Parthaloren Falls and in the middle of the Nidwalden River, she had raised a tower. Stone had been stretched upward, imitating an explosion of water frozen at its apex. High above the thunderous cataract, the stone splintered, bursting in a bouquet of slender points that tapered to the size of a finger. This was a sculpture done in the scale of creation. Nothing Mawyndulë had ever seen compared to it. The tower was beyond beautiful; it was evidence of what the Art could achieve with enough power, skill, and talent. Avempartha was as close to divine as the Fhrey had ever come— a temple to the Art.

Fenelyus had made it.

It took her three days.

The first time Mawyndulë laid eyes on Avempartha all he could think about was that old, wizened fane who drooled on herself. How had *she* made *this*? Seeing it for a second time, Mawyndulë thought the same thing.

Entering the tower was always a thrill. Fenelyus had made Avempartha to be an amplifier that conducted the intense power of the falls upward. Walking in, Mawyndulë experienced the rush. It literally staggered him. This drew odd looks from the non-Miralyith soldiers who trooped alongside.

How can they not feel it?

The year before, Gryndal had spent the night in the tower speaking to him of how Miralyith weren't Fhrey, but new gods. Vibrating with raw power, he found the idea impossible to argue. Mawyndulë was convinced he could remake the whole world from inside those soaring walls. That visit, in the company of Gryndal, had been wonderful, full of excitement and expectation.

This time was different.

"You're not taking the child with you, are you?" Jerydd asked, staring at Mawyndulë as if he were a stain on the floor.

"He asked to come, and I thought the experience might do him good," Lothian replied. "He might be fane one day. He should know *something*."

As always, his father was overwhelming in the defense of his son.

"It'd be better if you left him here with me. Let me teach the child something useful."

Mawyndulë cringed at the very thought of being left with the old kel. The steward of the tower was a month away from his own bout of uncontrolled drooling. He didn't even shave his head anymore and had a wreath of white stubble growing around a natural bare spot. Mawyndulë vowed that he'd kill himself before getting so old. There was a limit to what life should endure.

"He's been attending the Academy for the Art back in Estramnadon," Lothian said. "He's only done two seasons; I doubt he's acquired enough of the basics to even understand your lessons."

"The academy." Jerydd said the word as if it were a bad joke. "They'll ruin him. All those instructors with their rules and lesson plans. They keep tight control, afraid of mistakes. You and I didn't learn that way. Your mother pushed us to make mistakes—only way to learn—remember?"

Lothian nodded. "Perhaps on the way back."

The comment made the hairs on Mawyndulë's arms rise. *Then I hope I die in battle.* Mawyndulë could avoid being enslaved to Jerydd and the horrors of growing old in one act. He imagined the moment as heroic and thought the place of his death would be revered in the same way as the two boulders on the riverbank where Fenelyus stood to create Avempartha.

Kel Jerydd, Fane Lothian, Mawyndulë, Vasek, and Taraneh were all seated in the kel's personal study on the second level. Sile and Synne did not sit. Probably wasn't a chair big enough for Sile, and Synne couldn't sit still. Those seated shared a bottle of wine, but Mawyndulë wasn't offered a glass. His father didn't appear to notice. Insulted at his exclusion, Mawyndulë displayed his indignation by getting up and walking to the window. Although he didn't expect anyone would see his action as a protest, he knew, and that was all that mattered.

Outside, the moon shimmered on the river below the Fhrey army as they marched across the Nidwalden on a bridge that ran from bank to bank. The span was temporary, ordered by the fane, and created by Avempartha Miralyith. Once the army was across, the bridge would dissolve.

"I don't expect this war will take long," his father said. "We have nearly two thousand soldiers and almost fifty Miralyith. When we get there, erasing this insurrection and reclaiming Alon Rhist shouldn't take more than an afternoon. I won't bother to stay for the longer process of eradicating the Rhunes. It could take months to get them all. I'll leave it to the new lord of the Rhist." He nodded toward Taraneh.

Addressing Jerydd once more he said, "I should be back in a few days. You can have Mawyndulë then."

"Wonderful. It'll be good for the lad to get out of that viper's nest you call Estramnadon," Jerydd said. Then his voice grew a tad louder as he added, "I heard you got yourself in with a bad crowd there."

Bad crowd. In his mind, Mawyndulë saw the fleeting image of Makareta's face under a bridge, lit by magical light—the way he always remembered her. She was probably dead. He'd never found out, and the lack of knowing was difficult to take. The memory of her always hurt, and he wished it didn't. Makareta had used him, tried to kill his father, did kill dozens of good people, and yet in his mind he still saw that beautiful face and remembered how being with her had felt.

No one had said anything for several seconds, and Mawyndulë realized Jerydd had been speaking to him when he made the comment. They were awaiting his reply. He turned back from the window to see everyone watching. He focused on Kel Jerydd. The old Fhrey looked far too satisfied. "Bad crowd? Perhaps. All I know is that I was invited to a casual gathering by people considerate enough not to drink in front of me."

The fane stiffened. "Mawyndulë, show respect for the kel."

"Of course, Father. I shouldn't wish to insult such an accomplished Fhrey." He continued to stare at Jerydd. "I heard you got yourself in with a *bad crowd* of giants . . . Oh, and congratulations on killing Arion. You did a superb job there."

"Mawyndulë!" his father erupted.

Jerydd held up his hand to settle him. "It's fine. The child is wild. I'll fix that. Mawyndulë, you might be a prince in the Talwara, but here you're an infant. If you want grape juice, make your own. You're Miralyith, aren't you?"

"The Art doesn't create," Mawyndulë said.

"No?" Jerydd held out his hands, indicating the walls around them. "What's all this, then?"

"Fenelyus drew up stone. She didn't make it."

"Really? Touch the wall there. What kind of stone is that, do you think? Granite? Limestone?"

"I'm not an Eilywin; I don't know rocks."

"What you don't know is vast," Jerydd said. He snapped his fingers and a goblet appeared on the windowsill. Rather than wine, it was filled with a stack of strawberries. "There," he said. "Try one of those. They're perfect. With the real thing, you can never find them at their peak. Or if you do, they're always too big or too small, too tart or sweet. No, I must admit, I pride myself on creating a good strawberry."

Mawyndulë stared at the cup of fruit, stunned. Even Gryndal never *created*.

He was scared to touch any of the berries, but curious about how they would taste. Were they real? He reached out, plucked one off the top and bit into it. *Perfect.*

Across the room, the kel of Avempartha smiled. "Still think I can't teach you anything?"

"I never said—"

"You didn't have to. Even without the Art, you're an easy riddle to solve. You're the heir apparent to the Forest Throne. But you don't get the job unless you can win the challenge. If we held it right now—if your father dropped dead this very minute, and Imaly gave me the Horn of Gylindora to blow—who do you think would win? A child who whines about not being given a cup of wine, or an old Fhrey who can snap perfect strawberries into existence? If you want wine—if you want anything, Mawyndulë—you make it yourself or go without. Don't rely on anyone but yourself."

Mawyndulë was up early, standing on the south balcony. This was something Gryndal had shown him when they were last there.

The First Minister had roused Mawyndulë from a deep sleep. The prince wasn't used to getting up before midday, and being up before dawn was unconscionable, but Gryndal had whispered for him to follow. The whisper had caught his attention. Whispers were for secrets. Maybe Gryndal was going to share something personal, Mawyndulë thought. And indeed he had.

That morning, just a year ago, Mawyndulë had slipped out with Gryndal to observe the sunrise over the Parthaloren Falls. The light sent shafts across the brink, and through the spray vivid, brilliant rainbows formed. Standing on the damp edge of the balcony, he stared in awe at a world that appeared more magical than he knew it was.

The view this morning wasn't as grand as before. Mawyndulë had wanted to recapture that moment when he and Gryndal had stood side by side on that balcony and watched the glory of the world awaken—one of his best, untainted memories. But what had once thrilled him now left him feeling dull, empty, and lonely. Gryndal was dead. Even Avempartha felt smaller.

"Beautiful, isn't it?"

Mawyndulë spun to see Jerydd in the archway. The ancient Fhrey wore a heavy cloak that he clutched to his wrinkled neck with bony hands.

What's he doing here? What's anyone doing here?

Fenelyus rightly assumed that people would want to look out into the falls, and as a result, she'd created hundreds of balconies. Mawyndulë, like Gryndal before him, had selected a remote one. Yet here was Jerydd.

The kel smiled and shook his head. "Poor situational awareness."

"What's that supposed to mean?" Mawyndulë pushed back against the short rail. He felt trapped. Before him, the nasty old man was grinning with malevolence; behind him, the roar of the falls proved more frightening when he couldn't see it. Jerydd, feeble as he was, appeared dangerous as he blocked the way back inside.

He fell, my fane. Sometimes people do that. And as we both know, your son wasn't the brightest star in the heavens.

Yes, Mawyndulë has always been a disappointment. Let's not waste any more time on him. How about another cup of that marvelous wine and maybe a strawberry?

"Your mastery of the Art has been stunted," Jerydd said. "If you were one of my students—and you will be—you'd have known I was coming before I arrived."

"So you can tell the future, too?"

He's blocking the exit on purpose. I'd have to push him aside to get by. I'd have to touch him. Mawyndulë had no desire to be in the same world as Jerydd; he certainly wasn't going to touch him. Mawyndulë slid his hands along the little wall of the balcony. *Maybe I can climb down.* The stone was polish-smooth and even at that height still damp from the mist. He might as well have been leaning on ice.

"I can do many things. Gryndal could, too. Did you know he could see what was happening hundreds of miles away? It's called *clairvoyance*. Even Fenelyus couldn't do that."

"Doesn't surprise me. Gryndal was far better than—"

"Don't even think of finishing that thought." Jerydd stepped out onto the balcony with a raised hand.

Mawyndulë remembered how Gryndal had exploded the Rhune with a snap of his fingers and froze.

"Gryndal had some promise, some talent, but he was consumed by his own arrogance. I gave up on him years ago."

"Gave up?"

"I taught him the Art."

"*You* taught Gryndal? My father said he went to the academy. Said he learned from my brother."

Jerydd smiled. "You'll find many teachers over the course of your life, Mawyndulë. So did Gryndal. He did indeed attend the Art school, but, just as with you, I offered to take over his instruction. Being smarter than you, he thanked me for the opportunity. And after I gave up on him, he found another mentor."

"Who?"

"The same one who taught Fenelyus."

Mawyndulë narrowed his eyes. *No one taught Fenelyus. She invented the Art. My father said so. He's just boasting, trying to sound important.*

Jerydd shook his head. "You're too much like Gryndal. I can see the imprint he placed on you, but I can't see why. He was using you for something, but what?"

"Gryndal was my teacher."

The kel laughed. "Gryndal had no interest in teaching anyone anything. He had one goal—power. That's why he came to me for instruction, and why he left me for what he believed to be a better teacher. Power had always been his goal, and somehow you were part of that path for him. I just can't see how." He sighed. "Doesn't matter. The Fhrey is dead, consumed in the fires of his own arrogance, his plans gone with him. My task will be to fix you. Normally, I wouldn't bother." He waved at Mawyndulë with a dismissive gesture. "Hardly any raw material to work with, but you are the prince, and that gives you a shot at the throne. Through no virtue other than your birth, you'll have a chance to be fane. I owe it to Ferrol and our people to at least try and make a worthy Fhrey of you."

"I'm not broken."

"Ah, but you are, and in oh-so-many ways. Luckily, you have hundreds of years to make up for lost time."

"And you're going to teach me?"

Jerydd smiled. "You think learning from me will be boring—a bunch of dull exercises like those they drill into you at school, eh? What do you say we start our first lesson right now?"

Mawyndulë sensed a vague threat in that suggestion. *First lesson: I'll throw you over that railing, and you can learn to fly!*

"Sorry, my father says we're marching this morning. He's in a hurry to kill some people, and I get to watch."

Jerydd nodded, that smile stretching wider on his old shriveled lips. "How would you like to do more than watch? Your father tells me you hated your old teacher. She stopped you from exacting justice after Gryndal's death. You want to punish her for that, don't you?"

"She's a traitor. She should die. That's the law."

"Yes, yes, the law, of course. But how would *you* like to be the one to enforce it? To be the one to *execute* her?"

Mawyndulë stared at the withered old man. The wind wafting in updrafts flapped his pale cloak and blew several strands of white hair against the grain.

"What are you saying?"

"You were right last night. I failed to kill her as your father ordered. I won't make the same mistake twice, but I'm a little too old for extended travel." He gestured up at the tower rising behind them. "As you can feel, this is an extremely powerful source. From here, I can launch an attack on Alon Rhist if I wish."

"That didn't work on Arion before."

"No, it didn't. There are limitations. Avempartha allows me to see and hear and direct the Art over vast distances—just not all at the same time. I was able to find her; then I had to disengage and swing blindly. Locating her was difficult after she knew what was happening. If I had someone on the ground, someone right there in the thick of it who could send me updates and direct my attacks, combating Arion would be a simple matter. I just need someone I can work through . . . someone like you."

"How could I do that?"

"That's where the lesson comes in—that awful teaching part."

"I don't have time to learn—"

"Just as Gryndal knew how to see long distances, I know how to speak across leagues. I can show you right now how to hear me and then continue your education as you travel on toward Alon Rhist. By the time you arrive, you'll be able to help me target Arion. Through you, I'll be able to erase my mistake, and you'll have your revenge. Then when you return, I'll show you other things the next fane ought to know, things that will make you invincible in the Carfreign Arena."

Mawyndulë found himself nodding.

"Beautiful sunrise, isn't it?" Jerydd said.

Despite himself, Mawyndulë couldn't disagree.

CHAPTER FOURTEEN

House of Bones

Strange how life often delivers the worst with the best, the highs with the lows, happiness with sorrow, and joy with screams that haunt a person forever, making it impossible to sleep in a room with a window. Then again, that might just be me.

—THE BOOK OF BRIN

Despite the beautiful spring afternoon, Brin continued to glance nervously over her shoulder as she crossed the corbel bridge that connected the Verenthenon to the Kype. Memories of that damp hand clamping over her mouth continued to send chills through her.

Relax. Don't struggle.

Brin had to tell someone.

She would have gone to her mother if that had been possible. Hearing her say that everything would be fine, while giving Brin a tight hug, was what she needed. Her mother was always good at that. But her mother was dead.

I have you now.

Brin banged on the door to the Kype, and the little window in the door slid back.

"I need to see Persephone," Brin said.

The door opened. They knew her. She was the Keeper of Ways and had the run of the place by order of the keenig.

"She's up on the high floor," Elysan told her, jerking his thumb at the ceiling. The Fhrey closed and bolted the bronze door behind her, sealing out the sun.

Brin should have felt safer behind that heavily secured door. She didn't.

Just need to get you back to the pile.

"Brin!" Persephone was all smiles when Brin poked her head into the meeting room. The keenig sat at one of four tables filled with chieftains and Fhrey, each wearing serious faces. This wasn't a council meeting. They were held in the Verenthenon. But Persephone looked just as frustrated. Before Brin could say anything, the keenig was up and walking toward her.

"I don't want to interrupt, I just—"

Persephone raised a hand, stopping her. Looking back at those in the room, the keenig said, "I'm sorry, you'll have to excuse me a moment. Lipit, continue and I'll be back in a few minutes." With that, Persephone grabbed Brin by the hand and hauled her into the corridor.

She closed the door, threw her back against the wall, gritted her teeth, and began to bang her head against the stone.

"Seph!" Brin said. "I'm sorry, I didn't mean to—"

Again, she held up a hand. "It's not you. Trust me—I could kiss you for getting me out of there. I hate it when they bicker. The Gula think I'm trying to enslave their clans through a dependence on Rhulyn food; the Rhulyn chieftains are terrified because I'm making them farm while the Gula-Rhunes train. Our people are convinced the Gula will turn on us. And every day there are more reports of incidents, insults, and conflicts between Fhrey and Rhunes."

Brin smiled. "I'm glad I missed it. Lately, all your meetings have been the same. Not really worth writing about. Even the council meetings have been pretty repetitive."

Persephone took a deep centering breath. "Raithe was right for turning down the job." She pushed herself off the wall. "Do you ever see him? Raithe, I mean?"

Brin looked puzzled. "Isn't he in there right now?"

"No, this is primarily a discussion about clan grievances, and he doesn't have much of either. He doesn't even come to many of the council meetings anymore. But that's not what I meant. I was referring to a more informal setting. One not based on *official matters*. Do the two of you talk?"

"Sometimes."

"Does he seem all right?"

"I suppose."

"What's he been doing?"

"I don't know." She shrugged. "Mostly, I guess he's been teaching the young men in the courtyard. That's where I usually see him. He and Suri also go on a lot of walks. Neither one of them likes being in the city much. Why don't you ask *him* what he's been doing?"

"I was just curious." Persephone smiled. "Never mind. Did you want something, or were you just coming to save me from going crazy?"

Brin hesitated, biting her lip.

Persephone's eyes grew concerned. "What is it? What's wrong?"

"I think we have a raow."

"A raow?" Raithe asked. "In Alon Rhist?"

Tesh nodded.

They stood between the great towers on the parapet above the main gate that afforded an unrivaled view of the Grandford Bridge and beyond it the plateau of Dureya. Tesh knew he'd find Raithe there. The parapet was one of the few places to look at their home without having to climb a few hundred steps to see over the walls. And he knew Raithe liked watching the sunset from there. Perhaps looking out at his old home had a way of reminding his chieftain of how far he'd come, which when measured in physical distances wasn't far at all. Raithe had his sword out, rubbing the blade with an oily rag. Roan had told everyone to do that once in a while. Said otherwise the metal might *go bad*, like it was meat or something. Raithe was always oiling his. He took care of it like a woman with a newborn.

Unlike the rest of them, Raithe's blade wasn't made by Roan or one of her army of workers. The sword he cleaned was dwarven, the one Persephone had brought back from Neith. Not only was it an excellent weapon, it possessed a remarkable legend. Many believed its markings were magical because the sword was reputed to have destroyed a mountain, made Persephone the keenig, and slain a dragon.

"Raow don't live in cities and certainly not fortresses," Raithe explained.

"Brin is convinced it's a raow," Tesh said. "She ought to know. She says she heard it one night, and I saw a clawed footprint near her house, then another one when we were down in that maze of corridors and rooms under the Verenthenon."

"Wait. What? You and *Brin*? What in Mari's name were you two doing down there?"

Tesh shifted uneasily. He wasn't trying to avoid the question so much as trying to find the right way to answer. He didn't want to admit it hadn't been his idea, that Brin had led him down there.

Raithe scowled. "Tesh, the girl's only fourteen!"

"Fourteen? She is not! She's sixteen . . . her birthday was months ago."

"And what about you?"

"I'm sixteen, too."

Raithe rolled his eyes. "I know how old *you* are, but where's your house? Where's your livestock, your crops, your furs, your fields, your traps? How are you going to take care of her? How are you going to take care of a child?"

"A child? That happens from kissing?"

Raithe smiled. "Never mind. Now, what's all this about a raow?"

Tesh watched as his chieftain carefully slid the magic blade into a scabbard that was decidedly less impressive.

"We think someone is hiding it. Taking care of it."

"Like a pet?"

"I guess."

"No one keeps a raow. Why would they?"

. . .

"Outside my window, I heard two people talking," Brin said. "One was a man, the other a raow—I'm sure of it now. I could tell by the voices." She looked at the keenig until she was certain she understood. This was another reason Brin had wanted to talk to her; Persephone didn't need her to explain. "I've been thinking about it. I remember that the man said something about an agreement they had."

"Agreement?"

Brin nodded. "I think the man was hiding it, feeding it somehow. He mentioned someone by the name of Jada. I think he might have lured Jada to the raow."

Persephone was shaking her head. "Why would anyone keep such a thing? How could they?"

"Under the Verenthenon are all these little rooms. I saw a footprint in one of them—a raow footprint."

"It's called the duryngon," Persephone said. "A prison. I don't think there are any people down there anymore, but Nyphron mentioned they used it for studying creatures. You shouldn't be going down there."

"Well, trust me, I won't anymore. But what if there had been a raow there and someone let it out?"

Persephone rested the back of her head against the wall while her tongue slipped back and forth across the front of her teeth. "Who would do such a thing? And why?"

"I don't know, but I think it was a Rhune."

"How would a Rhune get access to a raow from the duryngon? It'd have to be a Fhrey. They are the only ones who know about that place and have access to it."

Brin shook her head. "I found the duryngon. Maybe someone else did, too. The night I heard voices under my window they were speaking Rhunic."

"Nyphron speaks Rhunic—a lot of Fhrey do."

"But not when they are by themselves. And it's possible raow only speak Rhunic. The one that grabbed me did. It's just that he—the one talking to the raow—didn't sound like a Fhrey. He sounded like a man."

Persephone frowned with a skeptical look. "You're still having the nightmares, aren't you?"

"It's not that. I know this sounds like—"

"Brin, it hasn't been that long. I still wake up covered in sweat, and I wasn't taken by that thing."

"It's real."

"Okay, let's say you're right. How would a Rhune learn about a raow trapped under the Verenthenon? And why would he be willing to hide it?"

"Do you remember that house in the city the first day we arrived?" Raithe asked, making the switchback turn near the rain barrel as they headed down the stairs. "The one Malcolm used to live in?"

"The one where he got in the fight with that fussy fellow?" Tesh replied.

Raithe nodded and came around the third switchback. The two were practically dancing down the staircase, but because of their worn boots, the only sound came from the slap of scabbards. They had left the parapet and begun walking back toward the open-air kitchen, which had been set up in the training yard. No discussion, no comment. They both just started walking the moment they caught the smell of smoky roasting meat wafting from that outdoor spit. Mealtime had a way of pulling people that way.

"Yeah, Meryl said he was living there alone, but I saw someone in the upstairs window."

"I think I remember you saying something about that, but I didn't see anyone." Tesh's stomach rumbled. He was starving. He went for hours working the rings, running the obstacle course, or sparring, and then he'd smell food and start salivating.

"There was definitely a pair of eyes up there. Drew away the moment I spotted them."

"What? Are you thinking that was the raow?"

Raithe shrugged. "Why did Meryl say he lived alone?"

"Maybe it was a woman? Maybe a Fhrey woman?"

"I thought of that, but why would he hide such a thing? Why would he care what we thought? Didn't Malcolm mention something about him lying? That's bothered me ever since. Why *would* he lie?"

By the time Brin left Persephone, it was obvious the keenig didn't believe her. Otherwise, Persephone would have done something. Instead, she insisted that Brin stay and eat, proving by her lack of urgency that Persephone thought she'd only had a bad dream.

As frustrating as it was to be ignored, Brin conceded that she needed to eat. During the meal, Persephone made a point of asking numerous questions on random, unimportant subjects, none of which had anything to do with raows, dangers, or sleepless nights. They talked about how Roan was killing herself at the forge while trying to create the *perfect metal*. How the dwarfs had become Roan's devoted slaves. They also discussed a quilt Padera was making with squares that depicted scenes from the last year, including one showing their fight with Balgargarath. The story squares had been Brin's idea, but she thought it too arrogant to say so.

And they also talked at length about *The Book of Brin*. Brin had thirty pages written that covered the origin of the gods, how Ferrol, Drome, and Mari had created the Fhrey, dwarfs, and men, and how the Evil One, called Uberlin, was born, and this somehow made the children of Erebus turn against their father and attack him. That whole area was murky. Some of the words were ambiguous enough to be confusing, and at times reading the Ancient One's markings wasn't easy. This history of the gods was the first officially completed portion of *The Book of Brin*—aside from the metal formula that she did especially for Roan—that she had set aside within an envelope of sheep's skin and placed in a drawer for safekeeping. She explained to Persephone how she thought she would do the whole book that way, section by section, putting the completed parts away in separate places to avoid the disaster of her life's work all being destroyed by some awful accident. At some point—after the whole work was completed—she would create copies and bind them all together into one great volume.

By the end of the meal, she had nearly forgotten about the raow, which she guessed was the whole reason Persephone had asked her to stay. If it had been just a dream, the meal and carefree conversation would have made her feel better. But it hadn't. The raow was real, and the fact that the sun was casting long shadows by the time Brin left the Kype brought the worry back.

I won't get home before dark.

She had just reached the steps down to the city when she heard him. "Hey! Brin!"

She spun to find Tesh leaping down the steps from the fortress, taking three and four at a time to reach her. She stopped and waited, clutching her satchel to her chest and gritting her teeth in a war with her lips in an effort to keep from smiling. *He likes me!*

"Let me walk you home, okay?" He was puffing from the run, his chest rising and falling. He raked back the hair from his eyes and wiped the sweat from his brow. The evening sun splashed across Tesh's face, highlighting the wisps of beard coming in unevenly on his chin, cheeks, and upper lip.

By Mari, you're beautiful.

"Afraid something might happen to me?"

"Kinda, yeah."

Brin had been joking, flirting. She didn't expect him to say yes. He wasn't there to charm her; Tesh had come to protect her. While his concern was thoughtful, it scared her. "Really? What did Raithe say?"

"He doesn't think we're crazy. More importantly, he reminded me about someone named Meryl who lives in the city on Yolanda Hill. He says he lives alone, but Raithe remembers seeing someone looking out through this guy's window."

"And you think he's hiding the raow?"

"Not sure. Technically, we only know he's lying. Well, that and he's hiding *someone*. Raithe is going to talk to Malcolm because he used to live with Meryl. What did Persephone say?"

"I don't think she believed me. She thinks I just had a nightmare. But I did learn what those little rooms are. It's called the duryngon, a prison.

Persephone says the Galantians use the cells to study creatures, so maybe they had a raow."

"Oh, so you don't believe me now, either?" Brin was getting more than frustrated with everyone not—

"I didn't say that. I believe you. I'm just wondering how someone could do that."

"Oh," she said softly.

"I mean, my mother described raow as monsters that slaughtered whole villages, making huge mounds with bones of the people they killed. For someone to be keeping one . . . well it'd be like a mouse keeping a cat, you know? Doesn't make sense."

"During the conversation, I overheard the guy—or *mouse* if you will— mention an agreement."

"How does a mouse make an agreement with a cat—a hungry cat? Do you think he has a magic weapon or something? Maybe a necklace that allows him to control it?"

Brin paused and stared at Tesh curiously, then shook her head. "How did you come up with—never mind. No, I don't think there's a magic medallion. But if the raow was in a prison, how did it get out? Perhaps it was let out. Maybe that's when they made the agreement. You know, I do this for you, you do that for me?"

"So, the mouse freed the cat on the promise that it wouldn't eat him?"

"Well, sure, but the mouse would want more than that. After all, leaving the cat in the duryngon would take care of that. The mouse would want something more."

"Like what?"

"Something a raow would agree to. Something it would like to do anyway."

"Kill lots of mice?"

"That night, when I heard them talking, one of them said something about waiting for spring. Nyphron thinks the Fhrey will attack in spring. That might not be a coincidence."

"It's spring, right now," Tesh told her. "You know that, right?"

They continued walking down the steep sloping street of paving stones, past dozens of buildings with lit candles and closed drapes. Fhrey were inside, and Brin wondered if they were peeking out, watching them pass. What did they do in there? And how did they feel about all of the Rhunes running free on their streets?

"You said Meryl lives on Yolanda Hill?"

Tesh nodded.

"So he's a Fhrey, then?"

"Actually, no, he's human. Was a slave, like Malcolm. Seemed like he inherited the house when Shegon died."

"Oh," Brin said, then sighed.

"What's wrong?"

"Well, if Meryl was a Fhrey, then I could see him wanting to release a raow to devour all the humans right as the Elven army arrives. Great plan—horrible and unimaginably evil, sure—but still pretty smart. But a human slave wouldn't want that. Meryl's on our side."

"I'm not so sure," Tesh said. "I think he liked being a slave. Malcolm said Meryl saw himself as one of them, and while a lot of the Fhrey loyalists—at least the non-Instarya ones—packed up and went back across the Nidwalden when we moved in, a human slave wouldn't be able to do that no matter how much they wanted to be a Fhrey."

"Really?" Brin bit her lip. "Is it me, or is this starting to make sense?"

"What do you mean?"

"I'm thinking that Meryl really could be planning on letting this raow loose. But how can I get Persephone to believe that?"

"We need proof," Tesh said. "I know where Meryl's house is. I'll go have a look. I'll go right now."

"You mean, we'll go."

Tesh gave her a serious look. "*No*, I mean *I'll* go. If you're right, Brin, this could be really dangerous."

She frowned, nodding. "I know that more than you, believe me. That's why I can't let you go alone." She looked at the two swords on his hips and recalled the sparring bouts in the courtyard. "What do you think? Can you defeat a raow? Maybe we should—"

Tesh straightened up and placed his hands on the pommels of his weapons. "With these, I'm better than anyone but Sebek. I can handle a single raow."

"So, what's the problem, then?"

Tesh conceded, "Okay, fine. Let's go visit Mister Meryl and see if he really does have a guest."

Unfamiliar with that section of the city, Brin followed Tesh. She watched him stop and pivot around more than once. The streets in the city of Rhist were a haphazard maze, the houses packed close and set on tiers such that Tesh often looked down at a street he wanted to get to, but he saw no means to reach it. Brin was starting to worry that they wouldn't be able to find the place when Tesh abruptly stopped.

"That's it," Tesh said. He was pointing at a home with a sword and shield for a door knocker.

"We walked by this twice," she told him.

"Yes, but from the other direction," Tesh explained, but Brin didn't think that explained anything.

By then, all the other homes had lights burning. This made Meryl's house stand out all the more. The place was dark.

"Do you think it's empty? Abandoned?" Brin asked.

Tesh pointed at the flower boxes under the windows. "Nope. Someone has been taking care of those."

"Then why so dark?"

"I think there are blankets over the windows," Tesh said.

"The Fhrey call those drapes," Brin explained. "Have them in the place I live, too. They're nice, but they don't block out *all* the light. If lamps were lit, you could see it. Is it possible no one's home?"

"Could be, but I doubt Meryl takes *it* for walks. Probably just likes it dark. Do raow need light?"

"I don't think so. The one that grabbed me didn't. I think it could see just fine in the dark." She looked at his swords again. "Those might not be as useful when you're blind."

Tesh grinned at her. "I think you'd be surprised."

This should have made her feel better, and it did, sort of, but Brin could still remember the feel of that hand on her face. Strong, cold, and damp, the long bony fingers squeezed her cheeks, and she had felt the sharp points on its fingertips.

"Really? You're *that* good?"

"Good enough to only be concerned about you."

Another warm flush bloomed on her cheeks. She was glad it was dark.

"So, what's the plan?" Tesh asked.

"How about we knock?"

Tesh raised his brows. "Best advantage in battle is surprise."

"This isn't a battle. I think we should start by speaking to this Meryl fellow. Challenging him. Even ask to search his house. If he refuses, or acts suspiciously, then we can go back and tell Persephone."

Tesh shrugged. "Okay, we'll do it your way." He knocked.

There were a few faint, unseen voices speaking in Fhrey down the street. Funny, she thought, how sounds carried in the night in ways they didn't during the day. Brin rarely saw, or even heard, the natives in whose homes they lived. The Fhrey were excellent at hiding. They came out at night after the streets were empty. For some time, Brin had been convinced the Fhrey could see better in the dark than humans. They were certainly faster and more agile. On occasion, she thought she saw one out of the corner of an eye, but when she turned, all she saw was a shadow. She thought of them as ghosts, spirits that she heard at night. She imagined they came to the Rhune District in the late hours and gathered to complain about how the Rhunes were ruining the place. The idea of them coming out at night made her think all of them were a kind of raow.

Standing in the street in the dark in a populated Fhrey section of the city, Brin knew this was a place she shouldn't be.

Am I insane? she thought. *Maybe.*

Almost nine months had passed since she was taken, and she was still having nightmares. The raow hadn't so much as bruised her, but it had left her broken. As a little girl, Brin used to be afraid of the dark, and her mother had let her fall asleep with the lamp burning—a costly custom to ease a child's fear. Brin had forced herself to face it, to lie stiff in her bed shivering, listening to every creak or gust of wind, waiting for . . . she never knew exactly what. The next morning, she felt free. Brin was hoping something like that would happen with the raow. That she would grit her teeth, face it, and finally be free. Even so, Brin wouldn't have gone to this house alone. *I might be insane, but I'm not crazy.* She had pretended ignorance when speaking to Tesh. She had spent all winter watching him train; she knew he was a superb warrior. Brin couldn't have a better protector. And yet . . .

The last time it took a dragon—no, she thought—*a Gilarabrywn.*

No one answered the door. Tesh rapped again. Again they waited. Nothing.

Brin sighed. "I guess we'll have to come back at—"

"You should wait here," Tesh told her.

"Wait? What do you mean *wait?*"

"It will be safer." Tesh lifted the latch, and, laying a hand on a sword, he pushed the door open.

"You can't go in!"

"No one is home."

"I know. That's why you can't go in!"

Tesh looked at her, puzzled. "It's probably listening to you."

This shut her up, and Brin clamped both hands to her face.

Raow love faces.

Tesh disappeared over the threshold, leaving Brin on the doorstep, terrified.

She stared after him into the darkness. It looked like a pit, a tunnel into some horrible void. Tesh was walking into a monster's nest. She waited. And waited.

Brin felt as if she'd stood there a month, maybe two, and in all that time she never moved, didn't breathe, and would have bet the year's wheat crop that her heart never beat once. She held herself rigid, staring into the dark hole of the house, listening. Tesh was quiet and as nimble as a Fhrey. Still, she heard some sounds. A faint rustle, then the creak of a board.

More waiting.

No more sounds.

The quiet is good. I'd hear a struggle if he's attacked . . . and yet . . . what if it grabbed him from behind? Raow are good at that. It could have him right now, that horrible hand on his mouth preventing him from making a sound.

Her heart was beating after all. How could she not have noticed the pounding in her chest?

I can't just wait here.

She took a step across the threshold but halted when a light appeared inside. It floated toward the door. An instant later, she saw Tesh holding a candle on a little copper plate with a finger ring.

"Place is empty," he said.

"Really?"

He nodded.

"Did you . . . did you go upstairs?"

He smirked. "Of course I went upstairs."

"Did you find anything—well—anything unusual?"

He curled his finger for her to follow and led her inside.

"If you didn't find anything, that's fine. I don't need to see. I believe you."

"No, I think you should see for yourself. Trust me. There's no danger. No one is here. Not Meryl, not a raow."

Brin's surge of courage was quickly draining away now that Tesh wasn't having his face eaten. She didn't want to go in; everything about that house was screaming for her to keep out. They were intruding, it was dark, and . . . there was a smell. Brin had no idea what it was, but it wasn't nice. "Not really necessary."

He was already halfway across the entryway, disappearing back into the dark, when she gave in and chased after him.

The home was, in many ways, like the one Brin was living in, although not quite as nice. The place was masculine, with less lace and more boots. Five pairs of high-top leathers were set near the door. She found no stenciling, vases, or wall hangings. The place was sparse. No knick-knacks, no plants. One thing did catch her eye: A beautiful harp stood in the far corner across from the fireplace. Formed of lacquered wood that was curved and carved, the thing was as much a piece of art as an instrument.

Tesh took her right to the stairs. Here the smell was stronger. The scent was rancid, like rotting meat. Tesh didn't pull or coax. He merely waited, watching her with sympathetic eyes. He probably thought she was a terrible coward. *He'd* certainly had no trouble marching through the house. Why was she so terrified?

What part of "they eat people's faces" didn't you hear?

Tesh said the place was empty, but raow, like Fhrey, might just be very good at hiding.

Brin clenched her fists, set her jaw, and followed Tesh up the steps. As they reached the second story, Tesh held the candle high so she could see.

The whole upper floor was one big mound of bones.

Long, short, thick, and thin, some were white, others yellowed. There were so many—a huge pile. Brin stepped away from the banister and moved into the loft, carefully placing her feet on bare patches of floor.

This is it, she thought, spellbound. *The pile.*

Brin stood in the midst of the mound, overwhelmed at the sight. Every bone had once been part of a person. She saw arm and leg bones, wide paddle-shaped pelvises, racks of ribs, and skulls. *How many has it killed? How many like me did it grab? How many screamed as it ate their faces?*

Then she realized the bones weren't just a pile. The arm bones were all together, each aligned in the same way. The same was true of the leg bones, and the feet and hands. Every part was carefully placed in some twisted design, right down to the ring of skulls with all the faces pointing out like watchmen.

That's its bed. Those skulls keep it safe while it sleeps.

"Brin?" Tesh said.

She barely heard him. She stood frozen.

"Are you all right?"

Brin honestly didn't know. She was crying, sobbing, tears running down her cheeks.

"I—" she started to say. Then she spotted the shawl.

The discarded wad of cloth lay on the floor, revealed by Tesh's little candle. The wool was the traditional Rhen pattern of green, black, and blue, and Brin had no trouble recognizing the weaving work of her mother. She picked it up. "This is Seph's shawl."

Tesh picked up a shimmering blue-and-gold cloak. "This is Nyphron's."

"Meryl stole them."

"Why?"

Brin's eyes went wide. "Meryl isn't going to use the raow to kill a bunch of people. He's targeting *specific* ones. C'mon. We need to go." Brin was already moving down the stairs. "I know why it's not here, and I know where it's going to be."

CHAPTER FIFTEEN

Through a Narrow Window

Most people like windows, but I think they look like eyes—soulless eyes that invite things a bolted door is meant to keep out. Yeah, it is probably just me . . . well, and Persephone.

—THE BOOK OF BRIN

Persephone sat in the quiet of her bedroom, rubbing the silver ring that hung from the chain around her neck—Reglan's ring. She tried to remember who had given it back to her. Konniger had been wearing it when he died. Someone must have delivered it after burying him, but she couldn't remember who. Tope maybe, or Wedon, or—no, it was Tressa. Persephone nodded to the stars outside the open window across from her bed.

Yes, it was Tressa.

She had dutifully delivered the chieftain's ring.

How could I have forgotten that?

Tears had been in Tressa's eyes, her cheeks worn riverbeds from facing the loss of a husband. Persephone knew what that felt like.

Persephone had lied, telling everyone that Konniger died while hunting the bear. No need to speak ill of the dead or embarrass the living, but word had escaped. Word always got around in a dahl. Persephone had no idea how Tressa learned the truth, or who might have told her. Maybe Tressa herself couldn't accept that her husband was a martyr, and had asked questions.

Tressa knew the truth, and yet she still brought the ring. Tressa was a bitch, but she was no coward.

The silver ring that had lived on Persephone's husband's hand for more than twenty years was all she had left. Some of that silver had been tarnished. Reglan had given Maeve a daughter, then ordered her taken away to die in the forest to hide his transgression. The man she'd loved unconditionally for twenty years, the man she'd trusted, had done more than just deceive her. He'd been a monster, killed a child—or thought he had. Such an idea was difficult to reconcile. Such tarnish was impossible to remove.

She drew the ring off the chain and held it up in the flickering light of the candle that rested on the little table. It had been a year. The mourning was over.

"I know you loved me," she told the circle of silver. "And I still love you no matter what you did. Can't stop that. Can't make it not be. And . . ." She swallowed hard. "And I miss you. I miss you so very badly. Still remember how you smelled, you know that?"

A tear slipped, rolling down her cheek. She let it fall.

"We were a great team, you and I." She bit her lip. "And it's stupid the things I keep thinking of: the way you bounced your foot at meetings or the silly sound of your laugh. I sometimes think I hear it in a crowd. I look, but it's never you."

She drew in a shaky breath. "Things have changed."

Persephone was alone in her room, isolated high in the Kype, surrounded by several feet of Fhrey-quarried stone. There was only the one narrow window, and it faced away from the rest of the Rhist. The door to the bedroom was closed. No one could hear. Still, the words were hard to say. She needed to hear them, needed to say them out loud to make it real. And maybe Reglan was listening. She hoped so because she needed to explain. "Things are different now that you're gone. You understand that, right? You were always so practical, and I'm the keenig now. Yeah, can you believe that? Me, keenig." She let out a little miserable laugh. "I have responsibilities, things I have to do. You taught me that."

She let the ring slip into her palm where she squeezed it. She closed her eyes and more tears fell. "I forgive you," she said in a whisper, but the words were loud in her heart. "I forgive you, my love. I hope you can do the same for me."

She reached out her arm, opened her hand and let the ring drop. She heard the small circlet hit the floor and roll away. "Goodbye, Reglan."

She cried then, deep and hard into the palms of her hands. After what felt like a long time, she wiped her face and took a breath. She felt exhausted, all the muscles in her body sore and weak as if she'd been in a fight. And she felt empty and alone, so very alone.

She sat with her eyes closed and head back, listening to herself breathe.

Then she opened her eyes and screamed.

Brin was known for being a fast runner, but she hadn't been training daily for nearly a year the way Tesh had. She had slowed down to an air-gasping walk by the time they reached the second gate. That was where he finally caught up to her.

"Keep . . . going . . ." She waved at him.

Tesh didn't bother wasting air replying. He couldn't run, but he could still jog.

"Right . . . behind . . . you . . ." he heard her say as he passed by. She still had a terrified look.

At first, Tesh didn't understand how those two pieces of clothes meant anything. So, Meryl was a thief. Who cared about that when he was harboring a monster? Brin hadn't bothered to explain; she'd just bolted. Tesh finally put it together when they reached the steps to the first gate, where the Asendwayr kept their kennel of hunting dogs. Meryl was going to use his pet to assassinate the leaders of the rebellion. But Persephone was in the Kype, the safest place in an impregnable fortress. Even Raithe couldn't get in there without an invitation.

But could a raow?

In the long dark of a Dureyan winter's night, the older villagers told stories, tales recited by parents. Being Dureyan, the stories were never pleasant, always tales of woe and warning. The legend of the raow was typical:

> Roaming hills and forests deep,
> On human bones it makes its bed.
> But weary raow cannot sleep,
> 'Til once again the pile is fed.

> It prowls beyond the fire's light,
> Warrior, hunter, girl, and boy.
> The raow savors every bite,
> A succulent face the monster's joy.

> Steer clear of lonely hills at night,
> The sunset shadows you must race.
> The raow's grip is oh so tight,
> As deeply she bites into your face.

Tesh charged the last steps to the Verenthenon, following the spiral steps that circled the inside wall and spilled out to the long corbel bridge. A quick final sprint and Tesh reached the Kype.

"Open up!" Tesh hammered on the door. He bent over, supporting himself with his hands on his knees, and took deep luxurious breaths. "I need . . . to see the keenig."

The little window in the door opened, and a pair of eyes peered out. "Too late. Come back in the morning."

"Can't . . . it's urgent."

"Who are you?"

"Tesh of the Dureya."

"Dureya, huh? Try coming back tomorrow."

"But you don't understand. I have to see the keenig."

"She's already gone to bed."

"I don't care—this is important!"

"Did Raithe send you?"

"Raithe? No."

"Then why do you need to see the keenig?"

"Because—"

"Techylor!" Tesh heard a familiar voice behind him.

Turning, he spotted Sebek coming out of the Verenthenon and walking toward him across the narrow bridge.

"Sebek!" he shouted with relief.

"I thought I saw you run up here. I was hoping to catch you below, but you went right by me."

Sebek was dressed in his breastplate and shoulder guards. His bronze armor was customized, smaller, thinner, and lighter than the others. Even so, he rarely wore it even in sparring matches. He always complained that the metal sheets were hot in the sun.

"Yeah, listen, you need to help me."

"I plan to."

Tesh looked at him, surprised. *Did Brin already talk to him? Smart girl.* He hooked a thumb at the door where the little window had already slid shut. "This idiot won't let me in."

Sebek approached, quickly drawing Thunder and Lightning.

For a confused moment, Tesh couldn't make the connection. *Is he going to use his swords on the door? How will that help?* "What are you doing?"

The Fhrey smiled. "Time for another lesson."

"Lesson? Didn't Brin tell you? We need—"

"You need to defend yourself."

Sebek closed the distance and attacked.

Tesh dodged the blow purely out of instinct and spun solely out of reflex. Then he drew iron from both scabbards. "This is no time for a lesson!"

Sebek grinned. "Winded, are you? Looked like a long run. Can't expect enemies to be courteous and only attack when you're prepared. Sometimes they catch you off guard in awkward places where you can't retreat."

He attacked again, and Tesh noticed something different in his assault. He imagined no one else in the world would have noticed, but after so many bouts, Tesh knew Sebek's technique—this wasn't it. The attack was more aggressive, more dead-on—and it was faster.

Tesh intercepted the blades and thanked Roan and the gods for the iron swords. Anything less would have given way. As it was, he felt the bone-jarring impact that nearly kicked them from his hands. In the past, that's what always happened, but Tesh had learned a new grip, and a new way of deflecting a straight edge-to-edge stroke, sparing him the loss of his weapons.

He saw the look of surprise on Sebek's face when he didn't lose his blades, and Tesh took that moment to strike back and to shout, "Stop it! We need to save—"

That was all the time he had before Sebek came at him again.

He swung straight on. No one ever did that. They all learned not to swing a deathblow. Instead, they were taught to angle the stroke so that a missed follow-through wouldn't kill. Sebek was breaking that rule. If Tesh failed to block, Lightning would cleave him in half. What's more, Sebek was stepping in, putting excess force into the blows.

What's he trying to do, kill me?

None of that bothered Tesh too much. Sebek, unlike the other trainers, didn't coddle. He pushed, and pushed hard. Famous for wounding students, Sebek had always upped the level of threat every time they fought. This was just another level. Tesh might have been flattered by the respect of no quarter shown, and he would have except for one thing—Sebek wasn't smiling. Sebek always grinned in battle. The Fhrey loved combat, and the better the fight the more he grinned. At times, he'd even laugh. This was proving to be a very good fight, but Sebek wasn't laughing, wasn't grinning, wasn't smiling. Sebek looked . . . miserable.

Flashing metal jolted as Tesh caught another stroke.

Sebek spun. *Crash* came the second blade. *Lightning followed by Thunder.* Sebek had never explained the names. After fighting him, he didn't need to.

Flash! Crash! The attacks came faster and faster, call and answer, and

Tesh was tired from the run. He had built up stamina but not this much. He was finding it hard to breathe, and Sebek wasn't giving him a chance to catch his breath.

"What are you doing?" Tesh heard Brin's voice. "Stop it!"

She was behind Sebek, and the Fhrey instantly pulled back and whirled to face her.

"Get out of our way!" Brin stood on the bridge.

Sebek had one blade facing Tesh and one extended, pointing at Brin.

For a flash of an instant, Tesh sensed death. He could smell it, feel it radiating off his mentor. Sebek would stab Brin through the heart, a clean, fast blow that wouldn't alter his stance, allowing him to parry any retaliation from Tesh. All of this was so clear, so obvious. Tesh was seeing three moves ahead and witnessing an unspeakable horror. Like any wild thing, the true nature of the Fhrey revealed itself.

Then it was gone.

This time the flash wasn't answered. Thunder didn't follow lightning. Sebek's shoulders relaxed, and his weight shifted to a neutral stance.

Brin pushed past the Fhrey, shoving him back against the stone wall as she barreled on.

Sebek didn't move. He watched her, and then Tesh. Still, no smile.

Reaching the door, Brin hammered on the bronze with all her might. "Open up!"

The window opened. "Who is—Brin?"

"If you don't open this Tetlin Witch of a door in the next two seconds—"

That's when they heard the screaming.

Persephone screamed as she watched the thing come in through the window, pale as the dead, long and lanky, and with black oily hair that hung to the floor. Seeing it, staring at it, Persephone still couldn't understand how it was getting through such a narrow opening. *Mice do the same thing, squeeze themselves down like that.* But this wasn't a mouse. Persephone had seen its like before and backed away in horror. She bumped the bed with the backs of her thighs.

I need to get out of here!

She spun and ran for the door. Grasping the latch, Persephone lifted and shoved. The door unlatched, then hit something and refused to open any farther.

"Help!" she screamed out the little crack.

"No one is coming," the raow told her, its voice the sound of snapping bones and hissing snakes.

The thing was still squeezing through the window, oozing inside, the fleshy goo of its body revealed to be a boneless bag of skin.

"Can't get away," it whispered.

"Help! Someone! Anyone! Open this damn door!" she shouted again and rammed the door with her shoulder, hurting herself.

"Nowhere to run, nowhere to hide." The raow used a singsong tone. Its head and shoulders were already in, the thing busily working on getting its hips through, twisting and pushing against the walls.

If it gets all the way in, I'm dead.

Persephone wished for the dwarven sword she'd once carried, but settled for a two-foot-long, four-prong brass candleholder. *Keep the sword up.* She heard Moya's voice. *Hold it back like this. Keep your left foot in front, and when that thing comes at you, step forward with your right as you swing.*

Across the room, the raow grinned, revealing jagged teeth. The thing was drooling. Long strings of anticipation glistened from its lips. Its red eyes glowed bright and wide with excitement as it stared at her. "Yes. Yes. Such a beautiful, succulent face."

With candelabra in hand, she charged. A good swing struck its head, but instead of hearing a satisfying crack, Persephone felt like she'd hit a bag of sand. She never got a second swing. Clawed hands struck fast as snakes. Persephone didn't feel the pain—not much, just a sting. She actually said, "Oww!" which was an absurd utterance, given the amount of blood that followed.

She backed away. The candelabra fell out of her hand. She hadn't let go, didn't mean to at least, but she'd heard the metal ring when it hit the floor.

Persephone hit the floor, too. Her legs had folded on their own. One minute she was standing, the next she was sitting with her back up against the bed. She clutched her stomach as a dull but growing pain spread. She wanted to get up, but her legs wouldn't have it. Something else—her nightgown clung, slicked to her skin.

How did I get so wet?

Her nightgown was shredded. The ivory cloth no longer white.

Persephone wanted to scream again but couldn't find any air. She wanted to get up and run to the door, but her legs refused to do anything more than slide around in the slippery puddle that formed beneath her. The only thing she could do was sit and watch as the raow continued to ooze through the little window. An outstretched and bony hand extended into the room, straining with grasping claws, reaching for Persephone's face.

"So soft, so sweet, so hungry. Don't move. I can taste you already."

Reaching the fourth floor, Tesh saw two spears blocking the corridor. They might have fallen that way, if there was any reason for two spears to have been left in the corridor. The pair of poles leaned at an angle, their points digging into the wood of the keenig's chamber door, bracing it shut.

Tesh was out front with Brin right behind. Sebek—who couldn't know the importance of the race—followed, a close third. Others were coming, too. Tesh heard the rapid footfalls of a dozen people, but they were far below and still had to climb the stairs.

Without effort, Tesh cleaved through the spears, freeing the door.

"Stay back!" he shouted to Brin as he flung the door wide.

Inside, Keenig Persephone sat slumped near her bed. Coming in that window was a ghoulish creature with red eyes, clawed hands, and black hair.

Raow.

The thing was about halfway through the narrow opening, still trapped at the hips, a single outstretched hand reaching for the keenig. The raow looked up, first at Tesh and then its eyes bulged when seeing Sebek. Its lips snarled, and with a hiss and one final swipe for Persephone that missed, the beast began to retreat.

Tesh stared in amazement, the way he'd once watched a snake swallow a whole mouse. *That's impossible,* he thought, watching the raow melt back out the window. *Almost like it doesn't have bones.*

Sebek didn't seem impressed in the least. Without hesitation, he leapt toward the window, drawing Lightning and Thunder as he went. The raow shivered and jerked as it struggled to escape.

Too late, Tesh thought.

The thing was trapped, caught as a rabbit in a snare, and Sebek was on it.

Tesh expected a quick death for the raow. Lightning and Thunder were coming, and the raow wasn't big and didn't look too strong. If anything, the creature resembled a shriveled old woman.

Just as Tesh would have done, Sebek thrust a straightforward stab. There was no need to complicate things. But to Tesh's surprise, the raow slapped the blade away. Its long nails made a teeth-grinding scrape across the bronze blade. Then, fast as an adder, it swiped with the other hand, forcing Sebek to block.

And then it was gone. The raow slithered through the opening with a grunt and fell out of sight.

Sebek stared at the vacant window. *"Culina brideeth!"* he shouted and slapped the stone wall.

Turning, the Fhrey glanced at Persephone. "She's hurt."

Tesh didn't need Sebek to tell him that; neither did Brin. "Oh, dear Mari!" she cried.

The rush of feet reached the stairs, and seconds later Moya entered, her bow strung, an arrow fitted. "What happened? We heard—" Seeing Persephone, she froze and dropped the bow. She shouted at Brin, "Get Padera!"

With a quivering hand over her mouth, Brin backed away in wide-eyed horror. "Moya?" she said in a pleading tone. "Moya, she's . . ."

"Go. Now. Get Padera! Run!"

Brin blinked, nodded, then flew out the door.

"We have a healer here in the Rhist," Sebek said calmly. "He's good."

"Get him!"

Sebek strode out of the bedroom, leaving Tesh to watch as Moya fell to her knees beside Persephone and applied pressure to the gaping wound. The keenig's eyes were open, staring at nothing. Her mouth hung agape, but she made no sound. Persephone was soaked in blood, her nightgown trapping puddles in its folds. She was breathing—that was good. That was about all that was good.

Moya put an arm around the keenig, helping to hold up her head, which had flopped to one side.

"Moya?" Persephone said in a soft voice. Her eyes found the woman's face and a small smile appeared.

"I'm here. I'm too damn late, but I'm here." Moya held Persephone's head with both hands, focusing on her eyes. Tesh wondered if she did that to help the keenig see her or to avoid looking at all the blood.

"I'm hurt," Persephone informed Moya.

"I know—I know. I'm . . . I'm sorry I wasn't here. I was told . . . someone said you wanted me downstairs. I didn't even know you'd gone to bed."

"I'm hurt, Moya. Real bad, I think." Persephone's head was bobbing up as her body jerked.

"You're gonna—" Moya swallowed. "You're gonna be fine. You're gonna be all right, okay? We're gonna take care of you."

"You're crying," the keenig told her.

"Am I?" Moya asked. "I'm sorry."

"Moya . . ." Persephone said. "I don't think I'm going to—"

"Shut up!" Moya yelled at her so loudly and violently that it startled everyone in the room—everyone except Persephone. "Yes, you are, dammit! You're going to be fine! You hear me?"

Moya hugged the keenig's head to her neck and kissed her hair. "Don't even think that way. Don't you even—you're strong, dammit. You crossed the sea, you led us to victory against Balgargarath, you killed a bear with a pissant little shield! You can beat this!"

"I'm bleeding."

"I don't care!"

More guards entered the room, both Fhrey and human. Each wore solemn masks of worry.

Tesh moved toward the window to get out of their way. Standing in front of it, he put his own head to the opening that was too narrow to allow it to pass. He looked down. It was quite a fall.

But what if it hadn't fallen? What if it wasn't dead? Was it on its way back to Meryl's house?

From outside, he heard a loud ringing chime. Tesh had never heard that before. *Must be an alarm. News of the attack must have spread.*

A Fhrey he'd never seen before entered the bedroom. He actually looked old, with a gray receding hairline and a few wrinkles. *How old does a Fhrey have to be to look like that?*

He barked an order in Fhrey, then switched to Rhunic. "Get her up on the bed." He had a bag with him that he placed beside her. "So, what do we have here? Severe lacerations, and, oh—"

"What?" Moya asked.

The healer dug into his bag. "I need water, and I need that gown off, right now."

"Dylon, get water," Moya told one of the Fhrey as she began to untie the keenig's nightgown. Then she saw Tesh standing next to the window. "Tesh, out! The rest of you, too. Stand guard outside; we don't need spectators."

Tesh left the room.

Outside, the corridor was crowded with more people. Most of the faces he didn't know.

What if it isn't dead? And if it isn't, if it's starving, would it really just leave? We found a shawl . . . and a cloak.

Tesh shot up the stairs, taking the steps three at a time until he landed on the top floor where Nyphron's personal quarters were. Tekchin had pointed it out once, but Tesh had never been inside. He didn't wait, didn't pause or knock. Tesh pulled the latch and walked inside. The Galantian leader wasn't there. The room had no bed, just tables, chairs, a fireplace, and a rack of weapons. Nyphron had a lot of weapons. Also hanging on the walls were shields, swords, spears, and helms. Such wealth was impossible for a Dureyan to imagine, and Nyphron used them as decorations! There were two more doors, so the bed must be in one of the other rooms.

"What are you doing in here?" Nyphron asked.

Tesh whirled to see his lordship come in from the hallway. Dressed only in a robe and sandals, he appeared more irritated than surprised. He also looked in a hurry. "Front gate send you? How many are there?"

"Just the one, I think."

"One?" Nyphron looked at Tesh like he was insane. "What do you mean *one?* They don't ring the bell for one."

"The bell? They don't?"

Nyphron pushed past him and started to enter the room on the right. Then Nyphron stopped and looked back at Tesh. "What's their position?"

"Their—*position?*" Tesh asked, baffled.

Nyphron stared at him incredulously. "Why are you up here if you don't know anything?"

The leader of the Galantians' eyes shifted to Tesh's swords.

Behind Nyphron, the interior of the room was dark, and the candles from the sitting room cast a sliver of light, just enough to reveal the corner of a bed. Tesh saw movement. He drew both swords and charged.

"What are—" Nyphron dodged to one side with the usual Fhrey speed.

Tesh ran through, kicking the door wide open.

The raow was there, caught in the lamplight. The thing hissed and lashed out with both claws. The raow was faster than Sebek and no longer trapped.

"Out of my way," it hissed. "Need the one that smells of thistles and lies."

The raow raked at Tesh again.

He got his blades up to save a slashing, but the force threw him against the wall.

It lunged at Nyphron. The leader of the Galantians, clad in his bathrobe and sandals, was caught off-balance. Tesh sympathized. No one over the age of seven expects a raow in their bedroom.

Tesh didn't have many options, and, as stupid as it felt, he did the only thing he could. He threw a sword at the creature. This wasn't a technique taught in the courtyard and it showed. The sword slapped the raow on the back, not at an angle that could have cut it, but the force was enough to catch its attention. Only a split second was bought, but for a Fhrey that was plenty. Nyphron leapt back. He retreated out of his room into the hallway, but the starved raow raced after. "You!" The thing's voice went shrill with recognition. "Yes, you—you and that other one! I'm out—free again. Oh, yes! And hungry. A feast—a banquet I will have this day before I sleep!"

Tesh followed. Outside the room's doorway, Nyphron crouched like a wrestler, looking nervous as the raow salivated and curled its claws. "Such a sweet-looking face."

Then the creature stopped, its sight drawn to the stairs.

Tesh reached the door's threshold just as Sebek appeared with both blades drawn and a determined look on his face.

"Sebek, it's the—" Nyphron said.

"I know—I know," Sebek replied.

Nyphron fell back as Sebek stepped up. The creature turned his attention toward the threat with two blades.

"Where's a cage when you need one?" Sebek asked.

"I admit, trapping it seemed like a good idea all those years ago—not so much now." Nyphron said. "The real question is . . . can you take it?"

Sebek didn't reply immediately.

"I think not," the creature said.

For the first time that Tesh had witnessed, Sebek did not initiate combat. The raow did. The fight was inhumanly fast and vicious. Blades against claws slashed and jabbed. Sebek got in a cut, but the raow raked him back across the thigh, winning a grunt. Tesh had never seen Sebek touched in a fight. Wounded, Sebek moved wrong, shifted slower, weaker. The world's greatest warrior was going to lose. With one sword left, Tesh considered helping, then he noticed something strange. The raow broke off its attack to avoid getting too close to a lamp.

It prowls beyond the fire's light,
Steer clear of lonely hills at night,
The sunset shadows you must race.

Maybe there was a reason that tale was told through the generations, and not just to keep children close to home.

The raow lunged, and Sebek was hit again. This attack caught him across the chest. The claws tore his armor free so that the metal plate flapped uselessly, the broken wing of a bird of prey. A fast second strike stabbed Sebek with three dagger-claws. The Fhrey staggered to one knee. But the raow didn't want him.

It has a deal with Meryl, Tesh thought, *and, surprisingly, it plans to honor it.*

The raow turned to kill Nyphron. "What a face," it whispered.

Leaping up, Tesh pulled the wall lamp down—a clay cup filled with oil, its burning wick protruding from a spout. The lamp shattered when it hit the floor. Oil splashed, and the fire followed it, but little of the liquid got on the raow. The slow-to-burn oil merely pooled around the raow's feet. Tesh was frustrated to see that the resulting fire wasn't large, not even dangerous. Anyone could have stomped out the flames or just stepped aside. Instead, the raow shrieked in terror. Wide bulbous eyes filled with panic; it ran—and ran the wrong way. The raow fled into Sebek. Lightning pierced the raow's chest, the tip passing all the way through its body. The Fhrey pulled himself up by the handle of his sword, and then Thunder answered, coming around and severing the raow's head. It fell, bounced, and rolled to the stairs where it had just enough momentum to fall down the first step, then the second, and third. On it went while Nyphron, Tesh, and Sebek stood around the oil fire listening to the *thump, thump, thump* of the raow's head bouncing its way down the steps.

In the gathering cloud of black smoke, Sebek dropped both swords and fell to his hands and knees.

"Tesh, get Anyval." Nyphron moved to Sebek's side and helped his friend move away from the fire.

"Who?"

"He's our healer. You'll find him down on—"

"It's okay. I know where he is. You were the second target tonight."

Tesh ran for the stairs. His legs felt rubbery. Training had helped, but nothing matched the demands of the real thing.

"Second?" Nyphron's voice stopped him. "Tesh, did you come up here because you thought that thing was going to kill me?"

He nodded.

"You saved my life?"

Tesh wasn't sure if that was a question or not. "Yes."

Nyphron looked puzzled. "Go—go on! Get Anyval."

Tesh ran down the stairs. As he descended, Nyphron shouted down to him, "Then wake everyone in the Rhist. That bell you heard ringing is from the parapet at the front gate. It means they're here. The fane's army is here. The war has started."

CHAPTER SIXTEEN

Lighting the Fire

*When people discover I was in the Battle of Grandford, they as-
sume I am a hero because they think that about everyone who was
there. That is the nature of myths. But the truth is, in the whole
battle I only had one lousy job. One! And I failed. Well, maybe not
failed, but no one could say that what happened was a success.*

—The Book of Brin

Like most of the men of Alon Rhist, Raithe had no idea what the ringing
bell meant, but he guessed it wasn't good. In his experience, sounds of
unexpected announcements like horns and drums were never followed by
welcome news, but he was also Dureyan. He had been trained from birth
that anything new—especially if it was loud—was a threat. Raithe was the
first to the top of the parapet above the front gate because he was already
on his way there when the bell began ringing. He'd gone to find Malcolm,
to talk to him about Meryl, but when he didn't find him, he decided to return to his ritual. Each evening after training, he climbed up to look out
over the river at the land of his birth. He usually just leaned against the
wall, stared, and asked *why?* He never expected to find an answer, but he
felt the question needed to be asked for all those who no longer could.
That he should be the only one left to mourn the passing of a clan he had
so desperately wanted to leave was more than ironic; it was sickening.

While Raithe was the first to reach the parapet, he was far from the last. Drawn by the sound, dozens came up, asking one another what was happening. Once on the parapet, no one asked anymore. Everyone could see the lights.

Raithe remembered being on the wall at Dahl Tirre, looking out at the multitudes of the Gula-Rhunes. All those campfires had been a frightening sight, a multitude of flickering yellow stars. This was different, and Raithe didn't care for the change. Out beyond Grandford were fewer lights than in Tirre, but these were arranged in neat, straight, evenly spaced rows. Raithe wasn't an expert on warfare, but he guessed that such precision wasn't a good sign.

"Thought I'd find you here." Malcolm nudged in beside him as the space along the front wall grew crowded. "Not so many as before, eh?"

"Is that all?" Farmer Wedon asked, standing on Raithe's left.

The farmer had spent the winter becoming First Spearman Wedon of the Second Cohort of the Rhune Legion, but Raithe still saw him as the wheat farmer he'd first met in Dahl Rhen. The same was true of Tope Highland and his three sons, all of whom were assigned to the forward principal line as members of the First File, First Cohort. Bergin the Brewer and Tanner Riggles were back spears. Bruce Baker and Filson the Lamp were part of Moya's special Archery Auxiliary. They all gathered around to peer out at their first glimpse of the enemy they had heard so much about.

"How many do you think there are?" Bergin asked.

"Don't know, two thousand, maybe?" Tope said.

"Roan?" Engleton called down the line of spectators. The woman in her leather apron stood staring like the rest of them. *Did she ever stop?* "Are my shoulder plates done?"

"Almost," she replied.

Raithe could have answered for her. For the past six months, *almost* was nearly all Roan ever said. Even if she hadn't started on something, even if the inquiry was the first she'd heard that something was needed, or wanted, the answer was always *almost*.

"Do you think they'll attack tonight?" Grevious asked. The carpenter from Menahan was one of the last to reach the parapet, but he arrived in full armor and gear: chest and shoulder plates, iron helm, leathers, shield, and spear.

Bergin saw Grevious and looked worried. "Are we supposed to be suited?"

Grevious shrugged. "Just playing it safe. Don't want to be scrambling at the last minute."

"Should we be forming up? Does anyone know?" Heath Coswall asked. "Wedon, you're First Spearman, what are we supposed to do?"

"I don't know."

"They just got here," Raithe replied. "Doubt they're planning a night assault after a long day of walking. But tomorrow is likely to begin early."

"We gonna wait for them, or are we going out to attack? Anyone know?" Kurt, one of Tope's sons, asked. He was about the same age as Tesh.

Raithe looked around. He was tall enough to see over most everyone's heads. Tesh wasn't there. *Back with Brin again.* Kid picked a lousy time to fall in love.

Heath was leaning out over the edge, trying to get a better look. "Wish they *would* attack tonight. I'm tired of waiting."

"Let's hope they don't agree," Raithe said. "There might only be a couple thousand out there, but we have less in here."

He looked up at the Spyrok. It was dark.

Why hasn't Persephone ordered the beacon lit?

Persephone knew she had to be either dead or dreaming. As she didn't have any experience with being dead, she chalked it up as a dream. Her first clue was that Reglan was sitting next to her. They were on the raised stage in Dahl Rhen's lodge, but in the wrong chairs. He was in the Second, while she was in the First.

"Bad times coming, Seph," her dead husband said. He looked thoughtful.

She could tell by how he sat leaning forward, his hands clasped together the way he always did—had—when something terrible happened. "Very bad times. You need to be ready, girl."

She spotted the silver ring on his hand. "Are you mad at me?"

He looked down at the metal band, smirked, and shook his head. "Surprised you wore it that long."

Persephone heard a roar and turned.

"Don't look at it!" *Reglan shouted.*

"What is it?"

"You know what it is."

She didn't, but she thought she should. There was something familiar in that sound, and the feelings it generated were both powerful and contradictory: tremendous hope and unmeasurable sadness. "I don't know. Tell me."

"I can't," *Reglan said.* "I'm surprised I can talk to you at all. Usually, it's only one way—I watch; I listen; I talk, but you don't hear. You must be very close to death. The walls between the worlds can get thin then. Still, I can't tell you what I don't know." *He rocked back in the Second Chair and rubbed his old hands up and down on his arms.* "I don't think I ever actually sat in this chair."

The roar again. Persephone shivered at the sound but didn't look.

"You're running out of time, my love. It's coming."

"What is?"

Reglan only smiled. "You always worked too hard. You put others before yourself. Never learned to be selfish. That's your problem. Sometimes you have to. Sometimes if you don't, bad things happen."

"Like what?"

He pointed toward the sound of the roar.

"Reglan, tell me. What is that?"

"I told you, I don't know. But you do. You don't want to see it, but you will. And when you do, remember this: Truth lies in the eyes. The eyes are windows, and the view through those eyes will be the same."

Persephone woke up feeling like her stomach was on fire—not so much a big bonfire as a bunch of little flames dancing all around, searing her skin.

The dream had left her muddled, and it took a long moment to realize she was on her bed in Alon Rhist. Padera's was the first face she saw, which meant Persephone had nearly died. Nothing short of that would have forced Padera to make the trip from the city to the fourth floor of the Kype.

"Welcome back, honey," the old woman said with those familiar withered lips and squinting eyes.

"Ow," Persephone whimpered.

"I bet." The old woman nodded, her lips rolled up in a sort-of-smile.

"You're awake!" Moya sounded as if Persephone had just performed a great feat. "Thank Mari, and Drome, and Ferrol!"

"Not leaving anyone out, are you?" Padera chuckled.

To her left, working at a small table that hadn't been there before, an unfamiliar Fhrey was cleaning up bloody rags. His was the first gray hair she'd ever seen on a Fhrey. Brin was there too, scrubbing the floor near the window with a bucket and brush. They all smiled at her.

"She's going to be fine now," the old Fhrey said.

Persephone tried to sit up and failed. Sharp, stabbing pains ripped through her torso.

"Don't move!" Padera scolded.

"We just got you stitched," the Fhrey said in a far more sympathetic tone. "Don't ruin our nice work."

Persephone saw that the Fhrey's hands, upper arms, and shirt were stained with blood in various stages of drying.

"How bad am I?" They had the covers pulled to her neck, and she was frightened to look down. "It cut me, didn't it? I remember that."

The old woman nodded. "Three deep slices opened up your belly. Muscle and skin mostly. You're lucky."

"Don't feel lucky."

"You passed out before the sewing. You *were* lucky."

Persephone had never suffered any serious injury. Even as a child she'd never gotten more than a scrape or a bruise. The rest of her life had been that of a sheltered chieftain's wife. Persephone liked to think she avoided harm because she was smarter than others, but she also had to wonder if perhaps she just hadn't lived as fully. This was different. She was alone in her bedroom and something had come after her.

"What happened?" She looked at each of them, then found Brin. "That was your raow, wasn't it?"

The girl nodded.

"How did it get up here?"

"We think it climbed."

"Did it—did it get away? I don't remember that part very well."

"Tesh, Nyphron, and Sebek killed it. Meryl is still missing."

Meryl? Persephone didn't know what that meant, but let it go.

"Some good news," Brin said with a bright if not entirely sincere smile and held up her hand. "I found Reglan's ring. It was on the floor here."

"Sorry I didn't believe you, Brin," Persephone said.

Brin offered a pained smile.

"Anyone else hurt?"

"Ah, well, yeah. Sebek," Moya replied. "Looks like he'll live, too. Not nearly as bad as you are. We're going to be moving you upstairs to the Shrine just in case."

"In case of what? It's dead—you said it was dead. Are there more?" Again, Persephone looked at Brin, expecting the girl to say, *Sure, there are hundreds and hundreds.*

"Anything is possible now," Moya replied. "I want you in a secure room. One without a damn window. The Shrine is the safest. I got some pushback from the Fhrey." Moya glanced at the healer, who was washing his hands in a basin. He didn't even look up. "But Nyphron supported me. We'll move you up in a few hours."

"What do you mean anything is possible *now?*" Persephone looked from one face to another. "Why now?"

"Seph . . ." Moya began and looked very serious, even a little frightened. "The fane's army is here."

"What? When?" She tried to sit up and again suffered for it.

She gritted her teeth, sucking in a quick breath. She really couldn't move. Her head and arms were fine, but even moving her legs tugged at her abdominal muscles—not that she wanted to do much moving. She was incredibly weak. Simply holding her eyes open was a struggle.

Moya took her hand. "Easy, easy. They aren't attacking yet. They only just got here, maybe an hour or two ago."

"Did someone light the signal? Did they—" She turned to look, and heated daggers sliced into her again. *Dammit! I'm just turning my head!* Which wasn't true and she knew it, but the frustration was nearly as agonizing as the pain. "Brin, is there a light on the top of the Spyrok?"

"The signal." Moya's eyes widened.

Brin looked out the window and shook her head. "Hem's on watch. Why didn't he light it?"

"He needs the order." Moya was shaking her head. "Hem only sees torches and campfires; he doesn't know who they are. For all he knows, it could be our troops on a training exercise. Nyphron was busy with Sebek, and I was—"

"Send a runner to the top of the Spyrok," Persephone ordered. "Tell Hem I authorize lighting the signal fire. We have to get the tribes back. We need to get everyone back."

"No one runs faster than me." Brin jumped up. "I'll do it."

The girl dodged around the bed and sprinted out the door.

"How many are there?" Persephone asked.

"I don't know, but not a lot. Not as many as the Gula." Moya glanced at the door. "Others want to see you, if you feel up to it. Do you?"

She didn't. Persephone didn't feel up to breathing. She wanted to sleep. She wanted to sleep forever and then some. *Almost did by the sound of it.* "Send them in."

Brin had always been fast. She could outrun anyone in Dahl Rhen, even Hory Killian, and he was two years older. He wasn't anymore. Hory was dead. The same giants that killed Brin's parents had killed him, too. As she pounded up the steps of the Spyrok, she wondered if the Fhrey had brought more giants with them. She'd only gone up the Spyrok one time before;

once was enough for anyone. Until reaching the top, it was just an endless spiral of steps with a disappointing lack of windows. This time she managed to reach the fourth level before slowing to a walk. By the time she reached the seventh floor, the burst of enthusiasm that she began her race with was gone. The pounding had become a plod.

Persephone looked like she was going to be all right. That's what both the Fhrey healer and Padera said. Brin hadn't been convinced until Seph's eyes opened. Since Brin's parents' death, she'd grown skeptical of such things as hope. Padera said she was growing up. Brin had always thought that meant a handsome husband, a home of her own, no bedtimes, and a greater voice in clan meetings. But she had come to realize growing up meant sadness, pain, and regret. Not until she hit the eighth floor did she realize that she and Tesh had saved Persephone's life. A smile climbed onto her face, and she carried it up the next two floors.

At the tenth level, there was a tiny window. Here Brin paused to catch her breath and peered out eastward. Lights were arrayed on the plain on the far side of the Grandford Bridge, a grid of evenly set squares. She couldn't see giants, but it was too dark to see anything but the lights.

It had taken so long, Brin had actually allowed herself to believe that they might never come, that the war had already ended. Optimism had disappointed her again—a childhood friend who made many promises it couldn't keep. Death, fear, blood—the only shining light in all of it was Tesh. He was the one good thing of her blossoming adulthood. While not exactly how she'd thought, how she'd dreamed of a sweetheart, she found she liked the real Tesh even more. And he seemed to like her; but she wasn't convinced. He was certainly eager to kiss her, but she wasn't so naive as to think a kiss meant love.

Maybe it does, optimism told her, but pessimism was quick to point out, *Maybe he's just yearning for any girl. Not a lot to choose from here.*

She remembered the feel of his hand on the back of her neck. Just thinking about it raised hairs, in a good way.

Where is he now?

She imagined he'd be back with Raithe, preparing to fight. There would be a battle in the morning, or the one after. Tesh would go out with the rest. He might be a fantastic warrior, but even optimism had a hard time selling her on the idea that such a thing actually mattered on a battlefield. If he died, Brin didn't know what she'd do. While only having really known him for a few days, she realized he was her first thought in the morning and her last at night. She had a glimpse into how Persephone must have felt when Reglan died. And while she had hated Tressa along with everyone else, she'd lost her husband, and that sort of pain deserved sympathy no matter how awful the man had been.

The top of the Spyrok was a stone parapet open to the sky and filled with a two-story building's worth of stacked logs that sat in a basin ready to be filled with oil. Hem, a member of Clan Melen, was a short, balding fellow with pudgy fingers and sad eyes. His watch would have only just started, but already he had a blanket around his shoulders and pulled tight at the neck. Hem was at the railing, looking east. He jumped when he heard her.

"Is it . . ." He pointed at the field of lights far below as the high wind blew what little hair he had. "Is it the Fhrey?"

Exhausted from the mammoth climb, Brin took a breath and said, "Light it!"

CHAPTER SEVENTEEN

The Signal

I still feel as if it was my fault, which I understand is stupid. But like I said, I only had the one job.

—THE BOOK OF BRIN

A fire ignited at the top of the Spyrok.

Mawyndulë was just outside his father's tent, which was still being raised by a team of Eilywin busily pounding stakes with mallets. Ever since his first visit, Mawyndulë had thought of the great tower of Alon Rhist as an upthrust spear punching out of the ground, stabbing at the sky. Now the tip of the spear burst into flame.

"Does that mean they've seen us?" Mawyndulë asked his father.

Fane Lothian was observing the construction of his battlefield home, which, when completed, would be a circular purple monstrosity held up by twelve-foot poles. He turned and squinted at the fortress; then, without a word, he marched across the camp.

Mawyndulë followed his father, who was already shadowed by the ever-present Sile and Synne. The silent twins who looked nothing alike—

the giant and the hobgoblin—went everywhere his father did. *What has the world come to when the fane needs constant protection?*

The four of them weaved between tents and cook fires. Why the evening meal was taking so long, he couldn't imagine. Remembering Jerydd's trick of making strawberries, Mawyndulë made a silent vow to master it.

The only thing worse than his hunger was the soreness and exhaustion from riding. They'd traveled far that day, his father pushing them, anxious to end the ordeal. All the Miralyith rode horses, and Mawyndulë was certain his animal was the worst of the lot. The beast wouldn't obey, and Mawyndulë spent most of the trip pulling its reins and kicking its sides. By midday, he'd found himself thinking that walking would have been a better choice.

The fane arrived at Kasimer's tent, which inexplicably was up before the fane's own. Lothian shouted for him to come out.

"My fane?" Kasimer asked. He was in dark robes and still wore the Spider helm.

Mawyndulë's father pointed at the spire, which, now that it was burning, reminded Mawyndulë of a candle. His father apparently thought the same, saying, "Blow it out."

"My fane?"

"It's a signal. Put it out now!"

"Yes, my fane."

Kasimer shouted to his troops. The Spider Corps had trained to work as a group. This wasn't easy. Miralyith were by nature a pack of individualists. Artists enjoyed meeting and talking, but collaborating on a project was the behavior of the Nilyndd or Eilywin—two tribes that needed to team up to accomplish anything worthwhile. The Art was personal, and Artists rarely needed help manifesting their dreams. Execution was also always part self-expression, and suppressing the instinct to act freely was difficult. To follow another's lead was counterintuitive and took months of practice, but the benefits were obvious. Like a dozen oarsmen on one ship, a handful of spiders could weave bigger, stronger webs. In this case, a team of Miralyith could snuff out a massive bonfire at a distance no individual could manage alone.

Mawyndulë watched as they rapidly assembled, forming in a circle around Kasimer, who acted as lead Spider. Everyone else would *feed* him power.

I could blow that candle out all by myself, Mawyndulë thought.

Not really *by himself,* but without the aid of the Spiders or anyone else at the camp. In the same way the Spiders fed Kasimer, Mawyndulë had a direct line of power to Avempartha. Jerydd waited on call. Anytime Mawyndulë wished, he could contact the kel and summon up the awesome power of Fenelyus's tower. Jerydd had taught him the technique before he left Avempartha, and they had practiced every day. By the time the troops reached Grandford, Mawyndulë was able to listen and monitor everything Jerydd said all day long. The kel knew he was listening and rambled on about the origins of the Torsonic Chant and the usefulness of the Plesieantic Phrase—two topics Arion had bored him with. He had always tuned her out, but it was more fun with Jerydd. Mawyndulë took great pleasure in having the kel's voice in his head, a voice that no one else could hear. He was positive that none of the Spiders—not even Kasimer—knew how to eavesdrop at unlimited distances.

After establishing the connection, all it took was a little concentration, and unless his horse stumbled, he managed just fine. He also had to pay attention; he couldn't let his mind wander. In the few days it took to ride from the Nidwalden through the Harwood and across the plains to Alon Rhist, Mawyndulë had learned more than in the three years with Arion.

"You just want us to put it out?" Kasimer asked.

"Blow it out so it can't be relit," the fane ordered.

Kasimer turned and faced the tower. Around him the other Spiders hummed in harmony, their hands and arms moving in perfect synchronization, performing the same motions in concert. Watching them, Mawyndulë thought the group looked creepy, like a real spider—a really *big* spider. Then Kasimer made a cutting motion with his arms and a slicing with his hands. A mile away, the light at the top of the tower grew brighter, then went completely out.

. . .

The top of the Spyrok exploded.

Brin had already started back down. Exhausted after her race up the stairs, she was taking her time, and she was only five levels below the observation deck when the top of the tower sheared away. Screaming as rubble and dust rained down, Brin cowered on the steps in a ball, covering her head and crying. She would have died, but most of the stone, glass, and timber blew west.

She stayed huddled, clutching herself and shivering. Terrified and bewildered, she didn't know what to do. Then in a burst of decision, she ran. Down the steps she flew, leaping as far and as fast as she could without killing herself, although a few times she came close. Brin kept her arms up for fear something might fall, or another explosion would rip through the tower. In minutes, she was down and running for the Kype.

"What happened?" several people asked as she flew by. Brin didn't stop. Then Tekchin caught up. He grabbed her with both arms and pulled her to him.

"Let me go!" she screamed, jerking hard. She didn't know why. By then, she wasn't even sure where she was heading.

The Fhrey held on. "Calm down. Relax. You're safe."

She stopped struggling, her strength gone. Her legs gave out and she collapsed.

Persephone felt, as much as heard, the explosion. It shook the fortress, rocking her bed, swaying the curtains. The men and Fhrey in her bedroom steadied themselves against walls and dressers whose drawers rattled. Tegan and his Shield, Oz, both drew swords, looking around for the enemy. Nyphron was at the window—*the raow window* as Persephone now thought of it—and looked up.

"What happened?" she asked.

"Miralyith blew the top off the Spyrok," he told them so matter-of-factly that Persephone wondered if he was kidding. "Don't want us sending signals."

"Oh, dear Mari, Brin!" Persephone said. She glared at Moya and again tried to get up, and again she suffered for it, this time gasping audibly with the pain ripping through her.

"You can't be trying that," Padera scolded. The old woman frowned with irritation, as if Persephone's wounds mattered.

Moya bolted out the door. Everyone else except Padera and Nyphron followed her. Padera busied herself, checking what damage Persephone might have done, while Nyphron, dressed in a comfortable robe, continued to stare out the window.

Persephone lay prone, eyes on the ceiling. She despised being helpless. She wanted to run, to check on Brin, to see the damage. But even if she managed to stand up, she'd collapse immediately. The dizziness plagued her. Even her fingers felt heavy. *How can I be an effective keenig lying on my back?*

"Did they see the signal? Did the message get through?" Persephone asked. "Is the bonfire at Perdif burning?"

He shook his head. "I doubt it. The bonfire burned for only a few minutes. I can't imagine anyone at Perdif is watching every second. Even if they were, they'd likely believe it was a mistake, a test, or a mirage. Why else would it vanish so quickly? But I'll go check."

With that wonderful assessment, he walked out, leaving Persephone alone with Padera. The old woman rinsed a towel in the basin, then wiped Persephone's face. Despite an inability to move, the keenig continued to work up a sweat.

"What is Perdif?" Padera asked.

"A small village of shepherds—a raised place in the High Spear Valley. There's a bonfire built on a hill there that can be seen by the Gula and the Nadak. They're supposed to light their fire when they see ours. The alert is then supposed to be relayed across Gula and Rhulyn, fire after fire, as the signal for all warriors to hurry back."

"And if they didn't see it?"

"We'll be on our own here with too few men to fight."

Nyphron returned. He was shaking his head. "There's no fire at Perdif."

"Build another," Persephone ordered. "Tell—"

"Can't. They didn't just blow the fire out. They blasted the top off the Spyrok. Even if we could, they'd just blow that one out, too. You'd be giving them targets."

Blew the top off the Spyrok? How could anyone blow the top off that huge tower? And if they can do that, how can we hope to survive?

Persephone felt herself sink farther into the mattress. They needed to signal Perdif. They *had* to signal. She'd sent everyone home based on the idea that she could call them back if the Fhrey attacked. The whole idea seemed so simple—too simple not to work. Persephone recalled patting herself on the back for her ingenuity.

"How did the fane's army get here without any warning? Our scouts—"

"Our scouts were Rhunes," Nyphron said. "All dead, I suspect, killed by Fhrey scouts."

This isn't how it's supposed to happen. This isn't fair. She had a plan, a good one. *And I can't even get out of bed because of some stupid raow!*

"Wait!" Persephone said. "What about Arion? Couldn't she make a signal?"

"Already sent for—" Nyphron smiled as Arion and Suri knocked on the doorframe.

"The fane is here, I take it?" Arion asked.

The Miralyith was rubbing her eyes, looking sleepy. Suri was alert, but then Suri had always been a night owl. The mystic stared at Persephone, puzzled. She glanced at the window, and her expression darkened.

She knows. No one told her, but she knows what happened.

Persephone had spent the winter watching Suri blossom. The most noticeable change came with the first snows when beyond all expectations Arion persuaded Suri to abandon her old filthy dress and ruddy wool cape for an asica. The transformation was remarkable. The onetime feral mystic, who had all the fashion sense of a hedgehog, had become a swan. She hadn't conceded completely. Arion had wanted to shave Suri's head, but the girl had refused. They compromised on her taking regular baths, which had done wonders. Only the tattoos remained of the mystic's former self, but even they looked different. With Suri dressed in the formal robe, what had once appeared as just another bizarre ornament now lent an aura of mystery and worldly wisdom.

"The fane blew out our signal," Nyphron told her.

Arion moved to the window and peered out. "Of course he did. Are you saying you didn't expect that?"

Nyphron frowned.

"The signal was my idea," Persephone said.

"But you aren't an experienced military commander. Nyphron should have known better and warned you."

"My *experience* is against normal adversaries. I'm not accustomed to magical warfare. Besides, the thing only needed to burn for a little while."

Persephone had never seen Nyphron offer excuses before. *They rattled him. Now he's wondering what else he missed.*

"Welcome to your first lesson." She faced Persephone. "You want me to make a new one," Arion said, not a question, but an understanding, an acknowledgment. Arion and Suri were both a little eerie that way.

Persephone had asked Suri once if she was learning to read people's minds. The mystic shook her head and replied, *I'm learning to read the mind of the world.*

"What do you think, Suri?" Arion asked.

Arion did that a lot, too. In every instance where they called Arion in for advice, she always made Suri answer first. The mystic paused and thought a moment. She moved to the window and looked out, then turned back and shook her head.

"Why?" Arion asked.

"Pointless and dangerous."

Arion smiled at her apprentice, then turned to Nyphron and Persephone. "Jerydd, or whoever they have leading the Spiders, is watching. They're looking for two things. A new fire—that they will blow out—and me. Can't see me now. Might not even know I'm here. But if I use the Art, they will." She glanced at Nyphron. "You'll lose your precious advantage of surprise as they alter their battle plans to include me, or they'll just launch another attack and try to do to me what they did to that tower. Honestly, I believe they're hoping I'll try."

Nyphron was nodding, his face tense and thoughtful.

"And the same applies to Suri?" Persephone asked.

"More so. She's your *real* secret weapon."

"So, no signal," Persephone said.

"Can't we just send someone to Perdif?" Padera asked.

"Perdif is forty miles away," Nyphron replied. "Take a person two days just to get there. Two more days for the army to get back. I'm optimistic, but even I don't think the fane will delay his attack that long."

"Naraspur," Arion said.

Persephone assumed this was a Fhrey word she wasn't familiar with, but she saw just as much puzzlement in Nyphron's eyes.

"Naraspur is the horse I rode here. I left Naraspur with Petragar. If she's still here, someone could ride—"

"Alon Rhist has a dozen horses," Nyphron said, then began shaking his head. "But being a fortress, the Rhist is designed to be hard to invade. A natural cliff protects the citadel and the city below, and we have only the one, well-fortified gate. To escape, a rider would need to cross the Grand-ford Bridge. There's just no other way for a horse to leave, and the fane's army is camped on the far side. Our messenger would be required to ride through a thousand Fhrey."

Arion frowned. "And the Spiders will kill anyone leaving the fortress. Especially on a horse, and for the same reason they destroyed the tower."

"I can't ask my people to commit suicide, not when . . ." Nyphron looked at Persephone. "So far, the rest of the Instarya are innocent of my crimes. If we fail, there's a chance at least that the fane will punish me and pardon them."

"What about a human?" Padera asked. She had dropped the towel back in the basin, throwing her full attention to the conversation. "What about a Rhune?"

Nyphron replied to Persephone rather than Padera. "A Rhune would stand far less of a chance. Members of the fane's army might hesitate to kill another Fhrey, but they would have no such qualms with a Rhune. And there isn't a Rhune alive that can ride a horse." He looked as if he were going to say more, then stopped.

"What?" Persephone asked.

Nyphron looked pained. "I am embarrassed to say we Fhrey are not above petty amusements. Rhunes have been forced onto the backs of horses as entertainment. It never ended well. No Rhune has ever managed to sit on a horse, much less ride one."

"Never?" Padera asked, but the tone of her voice was odd, as if this was a good thing.

"I'm sorry. I don't mean to be rude; it's just that humans don't have the required agility."

Arion nodded. "He's right. Riding a horse isn't easy. It is, in point of fact, dangerous."

"Racing through a camp of a thousand Fhrey, some of them Miralyith, would be impossible for anyone," Nyphron explained.

"It would be a *race*, wouldn't it?" Padera said. "A race for the fate of all our people."

Nyphron sighed and leaned against the wall. "Suicide is what it would be."

"But if someone could do it—if someone could cross that bridge and get past the army . . ." Padera looked in Persephone's direction but not at her. That one visible eye seemed out of focus, searching for something else entirely.

"It would be a miracle," Nyphron told her.

"Yes, but if they did, could they make a difference?"

"If they did, and if they rode hard, they might reach Perdif in less than a day—half a day maybe, though it might kill the horse, and honestly, wishful thinking would be more likely to work. But if you'd like to find candidates to try it . . ."

"No," Persephone replied. "I won't ask anyone to throw their life away."

"Of course," Padera said, "trying to ride a horse through that camp is something only a fool with nothing to lose would even think of."

"And we aren't that desperate," Persephone said. "We still have walls, near equal numbers, and our secret weapons." She looked at Arion and Suri.

Moya came back in. "Good news," she said and pulled Brin in behind her.

Seeing the girl safe and unharmed, Persephone smiled. She had a feeling she wouldn't be doing much of that anymore.

"That should wake them up." The fane sat on the ornate chair, which had been placed in the dusty field. A dozen Fhrey had stomped down the yellow grass around him so that blowing tassels wouldn't bother the ruler of the Fhrey. He wore a smug smile as he stretched out his feet and folded his arms. "It'll make it hard for them to sleep tonight, too. In the morning, we'll finish the task."

The Spiders continued to hum and chant, and Kasimer wove his fingers at the tower across the chasm.

"No sign of her?" the fane asked.

"Arion is not foolish," was all Kasimer replied.

"She turned against her fane in favor of a bunch of barbarians," Mawyndulë said. "She prevented me from rendering justice on Gryndal's murderer. How exactly would you classify that? Wise?"

A smile tugged at the corner of Lothian's mouth, and in his father's eyes, Mawyndulë thought he saw, for just a brief moment, a glimmer of . . . something. *Pride?*

Well said, Jerydd spoke in his head, and Mawyndulë nearly jumped. Always in the past, Mawyndulë had initiated their conversations. He opened the link. As a result, Mawyndulë had come to believe that only *he* could establish their connection. Mawyndulë found it disconcerting to discover the kel could be listening to *all* his conversations. *Kasimer means well. What he should have said is that Arion is not to be underestimated. That she's dangerous and cunning—which she most certainly is. You made points with your father, but it is better to have Kasimer on your side than against you. Let him off the hook and build a bridge.*

Mawyndulë considered this for a moment, then said, "I think you meant to say she's not to be underestimated, which I agree is very good counsel."

This brought a new look from the fane, one of surprise and accompanied by a smile.

"Yes, that's exactly what I meant," Kasimer said. Then he, too, looked at Mawyndulë and nodded at him. Mawyndulë had never seen the gesture before. A solemn look had accompanied the bowed head, and the prince realized it was an expression of respect, perhaps even a thank-you, like the little bow that fencers made at the end of a session.

See, that wasn't so hard, was it? As fane, you'll need people like Kasimer.

Mawyndulë fought the urge to nod.

Now you really should get some sleep. Tomorrow will be a big day, and it'll start early.

Normally, Mawyndulë would chafe at being told to go to bed, but it was different when a voice inside his head said so. He knew it was Jerydd, who was sitting in his study in Avempartha, probably sipping wine with his feet up much the same as his father. But coming from his head, it felt like his own thoughts. Jerydd was also a secret, and what good was a secret if he didn't take advantage of it?

Get some sleep, and tomorrow we'll kill Arion.

CHAPTER EIGHTEEN

The Race Begins

If there is one thing I have learned, it is that people will astound you. But the moment they do, or shortly after, you will realize you should not have been surprised. Ultimately, the problem was you, not them.

—THE BOOK OF BRIN

The first thought that entered Gifford's head as Padera shook him awake was that the Tetlin Witch was real—real and trying to kill him.

"Wake up, you lazy fool!" she whispered in the darkness of Hopeless House.

"I'm not lazy. It's the middle of the night!" Gifford replied in a hushed voice as he tried to avoid waking Habet, Mathias, and Gelston. Unlike Brin's new home, which had separate rooms, Hopeless House consisted of just one. "Why is you—"

"It's time," she said, letting go.

Gifford lay on his bed, looking up at her in the darkened room of snores. "Time fo' what?"

"Your race."

Gifford sat up, scrubbing the sleep from his eyes. The old hag was nuts.

This time she actually looked crazy. In moonlight that entered one window and slashed the side of her face, Padera was pale, her hair and eyes wild. He'd never seen the old woman so animated, so intense. It scared him.

"Time for you to fulfill your destiny, boy—to run faster than any man ever has."

"Yew insane, old woman."

"And you're going to win this race because I'm going to give you magic legs."

Magic legs? She really is the Tetlin Witch!

Far stronger than he imagined, Padera grabbed the collar of his shirt and dragged him up.

"Have you been dwinking?"

"It all makes sense now," Padera yammered, more to herself than to him as she continued to pull him along toward the door. She had hold of his wrist, but if he had resisted, Gifford suspected she would have grabbed his ear. "You had to be crippled; you had to suffer; you had to have nothing worth living for. I was such a fool to doubt. Tura was right. She was right all along."

"Where you going, Giff?" Habet asked in a groggy voice.

"He's going to save mankind," Padera replied.

"Okay." Habet turned over and went back to sleep.

"Can I get my shoes?"

"You won't need them." The old woman cackled. She was so much like a witch he shivered.

The Tetlin Witch has come for me at last.

"We need to hurry; we need to see Roan."

"See Woan? Why didn't you say that to begin with?"

The two made a fearful sight hobbling together through the dark streets of the city, a pair of goblins out for a stroll. The avenues were cold, the night biting, and he cursed first Padera and then himself for not taking time to grab a wrap and his shoes. After they left the Rhune District, Gifford spotted a few Fhrey watching them from a distance. The old and the twisted must be quite the novelty to their perfect eyes.

Monsters on parade. They invaded their homes, took their city, and wandered their streets. *See, honey, that's why mommy told you never to go out alone. See them there? See how horrible they are?*

In reality, he never heard them say a word as they passed. Those were just the sorts of things Gifford always imagined people saying about him. Usually, he was right.

Is that part of the magic, too? Can I actually hear their thoughts somehow?

He still wasn't sure if he could swallow all of what Arion had told him about his being a magician, his ability to wield cosmic power. Gifford, who had been the butt of jokes and tormented since birth, wasn't easily duped, but a few things didn't make sense. Why would Arion, a high-ranking Fhrey whom he'd never spoken to before, seek him out just to lie? What little he knew of her, and of Suri, suggested they weren't the sort to mislead or make fun of others. Persephone trusted them, and Gifford had always respected the keenig's opinion.

So, why did she do it?

After they left, he'd tried boiling water, catching twigs on fire. Nothing even got warm. He was positive she'd lied to him—just couldn't understand why. This unanswerable question, this strange doubt left the door of possibility open just a crack, just enough so that whenever anything unusual did happen, he wondered.

To a man with so little, hope is a barrel of ale. It alleviates pain for a time, becomes a crutch, but it also ruins what little good a person might otherwise squeeze out of life. Gifford wanted to think he was special. He wanted to believe that somehow the gods had a plan, and all his suffering was for a reason. But he couldn't bring himself to believe it was true. Those were dreams that ended in nightmares.

The pair was stopped at the lower gate by two Fhrey guards who had never been there before.

"I'm personal healer to Keenig Persephone, and this is my grandson who helps me," Padera told the soldiers.

"Helps you with what?" one asked, looking Gifford over skeptically.

Gifford smiled at him. He'd heard the same from hundreds of others. *What good could he possibly be?*

"It's true," the other guard said. "She's the Rhune healer. Padera, right? She was at the Kype earlier, after the keenig was attacked."

Persephone was attacked? Gifford stared at the guards, neither of whom was looking at them anymore.

"What happened?" the first guard asked.

"Raow gutted her," said the second.

"What!" Gifford shouted, surprising everyone.

"She'll be fine." Padera grabbed his arm again. "But I need to see Roan at the smithy, get some more needles from her. Are we free to go?" she asked the Fhrey.

"Sure, go ahead."

Padera jerked him forward. "Keep walking. You're slow enough as it is, and you don't have much time. There's so much we still have to do."

"What *is* we doing?" Gifford asked as he hobbled after her up the slope.

"Roan and I are going to make you a hero."

And I thought I'm supposed to be the magician!

They entered the smithy, and even at that late hour, it was no surprise to see Roan hammering on the anvil. What shocked Gifford was that Frost, Flood, and Rain were there as well. Each of them rushed with a terrible urgency.

As Gifford entered, they all paused to stare at him. Each showed the same horrible expression of sympathy. Roan looked as if she might burst into tears.

"Okay, will someone tell me what's going on?"

"The elven army has arrived," Padera said as Frost trotted over with a length of string and began measuring the width of Gifford's shoulders. "Hundreds of them have fanned out in front of the Grandford Bridge, maybe more. Hard to tell in the dark. They'll likely attack at dawn."

"Oh, holy Ma-we, you sewious?"

"Thirty-three," Frost shouted.

"Thirty-three," Flood repeated.

"What's more," the old woman went on, "the signal fire that was supposed to let our army know it's time to come to our aid was blown away by elven magic."

Frost lifted Gifford's arm and stretched the string down his side. "Fifteen."

"Fifteen," Flood echoed.

"We're all trapped here and will certainly be slaughtered to the last man, woman, and child unless the signal fire at Perdif is set alight."

Frost drew the string around Gifford's waist. "Twenty-nine."

"Twenty-nine? Seriously? Are you sure?" Flood said.

"Not everyone is as fat as you! Yes—twenty-nine!"

"Perdif is forty miles away," Padera told him. "Someone has to race there and light that fire by midday tomorrow or everyone in Alon Rhist will die, and after that, the rest of mankind."

"And you want me to—I can't get to Pew-dif by midday. I'd be lucky to walk back to Hopeless House by then."

"Here she is." Gifford spun to see Raithe's friend Malcolm. He entered the smithy leading a beautiful white horse. "They didn't even ask me what I wanted her for. The Instarya aren't overly fond of horses. In general, Fhrey prefer to keep their feet on solid ground."

Gifford had seen horses before, but never this close. He sometimes spotted them along with deer in meadows near Dahl Rhen, and on occasion—also like deer—they were hunted for food.

"Her name is Naraspur," Malcolm explained, rubbing the animal's muzzle. She snorted and stomped a hoof, making a disturbingly loud noise on the stone floor.

She's huge.

"You are going to ride her, Gifford," Padera said with admiration, as if he'd already done so.

Gifford looked up at the towering animal. "No, I'm not."

"On the back of that animal, you'll run faster than any man in history."

"How will I stay on?"

"You hang on to the mane," Malcolm said. "Lean forward, lie low, and just hang on tight."

"The gods made your arms strong for a reason," the old woman told him.

"How will I make it go the way I want?"

"With this." Malcolm came over then, holding a piece of metal with straps and buckles tied to it. "It's called a bridle. Slip this metal piece between her teeth, slide it all the way to the back of her mouth, then buckle it around her head. These long straps will make it possible to turn. She'll go where she's facing."

Malcolm put it on the horse. Then Roan hurried back to the worktable, grabbing up wads of cotton padding.

"Relax," Padera said. "The horse is the least of your worries."

Frost waved for Gifford to bend over as if he planned to tell him a secret, then he wrapped the string around his head. "Fourteen and a half."

"Fourteen and a half," Flood repeated.

"Why they doing that?" Gifford asked.

"The hard part will be getting past the elven army," Padera explained. "You have to ride across the Grandford Bridge right through their camp. They'll know you're trying to carry a message, and just like when they destroyed the Spyrok, they'll want to stop you, too."

"They'll kill me."

Padera nodded. "They'll try." She might have been smiling. "According to absolutely everyone, what you're about to do is suicide. That's why *you* have to do it. Don't you see? It's perfect. You have nothing to lose."

"My life. I could lose my life."

"Like I said, nothing to lose."

Gifford didn't have an answer. He knew he ought to, but he didn't.

"Don't look so miserable," she said with a grin, that one eye glaring at him. "I'm not sending you to your death. You won't die. I know it. Your mother knew it, too. Now pay attention, Roan has a present for you."

He looked over to see Roan and the dwarfs carrying over a suit of armor. All silver, the thing looked like sunlight on a lake; so shiny, he could see his face looking back at him.

"I fashioned this from iron," Roan said. "But it's not iron. This is a new metal, something I've been working on. I made it using a new percentage of charcoal—a better mix. It's harder, lighter, tempered. And I polished it. I figure the smoother it is the less chance a blade will catch." Frost, Flood, and Rain all nodded.

Malcolm stepped in and lifted the big plates hinged together by leather straps over Gifford's head. One plate covered his chest, the other his back, and the straps rested on his shoulders. Then Malcolm and Roan swung shoulder plates over the top and began buckling them on.

"The best part is"—Roan took the matching helm and turned it over, revealing a series of etched markings—"all of the metal has been engraved with the Orinfar runes. So, not only will swords glance off, but magic should, too."

Padera grinned so that both eyes were squeezed to slits. "You're going to make your mother proud, boy."

Roan struggled with tightening the helmet straps. She punched a new hole, having underestimated the size of his head. He tried to make a joke about it, but Roan, who was always too serious, was downright grave. She refused to look him in the eye as she set the helm on his head with a ceremonial formality as if he were a chieftain—*or sacrificial lamb.*

"Dammit!" she cursed and pulled the helm off again. "Still too small. You said fourteen and a half. It's more like fourteen and three quarters."

"Woan?"

"Yeah?" she said, turning back to the worktable and pulling the buckle out.

"I want to tell you something."

Padera had kept him breathless for the last hour, but as the dwarfs painted the Orinfar markings over the white horse, and Roan continued to work the armor to fit, Gifford had a moment to think. It had never crossed his mind to refuse. The old woman was right. He would go. He would ride across that bridge, not for mankind, or even his mother, but to save Roan. Already he'd thanked Mari five times for even this slim chance to *do* something. All his life he'd watched others play, run, fight, marry, have kids, build homes, hunt, farm, raise sheep, and dance. Gifford never did anything but make cups and look foolish. In an emergency, he couldn't even run for help. He'd always been a burden, always a mouth to feed with the labor of someone else's work. His pottery was a way to give something back, which was why he worked so hard to make it the best it could possibly be, but it wasn't really needed. Gifford had never been needed by anyone.

I'm going to die.

The thought wasn't painful, or scary, just heavy, sobering, like the end of an era. He felt nostalgic rather than frightened, which was strange because Gifford had few good memories. But those he had—every one of them—involved Roan.

"Woan . . ." he began. "I know about Ivy. I know Padewa killed him to save you." Bad time to bring it up maybe, but time was running out. He knew she felt guilt for Iver's death, for what Padera had done on her behalf. He wanted to help her understand it wasn't her fault. This would be his last gift to her, his last amphora.

Roan dropped the helmet on the ground. It rattled and did a half-roll, bumping up against her foot.

He waited.

She slowly turned, her eyes wide, but this time she looked right at him. He loved those eyes, those windows to worlds of marvels yet undreamed.

"I—I know this is a bad time to be . . ." he started, then paused and took a breath to center himself. "I'll pwobably not see you again, and I just wanted you to know that—"

"Padera didn't kill Iver," she said in a weak voice. "I did."

The words spilled out of her in one breath. They fell between them like the helmet, with a rattle.

Gifford stared, confused. "*You* did? What do you mean *you*—"

Roan looked down, maybe searching for the helmet; he couldn't tell.

"Woan?"

Her face came back up, pulled by her name. She wanted to take the words back. He could see it in her furrowed brows and lips squished in a sour frown.

"Tell him, Roan," Padera said as she rubbed the horse's nose.

Roan glanced at the old woman, then back at him, then at the helmet still on the ground. "Plants," she said. "Certain plants and rocks—you grind them up." She made a pestle and mortar action with her hands. "I fed what I made to mice I kept in a cage. Some just made them sick. Others . . ." She looked at her feet. "I had to know if it would work on something bigger. So, I gave it to one of Gelston's sheep. Mixed it in with the feed. Next morning it was dead—a froth around its mouth."

Gifford couldn't believe what he was hearing.

"Gelston cursed the gods, but it had been me." Roan bent down and picked up the helm. "Iver killed my mother. He beat her to death. I watched him. He wanted me to see, wanted me to remember. I did."

"You don't need to justify anything to me," Gifford told her. "Honestly, if I'd known, I would have killed him myself. I think anyone in the Dahl would have."

She looked up at him with tears in her eyes. "But I was his slave. I was his property. He had every right to—"

"No, he didn't. No one has such a *wight*. They want you to think so. Twust me, Woan, I know about this."

"But he *owned* me. Me and my mother."

"How?"

"Because he bought my mother."

"How?"

"He traded wood and grain with a man in Dureya."

"And how did that fellow get to own anyone?"

"My mother was Gula. She was captured in a battle. Her husband was killed; she was taken as a slave."

"Was that wight? Was it wight she was taken? Husband killed? Made a slave? Was that wight, Woan? And what did you do? If it was wight fo' a man to kill a husband and make his wife a slave, how can it be wong fo' a child of that same woman to kill a man to be fwee? The man who made a slave had no *wight* to do that, just the *ability*. You had the ability to fwee you self, Woan. You had the ability and the wight."

"I killed a man. I'm a murderer."

"You killed a fiend. You a he-wo."

"How do you know? How can you tell the difference? A lot of people cried at his funeral. I saw them. I watched my neighbors, my friends, weeping over his grave. I caused all that pain. It was me. Iver always told me I was a curse to everyone who cared about me. That's what I am, a curse, an evil curse, and I deserve everything that happens to me." She was starting to cry.

"That's not twue."

"*It is!*" she shouted, so loudly that the dwarfs and even Naraspur looked over. "You care. Don't you? You—you love me, don't you? Don't you?"

Gifford felt as if she'd reached into his chest, took hold of his heart, and was thumbing over it. He stood stiff and helpless under her teary gaze. He nodded slowly. "Mo' than anything in the woold."

"See," she said. "And look what it's got you. You're going to . . . you're going to . . ." She clenched her teeth and wiped her eyes. "I am a curse."

Gifford's arms started to rise. He wanted desperately to take her, to hold her, to hug her tight. This might be the last time he'd ever see Roan. He wanted, if nothing else, to kiss her goodbye. He saw her flinch and stopped.

"Got food here," Tressa said, running into the smithy with a leather satchel and a wine skin.

"You're optimistic," Flood told her as he put the finishing touches on the horse, then blew on it to dry.

Tressa shrugged. "The guy is due for a win. You can't lose your *whole* life, am I right?"

The three dwarfs looked at each other, not appearing to agree.

"Time to go, Gifford," Padera said.

The old woman walked toward him, holding a sword and a scabbard. Roan wiped her eyes and sniffled. She grabbed up the weapon and thrust it out to him. "I made this for you, too."

Gifford looked at the most magnificent sword he'd ever seen. Like the armor, it shimmered. "I don't understand. How—how was all this done so quickly?"

"Not quickly," she replied. "This sword, the armor . . . I was making a present. Padera said one day you would need all of it. And besides, I can't make a fancy vase. This isn't an amphora with a picture of you on it, but . . . it's the best I've ever made. I poured my soul into this. It's light, and stronger than anything; this sword is sharper than a razor, and it shines in the sun so bright it blinds."

"She's not kidding," Frost said. "This is the finest weapon I've ever seen."

Flood nodded, the two agreeing for the first time that Gifford had known them.

Gifford took the weapon from her, surprised by how light it was. "You all weal-ize I don't know how to use this."

"You *weal-ize* it's the thought that counts?" Padera took the sword and buckled it around his waist. "Time to go, Gifford."

The dwarfs had pushed crates beside the horse, allowing him to climb onto the animal's back. Malcolm stood in front, petting the animal's nose and neck, whispering to it, calming it. Gifford inched his good leg over. He could feel the beast breathing beneath him, pushing his legs out with every inhale. Gifford's hands shook as Malcolm handed him the reins.

"Tie the ends together so they don't fall," Malcolm told him. "Gifford, Naraspur is a smart horse. She can sense you're frightened. That fear scares her. She'll try and throw you off her back. So don't be scared."

"How can I do that?"

Malcolm smiled. "You're about to ride through an army camp of the Fhrey, who will attack you with swords, spears, and magic. Given that, do you really think you ought to be afraid of falling off a horse's back? Naraspur is a good horse, a brave horse. She'll help you if you let her. Hang on. Trust her. Trust her, and she'll trust you."

Gifford lay across the horse's back, holding on to the mane and the leather straps of the bridle as he listened to Malcolm explain how to get to Perdif. When Gifford could recite the directions back without error, Malcolm smiled, clapped him on the leg, and said, "You'll do fine. Now remember, stay to the dark areas and the mist. There's always mist this time of year. And don't stop. As soon as you cross the bridge, ride up the bank of the Bern to the north. Then when you see the sun, ride toward it."

"Good luck, Gifford," Tressa said. "And . . ." She hesitated and sniffled. "Thanks for being a friend when no one else was."

"Your mother is proud of you, my boy," Padera told him, her voice still abrasive enough to sand wood. She mushed her lips around, her eyes all but disappearing in that pile of wrinkles that some called a face. "I misjudged you. I'll admit that, and I'm sorry. Go be the hero your parents always knew you'd be."

Roan handed up the helmet, and he put it on, feeling the leather sit perfectly on his brow.

"Gifford, I . . ." Roan faltered. "I . . ."

"Just let me imagine the west of that sentence, okay?"

Malcolm took hold of the bridle and led the horse. When he was clear of the smithy, Malcolm gave Gifford one last smile and then made a clicking noise. The animal began to trot.

Staying on the horse's back wasn't easy. Gifford bounced and banged, slamming hard against the spine of the animal. It wasn't only difficult to stay on, it hurt. There was no padding where he needed it the most. Clapping as he was against the horse's back, only his tight grip kept him up. On the positive side, he wasn't afraid of the horse anymore. Having sat on her for so long, he'd gotten used to the animal. Even so, he nearly fell twice when the hammering caused him to drift too far to one side. What's more, Gifford knew the horse wasn't at top speed. Not yet. *What will happen when she runs? How fast is she? Are my arms that strong? Will I just fly off? And if she isn't fast . . .*

He hoped she was very fast.

Gifford caught many a strange look from the few people out in the courtyard and through the city streets as he traveled down through the tiers, but no one said anything until he reached the front gate.

"Where are *you* going?" the soldier there asked.

"To Pewdif. I'm gonna bwing back help."

The guard, a Fhrey in full armor, which included a plumed helm, looked at him with a smirk. "Is that a joke?"

He shook his head. "The Fhwey blew out the signal light. No way to light it."

The guard narrowed his eyes at him, then pointed at the gate with his thumb. "There's an army out there. You don't stand a chance. They'll kill you."

Gifford nodded. "You say that like it's a bad thing." While the soldier was puzzling this out, he added, "Open the gate."

The guard shrugged. "Your funeral."

Yes—yes, it is. This is my funeral.

Gifford had spent his whole life on a dirt floor, alone in a small home. He lived each day digging in the dirt, looking for clay, and occasionally working it into pots and cups. The nice people ignored him, avoided him as if his twisted back, gimp leg, and dead face were a disease they might catch. The others—the not-so-nice—insulted and belittled. Even the few very nice people, the ones he dared call friends, still made him feel useless. They didn't mean to. They thought they were being kind when they made a big deal of his pottery. *Look what the cripple managed to do!* Maybe they didn't mean it like that, but that's what he always heard. He was cursed. He was damned. The gods hated him, and he knew with absolute certainty that he would continue to invisibly dig in the dirt until one day he died covered in a slurry of silt. That was all he could ever hope for, that was the best, and he also knew he should be grateful. Anyone other than Aria's son would have been abandoned to the forest when an infant. That didn't happen to him—this did.

As the gate opened, Gifford, dressed in shining armor and wearing a gleaming sword on his side, sat on a beautiful white horse and looked out across the Grandford Bridge at the great pillars flying the Instarya banners. Beyond them, he saw the campfires of a vast army—the army he was about to single-handedly challenge on behalf of . . . of his lady.

I'm a hero like in a story or an old song. Me—Gifford the Cripple, also known as the troll boy—but not tonight. Tonight I'm a warrior, riding out of wondrous gates to do battle with gods.

He smiled then.

The guard noticed. "You really do want to die, don't you?" He lingered, staring up at Gifford.

"No, but all people have to, and can you honestly think of a mo' beautiful way to go?"

The guard gave him a sidelong stare, wetting his lower lip. "Are you sure you're not an Instarya?"

Gifford shook his head. "Just the son of a bwave woman."

"At least you'll have the advantage of surprise," the soldier said. "They sure won't be expecting *you*."

Gifford turned. "What's yew name?"

"Plymerath, but my friends call me Plym." The soldier looked out at the elven camp and then back up at Gifford. "Are you *really* going to attempt to ride through that and bring back help for us?"

"I weel-ly am."

The soldier nodded. He switched the spear he held to his left and reached up with his right hand, holding his open palm out. "Then you can call me Plym."

Gifford reached down and shook his hand. "Thanks, Plym."

Gifford urged Naraspur forward.

"Good luck," Plym said. "I hope you make it. You know what? Even if you don't, I'm going to tell the story of the shining, mounted warrior who rode out the gates of Alon Rhist on a white horse to meet his destiny wearing a smile. How could I not? And while the story might die with us, for a short time you'll be a hero."

Gifford looked back, waiting for it, for the snide comment, or the parting kick. The *you're all right . . . for a cripple,* or even the *you're brave . . . for a Rhune.* Instead, he watched as Plym silently closed the gate.

Gifford was alone. He was heading for the bridge that spanned the Bern River gorge dressed in magic armor, with a magic sword, on the back of a magic horse. *Not at all what I expected to be doing today.*

Naraspur walked across the bridge, her hooves making a lonely clip-clop on the stone. Wasn't hard to stay on her when she walked. Gifford sat up. No wind—everything was eerily calm. The faint growl of the cascades far below in the Bern River sounded like a cat purring. Some of the spray carried up. He could feel the damp on his face. Little beads of moisture formed on Naraspur's mane. Overhead, stars sparkled, and a near full moon guided him, bathing the world in a pale light.

Your mother was special, Padera had told him, *and you're supposed to be special, too. I've taught you to fight. To fight when every single person around you would walk away. I've taught you to strive for the impossible because that's what you'll have to do. One day, you'll have to do the impossible, Gifford. One day you'll have to run faster and farther than anyone has because that is the only thing that will save our people. That's why your mother died, and I won't let her death be in vain.*

He never knew his mother. Wished he had. From the stories he had heard, Aria seemed like a good person, a brave person, the sort of person he wanted to be.

"We need to go vey-we fast," he whispered to Naraspur. "Do you un-da-stand? I'm gonna be holding on fo' my life, so you'll have to handle most of the stee-wing. But we gonna want to go that way." He pointed up the river where, just as Malcolm had said, an early morning mist grew. "You paying attention, wight? I'm just saying this because any way that isn't up that bank will get us both killed. You don't want that, do you? Do you even un-da-stand Whunic?"

He saw no movement in the camp. The fires were down to embers with no one near them. Most everyone was asleep, lying under blankets in the open or in tents. Gifford's bare feet hugged the horse's body as best they could, and as he reached the far side of the bridge, he lay down low and once more hugged Naraspur's neck. Now that he was to it, now that he faced the end, he felt a sickness in his stomach. He was scared.

I really don't want to die.

He thought once more of Roan, of her in the smithy as some monstrous Fhrey broke in. He might not kill her. Why would he? She wouldn't fight. She'd cower. No. He'd take her and make her his . . . slave.

Gifford's teeth clenched. "*Wun,*" he told Naraspur, and gave her a kick with his feet.

He was glad for the strength in his arms as the animal lunged forward. Another kick sent the horse from that already familiar but agonizing trot to a gallop. He held tight, squeezing with arms and legs. The gallop was better than the trot, smoother, but the speed was terrifying.

Naraspur cleared the bridge but was still heading due east—she hadn't been listening at all! He had to turn her. Risking a horrible fall, he drew his left hand up and, grasping the rein on that side, pulled her head toward the riverbank, aiming north.

Turn!

With reluctance, the horse finally got the hint and left the road. A moment later, he was in the elven camp, dashing between tents and smoldering fires. Gifford didn't look. No point in it. He stayed low, hugging tight to Naraspur's neck. He heard shouts and a horn. Something hit them. Something hot. He saw a burst of light. Smothering warmth enveloped them both. No pain, just a sound like a flock of birds taking to the sky. While Gifford thought Naraspur had been running at top speed, at that moment he discovered he was sorely mistaken. Leaping over a sleeping Fhrey, she bolted forward, faster than he ever thought possible. The rhythmic *thrump*, *thrump* of her hooves became peals of thunder as she advanced to a full, eye-watering sprint.

After the initial jolt, Gifford found it easy to stay on her back. They were moving at an impossible speed, and yet there wasn't any bouncing nor jerking—just a steady back and the rushing wind. Nevertheless, Gifford clung to Naraspur in life-loving terror. They were going too fast for him to see grass, or rocks, or dirt; everything was a smear of lights and darks. Gifford was moving so fast he could have been flying.

One day you'll have to run faster than any man ever has.

Two more bursts of fiery light exploded around him, which only served to drive Naraspur faster. He could hear her snorting, breathing hard, driven by fire and fear. With the river gorge on her left, she couldn't go that way, and the attacks coming from the right drove her north.

More shouts erupted, and everything became incredibly cold. Ice tried to form around them but faded as quickly as it appeared. Then wind swirled, kicking up dust and tearing down nearby tents. Elven soldiers raced toward them, but they were too late to catch the panicked Naraspur, who understood quite well the idea of running for her life.

Spears were thrown. At that speed, the odds of hitting him were impossible—he thought—only these weren't men. The Fhrey were maddeningly accurate. Strangely, this saved them both. A miss might have killed Naraspur, but of the five who tried, all aimed for Gifford, and all hit him square. Four struck Gifford's back, and one exceedingly well aimed javelin hit his head. The blow rang off his helm, but Gifford continued to hug tight to Naraspur, both arms around her neck as she flew.

The shouting grew fainter, their course less erratic. And gradually, little by little, Naraspur slowed down. Soon she was back to a trot and finally a walk.

Gifford opened his eyes and looked up.

He was in a field illuminated by the rising sun. He was also alone.

Looking back over the rump of the horse, he didn't see the elven camp. He'd made it through.

Ha! I survived!

Then he cursed his idiocy.

"We need to keep wunning!" he shouted at Naraspur, who was puffing for air. "Maybe not quite so fast, but mo' than this."

He gave her a few minutes to rest, and then turned her toward the rising sun and kicked her once more. Off they raced across the high plain toward the High Spear Valley and Perdif—riding as the first rays of morning light filled the sky.

CHAPTER NINETEEN

Drawing Swords

So often I have heard that war is a noble and necessary thing, the answer to many problems. But I have found that when war becomes a reality, peace becomes the noble and necessary thing because there is no problem greater than war.

—The Book of Brin

Malcolm walked into Nyphron's bedchamber as the lord of the Rhist was using the chamber pot.

"We need to talk," the slave said as if he had such a right. Nyphron even noticed a dash of demand in his voice.

Malcolm had been more useful than Nyphron had expected, but the Rhune was taking too many liberties with their relationship, which had started out cobweb thin and over the last few months had begun to fray. Malcolm had already served his purpose, but apparently he didn't know that.

"Indeed, we do," he replied. He got off the pot and entered the sitting room where he found Malcolm on the cushioned chair near the fireplace. His legs were stretched out, his arms folded across his chest, a stern look in his eye. *I've let this go on way too long. Give a slave a pair of shoes and they will walk all over you.* "Let's begin with how you're not allowed to enter my chambers unannounced. For that matter, let's go over the fact that you're not even allowed in the Kype anymore. You're a—"

"I want you to tell Arion and Suri to hide the archers," Malcolm instructed.

"What?"

"Tell them to hide the existence of Moya and her archers from the fane's army. Then tell Moya to concentrate her attacks on the Spider Corps."

Nyphron was too stunned to reply right away, and he just stood staring in disbelief. The little Rhune was giving him orders—*military* orders. "You don't make demands of me, *slave*."

Malcolm had the gall to roll his eyes. He actually looked annoyed.

I've ruined this one. I let him think too much of himself. Letting him breathe free air for so long has overinflated his little Rhune lungs and poisoned him with a taste for things he can't have. Why didn't I see it before? I might have done something, but now—

"We've been over this." Malcolm pointed to the missing collar that wasn't on his neck. "I'm not your slave. And if you recall, not even your father, who had the right to do so, treated me as one."

The callous disregard, the lack of respect, was too much. "We aren't in Rhulyn anymore. This is Alon Rhist, and here you *are* my property." Nyphron was shocked to see Malcolm smile, as if the man found the comment amusing. Nyphron sneered back. "Did I say something funny?"

"You might be forgetting that Alon Rhist is no longer under Fhrey control. In this place, my people already conquered yours, so I wouldn't be so quick to throw around terms like slavery, property, or who owns who or what. You might find yourself on the wrong end of that discussion."

Surprise, which had shifted to sympathy and then irritation, gave way to anger. "And you shall find yourself on the wrong end of my sword."

Malcolm replied with a humiliating look of pity.

Nyphron, not ever having been the object of such an expression—from a Rhune, no less—paused for a moment. Intuition told him he couldn't be so far off in his assessment. Something was wrong. Very wrong. When a strong defending force retreated too easily, he knew to expect a trap. When a warrior was overconfident, he knew to look for a secret, a hidden dagger or an associate hiding in wait. Malcolm was too relaxed, too sure of himself.

"I'm not joking, Nyphron," Malcolm said in an oddly stern tone. "You need to do it, and do so now before anything is given away."

Nyphron took a threatening step toward him. Most men, most Fhrey, would have cowered. Malcolm didn't even flinch.

What am I missing?

Malcolm's expression turned from pity to annoyance. "I understand that you think of me as a common slave. Understandable, given that you grew up in a household where I played such a role. I also realize you have an ego the size of Mount Mador, but you need to set that aside and do as I say. If you want to be fane, then listen. I didn't work this hard, for these many long years, to have you ruin everything because you see me as being beneath you."

"You *are* beneath me. Very, very far beneath me."

"Yes, fine. I'm beneath you. Now please go tell Arion to cloud the archers."

Nyphron felt the blood throbbing in his temple. He was rarely ever this angry when not swinging a sword. Still, he held back. Every fiber of his being was telling him not all was as it seemed. There was something here, something unexplained. Discovering a surprise of this magnitude hiding beneath his feet was shocking to the point of being frightening. Nyphron hadn't been scared in centuries. He had been a little worried when Gryndal exploded Stryker, and he admitted to himself—and only himself—that he'd been quite concerned in Arwal when they had been surrounded and Tekchin had nearly died, but he hadn't been frightened. Only the unknown had the power to scare him, and Malcolm was creeping into the Realm of the Scary. For one thing, Malcolm was right; Nyphron's father had never treated Malcolm like a slave. The only work Malcolm had ever done was serve wine at parties and meetings—a perfect way to listen to conversations, Nyphron just realized. For as far back as he could remember, Zephyron always treated Malcolm as—

As far back as I can remember?

Nyphron thought hard and was surprised to discover he couldn't recall exactly *when* Malcolm had come to Alon Rhist. The bulk of Nyphron's life had been spent afield. He had no idea when he first noticed his father had a new slave. As far as Nyphron was concerned, Malcolm came into existence only when Nyphron first devised his plan to have a Rhune kill Shegon. Nyphron needed a disposable person, and he'd just inherited his father's household, his servants, horses, and slaves. He picked one whose name happened to be Malcolm.

But he'd been around long before that. He must have been . . . but for how long? Was it before the bad winter? Yes, definitely before then. Was it before Tekchin got his scar? Nyphron thought it was. Further and further back he remembered seeing him.

I must be mistaken. It had to have been a different slave, wasn't it? It had to be. Rhunes don't live that long.

Watching him, Malcolm offered a gentle, sympathetic frown, the sort a mother might show a son who had skinned a knee. "Nyphron, I want you to succeed. I want you to be not merely the fane but the ruler of the world. You can usher in a new age and build a civilization where the divisions of the past are healed. I can help you do that, but you have to listen to my counsel."

"How *old* are you?" Nyphron asked.

Malcolm smiled. "Just putting that together now, are you? Doesn't bode well for your chances of being an intelligent ruler, does it? Your father noticed right away—but then your father would have been a better leader."

Malcolm slapped his thighs with his palms and sighed. "But he didn't listen to me, either. Of course, the very reason he didn't listen is the same reason he would have been a better ruler. I can't explain how frustrating that is. You, on the other hand, are nicely spoiled. You just *want*—and you don't care who has to suffer so you can *have*. It's just not in your character to notice those you consider beneath you—like me." Malcolm paused as if something on the ceiling caught his attention. He looked up long enough for Nyphron to glance up as well. There was nothing there. Then Malcolm said, "That's how you'll die, by the way. This underlying blindness will be your doom, and even my telling you won't change anything because you'll forget. You're far too set in your ways and far too full of yourself. But that's the way of things. The ultimate irony is that *good people* can't always do what is needed because what's often required is bad, and they wouldn't be *good people* if they did bad things, now would they?"

Nyphron was truly worried and wondered if he should get his sword. Malcolm wasn't a Rhune; nor was he Fhrey. The problem was he had no idea what Malcolm was. Somehow, this person had deceived everyone, maybe for centuries. No, not everyone. His father had known—must have—that was why he had treated Malcolm differently, but he never told anyone, never told his son. *Why?*

"Why didn't my father tell me about you?"

"Tell you what?" Malcolm pressed the tips of his fingers together. A decidedly sinister action, the sort of finger expression he'd expect from a Miralyith. *Is that it? Is Malcolm Miralyith? Is he just making himself look like he's Rhunic?* He'd heard of such things. Malcolm could be a spy sent by the fane—only—no. He had been in the Rhist too long. Fenelyus would have had to send him, and she was dead. And why would a spy help kill Shegon and raise the Rhunes in revolt against the Forest Throne?

"Why didn't my father warn me that you weren't really a Rhune, that you weren't his slave?"

"So, we *are* finally past that—good." Malcolm nodded in approval. "I honestly don't know why your father kept you in the dark. I actually thought he had told you, and maybe he did, and you just never heard. You do that, you know?"

"Who are you, and how did you come to serve my father?"

Malcolm sighed. "This list of questions will have to wait. I've already wasted too much time here. Sun is coming up and you have a battle to wage, the first real battle of a very long war. The first step of which is to order Arion to cloud the archers. Tell her and Suri not to interfere at all with the Spider Corps. They *will* pinpoint her if she does. But the Miralyith can't protect themselves from what they aren't expecting, and the Spider Corps have never seen arrows before. Send out the first legion—Raithe's command and—"

"We have a fortress; it doesn't make sense to send soldiers out beyond the protection of the walls."

"Have you seen the top of the Spyrok recently?" Malcolm asked. "These walls are no protection against the Spider Corps. Now, as I was saying, send Raithe out with his spearmen and have Moya bring her archers up behind. Have them push until she's in range, and then direct all fire on the Miralyith. Do that and you'll actually stand a chance of surviving to see another sunrise."

Malcolm got up, causing Nyphron to take another step back. The never-really-a-slave started for the door, then paused as he laid a hand to the latch. "I heard that Tesh saved your life."

Nyphron nodded.

"Still planning on killing the kid?"

"I . . . I don't know." Nyphron narrowed his eyes at Malcolm as he finally understood that the ex-slave hadn't brought the topic up on a whim. The realization dawned that Malcolm probably never brought anything up without a reason. "What do *you* think I should do?"

Malcolm smiled back at him. This was a different sort of smile. Not sad, not a pitiful look, and not a snide or sinister grin. This was a genuinely pleased expression. "Now you're getting this."

The men of the First Spear stood in the courtyard before the front gate: five hundred men, shoulder to shoulder, the faint light of the morning's new sun revealing grim, apprehensive faces. Raithe walked up and down the rows, checking gear. They'd done this drill once a week for four months, and yet still many had failed to fasten shoulder straps or helms properly. They were nervous, scared, and distracted, and Raithe couldn't blame them. Farmers, shepherds, woodsmen—they were all becoming warriors that day, gambling their lives. Dureyans had it easier; their lives were never worth much. But these men had left wives, children, homes, and land. They all trusted him. He was the God Killer. Looking from face to face, Raithe guessed that more than half wouldn't live to see the sun set—maybe none of them would.

Raithe had ordered the men of the First Spear to suit up and assemble at the front gate just before dawn. Malcolm had awakened him in the dark, relaying the order. But when Nyphron finally came down to the courtyard, he appeared surprised to find them waiting, and for reasons that eluded Raithe, Nyphron gave Malcolm a look that might have been suspicion. A moment later, Moya and her archers appeared, filing into the back of the yard among the practice dummies. For so many people in one place, the yard was disturbingly quiet. A few songbirds sang happy tunes, sounding out of place on this particular spring morning.

"I know you're nervous." Nyphron stood on the Speech Rock, what everyone called the conspicuous thumb of stone that jutted up near the north end of the lower courtyard. He spoke in a loud, confident voice. "A few of you—quite a few—are outright terrified. Don't worry. It's natural. Everyone goes through this, but trust me, you'll get past it. Just remember your training, and you'll be fine."

Says the one person in the yard who won't fight.

Raithe didn't care if Nyphron's god forbade Fhrey from killing Fhrey; he found it impossible to follow someone who wasn't willing to march out in front.

"Spear leaders?" Nyphron waved them over.

Although the Spears were filled with a mix of clansmen, each was commanded by a chieftain. Over the course of months, the men who served changed out as several went home to deal with farms and family. The same applied to the chieftains. Tegan of Warric and Harkon of Melen were the lucky ones on duty that month along with Raithe and Alward, who had no homes and were always there.

"Third Spear." Nyphron looked at Tegan of Warric as he drew a crude map in the dirt with a stick. "You'll wheel left after you cross the bridge. Try to form up here and hold that line as best you can. Second Spear"—he turned to Harkon of Melen—"in the same way, you'll wheel right and form up here." He drew a line in the dirt. "Remember to keep the men tight and in formation, three deep. Raithe, you'll take First Spear right up the center."

"Lucky me."

"Moya, I want you to follow First Spear. There's a rise on the plain, a natural hill that—"

"Wolf's Head," Raithe said.

"Right—Wolf's Head. That's where they'll position the Spider Corps." Nyphron pointed at Raithe. "Your goal is to push close enough to Wolf's Head so that Moya and her archers can rain death." He turned to Moya. "I can't emphasize enough how crucial you are in this. All the Miralyith will be bunched together, making your job easier, but if you fail to kill them— well, the war might end right here." Nyphron pointed to the parapet. "I'll fly flags on the wall. Black means to form up. Green is the order to attack. Blue indicates we have the advantage and you should press the attack. Red is the signal to retreat—but remember to retreat in an orderly manner. Don't let the men just run. You'll need to march back together in the same order as you marched out or more will die. Any questions?"

"Where is Persephone?" Raithe asked. "Why isn't she down here seeing us off? She is the keenig. It's her place, not yours."

Nyphron looked down at the dirt map for a moment and took a deep breath. "Keenig Persephone was attacked last night."

Several erupted in surprise, but none were louder than Raithe. He shoved his way past Alward and Tegan to confront the lord of the Rhist. "By who?"

"A raow. It slipped into her room and might have killed her if it hadn't been for Sebek and Tesh."

Raithe turned around to glare at Tesh, who stood in the crowd of soldiers, looking guilty. "You didn't tell me?"

"You were asleep," the kid said. "And it was over, and there was this big battle today, and—"

"Persephone was hurt, but she'll be fine," Nyphron assured everyone.

Raithe fumed. He whirled back at Nyphron. "So, a raow is allowed in the Kype, but I'm not?"

"It wasn't *allowed* in, and this proves the necessity for tight security, doesn't it?"

That smug look, that lie told right to his face. Raithe wanted to kill Nyphron at that moment more than he'd ever wanted to kill anyone. Security had nothing to do with it. The other chieftains petitioned for audiences and received them, but Raithe was always refused. Not refused—no, nothing so definitive—he was merely delayed, delayed indefinitely. For months, he'd believed Persephone didn't want to see him. That's what he'd been told, and foolishly he believed it. Looking at Nyphron, he was now certain Persephone had become a prisoner in the Kype. Nyphron was keeping them apart, turning her into a puppet.

Maybe not even a puppet. Maybe there was no raow. What is to stop him from killing her and saying he's taking orders from her? She might already be dead.

Raithe took a step forward and glared at Nyphron. "After this battle, I'm seeing her whether you like it or not. Bar the door to the Kype, and I'll get Suri to melt that Tetlin bronze to a puddle. Do you understand?"

"We're all on the same side here," Nyphron said. "We're all allies in this fight."

"I doubt that. I'm not even sure you know what the word *allies* means."

"I'm not your enemy, Raithe," he said this with a steady, reassuring calm. "The *elves* are outside the walls."

Raithe narrowed his eyes. *One battle at a time.*

Tekchin found Moya near the front gate.

"I'm going with you," he said.

Moya jumped. He had a knack for sneaking up on her. "No, you're not. You're lousy with a bow."

Moya was filling her sack from the pile of arrows stacked under the parapet ledge. In only a few months, Roan had worked wonders. There were thousands, maybe tens of thousands, of the feathered shafts, each with a metal tip provided by Roan and her army of smiths. As with the bows, armor, and swords, Roan had taught others her methods, and they in turn worked each day adding to the pile. Moya's own bow—which she had named Audrey after her late mother because they were both so tightly strung—had been made by Roan from the heartwood of Magda. The weapon was special, believed by many to be magical. *How else could Moya—a woman—be so proficient with a weapon?*

"I don't need a bow. I'll be your Shield," he told her.

"Shields don't have Shields. You want to be a Shield, sub for me with Persephone. She needs protecting, and I can't be in two places at once."

"But Persephone isn't you."

Moya paused with a fist full of arrows and turned. "What's that supposed to mean?"

"You know what it means."

She dropped the arrows in the sack and slung the strap over her shoulder. "No, I don't. Enlighten me."

He frowned. "I'd be very upset if something happened to you."

Moya smirked. "Of course you would. But don't worry, spring is here, so you won't need me to keep you warm at night anymore. I'm sure there are plenty of Fhrey girls you can—"

"I don't want them. I want you."

"Why?" she asked, and looked Tekchin in the eye, daring him.

"Because I have feelings for you. I care about you."

"Not good enough." She hooked a skin of water around her neck and turned to her bowmen. "Filson," she shouted. "Make sure everyone has water."

"What do you want me to say?" Tekchin asked, frustrated.

She didn't mean to be cruel. *She* knew how he felt; Moya just wasn't certain if *he* did. "I don't want you to say anything. I just want to know if there's anything *you* want to say?"

"If I say it now, it'll be coerced."

She nodded. "I can see that."

"Then just let me say this instead." Tekchin circled an arm around her waist and pulled her tight. Holding her head, he kissed her hard. When he finally let up, she was desperate for air.

Taking a breath, Moya felt dazed. She nodded. "Very well put."

Tesh joined Raithe at the gate with the rest of the men, wearing a water skin and his dual swords. He was as tall as any of them, taller than some. Being sixteen made him a man in almost everyone's eyes, but to Raithe, he was still a kid.

"You aren't going," Raithe told him as he adjusted the placement of his knife on his waist belt.

"What do you mean?" The kid was a ball of energy, bouncing on his feet.

"I mean you aren't going. You're staying here."

"I'm a soldier in the First Spear, and I'm your Shield."

"And you aren't going."

Tesh's mouth hung open as his brows crashed down in disbelief. "Why?"

Raithe knocked on his own helm and then his breastplate. "You don't have any armor."

Tesh looked at the men in line—at his fellow spearmen—as if expecting them to speak up, to come to his defense. None said a word. They weren't even looking in his direction. "But Roan wouldn't make any for me. Said I had to wait until I stopped growing."

"No one without armor can go."

Again, Tesh sought help from his brothers-in-arms. Finding none, he turned to the walls of the fortress for understanding. "But that's stupid."

"It's not, and you can't go."

"Moya's archers don't have armor."

"Arion and Suri will be hiding them from the Miralyith."

Raithe picked out a spear from the rack. He didn't have a favorite. Spears weren't personal friends the way swords were. Weapons were different the way cats were different from dogs. People had a preference for one or the other. Raithe was a dog, sword, beer, loner sort. Spear people were strange. Malcolm was a spear person, and Raithe never could figure him out.

"How can you say that?" Tesh exploded. He threw his arms out and pointed to the men he moments before had turned to for help. "I've practiced harder than anyone. I'm better than all of them." Tesh took a step toward Raithe and glared. "I'm a better warrior than you are!"

Raithe nodded. "Maybe."

"You can't do this to me."

"Already done."

"I have a right to fight."

Raithe planted the butt of his newly chosen spear on the ground and looked at Tesh. "I'm your chieftain and your commander. You'll do as I say."

Tesh gritted his teeth, his eyes bulging, and he growled until he shouted as if in agony. "Why?" he yelled, his voice going too high. "I don't need armor. You've seen me fight. They won't touch me."

"They don't have to. You think we only have to worry about swords and spears? The battle would be a lot easier if that were the case." Raithe took his helm off and showed Tesh the runes etched inside. "This armor doesn't just protect against blades. You weren't at Dahl Rhen. You didn't see what they can do with a snap of their fingers. If you go out there unprotected, you'll be helpless—and dead long before we reach those blades you're so certain can't touch you."

"It's not fair!"

"Congratulations on identifying today's lesson." Raithe put his helm back on. "Life isn't fair. And don't worry if you don't learn it this time around. That lesson will come up again and again."

The beautiful blue sky began to darken. The courtyard fell into shadow as unnatural clouds stretched overhead. Raithe had seen this act before. So had the other survivors of Dahl Rhen.

"Find cover!" Raithe shouted at Tesh. "First Spear! March!" He ran forward. "Open the gate!"

CHAPTER TWENTY

The Battle of Grandford

The Battle of Grandford is remembered in song and story; a legend of mythic heroes and villains, an allegory of truth and courage; a rallying cry for a people. It is important to know that the Battle of Grandford got its name and reputation months after the fighting ended, bestowed by people who were not there. I am not saying there were not heroes, or that it was not a time of courage, only that the names of the heroes are wrong and the truths forgotten—and that the lessons of that day have yet to be learned.

—THE BOOK OF BRIN

The two forward towers that guarded the front gate of Alon Rhist were each far smaller than the Spyrok. The southern tower was known affectionately as the Downriver Tower. The northern one went by a less amiable nickname: the Frozen Tower, since it caught the brunt of the north winds and had no fireplace to warm it. At the base were a few tables, places for soldiers to gamble and drink, but in the small room at the top, there wasn't anything to sit on. Suri and Arion were forced to stand along the crenelated balcony, exposed to the wind and what, according to the clouds, was soon to be rain.

"Spider Corps?" Suri asked, pointing up at the sky.

Arion nodded. "Warming up for the show that's about to start."

"We don't do anything about that?"

Arion shook her head. "According to Nyphron, we don't do anything except hide the archers."

"But . . ." Suri looked up. She could sense the power draw, feel it like a breeze rushing past her face. "They're going to demolish this place."

"Maybe not."

Suri turned and looked toward the back of the fortress. She tilted her head up to view the severed remains of the Spyrok, the broken finger with a jagged pinnacle. Only one person had died in that attack. Most of the debris had been blown off the back of the fortress and rained down the barren hillside.

"No runes up there," Arion pointed out.

"None here, either." Suri gestured in a circle at their room, nothing but an observation deck with a wooden floor and a trap door in its center. An empty cask lay on its side in the far corner, surrounded by discarded cups, one of which had shattered. Someone *had* carved symbols into the wooden floor and even in the merlons, but the marks were profanities instead of runes.

"If there were, we couldn't do our job, now could we?"

"And we just have to hide the archers?"

"Actually, I'm going to do that," Arion said. "You're just going to watch."

Suri narrowed her eyes, puzzled. "If the Spiders can join their power, why can't we?"

"Oh, we could. I just don't want to."

Suri felt a sting of rejection.

"Don't look so hurt," Arion said with a frown. She took Suri's hand and gave it a light squeeze. "I just don't want them to know about you."

Suri liked the warmth of her fingers and was reminded of how long it had been since she had enjoyed the comfort of hugging Minna. Few things in the world were as good as plowing her face into white fur and feeling the beating heart within. Touch—physical contact—was more important than it seemed, but such things were never evident until they were lost.

Suri looked again at the sky and, remembering the lightning bolts in the forest, asked, "Should we go down a floor? Feels a little exposed here."

"Shouldn't be a problem. Hiding the archers is a very small thing. With all the siphoning they're doing, they won't notice."

"You weren't doing *anything* when you stood next to Magda."

"True, but I also wasn't paying attention. That's where you come in." Arion smiled and gave her hairless brows a mischievous quiver.

Strange that Arion was in such a good mood considering what was about to happen. Suri sensed a dullness between them, a wall of separation. Arion was visible to her eyes, but not to the Art. She was shielding herself against the forces of the fane, a prudent measure, but she was also blocking Suri. Maybe it was all one and the same, yet Suri suspected those cheery eyes and the whimsical smile were another veil hiding Arion's true feelings.

"Where I come in?" Suri asked.

"You'll be able to tell if they pinpoint me. You'll feel it. When they focus, it will be like the hairs on your neck will stand. Hard to miss, really. If you feel that, shield us. Just throw up a block like I taught you. Keep it tight and it ought to be able to resist them long enough for me to help. And if we must, we can run down the stairs to the safe room at the bottom." She was referring to the base of the tower that had Orinfar runes ringing it. Suri didn't like passing through that area, which felt like she was underwater. She couldn't feel the world the way she normally did until she climbed up above the safe room. "And if you feel your shield weaken, jump down, you understand? Don't wait for me."

"Why would I wait for you?" She grinned. Suri could play the unconcerned game, too.

Stepping to the edge of the tower, Suri looked down. The gate was open and the first of their soldiers began to pour out onto the bridge. "What about the bridge? Won't they destroy it?"

"How would they get in here, then?"

Suri thought a moment. "What if they don't want to get in here? What if they just want us all dead?"

This caused Arion to pause. She looked unsure, then said, "Let's hope that's not the case."

The sun was rising as Raithe led the men of the First Spear out of the bronze gates and across the Grandford Bridge. Looked like any other day—better even. Things he would normally take for granted all screamed for his attention: the way the light was so bright and golden, how dew glistened on everything in fine droplets, the blueness of the sky, and the warm and fragrant air. The little things were saying goodbye.

Raithe walked at the head of the army as any good chieftain should. The first target, the first casualty—these were the risks associated with privilege. Raithe had never gotten the lodge or the feasts, he only had a clan of one, maybe two—he still didn't know where Malcolm fit—but this *privilege* of being first in battle he had received often, at least since he had arrived in Dahl Rhen.

He tilted his head down slightly, the brim of his helmet blocking the glare of the sun—Roan thought of everything. On his left arm was the Dherg shield complete with runes; the design had been copied on all the new iron shields. Some of the men painted pictures on theirs. The less talented went with a big *X* or *T*; the more adept painted lions or dragons. Wedon, his First Spearman, had painted a target bullseye, saying he'd rather they hit it than him. Raithe left his blank. He liked the way it shone.

He would have bet against his reaching the far side of the bridge but imagined the gods enjoyed absurd poetics. Raithe, the quiet son of Herkimer, who had promised his sister and mother he wouldn't be like his father, would fall in battle on the plains of Dureya less than a day's walk from where he was born. Having accomplished nothing, making no difference to anyone, his failure couldn't possibly be more complete. And yet he walked quickly. Raithe, who had never before taken pleasure from a fight, was eager for this one. An explosion had been building in him for months. Frustrations caused by a shut door had wound him tight, and the coil screamed to be unleashed. If not for the fane's army, it would have been Nyphron. With luck, he would die and be free of it all.

They reached the far side of the bridge without incident. The only indication the elves knew they were coming was the darkening sky. Early morning looked like twilight. As they cleared the bridge, Raithe saw the fane's army—the rows and rows of tents set in perfect squares. In front, in gleaming bronze, stretched lines of elven soldiers. Two thousand formed a wall of spears and shields.

"It's too wide," Wedon told Raithe. "Too wide for us to form three-deep. They'll fold around. They'll flank us easy."

Raithe was impressed by the old farmer's transformation into a thinking soldier. "But it's thin. Look there." He gestured with his spear to a rise where a group of Fhrey gathered. "That hill, that's Wolf's Head. That's our objective. We aren't here to win, we just need to open a path and get close enough for Moya to hit that hill. Our three-deep will give us the endurance to get there."

"And our flanks?"

"Order the ends to fold."

"And if they surround us? How do we get back out?"

What makes you think we ever had any chance to get back?

Wedon sounded like a soldier, but he wasn't—not yet—and he certainly wasn't Dureyan. The thought of surviving a battle was far too optimistic.

Accept that you're going to get hurt, that you're going to die; embrace it, and you'll find the freedom to live. This was one of the many ridiculous things his father had told him that sounded less stupid every day.

"We'll make a full square if we have to."

"Not very smart tactically, but . . ." Malcolm gave Wedon a crazy grin. "Not much chance of anyone breaking and running."

"Would have thought something would have happened by now," Tope said, his head tilted up so he could stare at the clouds.

"Waiting for all of us to come out," Raithe told them. "Trying to lure us away from the safety of our warren. Probably overjoyed that we're leaving the walls."

They reached the edge of the crest. Raithe called for the break order, and the column fanned out. Each soldier took his prearranged place in a set of three rows, one behind the other. Raithe stood in the center, Wedon on his right, Malcolm on his left. Tope Highland and Gavin Killian stood side by side, their eldest sons Colin and Hanson with them. Their younger sons were in the second row with Wedon's boys, Bruce Baker, Gilroy, and Konniger's brother-in-law, Fig. Bergin and Heath Coswall were in the third row back. All of them stood with shields shining against the morning light, helms high, spears with butts on the ground. They really did look like an army.

Next came the following columns led by Tegan, who broke right, and Harkon, who broke left, forming up in the same fashion as Raithe's soldiers. Wedon was correct; the Fhrey line was much wider. Last came Moya and her archers, who fell in behind Raithe. Once in position, the world stood still—everything except the sky.

Everyone waited on Raithe. Even the elves waited. His was the final action—his order would call the clash and see hundreds killed. Feeling the weight of that great lever, Raithe looked back at the fortress. The black flags had been exchanged for green. Everything was on him.

Raithe thought of his father.

Maybe he'd misjudged the man. The way Herkimer frequented the High Spear battles, Raithe had always believed that his father and brothers were killers who longed for blood. Raithe had tried his best to avoid becoming like them, and here he was at the center of a line, in the middle of a battle, at the start of a war. Maybe his father hadn't wanted to be in his battles, either. Maybe he, too, only ever wanted a bit of land in a quiet meadow where his family could live in peace. War had a way of enslaving a man who had a talent for fighting. Battle was what Herkimer was good at, and just like Raithe, that talent gave him a home he'd never sought. Raithe imagined his father had stood many times where he was, in the middle of a line of men facing a wall of spears, and for that one brief instant as he raised his arm, he felt . . . perhaps not love but . . . understanding. In that understanding, he found forgiveness. And with the lowering of his arm, the war officially began.

A moment later, Raithe was hit by lightning.

Moya jumped and let out an undignified scream when the first lightning bolts hit. One after another, they rained out of the clouds, crashing with blinding flashes and followed by chest-rattling thunder. She watched as man after man was struck and illuminated brilliantly in the dim cloud-covered world. Raithe was the first hit, and Moya felt her heart stop, realizing he was dead. Gelston's luck—if it could have been called luck—was too rare a thing to happen twice. When the flash left her eyes, she expected to see a charred husk laying on the thin grass. Instead, she saw a miracle.

Raithe hadn't even faltered.

The man walked forward as if nothing had happened, and the rest of the army followed. Looking around, she saw that all of those struck remained on their feet. The elves saw it, too, and soon balls of fire rained from the sky, bursting through ranks of men. The soldiers hesitated, and some flinched, but the flames did nothing.

The runes.

Protected only by a leather tunic, Moya felt horribly naked. Neither she nor any of her archer auxiliaries wore metal or runes. No one had expected them to march into battle. In retrospect, Moya realized no one knew what to do with them. Archers had never been used in warfare, but the original idea had been for her cohort to stay within the protection of the walls and shoot down at the attackers. At the last minute, Nyphron had come up with the idea of sending them out behind the Spears to attack the Miralyith. Being outside the walls was bad enough, but he also told them they couldn't wear runes. The plan was for Arion and Suri to hide them, and they couldn't do that if runes protected the archers from the Art. He'd given his assurances they'd be safe, but Moya found that difficult to swallow. Luckily, the terrible light show was centered on the forward lines. Not a single bolt hit any of her archers. Thunder boomed, and flashes of lightning rained on Raithe's, Tegan's, and Harkon's men as they advanced across the open space, but those with bows walked under a quiet sky.

Fire came next. Great waves of flames washed over the front lines, so hot Moya felt her skin prickle. These sputtered out as Raithe and his front line closed on the enemy. Then Moya heard a new sound: the scream of metal on metal as men and elves clashed.

"Shouldn't we shoot?" Engleton asked.

"Our orders are to wait until we can hit that hill," Moya replied.

"But we could—"

"We wait."

. . .

With spears thrown, Raithe and the rest of the front line fought with sword and shield. Packed in a line, Raithe was elated to find that the greater mobility and speed of the elves was limited. Strength, courage, and sheer weight pushed the line forward. In these simple virtues, men were superior to Fhrey. He could see it—those beautiful sky-eyes were scared to die. He couldn't blame them. Men gambled with a few dozen miserable years of dirt, sweat, and cold, but elves risked thousands of years of ease.

Only a handful of thrown spears had done damage. The Fhrey were too agile. Raithe wasn't the first to kill. That distinction went to Malcolm, who slew the Fhrey across from him with a well-timed jab from Narsirabad. Despite all the iron, Malcolm still retained the old spear he'd taken from Dahl Rhen's lodge. Raithe killed his opponent a few seconds after. Wedon slew his, and they pushed forward a step, leading with their shields, driving with longer, stronger legs.

For all the training, for all the technique, there was little finesse in warfare. Formed in tight lines, violence came in two forms: slamming the shield and jabbing the sword. Raithe felt the effort just as much in his legs as his arms as he kept them bent, giving him the power to shove forward, driving the Fhrey off-balance. He discovered that an off-balance Fhrey was a dead one.

Blood sprayed. Men grunted and screamed—so did the Fhrey.

Some think the Fhrey, Dherg, and Rhunes are all related. Malcolm's words spoken a lifetime ago came back to him. He couldn't believe it then, but deadly combat—the simplicity, the totality, the desperation—changed his mind about a great many things.

You never truly know someone until you fight them, his father had often said. *Supposedly brave men are unmasked as cowards, and quiet, unassuming souls are revealed as heroes. Truths are exposed amidst blood.* The Fhrey were no different from men. This revelation swallowed him even as he fought. He knew he'd discovered something important, brushed against the profound, but he also knew he didn't know what that was, and before long the demands of battle smothered ideas with the practical needs of survival.

Exhausted and nearly blind with all the sweat and blood filling his eyes, Raithe called the switch. The front line stepped back, exchanging positions with the second line that moved up with renewed vigor and shoved forward in a burst of aggression. Even better than in training, the third line advanced, letting Raithe and his row sink farther back. There, they wiped their faces, took deep breaths, and swigged water from shoulder-slung skins. Looking around, Raithe found Malcolm still beside him, but Wedon was missing. So was Hanson, Killian's eldest. Old Killian had a worried look as he searched up and down the ranks.

Behind them, Moya and her archers walked at a slight distance.

Just as Wedon had predicted, the flanks swung in, but Tegan and Harkon had wheeled around and were holding them off as best they could, and their best was excellent. They appeared to be gaining ground. Crazy, buoyant thoughts of survival rose as Raithe saw their little force of men ripping through the elven lines. They had momentum. They were winning. If they caused a rout, the battle—the war itself—might be won that day.

Then the giants came.

Moya felt the ground shake with footfalls. Vast tremors caught everyone's attention. They came from the rear of the Fhrey lines, the same hulking monsters that had attacked Dahl Rhen. These were the big ones, standing three and four stories high, with fists the size of Roan's wagons. Wielding great stone axes and hammers, they cleared swaths in the lines of men. Bodies were thrown in the air. Helmets came off along with arms and legs. The forward push halted as the giants, acting as breakwaters, turned the tide.

Moya looked toward the Wolf's Head. She could see the rise, a barren patch in the center of the field, an exposed gray rock. On it, rings of Fhrey encircled one who stood in the center, a conductor flailing his arms, directing the others. They moved and writhed in concert, performing some rehearsed ritual. The lightning had ended, and the fires were gone. Moya couldn't imagine what they might be doing, but also couldn't imagine it was a good idea to leave them to it. They were still too far away—even for Audrey, even if Moya wound her tight. Raithe looked at her. She knew what he was thinking.

This might be as far as we can get. Tell me it's good enough.

It wasn't, and she shook her head.

Raithe frowned and his shoulders slumped, but he nodded.

Then Moya saw a giant turn their way. Raithe's cohort had pushed the hardest, driven the deepest into the Fhrey and made itself the biggest threat. As a reward, they drew the biggest giant. Large as an old tree, he charged the center line.

Raithe gave her one last look, a sad one, as he shouted, "First Principal forward!" Then he rushed ahead to take his place once more at the front.

The giant, dressed in patchwork rags and sporting a bushy beard and a thin-lipped sneer, swept men away like dirt from the floor. The only consolation was his speed, or lack thereof. Raithe knew it took a lot of time to get that much weight in motion. Once the giant made a swing, there were several beats before the return stroke. Fighting a hammer-wielding mountain had never been on the list of things Raithe's father taught him. The Galantians had skipped the lesson as well. Wasn't like he had a lot of options. All Raithe could do was attack the thing's feet. In that window between strokes, Raithe sprinted forward and shoved straight down; he pierced the beast in the foot with his sword just behind its big toe.

Grenmorian flesh was no tougher than a man's—softer even, since the bones were spread out—and the iron blade went deep. The giant howled and jerked, which for a slow behemoth was more of a slow lift of his weight-bearing foot. This did two things. As Raithe refused to lose his sword and hung on with all his might, the blade was pulled down, dragging razor sharp iron. He would have severed the toe but couldn't cut through the bone. Still, it caused the giant to stumble, which was good and bad. The mountain staggered—didn't look as if he had great balance to start with. The giant wavered, swaying back and forth. Formed in lines of combat, men and their elven enemy had no hope of dodging bed-sized feet. Dozens, maybe more, died beneath that monster's dance. Shining gems crushed underfoot, crackling like ice crystals.

The line broke. In panic, men and elves gave up their positions in favor of survival. The fight disintegrated into a melee, careful jabs replaced with wild swings. The giant continued to waver, tilting first toward the human line, then the Fhrey. Each combatant was forced to swing and block with one eye on their enemy and one eye on the teetering mountain. Raithe alone charged the giant. He tried to read the pattern of weight-shift. Anticipating where the next foot might fall, he ran for that spot. The odds were even that the foot would land either beside him or on him—no telling which. This sort of gamble, the overextension that left him vulnerable but could possibly win the fight, was one he'd learned to make in combat. Most men refused to take such risks. That was the strength of the Dureya, and the weakness of the Fhrey. Risk was the secret ingredient in combat— timidity invited death. Quite often risk invited death, too. Death welcomed everyone.

The foot came down close enough that Raithe felt the wind. Lunging and using both hands, Raithe slashed across the big tendon running up the back of the leg from the giant's heel. The cord was the thickness of a heavy rope, but in his hand he held much more than a stone spear. The same iron blade that broke the bronze sword in Tirre made the difference once more. The giant sounded like a howling wind on a frigid winter's night—a chilling cry that carried. With no support, the great tree fell. While it could have been better, it could have been worse. The giant crashed across both sides. Twelve people died instantly. Dozens scattered.

"Re-form the line!" Raithe shouted.

Wedon miraculously reappeared as he and Malcolm found Raithe and slammed shoulders with his. Both men were panting and slick with blood. He had no idea whose.

"Stay close, Moya!" he yelled. "Shield brace!" he cried and drove the line forward at a run.

We're going to succeed or die in the attempt!

The Fhrey hastily shuffled to defend as shields collided. Men were stronger and had momentum, but elves had elevation. Seeing the rush, fearing the penetration dividing their force, horns blew. Raithe saw the heads of giants turn and take their first lumbering strides toward them.

Finally, he thought with an odd relief, *this is where we die.* The Grenmorian herd ambled their way—his prize for being successful.

Then from behind him Raithe heard Moya. "Close enough."

The shot would be uphill, not at all ideal. There was also a wind, but not a whirlwind. If the Fhrey had had any idea what was coming, they might have raised a hurricane. Of course, if the Fhrey knew what was coming, Moya and her archers would have been charred in some magical fire. Instead, it was just the normal spring blow coming across the plateau, and Moya knew how to compensate.

"Aim just to the right of the hill!" she shouted over the cry of metal and men. "Don't watch the fly. As soon as you loose, fit the next shaft and draw!"

She clapped an arrow against the carved wood of Audrey's face, fitting the notch into the string. "Draw deep, aim high!" she shouted.

In five rows, fifty archers raised their bows and pulled. She heard the combined creak of wood, the angry growl of vengeful trees.

"Loose!" she yelled, and in one chorus, half a century of iron-tipped shafts flew.

"Load!" Moya shouted instantly. She already had her next arrow fitted. "Draw! Loose!"

The second volley was in the air before the first landed. From a distance and under the cloud-covered sky, the flights of arrows appeared like dark sheets of rain falling on Wolf's Head where a ring of Fhrey writhed and chanted. Too far to hear them over the closer chaos, Moya watched robes crumple. Those not hit looked up, confused, only to spot another shower of arrows.

Wolf's Head became a barren rock.

Freed up from her required assignment, Moya looked around. Two giants charged Raithe's line. They came on like bull moose, but many times larger. One on the left held two stone hammers. One on the right wore what looked to be a great metal pot on his head.

"Giants!" Moya cried, and pivoted her aim. Fifty archers mimicked her. "Draw! Loose!"

The burst of shafts didn't have far to travel this time. Nearly every arrow found its target, and the left giant dropped, as if he'd slammed into a wall.

The remaining giant reached the line and smashed through, wading into the formation and bashing men aside with a massive hammer. Moya watched as Wedon and Raithe were both struck and swept aside. They flew into Malcolm, and all of them went down.

Next up were the Killian boys, Wedon, and Tope's younger sons, who tried to stab at his legs but failed. The giant charged the archers, breaking through the lines of men as if they were waves on a beach.

"Draw!" Moya shouted, and heard the reassuring yawn of wood. She had no need to give the target; everyone saw the charging hulk looming overhead. "Loose!"

Fifty arrows leapt from strings with a stuttered *thwack!*

Moya's shot entered the giant's right eye. Others pierced his throat, mouth, and chest. Dead before the fall, the giant collapsed a few feet in front of Moya. The huge pot-helmet—the size of a bathtub—skipped and rolled, stopping at her feet.

Moya put a foot on its rim and prepared for another flight against the Spider Corps, but Wolf's Head remained empty of targets.

Lines of battle were a memory. The fight slipped into the chaos of a haphazard brawl where men paired off with elves, and the two sides mixed. In these one-on-one contests, the elves held the advantage, and Moya watched as more and more human bodies covered the grass.

Looking back at the walls of Alon Rhist, Moya spotted red banners.

"Fall back!" she shouted. "Grab the wounded and fall back to the fortress!"

Bergin lifted his head at the sound of her shout, then yelled, "Third rank, form up and bear the retreat!"

They tried to re-form. Bergin, the onetime brewer of bad beer, valiantly called to those around him to square shoulders, but the battle had moved beyond tactics. With the lines broken and spread out, death was certain. All that remained was for the elves to press their advantage.

They didn't.

In stunned wonder, Moya watched as the Fhrey let them go. Just as eager to disengage, the Fhrey fell back. A horn was blowing from the tents on the plateau. *How long has that been sounding?* Moya had no idea, but elves were falling back, and no more giants came their way. Grabbing their own wounded and dead, the forces of Alon Rhist withdrew from the field. Only then did Moya notice how it had changed. The whole plain that had once been a dull dirty yellow of sunbaked grass and bare dirt was scarlet red. Blood shimmered under the full face of a midday sun shining in a clear sky.

Midday? But it's just morning? It still has to be. I'm soaked with dew.

Moya looked and discovered it wasn't dew. Only then did the full force of the battle arrive. She'd seen the men dying, seen the blood, but until the clash of metal quieted and the screams became moans, until she had the chance to recognize the smell in her nose as blood, none of it had seemed real. With the warmth of the overhead sun, while standing in a field thick with bodies, Moya felt sick. Her hands shook, her legs weakened, but she managed to keep walking. She focused on the bridge, on the ford, and the great bronze gates of Alon Rhist.

The first day of the Battle of Grandford was over.

CHAPTER TWENTY-ONE

Casualties

We called it a victory the way in late winter we would call a bowl of thin soup a feast.

—THE BOOK OF BRIN

Mawyndulë had watched the battle at his father's side. The two had stood in front of the fane's tent where tables and chairs had been set up, spread with bowls of fresh berries, cheese, wine, and bread. Everyone had expected a party with a show—a display to entertain the fane. By midday, the tables had been knocked over, the berries scattered on the ground.

"What happened?" Lothian asked in a voice so calm it was eerie.

Before him stood a member of the Spider Corps, a middle-aged Miralyith holding a stick. Mawyndulë didn't know his name. His white asica had been sprayed red on one side, as if a huge bag of red wine had burst beside him. But the color wasn't right—less purple, more scarlet.

"We don't—" He faltered, reached up, and wiped his face, leaving a smear of blood across his brow. "Aren't sure. Everything . . . everything was . . . it was fine—working as planned, I mean. Then nothing worked.

Same as when that rider came through. The lightning didn't kill and the fire didn't . . . nothing worked at all—" He gasped for breath and ran the same hand through his hair leaving another streak of red.

Just stop touching your face! Mawyndulë thought, grimacing. *I have to look at you.*

"We couldn't understand it," the blood-covered Spider continued. "Then everyone just fell dead. I remember hearing a . . . a whistle, this wisp of air, and then everyone collapsed. No, not everyone, I guess. Some tried to run, only we didn't know where. We didn't know what was happening. It wasn't the Art. We sensed nothing—absolutely nothing. And a second later I saw them, these tiny spears falling out of the sky. I saw one go through Kasimer's skull." He held out a stick that was thin and straight, with feathers on one end and a metal tip on the other. "This is what killed us."

Mawyndulë's father didn't touch it. He just stared in disgust. "How many? How many Spiders are still alive?"

"Five, but Lym might not survive. He has one of these through his chest."

"They knew just how to hit us," Taraneh said. The Lion commander scowled, looking out at the field where bodies were being dragged.

"Of course they did," the fane snapped. "They had Arion and that Instarya rebel directing their assault. What about her? Did you kill *her?*"

The Spider shook his head. "We searched, cast nets, but found nothing. She didn't appear to take part in the battle."

Probably too terrified, Mawyndulë thought. She hid in that fortress, quivering now that the fane had come. That was the way with teachers, so smart when bullying a student, but in the real world that didn't work. Arion only knew how to juggle, make string patterns, and berate students for not paying attention. She was in trouble, and she knew it. *Swim out too deep, and I'm going to help pull you down.*

Mawyndulë stared at the stick in the Spider's hand. Not the one that killed Kasimer. The wood was clean; the point had a bit of dirt on it—so small and thin, just a tiny javelin. He could snap it in half, and yet these had decimated the Spider Corps in seconds. Mawyndulë couldn't help feeling shocked. Death was still a new concept for him, and the death of Miralyith was particularly disturbing.

How would it feel to have one of these sticks penetrate my skull?

And yet, Mawyndulë hadn't known any of the dead. He'd seen their faces, heard them speak to each other, but just as at home in the Talwara, Mawyndulë didn't socialize much. He actually juggled better than he made friends. Several years before, after a failed attempt to interest one of the younger guards in a game of Snakes and Hawks, he came to the sound conclusion that he shouldn't have friends. As heir to the Forest Throne, it was better that he didn't, less chance of favoritism that way. Mawyndulë saw it as his sacrifice for his people. Isolation was his gift. His experience with Makareta had chiseled that notion in stone. And once Jerydd started yakking in his head, he actively avoided others so he could talk back and not be viewed as insane. Outside of his father, the only one he spoke to was Treya. After his first trip abroad with Gryndal, he insisted that his servant join him. Mawyndulë was tired of fetching his own meals.

Arion was involved. There's no other way they could have managed it. Jerydd's voice startled Mawyndulë once again, although the only outward sign was a slight wince.

"Something wrong?" his father asked.

"No—just, well, it's disturbing."

His father nodded, looking at the tiny spear in the Spider's hand.

You don't have to keep me a secret. Your father might actually like to know you wield the might of Avempartha, especially now that most of his Spiders are dead.

"They took down the giants with these as well," Taraneh said. "I would think they could kill our soldiers even easier, and from such a distance, our troops could do nothing but act as targets. I imagine when we try to attack those walls, they will line the parapets and rain death on everyone who approaches. I would."

"How did they block the Art?" the fane asked. "Why didn't the lightning and fire affect them?"

I understand. You like the secret. You enjoy being special.

"Fetch a Rhune helm for the fane!" Taraneh shouted.

One of the Bear Legion soldiers trotted over carrying a bloody helm.

"Show him the inside."

The Bear spun the helmet around. Mawyndulë expected a gory mess, but the interior was clean. A strap and buckle hung from it and the inside netting was riveted, but underneath the netting were markings.

"Notice the runes?"

"Dherg markings," Lothian said. "The Dherg were rumored to have discovered a way to block the Art, something they called the Orinfar. We never knew what it was, only that their little underground warrens resisted us."

"These could be it."

"Dhergs, Instarya, tutors—is *everyone* helping these Rhunes? How massive is this confederacy?"

"Clearly, they are not as simpleminded as previously believed. This war appears well planned. I think there may be a real danger here, my fane."

Lothian took the stick from the Spider. "Obviously there is a danger."

"No, my fane, I meant . . ." He hesitated. "I think there is a chance we could lose."

Lose. That one word hung in a field of following silence. Those few who weren't looking—the servants cleaning up the mess of berries, the Spider Corps representative who had been trying to clean himself with his asica, even Synne and Sile, who continued to flank his father—all stopped and stared first at Taraneh, then at Lothian.

The fane huffed in disregard. "This is only the first day. Battles in my mother's time lasted weeks; some dragged into months."

"I don't mean to say that I think we will—or even that it is anything but an extremely remote possibility—but given what we saw today, I feel it is no longer the impossibility it had been. And I would like to advise caution where previously I saw no need."

"We were taken by surprise today," his father said. "We'll do better tomorrow. There are ways around the Orinfar."

We'll do better tomorrow, too, Jerydd told him. *Once Arion is dead, everything will be easier. Tomorrow, we go hunting.*

. . .

Raithe's left arm was broken, his shield a crumpled mess. Malcolm, who survived the battle without a scratch, had helped him back inside, and the two collapsed near the steps in the lower courtyard. Dying of thirst, battered and bruised, Raithe was surprised to hear cheering. All around them in the courtyard, up on the parapet on the surrounding battlements, and from the windows, people were shouting, hooting, hugging each other, and praising the return of the bloody mess of men.

"What's going on?" he asked. "I thought we lost."

"Maybe not," Malcolm said. "We are alive, after all."

"Looked like that hurt," said Tesh as he rushed up with a bucket of water and a cup.

Raithe regretted every bad thing he'd ever said to the boy. The kid knew exactly what was needed. Splashing his face with his good arm, he relished the cool water. It made him sigh and wonder if he ought to just dump the whole thing over his head. He might have if both arms had worked. Instead, he took the cup and drank. "Saw it, did you?"

"Was with the rest up on the parapet."

"I suppose *you* would have dodged or done some fantastic back flip, or blocked the blow somehow."

Tesh thought a moment. "I'm not sure there is a way to block a sledge-hammer the size of a house."

The kid was smiling, a big wide grin. Raithe took a moment to understand. *He's proud of me—proud and relieved.* Raithe hadn't seen that before, certainly not in his father's eyes. For the first time, he caught a glimpse of what he meant to Tesh. The kid he'd allowed to share his fire under the wool, the wild animal he'd tamed with discarded bones, had latched onto him more deeply than he'd believed possible.

"Now you went and did it, didn't you?" Padera hobbled over with a bag slung on one shoulder. "Broke that arm good." She set the bag down and pulled out boards and cloth straps. As she did, a smile formed.

"Why is everyone so happy?" Raithe asked. "Have the elves left?"

The old woman shook her head. "You didn't die."

Malcolm and Raithe exchanged looks.

"Doesn't seem cheer-worthy," Raithe replied as he struggled to put his back to the stone wall near the steps.

Tesh laughed. The kid was giddy enough to be drunk. The moment the thought appeared, Raithe wanted beer. *Dear Mari, a foaming cup would be marvelous.*

Padera pointed toward the front gate where worn, weary, and blood-covered men were still dragging themselves in. "This is the first clash. The first time men have ever fought Fhrey. No one knew what would happen."

Tesh was nodding emphatically. "Nyphron himself—he was standing next to me on the parapet—he said, 'This will decide it all.' Even he didn't know."

"You did great," Padera said as she felt his arm, squeezing here and there. "Walloped them good." Padera pressed on the broken bone. "Ah, there we are. Not bad, not too bad at all." She stretched his arm out and slipped a board underneath.

"You got the Miralyith like you were supposed to and proved men could fight. Nyphron says they're scared now . . . or ought to be. You're heroes."

"All their Miralyith are dead, then?"

Tesh shook his head. "Not all—a lot, though. Crippled them, we think."

"Still have giants," Raithe said, and he grunted as Padera used the boards to set his bone.

"You killed three!" Tesh was bouncing on his haunches. Then he frowned.

Raithe's eyes were watering, and he jerked a bit with the pain the old woman was inflicting, but still saw the kid's expression change. "What?"

"Gilroy and Bergin were talking about how many you killed—how elves aren't used to death. They were saying that this might be it. That they will leave now. That the war will end."

"And you're disappointed because you didn't get to fight?"

Tesh shrugged. "I just—I just worked so damn hard."

Padera wrapped the planks with a cord, tying it tight. And made a *harrumph* in Tesh's direction. "A man who builds a roof shouldn't complain when it doesn't rain; the gods might send a flood."

Around the courtyard other men were being tended to. They lay exhausted on the grass or sat, looking dazed. Some cried, some stared. A few laughed, but not in a good way. A handful continued to wander the yard, clutching their weapons and moving quickly as if they had someplace to be. But they only walked in circles with confused looks.

"Where's Wedon?" Raithe asked.

Tesh refused to look at him.

"The glancing blow that broke this arm," Padera said, "the farmer took square."

Raithe looked around again but couldn't find the farmer.

"They're leaving the dead down by the front gate," Tesh explained.

In addition to three sons, Wedon had a daughter named Thea. Raithe had spoken to her only once in Dahl Rhen. He remembered that she wore her hair braided, and she was rail thin and tall for her age. She had died in the giants' attack on Dahl Rhen a year ago. That's when Wedon stopped being a farmer and became a soldier. *I was just talking to him. How can the world change so fast?*

Padera created a sling to hook around his neck. As she tied it up, Raithe spotted Roan standing nearby. She had her heavy smithing apron on, the leather stained and scorched. Her face hadn't fared much better; her cheeks were smeared with soot. Arms across her stomach, she clutched her elbows and stared with worried eyes.

She shook her head. Then without a word, she walked away.

Raithe stared after her.

"She's worried about Gifford," Padera said.

"Gifford? Why? Where is he?"

"Only Mari knows, and I suspect even she might not be certain."

Raithe was confused. "How far can a cripple go?"

Padera smiled. "That, I think, is the question of the century."

CHAPTER TWENTY-TWO

The Pile at Perdif

I truly believe that hardship makes better people. Pain—assuming that it does not break us—provides the strength of knowing that such things can be endured and overcome. And I know of no one who suffered more than Gifford.

—THE BOOK OF BRIN

There was no one there; just a pile on a hill.

Didn't take long for Gifford to figure out why. Cresting the mound, he spied the village of Perdif below, the remains of five charred huts circling a well. He counted the people, too. Wasn't hard, only twelve—all dead. The bodies lay scattered—men, women, children, and two dogs. They lay twisted and splayed on the dirt, not a weapon visible.

Gifford fell off Naraspur's lathered back. No other way down. The ground was as hard as it looked, and he lay for a moment waiting for the pain to pass. The horse left him and walked slowly, wearily away. She'd be thirsty after their long morning race. Maybe she could smell water. Climbing to his feet and filling his lungs, Gifford called out. He waited, looked for movement below, listened, then called out again. No one answered.

The only sound was the harsh, dry wind that blew unabated and the flap of vultures' wings as they landed and fluttered from one body to the next.

The sun was high, and Gifford hoped minutes didn't count because he had no idea how to light the signal fire. They had sent him out with food, water, magic armor, and an amazing sword but nothing that could produce a flame. In that scorched land, he didn't think it would take much, but he didn't have *much*—he had *nothing*. No one expected the Fhrey would have visited Perdif first.

Most villages had braziers. Given the trouble and time that went into making fire, they just kept one going. Such a thing, he could see, was a luxury in Dureya. Not a tree visible for miles. There wasn't even much wood on the pile. Most of it looked to be sheep dung.

How well can that burn?

Persephone had likely ordered a mound of logs built last fall, but who could resist a giant pile of wood just up the hill from a village facing a cold winter?

He hobbled toward the pile as best he could, which wasn't good at all without his crutch. Giving up, he crawled. Within the ambitiously wide circle of stones, only three logs and a few dried dung patties remained. This wasn't a signal fire; this was barely a campfire.

Gifford lay on his back and let his body rest. His arms and legs ached, but he was alive. He'd done the impossible. Gifford had broken out of Alon Rhist and raced across Dureya in less than a day on the back of a horse. But now what?

He sat up.

What would Roan do?

She'd manage something ingenious, something that harnessed the power of the hot winds. Looking at the pile, Gifford didn't even see kindling. *I don't have so much as two sticks to rub together.* Crawling around, he found plenty of rocks. Gifford had seen Habet create sparks by striking two stones against each other, and he tried reproducing the process. None of the rocks he found worked.

I shouldn't have gotten off the horse.

He could have ridden farther. Perhaps there was another village nearby, one with a proper bow and kindling, or an eternal flame he could tap.

Searching around, Gifford realized he couldn't even see Naraspur, who had wandered off.

How long does Alon Rhist have? How long does Roan? What a great hero I am, to come so far to fail because I can't . . .

Gifford focused on the little pile of logs and dung.

What was it Arion had said? Something about holding a sunbaked rock, and . . .

People who are creative are usually that way because they are more attuned to the power and forces of nature. They can hear the whispers of the world, and it helps guide them in the right direction.

Gifford stared at the pile. He had no hope of lighting it, unless . . .

I want you to do me a favor, Gifford. I want you to move your hands like this.

He'd tried it many times since then, and it never worked. The attempts had always failed, but then he'd never *needed* it to succeed.

Have you ever wanted something to happen and then it did?

Gifford had never wanted anything more in his life than to light that fire.

Imagine my hands turning black as ash.

He stared at the pile and took a breath. Raising his hands, he made the plucking motions.

Concentrate. Close your eyes if you need to.

He did. He closed his eyes and imagined the pile bursting into flame: a loud *woof* followed by a burst of heat, the crackle of wood, and flame— lots and lots of flames.

He opened his eyes.

Nothing.

The few logs and the heap of dung remained unchanged. It didn't even smoke.

She had lied. He didn't know why but she had. Her and the mystic had— *The armor—it's covered in runes!*

Gifford threw off his helmet, and after finding the buckles, pulled off the rest of Roan's gift. He concentrated once more, and as he focused, an idea pushed into his mind.

Clap your hands.

The thought came unbidden. Was it a memory? Something the mystic had said? Gifford wasn't sure. Maybe she had, he couldn't remember. All he knew was that the thought had popped into his head, oddly clear, strangely certain. Fear and excitement gripped him then as he knew it would work. The answer to the puzzle was provided, and as so often was the case, it was obvious.

Oftentimes we hear it as our own thoughts telling us to go left, or just a sense that going right is a bad idea. Some might call it intuition, or a gut feeling, but it is the world speaking in an ancient language that you can almost understand.

The warm wind blew hard across his face.

Roan would use the wind, he thought again.

Gifford scanned the horizon. He knelt in that desolation, on the small knoll in the center of an endless plain.

Rediscovering how to speak our native tongue, how to tap and use that power in meaningful ways, is what we call the Art.

He was alone. No one could see or hear him. He closed his eyes again and this time he hummed. The wind came once more, a soft fluttering kiss that moved his hair. He held up his hands and let the air move through his fingers.

Nothing happened, nothing magical, except . . . *clay.*

Like the idea of clapping, this new thought came to him. He didn't know if it arrived from without or within. The effect, however, was powerful. Another puzzle piece fell into place and he was starting to see the bigger picture. The air—the air was clay. The way it felt passing between his fingers, the way it seeped and spewed. This was how he shaped his cups and pots and vases. This is how *he* created.

Gifford's stomach fluttered in excitement. Something was there, something that hadn't been before, something real; he was making a connection. This wasn't make-believe. This was a genuine thing. The Fhrey and the mystic hadn't lied. He'd found something, and it *was* inside him.

Clay. The wind, the air, the sun, the ground, it was *all* clay, and he could shape it.

He reached out and felt the wind as a malleable thing. His fingers felt something else, something strong, warm, and deep. He drew it back as he often did with the clay, squeezing, bending it to his will. Dirt and water spinning beneath his fingers became miracles of art. That's all he had to do—*make art.*

He formed fists and felt the heat build. The air swirled faster and faster, gusting his hair, pushing side to side, throwing up pebbles in a tiny storm. But when he opened his eyes, the pile was no different. There was no fire, no heat, no smoke.

Failure. Another in a long, long line.

Gifford's shoulders slumped.

Only this time, this failure . . . He thought of Roan dying or being made a slave again. He didn't just cry, he sobbed hard and loud. What difference did the wailing anguish of a cripple matter to the world or to the gods?

Clap.

Gifford's hands were still bent in two tight fists of rage and sorrow. He hated himself, the world, the gods, the vultures, the village, and most especially that awful pile of dung he knelt before.

"I love you, Woan." He spoke the words as a prayer, with tears spilling down his cheeks. Then, with all his might, he spread his arms and slapped his palms together.

The pile didn't catch fire.

Most of Perdif exploded.

CHAPTER TWENTY-THREE

Inside the Kype

Some moments we see clearly. We know they are important; births and deaths are just such times. Others sneak up on us, invisible from the front, but always, always obvious from behind.

—THE BOOK OF BRIN

The sun was setting when Raithe knocked on the door to the Kype. He wasn't alone this time. Moya and Malcolm stood with him as the little window in the door slid back. The same pair of eyes shifted, registering each face. The eyes didn't look happy.

"Open up, Por," Moya ordered.

The eyes focused on Raithe. "I, ah . . ."

"You're *ah* gonna open that door," Moya told him. "Or I'll put an arrow through that skull of yours."

The eyes blinked. The window in the door shut, then the big bronze door opened.

Poric was a surprisingly small Fhrey with white-blond hair who appeared to live in the nearby little room filled with dirty bowls, empty cups, and a pile of wood shavings. Twenty or thirty tiny animal carvings lined the shelves and tables. Poric watched Raithe enter with what looked like a mix of fear and anger.

"It will be fine," Malcolm assured him. "Raithe has a broken arm. Makes it hard to properly strangle a person that way."

"Hard," Raithe said, "but not impossible."

Poric's eyes widened, and a hand fluttered to his throat. This might have made Raithe smile if he hadn't been in such a foul mood. He didn't have anything against Poric. The Fhrey was only doing his job. Apparently, someone had told him not to let the Dureyan in except for official meetings. Raithe had enlisted the help of Moya rather than Suri or Arion. Suri, who didn't appear to care for Nyphron any more than he did, would have jumped at the chance for a little *fun*, but Raithe didn't want to cause that much trouble until he knew what was going on. Moya was the obvious choice. As Shield, no one could stop her from escorting him to the keenig. If Nyphron tried to, then Raithe might have a talk with Suri.

Moya led the way up the stairs. "Careful, the second one is crumbling. I usually just jump it."

Moya had denied any nefarious attempts on Nyphron's part to keep Raithe and Persephone apart, but Moya also said she had no idea why the keenig would refuse to see him. Under normal circumstances, she might have asked Persephone first before letting him in, but nothing was normal that day. The war had begun, Raithe was wounded, and Persephone had nearly died the night before. Time felt in short supply, and when Raithe had added, "How would you feel if you learned Tekchin was wounded, nearly died, and they wouldn't let you see him?" That was all it took.

They climbed seven flights to what Raithe realized was the top of the Kype. Just as sparse and cold as the rest of the fortress, the Kype made a poor home. While Alon Rhist exhibited power and elegance, this building was colder and more barren than Dureya. Despite the lack of food and the relentless winds, Raithe's people had songs, dances, and the laughter of children. The Kype was silent, their steps echoing.

"We have her in the Shrine," Moya explained. "Used to be the private chambers of Alon Rhist—the guy this place is named after. He was the only fane from the Instarya tribe, so they sort of worship him. Ruled for only five years before dying in some fight. They kept his rooms exactly the way he left them." She stopped and looked back. "You might not want to touch things. The Fhrey get a little sensitive about stuff like that."

If I find they've treated her badly, I'll do more than touch things.

They found familiar faces standing guard out in front of the chamber door. Grygor, Eres, and Tekchin all smiled at their approach. They were playing a game of Stones. Tekchin had the biggest stack.

"I asked *you* to watch her door," Moya admonished Tekchin.

The Fhrey shrugged. "I get bored easily. Not into wood carving like Poric. Left alone, I'd end up nibbling the ends of my fingers or something."

"Any change would be an improvement," Grygor said.

"Thanks." Moya expressed the one word with weight to all of them, then leaned in and kissed Tekchin. "You're a lifesaver."

Embarrassed, Tekchin turned to Raithe, pointed at his arm, and said, "Got a scratch, eh?"

"Had a disagreement with a giant," Raithe replied, glancing at Grygor, whose head nearly touched the high ceiling.

"They're animals," Grygor said. "Never trust one to keep a secret, or not bite the head off a Rhune just to make a point."

Eres and Tekchin nodded gravely, which made Raithe wonder—not for the first time—if the Galantians were joking.

Moya opened the door and Raithe walked inside alone.

The Shrine was a suite of rooms decorated with tapestries depicting battles and containing sculptures of half-naked Fhrey wielding spears or javelins, their muscles straining. Dark wood chairs with red-cushioned seats and gold vases and candelabras filled the space with an aura of opulence. This was by far the greatest assemblage of wealth Raithe had ever seen. To think such splendor existed across the river from the dung-brick home he was born in was shocking. Did any of the Dureyans ever have a clue? Did they even know such things were possible?

If we win the war, how can we ever return to lives lived in dirt? What will become of us if we're victorious? What will happen to the world?

And yet this room, too, while lavish, felt lifeless. Everything was so clean, so ordered. This wasn't a home to the living. It felt like a tomb, and he didn't like the idea that they had put Persephone in such a place.

He moved gingerly, creeping across carpets like an intruder. A door to another part of the suite opened, and Brin came out. She smiled and pointed at him with a hairbrush that she was holding. "You're in luck. She just woke up." Brin gestured at the door. "I'll wait outside."

Raithe stood in the center of the Shrine, watching Brin leave, then he looked back at the door.

Why am I so nervous? It's just Persephone.

He reached out for the latch and hesitated. For a moment, he thought to turn around, to just leave.

Maybe this is a mistake. If Moya says she's okay, then she is. If she were in trouble, Brin would have said something; Padera would have said something; Moya would have done something. They love Persephone, too. I'm being stupid.

Raithe knew Nyphron wasn't keeping Persephone a prisoner. He'd known it all along. He just didn't want to face the truth. He still didn't. Raithe turned away to leave.

"Raithe?" he heard her call. "Raithe?"

Too late.

He opened the door slowly and poked his head in.

Persephone lay on a huge canopy bed adorned with thick embroidered blankets and pillows of shiny cloth. There was no window, and the only light came from three oil lamps that filled the air with a sooty stench. There were other smells, too, unpleasant and unknown.

"I thought I heard Brin talking to someone."

"She, ah . . . Brin just left."

"Come in," she said.

Persephone looked beautiful; her face did anyway. The rest of her was covered by quilts. Knowing that a raow had attacked her, Raithe had been worried about what he'd find. As it turned out, she was pale, but other than that, she looked well.

He moved in slowly, noting his surroundings. Several tables were littered with bowls and glasses, pestles and mortars. Jars were filled with different powders—the source of some of the smells. Raithe crept up until he stood at the edge of the bed. "I heard about the attack. You all right?"

"I will be." She made a clawing motion to her stomach. "Some pretty deep cuts make it just about impossible to move, so I'm stuck here while everyone else fights. I feel terrible about that. I'm supposed to be the keenig, and sure, I didn't expect to be leading the attacks like Reglan did, but I thought I would be able to see them."

"I think your job was getting us here. Giving us this chance. Now *we* have to succeed."

She focused on his arm, and her face wrinkled with sympathetic pain. "Was it awful?"

"I guess that depends on who you talk to. According to everyone who watched, it was wonderful." He frowned. "Farmer Wedon was killed. So was Kurt, Tope's youngest, and Hanson Killian."

He saw the names' impact on her features and stopped himself. "Several others, too. I just don't know their names," he lied. "But it could have been so much worse." Filled with guilt at having falsely accused Nyphron, he added, "I hate to say it, but Nyphron's plan of putting those runes on the armor and having Moya's archers attack the Miralyith was . . . brilliant."

"Why do you hate to say it?"

He came closer, touched the covers on the bed with three outstretched fingers. "Because he's my rival."

"Rival?"

"Isn't he?"

She didn't answer. Her eyes searched the bedspread for one.

"I had it in my head that the reason I wasn't allowed into the Kype to see you was because of him, that he had given orders to keep me away. But he didn't, did he?"

"No, he didn't."

Persephone started to push herself up and cringed in pain.

"Easy," he told her.

She shook her head and made a dismissive wave as she struggled to breathe. "I'm fine. I'm fine."

"You sure?"

"Yes." The pain looked to have mostly subsided, and Persephone seemed more embarrassed than anything else. "You were saying that you tried to see me?"

"Yes. I came almost every day at first, then less so as winter came on. Guess I started getting the hint. I was always told you were too busy. I believed it because I needed to."

She didn't say anything. Refused to look at him.

"Do you love him?"

"It's complicated. He . . ." The words struggled to come out. She smoothed the covers. "He asked me to marry him."

Raithe didn't say anything after that. He couldn't. He was too frightened. When he was a boy, Didan had once crept up behind him and put a dagger to his throat, whispering, *Don't move.* That was how it felt when standing beside Persephone's bed, those words lingering in the space between them, dropped but not swept away. He waited, waited for her to say that she had turned Nyphron down, waited for her to laugh at the very thought. She didn't. Persephone said nothing at all, and the moment lingered until finally Raithe couldn't bear it any longer. "Have you slept with him?"

Her head jerked up. "No! It's not like that."

"Then how is it?"

"I don't see how my personal life is your business."

The words hurt. She wouldn't have said that a year ago when Konniger wanted her dead. Back then she'd welcomed him into her world, begged him to stay, wanted him to be part of her *personal life.* Back then, when he had asked for her hand, she had said the memory of her dead husband made remarrying impossible.

She must have seen the look on his face and read part of it correctly. "Listen, Raithe, I'm the keenig now. I have to think about what's best for the clans, and you're right; Nyphron is brilliant."

Why did I ever say that? He's brilliant, all right. He's twisted you to his will, that's how brilliant he is.

"He's given us the chance to survive. He and I have united the Rhunes and the Instarya. Together we can—"

"I'm too late, aren't I?" The phrase *he and I* was what did it. They were a team now.

Raithe looked away, his sight drifting across the shiny sheets, across the big bed—big enough for two. *Does he visit her, creeping in when it is dark, or does Nyphron live with her now? Does he sleep there every night? Which side is his?*

"I'm just saying that without Nyphron, we don't stand a chance. He knows how to fight them, and he keeps the Instarya from—"

"You've already decided. You're going to marry him."

She didn't answer.

"You are, aren't you?"

She looked away, refusing to meet his eyes. "It's what will be best for everyone."

Even Didan hadn't actually slit his throat.

No, not a slit throat, a stab to the heart.

Raithe stood still, feeling the pain slip in through his ribs—a fine spear thrust—very fine indeed.

I am too late. I just thought that she . . . He sucked in a breath. "Persephone, did you *ever* love me?"

He saw her stiffen. Her hands were clasped on her lap, a pile of pillows behind her head. Brin had likely propped her up and brushed her hair to receive him, so she could look her best for the execution. Persephone did indeed have loyal friends. Moya had led him there, and Brin had held the door.

"Raithe, this isn't about love. You have to be able to see that." Her tone became concerned. "If I were to refuse, if we were to lose Nyphron's support—"

"You refused *me.* Did I leave? Did I turn against you?"

"He's not you, and it's not the same thing."

"How is it different?"

"You were being selfish. You wanted me to run off to some mythical land of perpetual sunshine and a life without want. You asked me to abandon my family. Nyphron wants to help save them."

"Selfish? You're calling *me* selfish? I gave that dream up. I *stayed.* Stayed when I *knew* I was a fool to do so. You say Nyphron wants to save *your* people. But who volunteered to fight the Gula keenig? And why did I do such a stupid thing? For me? No—but I can tell you this, that's exactly what Nyphron is doing. He's the selfish one, not me. I didn't see him out there on that field." His words were spiteful and bitter. He didn't want them to be, but he couldn't stop. "I was the one who nearly died when a huge giant hit three of us with a sledgehammer—the same one that killed Wedon. I was the one out there saving *your family*. Where was Nyphron?"

"He can't—"

"He *could*. He just *won't*." Raithe's voice rose. "I asked you to come with me because I didn't think we stood a chance fighting the Fhrey, and because I know what war is like. I lived with men who made a profession of it. I've seen what it does to people, to those who fight year after year, and even more to those they leave behind. And maybe I was wrong about part of that; maybe we can win. But I was right about the effects of war . . . and still I stayed. And I know one more thing. I know I love you. Nyphron doesn't, but I do. And I thought—I thought you loved me, too."

She stared at him, a hard look on her face. *Stone. She looks like stone, cold and unmovable. A perfect keenig.*

"Did you? Do you?"

"No," she finally said.

Silence followed.

In a fight, it was possible to get used to the sound of the crash. The clang of metal on metal made a rhythm, a kind of music. Combat slipped into a duet, with each side playing their role until one attack slipped through a guard. Then the music stopped. Unexpected silence always followed, made loud by the expectation of the beat that never came. Raithe stood in that silence. His guard had been broken; her stroke pierced true. In her eyes he saw the shock and fear, the regret he often spotted on the faces of the trainees when a move worked and they actually hit him.

"Doesn't matter," Raithe said softly. "Even that doesn't matter. Doesn't change the way I feel. Can't say I know much about it, but I know that's not how love works."

Persephone's hands gripped the covers. She opened her mouth, but he no longer wanted to hear what she had to say, and he wasn't done. She deserved to hear all of it; at least the Persephone he knew, or thought he knew, deserved it. That's how it felt—not like she had rejected him, but like someone he loved had died. She had evidently passed away some time ago, but he was only now hearing the news. Not having been invited to the funeral, Raithe offered his eulogy. "I've loved you from the start. Maybe from the moment I first saw you in the forest, but certainly after you spoke to me like a real person, even though you knew I was Dureyan. And it doesn't matter if you can't love me—whether it's because you're still in love with Reglan's memory or because you want to marry Nyphron. None of that matters because . . ." His voice cracked. "Because even now . . . even now . . ."

His voice broke the way his father's sword had. He was left with the shattered, useless remains, except Malcolm wasn't there this time, and he wasn't saved. Raithe spun away and headed for the door. He'd wanted to see her so badly for so long, but at that moment he wanted nothing more than to get away.

"Raithe!" she called, but he didn't stop.

He moved past the group waiting in the hall. *Why do there have to be so many witnesses?*

"Raithe?" Brin called. "What happened?"

He headed for the stairs, wiping tears from his eyes.

There's just no winning for some people. Doesn't matter if you do everything right. Once the gods hate you, there's no happiness that can be achieved, and hope is just another torture.

CHAPTER TWENTY-FOUR

Dawn's Early Light

I honestly do not know what happened that morning. Only one person alive did, and I never had the courage to ask her.

—THE BOOK OF BRIN

Mawyndulë. Mawyndulë!

He opened his eyes to find a dark world where a stretched canvas tarp quivered in the wind. Took a moment to remember where he was: in a tent on the edge of a barren battlefield. Depression filled him. He had been dreaming of Makareta. He'd spotted her in a crowd on the streets in Estramnadon and had struggled to reach her, then woke up. That left him in the lonely dark, listening to the gusts and thinking about her again.

No one knew what had happened to Makareta, or maybe they did and chose not to tell him. He thought it possible that she was locked in the same cell where they had held Vidar. Or maybe they gave her to Vidar to make up for his wrongful imprisonment. As much as he hated Makareta for what she'd done, he thought he would kill the senior councilor if he'd hurt her. That's why he thought he might be in love with Makareta, and maybe that was also why everyone had lied to him about where she was.

A gust of inexhaustible wind made his tent sing a dull note. *I hope the stakes were driven in deep.*

Mawyndulë was bundled up in a pile of wool blankets topped by a bearskin. Only his head was exposed, and his nose felt numb. The sound of the wind made it worse. He couldn't actually feel it, but the howl spoke a rumor of bitter cold.

Mawyndulë, answer me.

Mawyndulë cringed. He'd thought it was fun to listen in on Jerydd's conversations or turn the kel into a personal storyteller as he rode. But having Jerydd invade his mind uninvited in the dark hours of the morning, left him feeling violated. While he knew Jerydd couldn't hear his thoughts, Mawyndulë didn't feel safe even in his own head.

He considered not answering. He could even pretend to snore. He was thinking just how annoying that could be when Jerydd spoke again. *I know you can hear me. I know you're awake. I've listened to you breathing for hours, and I can tell the difference.*

"I *was* sleeping," he said.

Sleep tomorrow. We need to get to work.

Mawyndulë yawned, wiped his eyes, then began to moan. He moaned a lot, a dull low tone that he was certain made dealing with life easier. "What kind of work?" He hoped it wouldn't be any more lessons. He was sick to death of them. At the academy, they made him do all kinds of repetitive tasks that made him wonder whether jumping off the Talwara balcony would really hurt so bad, or would it be better to just die instantly.

We're going to kill Arion.

Mawyndulë's head came up off the pillow. "How? The Spiders tried that yesterday. They can't find her. She's hiding."

She can't hide from Avempartha.

Mawyndulë pushed up, letting his covers slip and swung his bare feet to the ground. Forgetting that the floor of his tent was the field, he flinched when he felt the brittle grass poking against his soles and tickling his bare legs.

I thought the Spiders and Kasimer could handle it, but she's crafty. Should have guessed. Did you know Fenelyus named her Cenzlyor?

"What do you want me to do?" Mawyndulë wiped his eyes and ran a hand over his bare scalp, cringing as he felt the stubble forming. He hated hair. Couldn't understand why Ferrol allowed it to grow on Miralyith. The more it grew the dirtier he felt, as if the Rhune world was infecting him.

This won't be without risk, you understand.

"I don't care. I want her dead."

Good. Then I need you to go to where you can see the fortress. Get away from the camp, away from others, especially away from other Miralyith. Get in a nice lonely place where you have a perfect view of the whole fortress and then let me know.

"Right now? It's the middle of the night."

It's almost morning, and, yes, right now. I wanted to do this hours ago, but you sleep with the dedication of a depressed drunk. We need to do a search, and it'll be easier the quieter things are. Stillness makes hunting more efficient. So get up and—

"Okay, okay. I'm moving. It's not like where you are, you know? I'm in an awful tent. It's dark. It's cold. And there's a wind that doesn't stop blowing."

You whine a lot. I suppose that being the spoiled child of the fane people don't dare tell you that. They should.

"As I am indeed the son of the fane, how is it *you* dare?"

Because I know your father would side with me.

"Treya!" he called. An instant later, his bleary-eyed servant stepped in, rubbing her face and blinking repeatedly. Treya wasn't much to look at. Most of the time Mawyndulë didn't bother. She was an ever-present staple in his life, like his shoes or his goldfish—always there, never noticed. But he couldn't recall having seen Treya fresh out of bed. She was always up much earlier than he. At least it seemed that way. This was the first time since he was a child that she appeared unkempt. Her hair, which was always hidden in a wrap on the top of her head, was down. He was surprised to discover she had light brown hair—he was surprised she had hair at all. This revelation did nothing to enhance her appeal. Not only did Mawyndulë not find hair attractive on anyone, hers was an atrocious mess of tangles and jutted up in peculiar, inexplicable ways. "My sandals and cloak, get them, and pour water into the basin."

Just enough starlight pierced the canvas for Treya to find her way around.

"Shall I make a meal for you, my lord?"

Mawyndulë shook his head. Too early, his stomach wasn't ready for food yet. With sandals and cloak already on, he paused to splash water on his face. It was icy cold, so he opted to just dip his fingers and wipe his eyes.

"Are you going out, my lord?" Treya asked.

"Yes."

"Shall I come with you?"

Mawyndulë hesitated but shook his head. Best he did this alone, and he couldn't endure another minute near her hair. As much as he tried not to look, he'd catch sight of it out of the corner of his eye, bobbing and dipping like some ghastly puppet performing on her head.

He pulled back the flap on his tent as much to comply with Jerydd as to escape Treya. He had no idea how stuffy the interior of his tent had been until the fresh air greeted him. Damp and chilled, the world outside was alive with crickets and peeping frogs. All around were other tents and fires that had dwindled to glowing coals.

Stepping outside, letting the tent flap fall behind him, Mawyndulë didn't know where to go.

"Pits are that way, my prince." The duty guard stationed outside pointed to the south.

"Ah . . . thanks." Mawyndulë didn't know why he said it or why he turned and went south or why he felt he had to be secretive. He wasn't doing anything wrong, but it felt that way. He was on a clandestine mission following the instructions of the voice in his head. Some might even call that insane. *Look out! Look out for the mad prince!*

He slipped into the shadows and around to the south past two more guards, who just nodded respectfully. He picked his way, moving fast. Cold had a way of adding urgency to any endeavor. He passed the pits and kept going down the slope out beyond the pickets, then he veered to the west—toward Alon Rhist. In the starlight, he could see fine, and he pinpointed a pillar of rock rising from the plain. Looking a bit like a crooked finger, it jutted up and out. The crag appeared to have a small trail running up one side.

Where are you? What are you doing? Jerydd pestered him.

"I'm having breakfast with a family of bears, tarts with jam and cinnamon tea. Bears are very good cooks, you know."

Don't get flippant. This is serious.

"I'm climbing a rock to get a good vantage point to see the fort. That's what you wanted, isn't it?"

Are you outside the camp?

"Yeah, about two, three hundred yards, I guess."

Good. Let me know when you've found a spot—a quiet spot.

The trail was precarious, and Mawyndulë was regretting his decision to take it. Narrow, with a sheer drop on one side and the cliff wall on the other, he found himself shimmying along. By the time he reached the top, he was no longer cold. He was sweating.

"Okay, I'm at the top."

Have a good view of Alon Rhist?

Mawyndulë peered west. He was up only sixty feet, but it felt as if he could see forever. Below him, the entire Fhrey camp was visible so that he could see the orderly precision of the tents punctuated by the glowing red points of burned out fires. "Yeah. It's across this chasm: bunch of walls, big dome, massive tower—not so tall now that they cut the top of it off."

Just sit down. Make yourself comfortable. Keep your back straight, cross your legs, and just concentrate on Alon Rhist. Try not to let your mind wander. Just focus on the fortress.

"Okay."

And try not to scream.

"Scream? Why would I—"

Mawyndulë jerked as he felt a jolt of power slam into him. He didn't scream. He couldn't. All he was able to utter was a weak squeak as his mind and body were blasted with the indomitable force of the tower of Avempartha. Power flooded him so that he felt he might drown. Every muscle contracted, as if someone had dumped a barrel of ice water over his head.

He managed a weak gasp as the fortress rushed at him. In an instant, he was viewing the great bronze doors. They were close enough to touch. Then he flew through them. A moment later, he was standing in a courtyard where soldiers—both Rhune and Fhrey—stood or walked. Not needing to use the stairs, Mawyndulë flew upward to a higher courtyard and passed through barracks where men were waking up, getting dressed, and eating at long tables or with bowls in their laps. Next, he reached the dome and rose to a balcony overlooking a huge room filled with decorative weapons. He'd been there before when he and Gryndal had visited. Then he was whisked away, flying across a bridge toward a sturdy square tower built just in front of the decapitated Spyrok. This was the Kype, the fortress inside the fortress. Lamps were being lit. People were dressing. The fort was waking up, and Mawyndulë felt himself growing dizzy. He flew again, back this time toward the front of the Rhist. The jerking, haphazard motion was making his stomach queasy as he flew through the many rooms and hallways spinning left and right searching for—

He stopped.

Suri handed the steaming tea over to Arion. The two were at the top of the Frozen Tower. With the Spyrok gone, it was the nearest Suri could come to the out-of-doors. The closest she could get to feeling any kind of freedom. She'd always hated walls, and lately she had been confined behind a great many of them.

Although no one could actually stop her, Arion could put up a good fight, but Suri didn't think even she could do anything if Suri really wanted to go out. She had learned there were few things she couldn't do if she really wanted to. For the last month, her education with Arion had dwindled to discovering not what she could do, or how to do it, but the few things she couldn't. Flying was one, so was bringing back the dead—at least once they had crossed into that light, into the realm of Phyre. Another was pure creation—making something from nothing. These were all beyond the Art—well, sort of. Nothing was really *beyond* it. The Art was every-thing, the common thread that ran through existence, holding it together. Everything was part of the Art, but some things, like pure creation and raising the dead, were so complex, their cords so deep, no Fhrey or Rhune Artist was likely able to master the weaves or control the power needed. That was the realm of gods. The closest anyone had ever gotten—as far as she knew—was the creation of Balgargarath and the Gilarabrywn. Even they weren't *real*, not actually alive; each was a force of power held to-gether by artificial bonds, but independent of the Artist: an animated, self-sustaining, thinking thing that could feasibly continue to live even after the Artist who created it died. In that sense and by virtue of achievement, Suri was perhaps the most powerful Artist in the world, second only to the one who had created Balgargarath. Whoever had managed that feat had to be the greatest Artist, and only a little short of the gods themselves.

Despite her hatred of walls, Suri remained indoors. She stayed because Arion asked her to. Arion was afraid something bad might happen if Suri left. What that was, Suri couldn't sense or imagine. She had lived all her life in the wilderness among killer bears and hungry wolf packs, and that was before she could redirect the course of rivers and order the sky to rain. Suri also understood that Arion didn't want to be alone. Suri had discov-ered a comfortable companion in her fellow misfit, Raithe, but in this place, at this time, Suri was all Arion had. In the span of one short year, the Mi-ralyith had become Suri's mentor, substitute mother, dependent child, and best friend. Even though Arion was fully recovered, Suri still worried about the Fhrey's health, about her using the Art—not because of remain-ing symptoms, but because she could still see the scar on her head. The small white half-moon was always there as a reminder of how close Arion had come to death.

"So, what am I not supposed to do today?" Suri asked as the two looked out at the waking world over steaming cups of tea. That was another won-derful thing about Arion. She, too, got up early and enjoyed saying "good morning" to the sun.

"Same as yesterday—unless something unusual happens."

Suri looked down at the Fhrey camp being revealed by the growing light. "Yesterday they threw lightning and blasts of fire—what is it you consider unusual?"

"Yesterday they didn't know about the runes," Arion said. "Tactics will change. I'll try to counteract them. From what Nyphron told me, few of the Spiders survived. I think I can deal with those that remain. I don't want to boast, but now that Gryndal is dead, I think only Kel Jerydd and the fane himself could best me."

"You're Cenzlyor."

"That's right." Arion took a sip. "And you're Cenzlyor of the Rhunes—ah, humans. Sorry."

"What does that mean *exactly*?"

"When the first person to wield the Art names you Swift of Mind, the implication is that you're the best Artist in the world." Arion shrugged. "Honestly, I think it was just a pet name Fenelyus made up for me and had nothing to do with my skill, but the title impressed a lot of people."

Suri watched her standing at the wall resting, her cup on the edge while she was still holding it with both hands. Bright blue eyes looked out at the horizon, as if she could see something there. Suri had seen that look before.

"I don't think it was just a pet name," Suri said.

"Oh, really? You, who never met Fane Fenelyus, can tell me her mind?"

Suri nodded. "Don't need to know *her*—I know *you*. And I can see the same thing she did."

"Really? Okay, what does it mean?"

"Swift of Mind."

Arion smiled. "Well, yes. Literally, sure, but it doesn't mean I am the best Artist. Like I said, Lothian is more powerful; so is the kel. Even Gryndal—"

"Gryndal was a monster."

Arion neither nodded nor shook her head. "And if Raithe hadn't killed him, I'd be dead. But the question remains, why did Fenelyus choose to call me that? I clearly wasn't the best Artist."

Suri looked at her curiously. "It has nothing to do with being an Artist. She wasn't speaking about your skill in the Art at all, she was describing *you*. I can see the same thing. You're a lot like Tura. A lot like Magda, too.

I think Fenelyus called you Cenzlyor because she thought you were *wise.* That was why she wanted you to tutor the prince. Not to teach him the art of magic but the art of wisdom."

Arion stared at her with a look of shock. Then slowly a smile grew. "I suspect I'm not the only wise one here. You know what? You really are Cenz—" Arion looked out east with a concerned face. "Mawyndulë?"

Suri felt the hair on her neck rise. She began to put up the shield, but before she could, Arion shoved Suri backward with an incredible force. She stumbled and fell down the stairs, banging her elbows, pain jolting up her arms. She tumbled down a dozen steps before stopping.

"What was—" Suri began, when a flash of light blinded her and the whole upper portion of the tower exploded.

Suri felt the heat and heard a sizzle. This wasn't fire, and it wasn't lightning. This was raw, naked power, concentrated and devastating. Stone burst to powder, wood incinerated. Everything above was gone, including the room they had tea in, leaving Suri on the stairs of the now shorter tower. For an instant, Suri thought the worst, then she spotted Arion. She lay sprawled across three steps. Her eyes were open, but she wasn't moving.

She's not moving!

Suri was supposed to run to the safety of the runes below, but Arion didn't even look like she was breathing. She was . . .

Suri looked down from what had become the new top of the tower. Like a swan left a wake on a still pond, so, too, did the Art. Such a massive blast left a clear signature. This one traced back to Misery Rock. Filled with anguish and rage, Suri raised a hand and spoke a single word—nothing she'd been taught, nothing she'd figured out. It wasn't even a word she knew. Just as in Neith, she acted without thinking, pure reflex.

Power, she thought, and pushed out.

A blast tore through stone, exploding Misery Rock.

Suri thought she heard a cry or scream—not with her ears but along the same conduit that had sent the attack.

She waited. Nothing.

Suri reached out, searching, groping for the source. Power that strong should be easy to find, but she couldn't. The wellspring had dissipated—or the caster was dead. The fight was over.

From across the Grandford Bridge came the sound of horns. The second day of the battle was starting, but Suri didn't care. She ran over to Arion, who remained exactly where she had fallen. "Arion!"

Not a shudder, not a twitch, not a breath.

"No!"

Suri began chanting even before reaching Arion. She knew what to expect this time. She kicked the door to the spirit world open and leapt in. She dove head first into the waters of that awful river, dark and cold. She swam in search of Arion, calling her name as she went.

Arion! Arion! I'm here! I'll save you. Hold on, I'm here! Just hold on!

She shouted the words into the void.

But Arion wasn't there.

The river was empty. The dark waters clear.

Her friend had already been washed away.

Mawyndulë nearly killed himself on the trail coming down from what was left of the crag. The cliff-side path wasn't built for running, much less a panicked dash, and now it was strewn with debris. He slipped three times trying to get down and banged his knee hard enough to make his eyes water. He raced blindly through the choking dust cloud kicked up by the oh-so-close explosion that had ripped the world a new hole.

"What was that?" Mawyndulë shouted as he reached the bottom. He was no athlete, and he struggled to breathe, his lungs burning, his heart pounding. But he kept moving. He knew he needed to get away. "I thought we killed her!"

Silence.

"Jerydd? Jerydd, answer me!"

I don't know.

"What do you mean, you don't know?"

Which word didn't you understand?

"You act like you know everything, and yet, I almost died up there."

I told you there would be risks.

"But we killed her. I saw her die."

Yes. She's dead.

"Did she have some kind of trap on her? Some kind of defense that triggered when she died?"

No. Such things aren't possible.

"Then what?"

There was another person on that tower with Arion.

"Just some Rhune. She couldn't—" Mawyndulë remembered the death of Gryndal. How Arion had defended the Rhune and said, *This one has the Art.*

Couldn't what? Why'd you stop talking? What are you thinking?

"The Rhune," Mawyndulë said. "That Rhune has the Art."

That's impossible.

"I saw her before, when I was with Gryndal. She defied his silence. She has talent."

Talent is one thing; a knack is one thing, but a moment ago we were nearly hit by enough raw power to make me think Avempartha has a twin!

"*I* was nearly hit. Not *we*, me! I nearly died!"

You're alive. It's over. Quit making such a fuss.

"A fuss? What part of 'I nearly died' don't you understand?"

You're at war, not a tea party, and you wanted to go.

"I'm a prince, not some common soldier."

Funny how death doesn't discriminate. Makes you wonder about such privileges, doesn't it?

"I'm still running—or at least—walking very fast for my life here. Can you stay on topic? What does it mean if I'm right and a Rhune did that?"

A long pause followed; then, as Mawyndulë crossed back inside the pickets, he heard Jerydd's voice in his head.

Then Taraneh is more right than even he knows.

CHAPTER TWENTY-FIVE

The Art of War

*The best way I can describe that day was like watching the world
end with enough time to take notes—because it was, and I did.*
— THE BOOK OF BRIN

The smithy had a cot, water, and tools enough to do anything. Better than
Roan's roundhouse in Dahl Rhen, it had more space, a big forge, anvil,
trough, worktable with all sorts of tools, and no ghosts. That last amenity
was particularly nice. Iver had never set foot here, and no part of Alon
Rhist reminded her of him. Nevertheless, Roan still never slept on the cot.
The cot had been mostly for show, a concession to Gifford and the dwarfs.
Roan never knowingly used it. She worked until she dropped, sleeping
wherever she collapsed, which luckily had not yet been while working the
forge. She always woke up on the cot. The little men put her there, saying
she was in the way. She believed them the first few times, then realized she
always woke up covered with a neatly tucked blanket and with her shoes
off.

The foursome—whom everyone referred to as the Smith and Her Little

Crew, the Lady and the Three Dwarfs, or most often, She and They—had grown close. All of them diligent, single-minded workers, the four never talked much, but that didn't mean they didn't understand each other. When they did communicate, it was in grunts or gestures. A tilt of a head meant *add more coal,* and a nod said *pump the bellows.* The little men slept as infrequently as she did—not because they didn't want to sleep, but because if Roan worked, they did, too.

The labor was hard and all-consuming but never enough. In the past, all Roan had to forget about was Iver, and hard work was normally enough to manage that. She hadn't thought about the old woodcarver once, but it wasn't because of her workload. For the last two days, Roan hadn't touched her hammer—which she had named Banger the Heavy, and which she swore had developed wear marks that fit her hand. Since Gifford had left, she hadn't stoked the furnace, hadn't polished metal. Mostly, Roan sat in the corner holding the crutch he had left behind. Much of that time she spent crying. The rest she spent twisting her hair, biting her nails, or simply rocking in place.

Most of Roan's life had been spent in fear. In many ways, terror had become a familiar reassurance. She wouldn't call it a friend, but certainly fear was a visitor she could always count on to show up. With Iver's death, everything had changed. She now had the war, but that was as faceless and distant as worrying about famine or disease. Such things paled compared to being trapped in a small house with a huge man who had a propensity to torture. After that, she felt as if half of her life was missing. Part of her was gone, and that vacuum of fear had been filled with guilt.

She had killed Iver. No amount of justification made that right in her head, no matter how hard she tried. From this seed came thoughts that she must have helped make him what he was. Iver was never cruel to anyone else. The rest of the Dahl loved him. So it must have been her. She brought the evil out. And if she could do it to him, she might do it to others.

You'll be a curse to anyone who cares about you, Roan. That's what you really are, Roan, a curse, an evil curse, and you deserve what I'm going to give you now . . .

Then, just as she was beginning to think she might be able to live without the throat-clenching anxiety that drove her to beat Banger the Heavy senseless, the fear returned. But this time it was different.

She had watched from the parapet as Gifford rode across the bridge and through the Fhrey camp. She'd prayed to every god there was, and a few she invented, to keep him safe. And then he was gone. As horrible as it had been to live each day in dread of physical pain, worrying about Gifford was worse. There were precautions she was able to take with Iver. He wasn't always predictable, but most times she knew how to steer clear of real trouble. She knew to keep things clean, which items never to move; she knew not to speak, but to answer quickly when called; and never, never to protect herself from a beating—that always made him hit harder. And when he slept, she was free to relax, to breathe free air. But she could do nothing to help Gifford, and there was never any pause, no relief from the smothering terror that he might already be dead, and if he was . . . *one and one makes two, two and two makes four, four and four makes eight . . .*

She kept counting. The numbers distracted her, keeping her mind from wandering. When she lost focus, she started problem-solving. The challenge before her was the conundrum of how best to end her life. There was a vast array of possible choices, and picking the optimal solution wasn't as easy as might first appear. But if there was one thing Roan knew she was good at, it was solving problems. She'd already worked out a dozen excellent choices. Poison was the best, but she was far from isolating the perfect one. All she needed to do was . . . *eight and eight makes sixteen, sixteen and sixteen makes thirty-two, thirty-two and thirty-two makes—*

The smithy shook with a jolt. Dust kicked out of the corners, and all three little men stopped in mid–hammer swing to look at each other. A moment later, a second blast shook the place, and all of them ran out into the courtyard in time to see part of the Frozen Tower shear away.

Massive blocks of stone, sliced at an angle, just slipped and fell—mostly to the outside—but a few tumbled and rolled, smashing into the courtyard. One bashed through the roof of the woodshed, spitting a handful of split logs into the air.

A crowd rushed into the yard, everyone in nightshirts. This confused

Roan until she realized it was early morning, and only the dull suggestion of the light to come was in the sky.

"What's happening?" someone asked.

No one answered.

Roan guessed it was magic. She'd seen it before and had concluded that such things worked on different principles than ropes, pulleys, and wheels. Roan began wondering if magic wasn't just another methodology. People thought the bow and arrows she made were magic. Maybe magic was just something people couldn't understand. Perhaps, if she studied it, she might learn how magic functioned, how to harness its power in a practical, calculated manner. What a thing it might be if anyone, by the simple flipping of a lever, could illuminate a home with magic light.

"Roan!" Padera called. The old woman hobbled up, pointing at the damaged tower. "Get your bag and follow me. Now!"

Roan reached for her panic bag—a small satchel she kept filled with the most commonly needed emergency items—an extension of her pocket idea. Inside, she'd placed needle and thread, string, rope, a small but sturdy stick, salt, clean cloth cut in strips and some in squares, a tiny chunk of pure silver, willow bark, her bound knives, a tiny hammer—this one named Banger the Light—a cup, and a small saw. She grabbed it from the corner of the smithy and ran after Padera.

"Arion and Suri were in that tower," the old woman said as they hustled across the courtyard. A small cluster of men stood outside the Frozen Tower peering in at the open door. Roan and Padera pushed past those at the entrance. Then Padera stopped and grimaced at the steep stairs. "Go on, I'll wait here."

Roan climbed the shattered remains of the spiral steps. She only had to go a short way before finding both Suri and Arion, lying together.

"Arion? Suri?" Padera shouted from the bottom of the stairs. "Are they dead?"

"Well, they look . . . bad," Roan replied. She drew closer and bent down. "Suri is still breathing. Arion isn't. Yes, Arion is . . . Arion is . . ." She didn't want to say it.

"How is Suri?"

Roan shook the mystic's shoulder. "Suri?"

She didn't respond.

"No wounds but she's not waking up."

"Damn her," the old woman cursed. "She's tried it again."

"Tried what?" But Roan wasn't really paying attention to Padera any-more. She stared at Arion as she lay on her back, awkwardly bent, her eyes still open, staring up at the sky where the top of the tower had been. The Fhrey was thousands of years old, bald, and absolutely the most beautiful thing Roan had ever seen. Even in death, in that awkward position, she was still lovely. Roan reached over and closed Arion's eyes. That was bet-ter. *Now she looks like she's sleeping.*

"You there!" Padera shouted in her ragged voice. "Go up and carry them down. Bring them to the smithy."

"Is it safe?" someone asked.

"Safer than not doing what I tell you! Both of ya, get up there!"

Roan recognized the two men who came up. She thought their names were Glen, and Hobart, or Hubert. They were from Clan Menahan, as was obvious by the pattern of their rich blue, green, and yellow leigh mors. They approached the two Artists, looking terrified.

"Just pick her up! She won't bite," Padera shouted as if she could see them.

The two men looked at Roan with pleading eyes, searching for assur-ance or at least sympathy.

She nodded whatever approval she could give.

Suri and Arion were both tiny things, and the two men had no problem carrying them down, clutching the two like babies, heads slumped against their chests. By the time they were out of the tower and crossing the court-yard toward the smithy, the bells were ringing again. Day two of the war was about to start.

Once more, Persephone cursed her lacerated stomach, the bed, the raow, and anything else she could think of as she struggled to sit up and suffered for it. Stabbing pains jolted her from gut to toes.

"We don't know exactly," the young man said. His name was Aland, a soldier from the Third Spear—Harkon's Clan Melen battle group. Short, young, and thin, he had been assigned runner duties and become the official voice of the war for Persephone. "I got reports of flashes of light near the north tower, explosions, and. . . ."

"And what?"

"The top has been ripped away, gone like the Spyrok."

"How many hurt? How many dead?"

"Ah—two I think, one Fhrey female and a Rhune girl."

Persephone, Moya, and Brin looked at each other.

"Well, which is it? Hurt or dead? Are you saying Suri and Arion are . . . are they all right?"

"I don't know their names, but one is dead and the other can't be woken up."

Tears were filling Brin's eyes, while Moya stood stiff, her jaw clenched.

"Anything else?" Persephone asked the young man standing at attention at the foot of her bed.

"Just that the men have formed up inside the gates, and the archers were ordered to the walls. Lord Nyphron has decided not to engage them today."

"And the Fhrey army?"

"Lined up on the far side of the ford, but they aren't advancing yet."

"Fine. Get me details on the two who were hurt in the north tower."

The young man started toward the door then paused. "Do you want me to tell Lord Nyphron you wish to see him?"

"Nyphron?" Persephone shook her head. "No."

Brin crossed the room. In her hands, she still held the cup of water that Persephone had asked her to get before Aland had come in. Brin's hands were trembling, making the water jiggle. "Suri and Arion?" She looked down at the cup as Persephone took it from her. "What do you think happened?"

Persephone shook her head. She'd learned through painful trial and error not to shrug.

"I should go," Moya said.

Persephone nodded.

"I'll send someone to watch the door again."

"Okay."

Moya lingered a moment longer, looking at her. "It doesn't end. It just doesn't end, does it?" Then the beautiful woman with the big eyes and the longbow named Audrey left.

"*You* killed her?" the fane asked for a second time.

Mawyndulë nodded, disappointed his father had put so much emphasis on the word *you*.

"Are you sure? How can you know?"

"I saw her."

"Saw her?" His father was still in his tent, standing in the light of three freestanding candelabras as two servants strapped on his armor. The sun was rising, but too weak and too slow to illuminate the tent's interior. "How could you have *seen* her?"

Tell him the truth. He won't believe a lie, and he'll find out eventually anyway.

"Kel Jerydd helped me. He's using Avempartha."

Since the start of the battle, Synne had been constantly searching for danger, but now she paused to stare at him. Even the servants stopped their work to look over. Both of Lothian's brows rose.

"He taught me how to talk with him before we left."

"You're in communication with Jerydd?" his father asked.

"Yes."

The fane continued to stare at Mawyndulë for several seconds, trying to digest this. Then he began walking around the tent in thought. The servants followed, struggling to finish their tasks. Sile, who was in his path, was forced to take a step back, pressing his massive size against the canvas. Another step and he might have brought the whole place down. "So that explosion was Jerydd channeling Avempartha's power through you?"

Mawyndulë nodded but was quick to add, "Yes, and I nearly died."

His father continued to walk in a circle, trailing his servants, showing no sign of having heard him. He stopped. "Ask Jerydd if he can do more."

I can do whatever my fane wishes.

"Yes, he can," Mawyndulë replied.

"Good—excellent. Come with me." The fane walked out of the tent.

The captains of the Shahdi—the Erivan military—had assembled around a bare patch of exposed stone where a small fire burned. Each was outfitted in full battle gear of bronze armor, blue capes, and helmets with bristled crests of horse hair, color coded to their regiment. Some were tall, some short, most old.

"My fane!" they all shouted, snapping to attention at his approach and clearing room around the fire for his father's entourage. Several eyes glanced at Synne. Most of them had been introduced to her in the usual fashion. As a result, none of them made sudden moves in the presence of the fane.

"Assemble the troops but don't advance," his father ordered. "We're going to do things a little differently today."

Tell him about the other one, about the Rhune.

"They have another Artist. She's still alive," Mawyndulë said. His father looked at him, confused. Mawyndulë found it nice that his father finally listened when he spoke, listened with real interest, but he felt it wasn't his words so much as Jerydd's he was listening for. "There's a Rhune Artist in Alon Rhist."

His father looked puzzled. "Did you say *a Rhune?*"

"We think she's freakishly powerful." He used the word *we* preemptively, knowing that his father would ignore any speculation of his.

She's not that powerful. I was just caught off guard. Now that I know she's there, things will be different.

"A Rhune? How is that possible?"

Mawyndulë shrugged for both of them.

"Does Jerydd think he can beat her?"

Not a problem.

Mawyndulë nodded.

"Well"—the fane began finishing the buckle on his breastplate himself—"tell Jerydd to warm up the tower. We're going to do some damage today."

Moya reached the parapet above the front gate. It was lined with her archers, Tesh among them.

"Are you supposed to be here?" she asked.

"Raithe didn't say I couldn't."

"You didn't ask, either."

"You don't know that," the kid said, adjusting the tube packed with arrows that was slung over his back.

He had twenty, maybe twenty-five in there—a bristling bouquet of white, black, and gray feathers. The other archers had a similar number. Moya remembered how she had fought a demon with only six, back when arrows had stone tips, and *arrow* meant a tiny spear with *a row* of markings. Now everyone had unmarked iron-headed shafts with three feathers placed to align properly with the notched end, and no one had any idea where the term *arrow* came from. Maybe one day if someone else learned to read Brin's writing, they would know.

Out across the ford, she could see the Fhrey army. *Such straight lines.*

"Don't let fly until I tell you," she shouted, and the order was repeated up and down the line. "Wait for my signal."

"How's Brin?" Tesh asked.

"You know, if you weren't here with me, you could go up to the Kype and ask her yourself."

"But then I wouldn't be able to kill elves."

Moya bent her bow, hooked the loop of the bowstring, then looked over at the kid. "You hate them, don't you?"

"Don't you? They slaughtered my family, my whole village, the entire clan. I just want to return the favor."

"We live with them, you know. I'm even—sort of—*with* one." She didn't know how else to put it. "Don't repeat that, by the way—not even to him."

"Tekchin?"

"Yeah, the ugly one." She tested the weight of the draw. "Not all of them are bad."

She caught a glimpse from Tesh that wasn't the look of a child. Too cold, too hard, too ruthless to be the eyes of innocence.

"C'mon, even you have to agree with that—you saved Nyphron's life."

That look again. He wiped it away and didn't answer, but in his eyes, she spotted something he sought to hide, something dark—an awful, pitiless hunger that had no place in the face of a man much less a boy. For that brief instant, Moya was reminded of the raow. They all had the same famished look, and for the first time, Moya felt frightened of this barely ex-child whom she'd taught to kill from a distance.

She was still staring at him when the world began to shake.

They had Suri on the cot, a blanket pulled up to her neck. Padera listened to the mystic's heartbeat while willow bark stewed on the furnace. At first, it was just Roan and Padera. The little men waited outside with the rest but came back in when Roan asked them to stoke the fire. Tressa came with them. She was the one who had filled the bucket with water for boiling the bark.

Roan had grown up three houses away from Tressa. Her primary memory of the woman was the parties held at Tressa's home; at least they sounded like parties. She had listened to singing and laughter late into the night and would lie awake imagining what it might be like to laugh like that. Roan was never invited. Tressa hadn't been the sort to mingle with the slave of a woodcarver the way Moya, Padera, Brin, or Gifford had. Roan always wondered why—not why Tressa had refused to acknowledge her existence, but why Moya, Padera, Brin, and Gifford hadn't.

Everyone hated Tressa because her husband, in his ambition to become chieftain, had killed Reglan, and he'd tried to kill Persephone, too. Tressa had steadfastly denied knowing about her husband's plans, but no one believed her. Moya despised Tressa. Brin hated her, too, and as a result, Roan felt she should as well; but she didn't. Roan understood what it was like to be the outcast, to be the one who didn't count. As a result, Roan smiled even while Padera scowled at Tressa.

Tressa drew back. "What are you grinning at?"

"Thank you for the water."

"I didn't bring it for you. I brought it for her." Tressa pointed at Suri.

"Since when do you do anything for anyone other than yourself?" Padera asked.

"Why do you care? Needed the water, right? Need it to make your witch's brew, so there, you got it."

"Fine," Padera said. "Now leave."

Tressa frowned and turned toward the door.

"She doesn't have to go," Roan said.

"She doesn't have to stay, either." Padera rinsed a folded cloth in the bucket.

"This is my smithy." Roan spoke with unaccustomed firmness.

This brought a sidelong squint from Padera and an incredulous look from Tressa.

"This isn't *your* smithy," Tressa said. "All of this belongs to the Fhrey."

"Which right now belongs to Persephone." Padera placed the cloth on Suri's forehead. "You remember Persephone, don't you, Tressa? The one you and your husband—"

"I don't care whose smithy it is," Roan said in a raised voice. "She! Can! Stay!"

Padera and Tressa and even the three dwarfs looked over, surprised.

The old woman went back to mopping up Suri's face without another word. Tressa continued to stare a moment longer. She ran her tongue along the full width of her teeth, then sucked like she had something stuck between them. Finally, she drew in a breath through her nose and gave a little nod. "Thanks."

Right about then Roan felt a little lightheaded—she got dizzy sometimes from not eating or when she went too long without sleep—but when she noticed ripples in the bucket resting on the ground, she realized the feeling wasn't coming from her. A moment later, the tools hanging from the overhead crossbeams began to clank against one another. Dust spilled down, and the shaking got worse.

Malcolm came running in. He looked at Suri, then at the rest of them. "We need to wake her, and fast."

Raithe was lying on his cot in the barracks when the rumblings began. He'd heard the bell, watched the others scramble, but didn't even pull back his blanket. No one stopped or asked why. He was wounded and wouldn't be expected to fight unless the Fhrey breached the gate. Only that wasn't why. At least, it wasn't the wound they knew about that kept him in bed.

It would take a man like Gath. Someone renowned, someone who everyone could agree was the bravest, strongest warrior among them. Someone who all the chieftains could kneel to and not lose the respect of their people. It would take a hero.

That's what Persephone wanted. Used to be him—now it was Nyphron.

When he closed his eyes, he could still see Persephone as she once was, climbing the creaking ladder to the top of Dahl Rhen's wall, wearing her black dress. That's how he best remembered her, how she used to be. The wind was in her hair on the night the Fhrey had arrived, the day after Konniger tried to kill her and they had all jumped off the waterfall. She was so lovely, and she had needed him. He had been her protector against the Fhrey, against Konniger. *He* had been her hero.

I wish I hadn't asked her to leave with me.

That had been a mistake—a huge one. Back then his mind was possessed by the lush fields that he and his father had found across the two rivers. He couldn't imagine that she wouldn't want to go. Her own chieftain hated her, and the Fhrey had invaded. His idea to find a better place should have been embraced with repeated *thank-yous*. But he hadn't understood Persephone's devotion to her people.

Lying on the cot, he stared at the ceiling. He could picture the two of them across the Urum, up on that hill. He saw a beautiful log house with an actual door, a field of wheat growing next to a field of rye, and a split-log corral filled with grazing sheep. The two of them happy and safe, far from the beat of drums, the claws of raow, the peal of bells, and the—

A crack ripped up the side of the stone wall of the barracks. Pieces of stone chipped and spat across the room, skipping off the wood floor. The ceiling rattled, and the floor shook so hard, Raithe no longer needed to get out of bed. The bed did the work for him.

Standing up, he found the shaking more noticeable, more alarming—as if he were in a little boat rolling over waves. He grabbed his sword belt and jogged for the door. He arrived in the courtyard just in time to see the remainder of the Frozen Tower collapse.

"Get off the wall!" Moya shouted as everyone watched the north tower crumble.

The massive stones came straight down, imploding and giving birth to a massive cloud of dust, dirt, and crushed rock. Below her, spider-web-thin cracks spread through the stone. Soon, the whole front wall of Alon Rhist began to waver, and Moya screamed.

Whether the archers had heard her or not, they ran for the stairs. Then the tower collapsed. It didn't implode; it toppled. Listing to one side, the stone staggered, then keeled over and fell across the upper courtyard, crushing the barracks and the kitchens, narrowly missing the smithy.

Moya was shoved from behind. She bounced off Filson's back and lost her footing on the steps. She would have fallen if there had been room. Too many bodies prevented her from going all the way down. A hand caught her by the wrist and drew her out of the crush. She pressed against the outer wall, letting the others run by, which they did without a glance. The stone she leaned on was shivering.

Stone shouldn't shiver.

The hand that had caught Moya belonged to Tesh. He waited beside her for the mob to rampage past while the wall they stood on quaked and quivered.

We're above the main gate. This is their target!

The idea was slow in coming but finally arrived. The Fhrey were trying to bring down the front wall, to lay the fortress bare. Moya heard the crack and snap of stone and the screams of more than a dozen men as the stairs disintegrated.

We're next.

Moya braced for the fall. She grabbed the ancient parapet, despite knowing that it, too, would fall. The stairs and the primary supports for the massive wall were gone. The whole thing was going down. It had to, but it didn't. The wall continued to shake and jerk back and forth. Tesh and Moya wrapped their arms around the merlons, clinging to the bucking wall. Still, it didn't fall.

Across the chasm, Moya spotted the Fhrey troops lined up at the foot of the bridge. They were waiting for the front of the fortress to come down. But the front wall of Alon Rhist refused to fall. Bewilderment filled every face as the great stones danced like a stack of juggled plates. Looking inside the courtyard, Moya saw why.

Standing amidst the rubble of the toppled tower, just outside the smithy, Moya saw the small figure of Suri flanked by Roan, her dwarfs, Malcolm, and Padera. She stood with arms outstretched, hands moving, head thrown back as if singing to the sky.

Not knowing if Suri was winning or losing, or just buying time, Moya didn't want to wait to find out. The stairs to the south were gone. The only way off was the steps on the far side.

"Up for a crazy run?" Moya asked Tesh and nodded toward the long expanse of crenelated parapet that wiggled like a snake.

"Always." Tesh turned his body and knelt like a sprinter. "Ready."

"You first. Go!" she shouted.

The kid took off and got several strides across before being buffeted between the battlements. He staggered and fell, got up, and ran again. Once he was three merlons down, she started her run. She could have been sprinting across a bobbing log in a rushing river for all the stability the wall was providing. A jerk nearly sent her out a crenel.

Not a log at all—I'm running along a rope used in a tug-of-war!

While remaining vertical, the wall was faring poorly from the struggle. Stone blocks were jiggled free and fell. Whole merlons were missing, and the parapet was no longer anywhere close to straight. While it changed from moment to moment, the wall had warped into an *S* shape. About the time Moya was in the very center, she heard a terrible *clang.* Fearing she was about to fall, she sucked in a breath, but the wall stayed up.

The doors! The great bronze gates are right beneath me. They must have been shaken off their hinges.

Ahead of her, Tesh reached the stairs, and once more he stopped. Turning back, he waved frantically for her and waited.

Kid has more balls than brains.

The wall jerked again, and she was slapped from one merlon to the other. She slammed one shoulder hard enough to make her cry out, then the other side of the walkway hit her in the chest, knocking the air out of her.

Tetlin's tit!

She forced her legs to keep moving. Moya wasn't sure where the strength came from—maybe Suri had buoyed her up, or Mari was lending support, or just plain old-fashioned fear fed her efforts—but she finished the crossing, and she and Tesh raced down the steps to the courtyard.

They were fifty feet away when at last the wall came down.

Suri used to try to catch fish with her bare hands. She'd seen the bears do it, so she thought it was worth a try. Tura had explained that her lack of claws was an insurmountable obstacle. Suri tried anyway. She had stood knee-deep in the stream where the fish swam in the shallows—the same place where the bears hunted—and she scooped up a nice river salmon. The scales were slick as oil, and the creature wiggled, fighting hard. She could feel the muscles thrashing back and forth as the fish struggled. She pulled it to her chest, but the thing was just too slippery, too heavy, too strong. After a titanic battle, it flew from her hands and back into the river, leaving her disappointed and realizing that she couldn't do everything.

Suri felt the same way when the wall was finally torn from her grasp and shattered into a heap of broken stone.

You just don't have the claws.

The land continued to shake. There were no runes on the ground to stop it. The Orinfar protected the primary walls, which was part of the problem in holding them up. She couldn't grab them with the Art. Instead, she was forced to use the air around them and anything else that wasn't rune-marked. No sooner did she stop one tower from falling, then another began to wobble. She tried to calm the ground but couldn't.

Where is all that power coming from?

All Suri was doing was holding things together, and she felt exhausted. The struggle over the front wall had drained her, the runes on it acting against her efforts, and the continued fight to withstand the impacts that shuddered the rest of the fortress was a marathon she couldn't finish.

Maybe it's because there are more of them. But Suri could only sense the one, a young Fhrey. She could almost see him, and there was something familiar in that connection. She knew this person. He'd been in Dahl Rhen. He was the one—

"The bridge," a voice said in her ear. "Forget the walls. Destroy the Grandford Bridge."

If the words had been screamed, she might not have listened, but the calm confidence was something one looked for in emergencies.

The bridge.

She felt them coming across—hundreds. They were in a hurry, afraid she would notice and terrified she wouldn't be distracted enough. Worried she might—

Suri let go—let the tower fall. Then, with all her remaining strength she reached out toward that delicate span, that thin vulnerable sliver of stone that crossed a very deep chasm. The bridge was just as protected with runes as the walls, but she didn't need to touch it any more than the elves needed to touch the walls of Alon Rhist to topple them. Destroying was so much easier than preserving. All Suri needed was to shift the cliffs.

Suri moved the east cliff just a bit to the south, and the west cliff a bit to the north. Like unraveling a string weave, or opening a knot, the bridge disconnected from both sides and came free. The span fell. She couldn't see it with her eyes, but she sensed it, felt the weight give way and heard the screams as hundreds of Fhrey plummeted to their deaths.

Suri whirled and reached out, looking for the next calamity. There wasn't one. The ground stopped shaking. She sensed nothing. The world returned to stillness.

Suri opened her eyes and saw the devastated remains of the fortress. The entire front of Alon Rhist was a ruin of crumbled stone and shattered wood. Malcolm laid his hands on Suri's shoulders and gave a gentle, reassuring squeeze. Roan was there, too, and the old woman Padera, and Tressa, and Moya, and Tesh, and Raithe. They were all with her, including dozens of men and Fhrey she didn't know, everyone looking relieved.

Everyone was there . . . everyone except Arion.

CHAPTER TWENTY-SIX

The Butterfly and the Promise

Voices of the dead have a way of compelling us that the voices of the living can never match—there is simply no way to argue.

—THE BOOK OF BRIN

The look on Lothian's face was terrifying. Not fear, not hatred, not disappointment, not even frustration, but a horrible mix of each—and a heavy dose of rage. His cheeks and ears had turned red, his eyes bulged, and the vein in his neck and forehead stood out.

"Those Fhrey . . ." The fane lost the ability to speak and opted to just point toward where the bridge had been. "All those brave Fhrey . . ." He gritted his teeth and forced a swallow. "They're all dead."

Mawyndulë didn't say anything. He knew from experience that nothing he said when his father was upset ever helped, and he'd never seen his father this agitated.

"How did you let that happen?"

We didn't exactly let it happen, Jerydd said from the safety of his head.

"It was an accident," Mawyndulë said.

"An accident!" his father shouted at him. "They're all dead!"

That's war for you. Aren't you glad you declared it? Did you think it would be all sunshine and rainbows? Besides, we killed three times that many when the wall crushed the people in the courtyard. Wait! Don't say that—he'll still see it as a loss. Your father doesn't think one Rhune equals a Fhrey, and rightly so.

Mawyndulë couldn't believe that Jerydd thought he'd relay any of that, but then again, the kel was safe, miles away from the fane's anger.

"She's incredibly strong."

"You had the power of Avempartha! Or so you said."

We do.

"I do."

But that Rhune bitch sucks power like a whirlpool in a hurricane, and she's as flexible as a ten-year-old. Plus, she's fast, really fast—Synne fast. And we couldn't get at her.

"There were runes on that wall between her and us, so we couldn't attack her directly. Still, we eventually won, and the wall came down."

"And so did the bridge with hundreds of my soldiers," the fane said through clenched teeth.

"Well, yeah, but that wasn't our fault. Everything was happening so fast. I'm shocked she was able to think about that given everything we were throwing at her."

The fane continued to fume, taking rapid deep breaths while glaring at his son. Then he turned to Taraneh and Haderas. "We still have five Miralyith, right?"

"Four, my fane," Taraneh replied. "Lym died last night from wounds to—"

"Okay, four. That's seven including Synne, Mawyndulë, and me. We'll take care of it ourselves. I should have known better than to rely on Jerydd. That's the second time he's failed me. He underestimates everyone. But no Artist can stand against seven. Forget all this marshalling of power. We'll each work independently. During the night, the seven of us will each form a bridge—and *hold* it. Then the Shahdi will cross. The outer wall has fallen, the gates gone. Their orders will be to slaughter everyone on that side of the river."

"All the Rhunes, you mean."

"I mean everyone."

"But, my fane," Taraneh said, shocked, "there are hundreds of Fhrey in Alon Rhist. Not all of them are soldiers, and those who are haven't participated in the fight. Well, not as far as we can tell."

"All of them!" Lothian ordered. "Everyone who wanted to go, left. No one over there is being held against their will. They chose that side of the river. They chose to defy me. Kill them all, Taraneh. Every last one."

Taraneh stared in disbelief for only a second, then bowed. "As you wish."

Your father sounds upset.

Raithe stood in the middle of what used to be the lower courtyard. What had once been a grand fortress of soaring walls and majestic towers was little more than a hillside again—a barren crag littered with piles of broken stone and broken bodies. Hundreds had been crushed by the collapse. Some were trapped when buildings came down, others were below walls that toppled. When it became apparent that the Fhrey had given up their assault for that day, the remaining inhabitants of Alon Rhist began the sad and exhausting process of digging out the dead. With only one good arm, Raithe was useless. He stood in the center of the rubble and simply watched as people he knew were pulled back into the sun.

A face here or a name there from Dahl Rhen, Tirre, Melen, Warric, and Menahan, folks he'd known for only a year. Thinking about it, he really didn't know any of them. Raithe had kept to himself, stayed apart, avoided friendships and connections. Better that way, he'd felt. No sense in establishing ties that might be hard to break. But looking at their bloodied faces, he discovered something terrible. He hadn't managed to remain as distant as he thought.

Tope Highland was laid beside his last two sons, Colin and Kris, both great dancers and singers, who'd displayed their talents on many a night after the late meal. Their mother was arranging marriages for the two lads with girls from Menahan, and neither was anxious to see whom their mother had picked. Tope's other son, Kurt, who was the same age as Tesh, had died the day before. Filson the Lamp was stretched out on a small bit of still-visible grass across from Tope's family. He'd been a quiet man, once the only full-time lamp maker in Dahl Rhen, but few knew him as "the Lamp" anymore. He was a soldier, one of Moya's archers. Filson had befriended a stray dog that wandered the Rhist. He fed the bony animal leftovers from his meals, causing the mongrel to follow him everywhere. Raithe caught him giving the dog as much as half his food. The fool was going hungry to feed a mangy mutt. Next to him were Gilroy and his wife, Arlina. Her head had been caved in. Raithe identified Arlina by the dress. She only had the one.

Before he knew it, Raithe found himself weeping. *I only stayed in Dahl Rhen for Persephone. She was all I wanted, all I cared about. None of these others mattered. So why in Tetlin's name do I feel so awful?*

"Raithe?"

He turned and saw Malcolm near Roan's smithy, one of the few structures still intact. The thin man was out of his armor, back to wearing the old wool clothes Brin's mother, Sarah, had made him. What a year ago had been clean and neat was as stained and tattered as Malcolm's old robe had been. The man was hard on clothes. He waved Raithe over, then went into the workshop.

Moving slowly, Raithe crossed the courtyard and followed him. Inside, the place was a cave, dark except for the eerie orange light thrown by the forge and the patch of sunlight entering the doorway. The dwarfs and Roan were there, which was to be expected, but Tressa also stood in the shadows. Suri knelt on the floor beside Arion, who lay on Roan's cot. A blanket was pulled to the dead Fhrey's neck as if she were sleeping. Raithe paused to stare at her a moment. The others probably thought he was paying respect or was overcome by grief. Neither was in his mind. A dead Fhrey was still such a strange thing. Arion was pale, but she always had been. Yet on that cot, catching most of the doorway light, she appeared ghost-like. So fragile was she that he found it difficult to accept that she had ever been alive. As he stared, Raithe realized with a good deal of reluctance that he had liked Arion. He had liked her a lot, though he couldn't remember a single conversation they had shared.

Suri's eyes were puffy and red, her cheeks streaked with tear tracks. Raithe knew how close the two had been. Suri had often spoken of Arion as if she were an older sister or even her mother. A strange way for a human to feel about a Fhrey, but Suri was anything but usual. That was what he liked the most about her. She could find the person inside the drapery, see the truth behind lies, and she cared for those uncared for by others. That he was Dureyan never mattered to her, and even if he knew nothing about the one called Cenzlyor, Raithe would have felt her loss because Suri loved her. He wished he could help, but knew from experience there were some things no one could fix.

Frost, Flood, and Rain busied themselves by adding wood to the furnace and jabbing pokers into the coals. Occasionally, they stole looks over their shoulders. Roan sat on her stool at the worktable, watching. She wore a leather apron looped around her neck and extending below her knees. Her dark hair was tied up out of the way, a lone lock dangling over her forehead.

Malcolm waited. He stood very nearly in the middle of the smithy between the assembly table and a stack of wooden buckets. Once Raithe moved away from Arion, Malcolm folded his hands before him in a deliberate manner that announced sincerity. "What I have to say to you now is incredibly important. More important than anything I've told anyone in a very long time. I might stumble here and there because it's not an easy thing to talk about, so please, bear with me."

Raithe had never heard him speak so gravely before, and for a moment he didn't sound like Malcolm. Not the man he met on a fork between two rivers, the one who had followed him blindly for a year, the one who didn't know which animals could be petted and which would attack. This was someone else.

"Want us to leave?" Roan asked. She was so convinced of the expected answer that she got to her feet.

"No," Malcolm replied. "What I have to say is for everyone here."

Roan stopped here, confusion swimming in her eyes. She eased back onto her stool. At the same time, the dwarfs put down the pokers and paused to listen.

"We have a problem," Malcolm began. "A very serious one. The Fhrey outnumber us three to one. Our rune-etched walls are broken, the only things protecting us are gone, and most of our best soldiers are dead." He gestured at Raithe. "Or wounded."

"What do we need walls for?" Raithe said. "The bridge is gone."

Malcolm shook his head. "Lack of a bridge won't stop them. They still have Miralyith. They will use the Art to extend the stone of the cliff walls. I told Suri to destroy the bridge only to give us this time to prepare."

"That was you?" Suri asked.

Malcolm nodded, then turned to Suri and offered her a sympathetic smile. "You can't stop them, can you?"

Suri shook her head. "I'm not strong enough." Suri touched Arion's hand. "She might have been, but not me."

"Arion couldn't have stopped them, either," Malcolm said. "And tonight the fane's Miralyith will create new bridges, and his army will cross over the Bern River with orders to kill everyone. You might disrupt one or two of the bridges, Suri, but you won't be able to take down all seven."

"Seven? Wait . . ." Frost said, rubbing his beard the way he did when he was pondering. "How do you know there will be seven? How do you know any of this?"

Malcolm shook his head. "That's not important at the moment. Just consider it a good guess. How we stop them is what we must discuss."

Suri looked back at Arion and shook her head. "We can't."

"You sure?" Malcolm asked.

"Pretty—" She didn't finish and the tears flowed again.

"Isn't this Nyphron's and Persephone's problem to solve?" His voice had an odd sound, more gravelly than usual. Raithe didn't understand the change. He sounded upset, and his anger grew each time he looked at Arion's face. It didn't make sense; the dwarfs had hated Arion. Everyone knew that.

"They can't solve this," Malcolm said. "But the people in this room can."

This conjured a round of puzzled faces as they looked to one another for hints of understanding. They found none.

"What can we do against an army of Fhrey that Nyphron and Keenig Persephone can't?" Frost asked.

"He means me," Suri said, shaking her head. "But I can't—"

"Actually, I mean everyone," Malcolm said. "Every single person in this room must do their part."

This brought a look of absurd disbelief from Tressa, who remained uncharacteristically silent.

"There's nothing I can do!" Suri was shaking her head. "If they hit me with the same power as before, I can't—"

"They *will* hit you, and with *more* than last time," Malcolm assured her. "Only one Miralyith fought you today. But after the bridges are made and the troops are across, all seven will focus on you. Once you are gone, we won't stand a chance. The Fhrey army will butcher every living soul while the Miralyith obliterates what remains of the city."

"If what you say is true, we don't actually *have* a problem," Raithe said. "We *have* a lack of hope."

"Gifford might return," Roan said, causing everyone to look her way. The sudden attention caused her to shrink back, drawing up her knees and hugging them. Still, she managed to add in an unusually proud tone, "He rode a horse to fetch the Gula."

Tressa was shaking her head, but Malcolm smiled at Roan, a warm, encouraging look accompanied by a confident nod. "Yes, I honestly think he will, but it won't be enough, and it won't be in time. And the Gula don't have armor—they lack the protection of the Orinfar. Were they here now, they would be obliterated by the fane's Miralyith."

Roan looked guilty.

"It's not your fault. You and your army of smiths did an amazing job. No one could have done more. There simply wasn't time."

"Then it really is over," Raithe said. "There's nothing we can do."

"No," Malcolm replied and shifted his sight back toward Suri. "She knows a way."

The mystic's tattoos drew together in a confused furrow on her brow. "But you just said I wasn't strong enough against all of them."

He nodded. "But you know something they don't. You know how to make something that the Miralyith's magic would be powerless against."

Suri appeared even more puzzled and was shaking her head. "I don't know what—"

She froze.

The tattoos around her eyes separated, and her brows jumped up. Her mouth opened, first in understanding, then in horror. The mystic's head began shaking rapidly. "No—not *that.*"

"You can do it," Malcolm said softly. "You've done it before."

"No—I can't." Suri inched back, withdrawing from him, from all of them. Her fear-filled eyes darted to each of their faces as if they all plotted her death.

"It's the only thing that will save us."

Roan had her hands up to her mouth, her eyes reflecting Suri's horror. Frost dropped the tongs he was holding, and Rain joined Suri in shaking his head.

"What's going on?" Raithe asked. "What are you talking about?"

Malcolm replied by looking at Suri, who refused to answer. No one else said a word.

"Everyone knows what's going on but me," Raithe said. He focused on Roan. "What is it?"

The woman lowered her hands, and after a fleeting glance toward Suri, she said, "He wants her to make another Gilarabrywn."

At the sound of the word, Malcolm turned with a curious look. "*Gilarabrywn?*"

Roan nodded. "That was her name."

Malcolm thought a moment, then nodded. "Oh—I see; yes, of course."

"I can't do it." Suri's head was down, her fingers raking through her short hair. She gripped and pulled, making herself wince.

"A Gilarabrywn would be immune to their magic," Malcolm told her. "It could end this battle. Might even end the war."

"But I can't!" Suri nearly screamed.

"I don't understand. Why can't you make this thing if it will save us?" Raithe asked.

Again, Suri didn't answer. She drew in her arms and legs, closing on herself, collapsing. She gazed at all of them. "Don't ask me to do that. Not again."

Raithe looked to the others, then finally just stared at Roan once more.

"To make a Gilarabrywn, she has to kill an animal," Roan explained.

"That's no problem at all," Tressa said. "There's a dog, a filthy mutt that Filson used to feed that—"

"No!" Suri erupted in anger. "Not an animal. I don't have to kill *an animal*." I have to . . . I have to kill . . . it has to be a *sacrifice*."

"Like a lamb?" Raithe asked. Lambs were animals, but that's what they always used as sacrifices in Dureya.

"No! Not like a *lamb*—not a killing—a *real* sacrifice. This isn't about slaughtering some innocent beast. It isn't about destroying what might have been a nice meal. It has to be *real*, not symbolic. And it has to be mine. I have to destroy . . . I have to take a life that matters to me. Don't you understand? I have to kill someone I love."

By the surprise on the faces, this was news to everyone—except Malcolm, who placed a comforting hand on Suri's shoulder. "In order to save the lives of everyone who went to Neith," Malcolm told Raithe, "Suri sacrificed Minna."

Raithe knew the wolf was missing, and he'd heard she'd been killed on their trip, but he had no idea that— "You *loved* Minna."

Tears slipped down Suri's cheeks as she nodded.

"Suri," Malcolm said. "You have to make another Gilarabrywn or everyone will die. Not just us, but the Gula-Rhunes, too. And if the Fhrey succeed in winning here, the fane will order his army into Rhulyn where he'll scorch the fields, burn the villages and dahls, and hunt every last human to extinction. As bad as that sounds, it won't end there. The fane has lost reason, gone mad." Malcolm looked to the three dwarfs standing by the anvil. "He knows the Belgriclungreian people helped. He knows about the iron weapons and the Orinfar."

"We didn't give either of those," Frost protested. "The Orinfar was found in an old rol, and as for iron . . ." He pointed at Roan. "We didn't give that. She stole it."

Roan got to her feet. "And you stole the same secret from the Ancient One."

"We didn't steal it. My ancestors made a trade."

"Which your ancestors didn't honor, which means you stole it."

Frost didn't answer.

"And this isn't iron." Roan let her hand run over a sheet of metal lying on the table behind her. "It has iron in it, but I changed the process. This is a different metal: harder, lighter, and it won't tarnish or rust. But you're right. I did steal the idea, most of it. I improved on the concept, but the majority I got from the rubbings." Still touching the shiny metal, she added, "I shouldn't hide that. Everyone should know the truth." She nodded. "Yes—I did steal this, so that's what I will call it—*steel*." Her lower lip quivered as she nodded. "Yes, that's a good name. There's no *rrr* sound in *steel*."

"It doesn't matter." Malcolm's voice lowered to a sympathetic tone. "What matters is that the fane believes the Belgriclungreians broke the agreement they had with Erivan. Lothian will seek to do what Fenelyus refused to. He'll march on Belgreig, slaughter his way south, and destroy Drumindor with as little problem as you've seen here." Malcolm stared at the three dwarfs. "Your people will be destroyed along with the humans. Two massive branches from the tree of life severed, and that's too much of a shock for the old gal to sustain. With no outside enemies, the Fhrey will devolve. Some have already broken their covenant with Ferrol, ignored the law of the horn, and killed each other. In time, more will seek to rid themselves of the Miralyith, or the Miralyith will seek to purify themselves and eliminate the other tribes. A population like theirs that reproduces so slowly can't survive a civil war. The goblins will see their opportunity and attack. Then it will be the Grenmorians against the goblins, and civilization will vanish, snuffed out before it ever had a chance to truly bloom."

Suri glared at him. "So, I have to do this or the world ends? Is that what you're saying? Is there anything else you want to add? How about the sun, will it go out? Will the moon fall? Will all the lakes, rivers, and streams dry up?"

"Actually, there *is* one more thing," Malcolm said, then looked down at Arion. "This is part of what she needed you to do—why you had to live and become a butterfly."

At the sound of that last word, Suri gasped. She clutched her body tighter and her breath grew shallower as she glared at him.

"Her Art," Malcolm explained. "Her ties with the world whispered the message in her ears. That was her gift, the one Fenelyus saw, but neither of them fully understood. Everything Arion did since coming to Dahl Rhen has led you to this point. She worked hard to provide you with the power to save your people and hers. The treasure you brought back from Neith wasn't iron or steel. It was the knowledge you gained from Minna's sacrifice. Suri, your sister didn't die to save the nine of you, she sacrificed herself to save the world." Malcolm offered a knowing smile. "She truly was the wisest of wolves."

The tattoos came together again as Suri bounced back from the blow Malcolm had delivered. She looked angry.

Minna was a subject Suri avoided. The wolf's death was something Raithe knew to step carefully around. Malcolm was dancing on the narrow ledge of a very high cliff.

"How do you know?" Suri demanded. "How do you know about the butterfly?" She pointed at Arion. "Did she tell you?"

"No," Malcolm said. "But that's not important."

"It is!" Suri rose up to her knees to face him.

"No—it isn't. What's important is that what I'm telling you is true. If it isn't, just say so."

Suri stared at Malcolm with a wild look that terrified Raithe.

The mystic was breathing hard, her teeth clenched as if she was deciding whether to make Malcolm explode or not. Her breathing slowed, and the muscles in her face relaxed. "Doesn't matter," she replied while looking over at Arion. "I'm all out of friends to kill."

The smithy fell silent then. From outside, the sounds of people digging and heaving stones entered the open doorway. Suri threw her head back and wiped her eyes. Roan stared at her worktable, and the dwarfs inspected their boots.

"Is she?" Malcolm asked.

"I'm clearly not in the running," Tressa said. "For once, being universally hated is a good thing."

"Is she, Raithe?" Malcolm looked at him.

"Is she what?" he asked.

Malcolm waited.

"Don't look at him," Suri said. "Why are you looking at him?"

Malcolm continued to stare. The man who didn't know how to use a spear and had never seen a dahl was gone—no longer the clueless ex-slave whom Raithe had saved from death in the wilderness. There were no questions in those eyes, no fear. All Raithe saw was sadness, sympathy, and patience as he waited for a response.

"Are you saying . . ." Raithe began, then faltered.

Is he saying what I think he is?

Malcolm nodded. "You wanted to make a difference."

The words punched him in the gut, and it was Raithe's turn to look devastated.

"You can make your life matter."

"You mean I can make my *death* matter."

"Wait, what?" Roan asked.

"He's suggesting that Suri kill Raithe to make a Gilarabrywn," Rain said.

Suri stared aghast at everyone.

Malcolm stayed focused on Raithe. "She gave you all the food. She took from herself and Kaylin, and gave it all to you. She did it so you would live. Just as Arion sensed the importance in Suri, so, too, did your mother understand that one day you would be needed. She wasn't a mystic or a Miralyith; she didn't need to be. Elan spoke to her just as it did to Arion, but your mother understood it as intuition, as belief. She sacrificed herself and your sister so that one day you would be here—and that you would have the courage to make a similar choice. Her sacrifice wasn't to save her remaining child, but to save everyone's sons and daughters."

Outside the smithy, the dead were pulled from the wreckage of the ruins of Alon Rhist. Inside that building, Raithe wept.

Trapped in the Shrine, without a window, Persephone lamented that she hadn't seen the sun set. It would be her last, and she wanted to say goodbye to the sun. Everything had gone so wrong so quickly—all of it her fault. She should have had a better plan to ignite the signal fire. That was a stupid mistake. She should have kept more troops in the fortress. She should have ordered the Orinfar runes scribed over everything, not just the outer walls—she should have had it tattooed on every person. When looking back, all of the mistakes were easy to see and so tragic because the first day had seemed so promising. Everyone thought they'd won.

A report had just arrived that the fane's Miralyith were creating bridges across the Grandford gorge.

"We'll make the last stand up here," Nyphron told the Galantians as they gathered around Persephone's bed, along with Moya, Padera, and Brin.

"You can't fight them," Moya said.

"If they come in here, I can and will," Tekchin replied.

"No, you can't." She was firm. "You can't kill another Fhrey."

"Yes, I can," Tekchin growled. He pointed at her with his sword. "If they try to kill you . . . trust me, *I can.*"

"I don't want you to."

"She's right," Persephone said. "It's not worth it. You've already sacrificed too much on our behalf. If we're going to lose anyway, what's the point of cursing your souls in the process? Maybe if you surrender, the fane will spare your lives."

"She's right," Nyphron said. "The fane's anger will focus on me. You can't break Ferrol's Law."

"I'm not going to just stand here and watch them die," Tekchin said.

"Then leave," Moya told him. Her voice was cold. "All of you should just go. I'm sure you know a way out. Some back exit, some warren hole. Go on and leave us."

"Moya!" Persephone scolded. "Don't be so cruel."

"She's not," Tekchin said. "She's being brave. She's being exactly what any of us would be. She's being a Galantian."

"She is, isn't she?" Grygor grinned at her. "Proved herself in battle, too, against a giant monster, in a one-on-one with a chieftain, and in a melee."

Eres nodded. "And she's the best in the world with that bow of hers."

They each looked at Moya critically. No one scoffed; no one laughed.

"A Rhune?" Nyphron asked them all with a smirk. "And a woman to boot."

Tekchin nodded.

"Look at me," Grygor said. "I'm no pretty Fhrey."

"I'm not sure that's an argument in her favor," Nyphron told the giant, but Eres kept nodding.

"What makes you think I even want to be in your lousy club?" Moya asked, but her tone lacked the usual bite.

"You don't understand," Tekchin said. "Galantian isn't a group or organization. It's just a word. A Fhrey word."

"Moya," Persephone said. "*Galantian* means *hero*."

"At its core, it means *the best*," Nyphron said. "In Instarya tradition, he is *Galantian* who epitomizes the best of the tribe's values: honor, martial skill, and bravery." He looked at Vorath and Anwir who both nodded, as did Eres. "And so seven once more becomes eight."

Moya looked from one to another, each smiling back at her. "As nice as all that is, and thanks for the vote of confidence, you really need to leave."

"Running away isn't very heroic, is it?" Eres said.

Anwir nodded. "We appear to be trapped by our own ideals."

Moya sighed and pointed to the east. "Seven bridges, people. They're making them right now. Climb what's left of the Spyrok and look for yourself. And we don't have walls anymore. Come dawn they'll kill us all. And since you can't help by sticking around, you ought to go."

"I will if you will." Tekchin grinned at her.

"You know I can't."

"You can," Persephone told her. The pain in her stomach was still awful, but she had a little more movement than before. She could sit up and she was, but sitting in a bed did little to enhance her authority. "As the keenig, I'm the only one who has to stay. This is my mess, and I bear the responsibility for it. No one else does."

"I do," Moya said.

"I know, I know, you're my Shield, and a damn fine one, but that doesn't mean you have to die with me."

"I won't leave you."

Persephone sighed. "You're being stupid. You all are."

Moya nodded. "Maybe, but if that's the case, there are a lot of dumb people in Alon Rhist right now because no one's leaving. I saw them on the way here. They're rebuilding the walls a stone at a time. Bakers, weavers, and former farmers are out there, stacking stones. I asked Bergin why he was bothering. I expected him to say it was to hide behind or something. But you know what he said?" She paused to swallow, an act that took effort. "He said, 'To protect the keenig.' I told him that was my job. He said, 'No—that's everyone's job.' "

"That's wrong. It's the keenig's job to protect all of you," Persephone said.

"Most of the time, maybe, but not today."

Moya picked up a bundle she'd laid near the door and placed it on the bed. Unfolding it, she revealed two long daggers of shiny metal. "Compliments of Roan." She handed one to Brin and one to Persephone.

"Are these to use on the enemy or ourselves?" Persephone asked.

"I suppose that's for you to decide." Moya started for the door. "Need to check things. You do, too, don't you, Tekchin?"

The Fhrey looked puzzled for a moment. "Check on . . . Oh, sure." He grinned. "Be back in a minute," he told the rest of them. "I have to check on things."

Moya waved to Persephone. "Might take him longer than that. I'll be back in an hour or two."

"Going down to the courtyard?" Brin asked.

"Ah—passing through it. Why?"

"Thought I'd walk with you."

"Brin, we—" Moya stopped. "You want to see Tesh, don't you?"

Brin blushed. "Maybe."

"Those who are sticking around," Nyphron said, "let's get back to reinforcing the doors. Those bridges will be completed sooner than we want."

"That means he's going to point at things he wants me to move." Grygor winked at Persephone as he and the others filed out.

"Nyphron?" Persephone stopped him.

The Fhrey lord lingered at the door, looking back as the others moved past.

He stood straight, that bold chin held high, the lamplight gleaming on him. *Dashing*, that really was the word for him. His blond hair was thrown back over his shoulders, his bronze armor polished to a dazzling shine, emphasizing his shoulders and chest. *Yes, dashing*.

"I've been thinking about what Arion said." Persephone struggled once more to sit up straighter. She always felt so small when talking to Nyphron. "About sending a bird to the fane and telling them about Suri."

"Can't do that."

"Why can't—oh . . ." She paused, concerned. "Was the pigeon loft destroyed?" So much had been lost in that last assault.

"No, Alon Rhist still has its full complement of those, but we've gone over this. You saw what the Miralyith did to Arion. Suri probably survived because they didn't know about her. Besides, I don't think you know how bird couriers work. They are trained to fly home. Home in this case is a coop in the palace in Estramnadon. The army is across the chasm. By all accounts, so is the fane. A message sent by bird won't reach him."

"But Arion was so adamant about it. So certain it could help save both our peoples."

"I hate speaking ill of the dead, but Arion was Miralyith. I've never trusted them. Now if there is nothing else, this is my fortress—what's left of it. I should see about securing it the best I can. Don't want to disappoint the fane. He'll be expecting a valiant last stand from the Instarya."

"Can I ask you a question before you go?"

"You're the keenig," the Fhrey lord said with a smile. "Your wish is my command."

She smirked. "I've been thinking about your proposal."

Nyphron chuckled. "Little point in that now."

"I actually think that now is the perfect time to think about it. There's no pressure anymore."

This appeared to puzzle him, then he shrugged it off and asked, "What did you want to know?"

"I was wondering—well, if let's say the fane and his army just vanished with the rising sun—do you think you could ever love me?"

"Love you?" The words mystified him. "I'm not even certain what love is. That Rhune word doesn't translate well, you know. And as far as my understanding takes me, it isn't all that clearly defined in the Rhunic culture, either. So, let me ask, do you?"

"Do I what? Do I know what love is, or do I think I could love you?"

"Take your pick."

"I think it's possible to love anyone."

"Well, there's your answer then."

"That's *my* answer. I want to know yours."

Nyphron stared at her and licked his lips. "You want an honest answer, don't you?"

"Yes. Yes, I do."

He nodded. "Honestly, as I said, I don't know if I understand what love is to begin with, much less what you may happen to think it is. I think you're a decent person, above average intelligence, you're practical, usually logical, and don't annoy me too much—except when talking about love. But if it helps, let me clarify my position. Should a miracle occur and we survive tomorrow, I would want to marry you for political reasons, as a means of uniting our people and increasing our power. I won't be faithful; you should know that. And as one-sided or as unfair as it may seem, I would insist that you be. Not because I would be upset if you entertained another man, Fhrey, Dherg, or Grenmorian for that matter, but because your children will rule the world we make, and my bastards won't have any claim, making my infidelity irrelevant. Make no mistake about it, our union would be a business arrangement, plain and simple, and one that would benefit me more than you. But ultimately our union would provide the most reward for the Rhune and Instarya peoples. Still, I hoped it would be based on mutual respect and honesty."

"I see." That was all she could think to say. What else could she say? "Doesn't matter anymore, I suppose."

"No, I can't see how it would. Anything else?"

She shook her head, and the dashing fellow in shining armor disappeared.

Staring at the empty doorway, Persephone remembered Raithe's words: *I've loved you from the start. And it doesn't matter if you can't love me— whether it's because you're still in love with Reglan's memory, or because you want to marry Nyphron. None of that matters because . . . because even now . . . even now . . .*

She remembered his voice, how it cracked and quavered, how his hands were squeezed into fists, the passion on his face.

You're practical, usually logical.

Usually, she thought.

Persephone shifted weight to throw her legs off the bed, but the pain ripped through her again.

Okay—okay!

She would wait for Brin or Moya to come back, then she'd send for Raithe. She wanted to see him before the attack. She needed to tell him the truth.

I have time. Another hour or two won't make a difference.

CHAPTER TWENTY-SEVEN

Malcolm

We called him Malcolm, but I realize now that was not his only name.

—THE BOOK OF BRIN

"Need a sword to put the name on," Roan said, concerned.

The smithy was silent except for the low thrum of the furnace. Always burning, the fire kept the big room hot and the walls shimmering. In that fiery glow, everyone watched Raithe. Everyone except Suri, who stared at the floor.

Roan's eyes betrayed a panic that Raithe didn't understand until he realized all the weapons she'd made had been handed out. Not a shield, spear, helm, or sword lay in the racks. Plenty of metal remained, most of it in a pile of rock beside the pile of charcoal, next to the pile of stacked wood.

Raithe felt the pommel of the weapon at his side. "Can it be any sword?"

"Doesn't even have to be a sword," Frost said. "Just something strong to etch the name on. But a sword would be best."

"What name?"

"Your name," Rain explained. "Your *real* name."

"Raithe is my real name."

Suri shook her head. "Not what your parents called you, the name Elan gave you."

Raithe didn't know what that meant but didn't think it important. He unbuckled his sword belt. Roan got up and reached out for it, but Suri shook her head. "That one already has a name."

Raithe sighed. "We're in the middle of a war and no one here has a sword?"

"What about your father's blade?" Malcolm asked.

"It's broken."

"We're in a smithy surrounded by the world's premier sword smiths. I think they can do something about that. Where is the blade?"

"I left it in the barracks."

Malcolm nodded and rushed out.

"Can you fix it?" Raithe asked.

"That blade is almost pure copper," Frost said. "Would make a lousy sword for such a noble thing."

"We have tin," Roan said, then looked at the dwarfs. "We could make a bronze sword. Be a lot faster to forge than iron."

"True," Flood said. "Copper and tin melt fast and don't need much heat, so it'll take less time."

Rain was shaking his head. "I think we can do better. We could make *black* bronze."

"Need gold and silver for that, lad," Frost replied.

Reaching up, Rain pulled free the golden torc from his neck. He held it out. "Use this."

Frost and Flood looked at their companion in surprise.

Rain frowned at the torc. "It's only a trophy. What good is it if Erivan invades Belgreig? Our people need to contribute something. If sacrifice can save all of us, then all of us should sacrifice, and in light of Raithe's contribution, this is indeed the least I can do."

"Still need silver," Frost said.

That's when Tressa stepped forward. Although it took a bit of work, she managed to wrench a ring off her finger. "I was supposed to give this back when I returned the chieftain's ring, but . . ." She looked down at it. "I'd lost my husband and thought I deserved to have something. And the ring looked better on my hand than the one Konniger had given me when we married. Consider it a contribution from Persephone and me." She held it out. "Take it."

Frost took the silver circle of metal and eyed it.

Malcolm returned with the broken blade, pausing to look at Tressa. "Strange, isn't it? How in the right moment, even a vain, selfish act, like keeping a ring you don't deserve, can be exchanged for a noble deed like this . . . and how a lost soul can, unwittingly it seems, take a first step toward redemption."

Tressa stared at him, her eyes widening. She raised her hand and pressed it against her mouth, muttering through her fingers, "Every single person in this room must do their part."

Malcolm nodded and laid the blade down. Herkimer's sword was the same as it had been, but in the light of the forge it appeared redder. Raithe could see the multitude of scratches, pits, and divots. The edge was jagged, unintentionally serrated where his father had damaged it in countless battles.

"My father died for this sword," Raithe said. "But not really."

Roan looked up at him, puzzled.

"It's pride—false glory purchased with and steeped in the blood of innocents." He looked at Roan with hopeful eyes. "If you can, I'd like you to make it into something better."

Roan nodded toward Flood, who stoked the furnace.

She placed the broken copper sword into the furnace. Flood worked the bellows, puffing the coals a bright, eye-dazzling white.

Frost took the circlet of gold. He measured off an amount, hewed it into two pieces, and added the larger to the furnace. Then he added Tressa's ring to the crucible. The glow of the open furnace lit up all of their faces as Flood pumped the bellows and the metals merged. Feeling the heat, Raithe turned away and found Malcolm sitting in a darkened corner opposite the one Suri had claimed. They all sought space for solitude, each pair of eyes staring down demons.

"Hey," Raithe said, overturning a bucket to sit on.

Malcolm, who had his back against the wall, his knees bent, glanced up and offered a sad smile.

"You've been holding out on me, haven't you?"

With a guilty look, Malcolm held up two fingers, indicating something very small.

"Did you know this would happen? When you hit Shegon with the rock, did you know about this?" Raithe gestured at Roan and the dwarfs.

"Which answer would make you feel better?"

"Well, on the one hand, if you knew, then you're something of a lying bastard who manipulated me for a year."

Malcolm nodded.

"On the other hand, if you hadn't hit Shegon, I'd have died a year ago—died alone and forgotten on a rocky fork of land."

Malcolm continued nodding.

"Don't suppose it really matters much, now."

Malcolm shook his head.

"So, what are you? Some kind of mystic like Suri?" He glanced at her as she sat hugging her knees, rocking as if in pain.

"I'm not a mystic."

"What then? And don't tell me you're just a slave. I'm not buying that anymore."

"I *was* a slave . . . sort of, only . . ."

"Only what?"

"Well, I'm not sure you can really call it slavery when I volunteered for the position. Took me three days to convince Nyphron's father to seal the collar around my neck. Zephyron was a wise, generous, and honorable Fhrey. He was my first choice."

"First choice for what?"

"Emperor."

"What's an emperor?"

"Like a keenig, only bigger. Instead of being the ruler of all the clans, an emperor would be the leader of the world. A single leader would have the power to end conflicts between whole peoples, to disperse knowledge, and bring lasting peace to everyone—to unite what was broken. But Nyphron's father had refused to listen—I suppose he wouldn't have been the right person for the task if he had. Now Nyphron will become the first emperor."

"Nyphron, not Persephone?"

Malcolm only smiled.

"She marries him, right?"

Malcolm sighed. "Certain things need to fall in a certain way. It isn't always nice, and it's rarely fair, but that's the way it has to be in order to fix what was broken."

"And what is it that was broken?"

No smile this time. Malcolm looked squarely at him and said, "The world."

Raithe laughed, but Malcolm wasn't joking, and he stopped. "Okay . . . so how was it broken, or don't you know?"

"Oh, I know. Believe me, I know. I was the one who broke it."

Malcolm had been a puzzle ever since they met, a fussy, delicate man who knew so little and so much. Raithe understood Malcolm had lied to him, or at least avoided the truth. What Raithe found surprising was that he didn't care. Maybe it was the lack of smugness. Raithe saw no malice, greed, or spite in Malcolm. He had no idea what benefit his friend might have gained from the deception. There didn't appear to have been any. And there was an overwhelming sadness and sympathy that spilled from the man, a sense of guilt that had Raithe feeling sorry for him.

"Malcolm? Who are you?"

At this, the onetime servant who Raithe first imagined as a weasel or a fox—the man who turned out to be a bit of both—frowned. "I can't tell you."

"It's not exactly like I'll be repeating it to anyone, you know."

Malcolm sighed. "Don't confuse *can't* with *won't*. That question can't be answered in any way meaningful to you, maybe not to anyone—not yet. Perhaps one day there will be someone capable of understanding the answer. Perhaps one day there will be someone who doesn't need to ask."

"So you don't know everything?"

Again, the smile. "Yes and no."

Raithe smirked. "Seriously?"

Malcolm looked squarely at him. "I'm being honest here, and you have no idea how rare this is." He smiled. "It's not my fault you can't understand what I'm telling you."

"I'm about to die—be nice."

Malcolm nodded. "Sorry. I suppose I could explain a *little* better." Malcolm picked a pebble from the floor. "If I let this drop, I know it will fall. I also know it will fall right about here." He pointed to the spot just below his hand. "We both know that, right? We both know this absolutely, but . . ." He let go of the pebble, and before it hit the ground, he brought his foot over and knocked the stone aside. "Things can change from moment to moment. Most of the time I'm right, but on occasion, someone's foot gets in the way. Does that make any sense?"

"How is that different from what anyone does? We all have expectations that don't always—"

"I don't have expectations. *I know.* I know everything that will happen—unless it is altered. I realize this seems like a fine line of difference, but it isn't."

"You mean you're like Magda the oracle?"

"In a way, but while I would say I know a good deal more than any tree, I'm far less wise."

Raithe made a point of looking him over. "I'm guessing you aren't human. Are you Fhrey? Is that why you didn't know our customs?"

"I once told you the Fhrey, the Dherg, and the Rhunes were all related. They are. The differences came later. The Fhrey had it the easiest and lived longer as a result. The Dherg found solace in caves and were stunted, and in more ways than they're willing to admit. Humans had it the worst of all. I've been late getting to them. You're going to change all that. I'm sorry about this, about how things turned out. If it were possible . . ." He sighed. "Never mind."

"Can you tell me one thing?"

"Not about Persephone, is it?"

He shook his head. "About my sister and my mother."

"Oh." Malcolm nodded. "You want to know if you'll see them again?"

"I think about it. I think about it a lot. I never got to say goodbye. I never got to express my thanks. I don't know how the afterlife works. Don't know if I'll go to Alysin, Rel, or Nifrel. And I don't know where my mother and sister are."

Malcolm thought a moment. "They gave their lives to save you. You're giving your life to save everyone else. I suspect the afterlife will look kindly upon all of that."

"You don't know? Or you can't tell me?"

He smiled. "You're going to find out for yourself very soon, but I don't believe you have anything to worry about."

"Can you at least tell me your real name? It's not Malcolm, is it?"

"It is now. I've been Malcolm for a few hundred years."

A few hundred?

"Names are temporary things, like clothes. They serve to make us look a certain way but are quite trivial and can be changed. It's like you're asking me what my *real* shirt is."

"What was your *first* shirt, then?"

"*That* was a very long time ago," Malcolm said, but Raithe wasn't satisfied and stared until Malcolm sighed. "Turin," he finally said. "Turin was the name of a very young, very innocent, very stupid person."

Raithe looked across at the forge where Roan drew out the glowing metal to begin the hammering. "And you're certain this is the only way to make the world right, Turin?"

"Unless someone's foot gets in the way. Speaking of feet . . ." He stood up. "I need to have a talk with Nyphron and make sure he keeps his on the ground, and doesn't do anything rash."

"I'm guessing that's a full-time job."

"It is with most people." Malcolm took two steps then paused, and looking back, added, "Including myself."

Nyphron was alone on the third floor balcony that ran around the outside of the Verenthenon when Malcolm found him. "So much for your plans," he told his ex-slave. "I think your prediction of me becoming the ruler of the world was a bit off."

"Try not to think too much; you don't have the talent for it."

Nyphron's brows rose. He was having trouble adjusting to this *new* Malcolm, this onetime slave who behaved as an equal. *No,* he thought, *he acts like my superior—like my father.* Nyphron had never cared for the easy authority Zephyron exercised over him, one of the many reasons he'd spent so much time abroad with the Galantians. And he cared even less for Malcolm. If either of them had more than a day in their futures, he might have voiced his objection, settled the issue, but as it was, he couldn't see the point.

"They're creating bridges right now." He pointed down at the seven tongues, each of slightly different lengths, reaching out toward their side of the Bern. "Come morning—"

"Not morning," Malcolm said. "They'll attack tonight." He looked up at the stars. "Two, maybe three hours."

Nyphron felt a surge of panic, then it subsided. *What difference does a few hours make? The result will be the same.* "Just as well, I suppose. No sense prolonging it."

Malcolm stared at him, perplexed. "You really think you're going to die?"

"The fane won't pardon me after this."

"No, I mean you're certain the fane will defeat us?"

Nyphron looked out at the campfires, and then down at the rubble below them. "We lost almost half our fighting force today, and that was without the fane bringing in his infantry. Yes, we will all die. Maybe not you. *Can* you die?"

Malcolm smiled at him. "What would it be worth to win this battle?"

There was no point in replying, so Nyphron simply waited. He had no idea who, or what Malcolm was—a Miralyith perhaps? But he'd never seen Malcolm perform magic. A crimbal lord? There were legends about them sometimes leaving Nog and visiting Elan. They possessed great powers and weren't bound by the same laws as Rhunes, Fhrey, and Dherg.

But again, there was that issue of a lack of magic, and crimbals were known to wallow in the stuff. He might be a demon or spirit. Stories spoke of such things walking the face of Elan and causing mischief to mortals. Whatever Malcolm was, Nyphron certainly didn't trust that smile.

"You'll owe me a favor," Malcolm said. "I will ask you to do something, and you must do it—no matter what it is."

"Scary promise."

"It is."

"I won't kill myself."

"No, it won't be that."

"And I will be ruler of the entire civilized world?"

Malcolm paused in thought. "Well, minus Belgreig. The Belgriclungreians are about to have a bit of a revival, but you'll be allies."

"Fine," Nyphron said. "I did say *civilized world*." He stared at the thin figure before him, who didn't have a trustworthy face, and he certainly wasn't a man. "Why do I feel like you'll twist this into something terrible?"

"You're right to be wary. I can tell you now that you won't like what I'll ask of you. Certainly not at the time I ask it. Wouldn't be much point in my making this agreement if it was something you'd agree to willingly. But it won't be anything too horrible, and in time, you'll agree that I was right."

They stood looking out at the torch- and star-filled night, watching the growing bridges—seven fingers of death.

"So, do we have an agreement?"

"If by some miracle we do win tomorrow—or tonight—how can I know it was you who made it happen?"

"If you agree to my demand, then tonight you'll see a dragon rise from the rubble of Alon Rhist. This"—he paused and allowed a little smile to creep onto his lips—"*Gilarabrywn* will fend off the worst of the fane's assault."

"The worst? And what of the rest?"

Malcolm pointed to the eastern sky. "The Gula-Rhunes."

Nyphron shook his head. "That's impossible. The fires were never lit."

Malcolm's eyebrows rose sharply. "Seriously? I just told you a dragon would rise up out of the rubble and do battle for you, but it's the coming of the Gula horde that you can't believe?"

"Okay, none of it is believable."

"So when it happens, when you see it all with your own eyes, and exactly as I've described, you'll know it was my doing, and you'll be bound to this agreement we make tonight, yes?"

Nyphron didn't need to think long. The bridges were growing at an uncomfortable speed. Malcolm was right about that much. The attack wouldn't be in the morning. "Agreed. I just wish you were telling the truth."

Padera and Malcolm were the first to enter Persephone's room after Nyphron had left. "That Fhrey downstairs is a terrible patient," Padera grumbled.

"Sebek?"

"Is that his name? Terrible, just terrible. Won't stay put. Won't listen." She pointed at Malcolm. "Even when he translates, it does no good. That Sebek gets himself bleeding. Stubborn fool." She smiled at Persephone, waddling over duck-like. "So, how are we doing?"

"I'm fine, but I need you to do a few things for me."

Padera glared with one eye. "I am; I'm checking your bandages," she said, tugging at the covers. "Wait, who are you talking to?"

Persephone held the blanket tight. "Both of you. Malcolm, do you know about the pigeon loft?"

He nodded.

"I want you to send a message." She paused, trying to remember what Arion had told her months ago when she had stood in the Karol and pleaded for Persephone to send word. Arion had a very odd way of saying it. Something about the limitations of the system they used to convey reports. The symbols used were few and specific. There was no symbol for beautiful, bumblebee, happiness, or eagle, just to name a few; the script revolved only around the needed ideas for military reports and orders:

numbers, supplies, deaths, births, seasons, and such, and all of it was in a shortened form so a message could be tied to and carried by a small bird. "I can't remember how Arion put it, but you need to convey that: *Rhunes are not animals. We are capable of the Art. All we want is peace. Are you willing to find a way to end this war?* That had been Arion's message. I'm only now seeing the wisdom in it. The fane won't see the message in time, but maybe after he returns home, he will. Once he has regained his fortress and we are no longer a threat, perhaps then he will read it. I hope he does, and it softens his heart so he won't kill all that remains of our people."

"I actually have some experience with the messenger pigeons," Malcolm explained. "I can handle it myself."

"Good, that's better. I was worried about trusting the Instarya to write it correctly. This is important, Malcolm. Thank you. You've always been there for me, haven't you?"

"As I will always be, until the very end."

Persephone smiled. Sometimes he said the oddest things. *No, it's not what he says; it's how he says it, as if he knows something I don't.*

"Let me see those stitches," Padera said.

"No, I need you to find Raithe. Tell him I want to see him right away."

"Of course, of course. Why not?" The old woman threw up her hands. "There's only a war on, and the place is an obstacle course of broken rubble. Why don't I rebuild the fortress while I'm at it?"

Padera and Malcolm left, and Persephone laid her head back down on the pillow. She had done all she could to save her people. That part of her life was over. Only one loose end remained between her and a peaceful death. She needed to make a confession to a man she had lied to.

CHAPTER TWENTY-EIGHT

Wolves at the Door

I can honestly say I was never more frightened in my life. It was not that I thought I might die—I knew I would. I knew it with the same certainty that I knew I was in love—all this and I was only sixteen.
—THE BOOK OF BRIN

Horns blew sometime past midnight.

Tesh had finally gotten used to the bell announcing attacks, but the bell had fallen along with everything else. Trumpets were the new heralds of doom, and they woke him from a nightmare-filled slumber where Brin was dying, trapped in the Kype. He couldn't reach her. No matter how many Fhrey he killed, more always came.

He hadn't planned to sleep, didn't even think it would be possible. He promised himself he'd just close his eyes for a moment, but after sixteen hours of moving rocks to help build a makeshift wall, his body had betrayed him.

Now, Tesh ran across what remained of the courtyard. Jumping onto the collapsed remains of the old Frozen Tower, he looked down and saw seven bridges that hadn't been there when he had gone to sleep. Across them, seven columns of soldiers flowed above the chasm. All around, men ran wildly, trying to find each other, trying to locate their leaders, trying to understand what to do.

"Has anyone seen Raithe?" Tesh shouted.

No one answered. No one knew. No one cared. Everyone had problems of their own.

He could join up with the men forming in the lower courtyard. He saw them from his perch, ragged lines coming together slowly. Both Harkon and Tegan were down there shouting. Raithe couldn't stop him from fighting this time. Now, no one had a choice. Tesh looked back over his shoulder toward the dome and the Kype. The nightmare was fresh enough that he had to resist an urge to look for Brin.

My duty is to Raithe. "Raithe! Raithe!" he called, standing on the tips of his toes to see better.

"There you are!" Tesh heard a woman yell at him as she hauled a bucket of water. Her name was Tressa. All he knew about her was that most people spat on the ground after she walked by. "Raithe is in the smithy. He's been wanting to talk to you."

"Is that where you're going?" Tesh asked.

The woman nodded.

"Let me help you with that, then."

Tressa looked at him in shock, as he took the bucket from her hands.

The courtyard was an obstacle course of fallen rocks and rushing people, and he dodged his way across to the smithy. The furnace was going. He could see the firelight leaking out from under the door. Inside, he found Roan and the dwarfs working at the polishing table, while Suri and Raithe sat in opposite corners of the room. Malcolm stood near the door.

"They're attacking," he announced.

Heads came up, but no one moved.

"Raithe?" Tesh said.

"I know," Raithe replied.

"They're forming up in the lower courtyard. What do you want me to do?"

Raithe stood up and walked over. His movements, agonizingly slow, made Tesh want to scream. This was an emergency; seconds counted and his chieftain was meandering his way through the stacks of charcoal and iron.

"We need to talk," Raithe told him.

"What? Now? The Rhist is under attack. They've got bridges. They're coming over right now. Seven columns!"

"Yeah, I know."

"You know?" Tesh couldn't see how Raithe could possibly know if he'd been sitting in the smithy.

"This won't take long."

"What won't?"

Raithe lifted his good arm and put a hand on Tesh's shoulder. "I want you to know that I'm proud of you, and that you're the closest thing I've had to a son. That if I had one, I would have wanted him to be like you."

"You think we're going to lose this fight." Tesh saw the defeat in Raithe's eyes. He'd already given up.

"No." Raithe shook his head. "We're going to be okay. I even think we might win the war."

Tesh scrunched his face up. "You said this was a lost cause."

"Changed my mind."

"Odd time for that."

Someone outside shouted for more arrows to be brought to the Veren-thenon. Tesh looked out at the action of soldiers running and hoped Raithe would hurry up.

"The victory will come at a price."

Outside, the trumpets blew again, and Tesh imagined that the Fhrey were fighting in the lower courtyard. "We can have this talk later, can't we?"

"No, we can't. Tesh, when—if anything happens to me, you'll be the last Dureyan. You should make sure that our people don't die with you. You like Brin, don't you?"

"I really don't think now is the time—look, I need to get down to the—"

"Now is the perfect time because I don't want you anywhere near the fighting."

"What? You *can't* be serious! You stopped me last time—and I can help!"

"You can help more by living through this night."

"What do you want me to do? Cower somewhere?" Tesh exploded. "You're being stupid. I can—"

"I want you to go to the Kype and protect Brin."

Tesh remembered his dream and lost some of his anger.

"And when this battle is over," Raithe said. "I want you to start a family. Raise children, and live a good and happy life—someplace safe and green, like on a high bank overlooking the Urum River. I want you to do what I never could."

Why is he telling me all this now?

Tesh noticed the others watching them, Suri and Malcolm especially. The tattooed girl had tears glistening on her cheeks. "Why are you—?"

"You have talents, and you've learned to use them, but don't let that be your whole life. Dureyans have always been known as warriors, but you need to change that. Promise me you'll do something good, that you'll make your life worth something more than killing."

"What's this about?"

"Promise me."

"But I don't understand why—"

"Promise me."

Tesh looked at Raithe. His eyes were desperate.

He thinks he's going to die tonight. Maybe the mystic had foretold his death. Tesh heard she had magic powers, and Raithe's eerie calm unnerved him. "Okay, I promise."

Raithe smiled. "Good. Now go to Brin. Take care of her. Be a good man and a good father."

Tesh, who had been eager to leave a moment before, lingered a moment longer. He was missing something. There was tension in the smithy, a strange silence.

"What's going on?"

"You'll find out," Raithe said. "For now, your chieftain has given you an order. Get going."

Tesh stared at him, trying to understand. But it was impossible, and memories of his nightmares pushed him out the door.

Brin couldn't find Tesh. Minutes felt like hours, and hours turned into an eternity. With each passing second, her desperation grew. When the horns started blowing, she knew her time was up.

With that sound, every man stopped what he was doing and rushed down toward the lower courtyard, forming up. *That's where he'll go,* she realized. *He wants to be at the front of the line.* The lower courtyard was no place for a Keeper of Ways, but she desperately needed to see Tesh one last time.

"Brin!" Chieftain Harkon shouted. "Get out of here, lass. The enemy is upon us. Run back to the Kype! Do it now!"

Brin ignored sense and joined the ranks of men rushing down the steps. She was shocked by the devastation of everything below the upper court-yard. Collapsed buildings and towers had blocked access to the city streets, but the stairs and a pathway had been cleared all the way down to the lower courtyard. Walking down to where the front gates had been felt like swimming out too far; she was going too deep, getting over her head. When she reached the bottom—where men were forming in lines to re-place the stone wall with one of flesh and blood—she still didn't see Tesh. The sound of marching made her look east. The seven bridges were com-plete, and the elven army was crossing.

With no place left to look for Tesh, she headed back, but each step she took hurt. She just wanted to see him one last time, needed to say goodbye, share a final kiss. She didn't think that was too much to ask. She didn't think it would be so hard. As she ran back to the upper courtyard, she felt her heart breaking—her desire to say goodbye had become a genuine need. She *had* to see him once more before . . . before the end of the world.

It's not fair!

Others had years. Padera had been blessed with decades. What did she and Tesh have? Not much, just a few days to love, to fight, to hold, and to cry. Brin wanted nothing more than to grow old with him, to live the life her mother had. She wanted to spend day after boring day in a tiny home and suffer endless nights listening to him snore. When he was sick, she would've brought him soup. On his birthday, she would've surprised him with a new pair of mittens she'd spent months knitting. Brin wanted to be cooped up through long winters beside him, the two of them curled up like a pair of chipmunks in a den. She wanted to give him children, watch them grow up, see them marry and have their own children. How would Tesh look with gray hair? How would it be to sip tea in front of their own home watching grandchildren play? She would never know.

I got one kiss, one lousy kiss!

"Brin!"

She whirled and saw Tesh running at her.

Brin flung her arms out and pulled him to her. Squeezing as hard as she could, she kissed him. Then she did it again and again. Her lips still against his, her hands making fists in his hair and shirt, she said, "I wanted to say goodbye."

"Goodbye?"

She let her cheek slide next to his and spoke in his ear. "You're going to fight with the rest, and by morning, we'll all be dead. I had to see you. I had to say goodbye. I had to—I have to tell you . . . I love you."

She hadn't planned on saying it. Brin hadn't even thought it before. The words just came out, but the moment they left her lips, she knew it was true. That was the real reason she'd been so desperate to find him.

"I love you, too," he said.

He loves me! She kissed him again.

Horns were blaring. She heard shouts and the clang of metal. She ignored it all. The world could fall apart, she no longer cared.

"Brin! What the Tet are you doing here?" Moya ran at them along with an onrush of swordsmen and archers. Her face was fierce, her bow strung. "The lower yard is overrun. They're coming up the steps. Get to the Kype! Move!"

Padera was just making her way down when the whole world started coming up. She was on her way to find Raithe, and the best place to start looking was the barracks. That was across the corbel bridge, through the Verenthenon, and down the long, narrow stairs to the upper courtyard. She only got as far as the bridge.

"Don't go out there," Grygor said. The giant stood guard beside the bronze door, which, for the time being, was left open so he could look out.

"Persephone wants me to get a message to Raithe."

Grygor shook his head. "Too late for that. The fane's army is across the ford."

The old woman stood with the giant in the doorway of the Kype, looking out at the end of the world. The sky was swirling again. Dark, unnatural clouds covered the stars, folding and unfolding, making threatening faces at the living. Lightning flashed between the shades of gray, brilliant bolts of white that cracked and boomed.

"I wish it would rain," Grygor said.

Padera glanced at him. No matter how she tilted her head, or how tightly she squinted her one eye, she could never manage to fill her expression with enough incredulity. "Did you say you wished it would rain? Why in the world—"

"Because it'd only be a storm then, wouldn't it? Just a spring rain. We could shutter the windows and bolt the doors, and it would blow over as all downpours do. But this isn't one of those storms, is it?"

From beyond the dome, she saw streaks of red light coming from the far side of the ford. One struck the remaining forward tower and sheared off the top.

"No," she said. "No, it's not."

Screams were carried on the wind. Cries of pain and horror rose up from the village and the lower yards. They were faint enough to be the wails of ghosts.

"My relatives have arrived." Grygor pointed down at the seven bridges as huge Grenmorians lumbered across, wielding great clubs that they used to bash chunks out of anything still standing.

"Why aren't you with them?"

"Don't get along with my family." He looked down at her.

"No one gets along with their family," Padera replied.

"They tried to kill me—twice. Sheer luck saved me the first time. Second time it was Nyphron. Didn't look back after that."

The world shook, and both Grygor and Padera staggered, reaching for the door frame for support.

"They're doing that again," she said. "Treating this fortress like a dog treats a rabbit caught in its teeth."

Another shake and the dome of the Verenthenon cracked like an egg. Just a tiny spidery line, but the fissure, jagged and terrible, declared a prophecy. A moment later, a horde of people spilled out from under the dome. A sprinting line of evacuees raced across the corbel bridge toward Grygor and Padera. Most were soldiers, including the chieftains Tegan and Harkon, but leading the pack were Moya, Brin, Tekchin, and Tesh.

The prophecy fulfilled itself as the dome fell. Dust of broken stone belched from the belly of the Verenthenon, a cloud that obscured the length of the span. Padera lost sight of everyone for a long awful moment. Then Moya appeared, slick with sweat, pumping her arms, her bow held high in one hand.

Grygor and Padera moved clear as dust-covered soldiers poured in.

"Seal the door!" Tegan shouted when the last survivor dove inside.

Grygor looked more than pleased to slam the bronze door shut and lay the metal brace.

"Everything on the other side of that door is lost to us." Harkon wiped the dust and grime from his face.

"They crushed us at the front gate." Bergin panted for air. "There's no stopping them."

Tegan placed a hand against the closed door as if willing it to hold. "There's too many."

"And then the light show started," Harkon grumbled.

"And now they have giants," Moya said, glancing at Grygor. "I'm going up to Persephone. I'll die with her."

The others didn't say anything, but many nodded.

"I'll stay here and hold this door," Tegan declared. "I hate stairs."

"Me, too." Harkon pulled his sword and weighed it in his hands. "Stairs are the gods' curse to men."

"I'm going to stay," Tesh told Brin, who took a step back as if she'd been pushed. "It's the best way to protect you."

"Why are you down here?" Moya asked Padera.

"I was sent to find Raithe."

Moya shook her head and pointed at the door with her bow. "There's nothing on the other side of that door now except bodies."

In the smithy, heads jerked at the sound of another explosion, but Malcolm seemed unconcerned. Tressa and the dwarfs stared wide-eyed at the door as screams came from directly outside. Raithe knew those sounds would come back to them in nightmares for the rest of their lives, *if* they survived the night. There were other sounds, too: deep booms, clangs, and the howl of whirlwinds.

Something banged against the little wood door, eight vertical maple boards held together by a Z brace with a simple brass latch.

Roan worked a foot pedal similar to a spinning wheel, but this one rotated an arm of soft cloth. Then she stopped and, pulling a rag from the waist of her leather apron, wiped the sword in her hands. Turning, she held the weapon to the light of the forge and nodded to herself. Then, still chasing down smudges with the rag, she carried the blade across the room and handed it to Raithe. Holding it out with both hands, she used the cloth so that no part of her skin left a print.

"I did my best," Roan said.

Long, shimmering, and with a rich black color, the sword was perfection. Roan's skill at a forge and anvil had grown beyond imagining. The object she placed in his hands wasn't a sword, wasn't a weapon at all; it was a work of art.

Everyone in the room stared at him as he looked at it.

This isn't a sword for me to wield. I'm looking at—I'm holding—my own death.

"I . . ." Roan's voice cracked, then just stopped. She bit her lip and started to cry.

"It's beautiful," Raithe told her. "The most amazing thing I've ever seen. Thank you."

She began to sob, to collapse; she ran back to the worktable but pushed the stool aside and sat on the floor, drawing her knees up. That's when Raithe realized the obvious. The sword had been her support, and not just the one he held. All the swords, the shields, and armor that Roan had made were the pillars she had lashed herself to in order to remain standing. The work had been her distraction, her world within the world, her retreat, but this blade was the last, and the war was finally knocking.

Raithe weighed the sword in his hands: heavy, well-balanced, and magnificent. He turned it, and the glow of the forge shone across its face.

More screams came from beyond the door. He heard a man cry, "Help me! Help me!"

Promise me, Raithe. He recalled his mother's voice, shaking with the cold and coming out in puffs of frost. *Promise me you'll do something good, that you'll make your life worth something.*

He walked across the room to Suri. She was sitting on the floor in the same cross-legged manner she had in Dahl Rhen, only now her hair and skin were clean, and she wore a lavish asica after the fashion of the ranking Fhrey. She looked up at him as he held out the sword.

"I guess this means I'll never learn to juggle." He meant it as a joke, something to break the tension.

Suri started crying.

"Sorry," he said and sighed. "So, how does this work? Will I remember who I am? Who I was? Will I have memories?"

"I don't know," Suri said, sniffling. "Minna . . ." She shook her head. "It really wasn't Minna at all—and yet I felt that part of Minna was there."

"And this sword." He looked at it again. "This will be used to kill me after I get done fighting the Fhrey?"

"You'll be killed in the making. I honestly don't know how much of you may linger in the beast. Maybe none. It might just have been what I put into the conjuration that made it seem like Minna. The sword will break the weave. If any part of you is trapped, it will be set free by the sword."

"So, what do I do now?"

She reached out and took the blade. "Just lie down," she told him.

He did, and she placed the fabulous sword on his chest.

"Doesn't it need my name on it?"

"Yes, but that . . ." Suri squeezed her lips together, turning the pink white, and her eyes tightened, squinting as if in agony. She took a deliberate breath. "When Minna died, I didn't have a sword or anything, so her name was imprinted on my mind by her escaping spirit. When your spirit leaves your body, it will pass through the sword and leave your name there. It will be you who writes it, using the language of creation."

Raithe nodded.

Something hit the door to the smithy again, something hard. The hinges rattled.

"We're running out of time. They're going to break in," Flood burst out, his voice an octave higher than usual.

"No," Suri said calmly, softly. "That door won't open until I allow it." She looked at Raithe. "And when it does . . . they'll wish it hadn't." Suri ran her hands along the blade. "Such a beautiful thing to be created for such an awful purpose." She shuddered and brought a hand to her face.

"I don't know who this is going to hurt more," Raithe said. "Me or you."

Suri lifted her head to look at him, tears running down her face. "Me," Suri told him without a hint of humor. "You—you won't feel a thing. But I will." A tear fell from her chin and splashed onto the shimmering blade. "I'll feel it every day. Every. Single. Day. For the rest of my life, I'll see your eyes as they are right now, the same way I still see Minna's. She had blue eyes, bright blue eyes—so very, very bright."

"Just so you know, I'm not leaving anything behind," Raithe told her. "In many ways, you're doing me a favor, if that makes this any easier."

Suri placed her hand upon the black shimmering blade. "It doesn't."

Persephone sat up in her bed. Propped by a pillow against the carved headboard, she listened to the sounds of battle. Explosions rumbled the stone so hard that the canopy above the bed quivered. In Persephone's right hand she held the little sword Roan had made; in her left, she squeezed the blanket. She held both so tightly her hands ached.

She was scared. *It will be over soon. Everything will be over.*

At any minute, a Fhrey would break in the chamber door, someone not unlike Nyphron. Her mind told her that. Her emotions imagined monsters: fangs, glowing eyes, claws, something similar to the raow—only bigger—much bigger.

Shouts, cries, the thunder of feet, then it finally happened. The door to the outer room of her suite burst in. Persephone flinched—almost screamed.

"They've crossed the corbel bridge," Moya said, panting as she entered. Her face and arms were shiny from sweat, the longbow held in her left hand, the sack of arrows slung over her right shoulder. Brin and Padera followed her. The old woman shambled through the archway and around the end posts with her famous frown and squinty eyes. In contrast, Brin was terrified. She raced in, cheeks streaked with tears.

"Up on the bed!" Persephone shouted, waving for them. Brin leapt up and hugged her tight. The girl was shaking.

Padera sat herself on the other side of the bed, and, taking off one of her sandals, she rubbed her foot.

Moya stood in front of the door, her bow out, an arrow fitted to the string, four more in her draw hand in between her fingers, five bunched in her left along with the bow shaft.

"What's going on?" Persephone asked them.

"The bridges are finished, and the elven army has crossed the ford," Brin explained.

"They came with hardly a warning," Moya said. "Hundreds pouring over the chasm, both beautiful and terrible, wearing shining gold and shimmering blue. With them came whirlwinds and giants. Nothing can stop them. They're coming still."

Boom!

"They're here," Moya said, looking out through the archway into the sitting room as if she could see them. "That would be them hitting the bronze door downstairs. Tegan and Harkon are trying to hold it with a handful of men." She looked at Persephone. "Gavin Killian and Bergin are with them."

Persephone didn't know why Moya told her about Gavin and Bergin. Maybe she felt it would be comforting to know that men of Dahl Rhen were defending her. At the sound of their names, Persephone remembered her home of long ago and far away, a world of another time that was only a year lost. She saw the stone table and Mari between the braziers at the foot of the lodge steps. She recalled the summer fairs where Bergin served honey mead, barley ale, and strawberry wine and the dark winter nights when Gavin told his ghostly tales around the lodge's fire, scaring Habet into adding more wood than was needed. That whole existence was gone. Even its memories were being hunted down and erased.

I came to tell the chieftain we're going to die. Suri's voice came back to her, eerily innocent, spoken in that detached-from-reality manner that had so confounded Persephone.

Who's going to die?

All of us.

All of whom? You and I?

Yes—you, me, the funny man with the horn at the gate, everyone.

Persephone had thought the girl was merely looking for food. She also believed Suri was lying. Persephone had been wrong. The only thing Suri had lied about was the possibility of hope—that heeding the counsel of the trees could help. Persephone had done everything Magda had said, but none of it had saved them.

Suri had been right. *We're all going to die. You, me, the old woman. The young girl. The people outside. Everyone.*

Raithe had been right. They couldn't win, but he had been wrong, too. Even knowing how it turned out, Persephone would have still chosen to stay.

Death is inescapable. Everyone spends their days, buying unrealized dreams. I gambled mine on hope, not for myself, but for all those who would follow.

The Kype rocked as something powerful impacted its base. Dust fell from the rafters, and out in the sitting room, a golden cup fell from its seat on the stone molding and rang on the floor.

"I'm so scared." Brin hugged Persephone tightly, pressing her head against Persephone's side. "Will it hurt terribly, do you think?"

"No, child," Padera answered for her. "The Fhrey are not ones for sport."

"She's right," Persephone assured, although she had no idea if it was true, and she knew Padera didn't either. "It will be quick, and we'll all be together again. Your mother and father, Mahn, Reglan—"

"Melvin and my boys," Padera added. "Been too long since I seen them."

"Maeve?" Brin said hopefully.

Persephone nodded and brushed the hair from the girl's eyes.

"Farmer Wedon, Holliman, the Killians . . ." Moya listed them as if making sure to invite everyone to the after-party.

"And Aria." Persephone glanced at Padera, who managed to find a smile in those lips after all.

And Raithe, Persephone thought. *Would they really all be there?*

The door of the suite opened, and Moya's bow stretched.

"Nyphron!" Brin shouted, warning her off.

The leader of the Galantians entered with a half-dozen men, as well as Vorath, Eres, Grygor, and Tekchin.

"Brace the door!" Persephone heard Nyphron shout.

Tegan and Tekchin carried Harkon into the bedroom. The Melen Clan chieftain was bleeding from several wounds, the most obvious being a gash in his skull that ran a stream of red into the man's eyes. All of them were covered in blood. Even Tekchin.

"Did you . . . ?" Moya asked him.

He threw an arm around Moya's neck, pulled her to him, and gave her a long kiss. "No," the Fhrey said with a pronounced tone of disappointment that bordered on self-disgust.

"They certainly *helped*." Tegan jumped to the Galantian's defense as he used his sword to cut into the foot of Persephone's bed sheet. "Pardon, Madam Keenig."

"Take the whole thing if you need it." Persephone's heart was pounding. Seeing the blood made the nightmare real.

"We have bandages on that table," Padera pointed out. "Needle and thread, too."

Tegan looked over.

"Give me that thing!" Harkon yelled and stole the cloth from Tegan's hands and began to wipe his face.

"You can worry about seeing later," Tegan growled and took the cloth back, pressing it against the wound. "Need to dam this bloody river you have flowing."

At the bedroom door, Grygor peeked in.

"You made it," Padera said.

The giant grinned at her.

"What happened to Tesh?" Brin left Persephone's side, and took bandages from the table, and handed them to Tegan.

"Don't know," Tegan replied. "He was with us. But when the door was breached, we all ran. I was too busy worrying about myself to pay attention to where everyone went."

"The Fhrey saved us," Harkon said while helping to hold the new wad of cloth to his own head as Tegan and Brin worked to tie a bandage around it. "Threw themselves in the way. Blocked their attacks. Gave us time to—"

"Here they come!" Eres shouted from the sitting area.

Tekchin leapt out of the bedroom to join him, and Moya raced to the archway, stationing herself between the two rooms, Grygor to her left.

Persephone heard a thud, then a bang, and finally the sound of wood splintering as the door to the hallway broke open. Moya let her first arrow fly and had another nocked immediately. Shouts and cries filled the sitting room.

"Get me up! Get me up!" Harkon ordered. Tegan lifted the chieftain and put his sword back in his hand.

"Can't see!" Harkon wavered. "Blood's in my eyes!"

"Relax, I'll tell you when to swing," Tegan said.

Looking past her Shield, Persephone saw the Fhrey force their way into the sitting room. Just as Moya had described, they were both beautiful and terrible, wearing brilliant gold and shimmering blue. They killed Tanner

Riggles in the blink of an eye. Three other men were cut down as the fane's army forced its way in. Moya fired arrow after arrow. Many found their targets; gold-and-blue uniforms littered the floor.

"Get the little spear thrower!" someone shouted in Fhrey.

That's when Tekchin rushed them, or tried to.

Grygor threw the Fhrey aside and stepped in the way. "You have an after-life to go to. Grenmorians just turn to dust." Grygor unleashed his massive sword, moving with surprising speed and not-so-surprising strength. The bronze armor prevented the Fhrey from being cut in half, but his strokes must have shattered bones. Whomever he hit didn't get up.

For a moment, Persephone thought there might be hope. If the Galantians could hold them, and Moya could shoot—but then the wall to the hallway exploded and Fhrey poured into the sitting room. Grygor took a spear thrust to his shoulder and another to his side. He staggered. Vorath rushed to his aid and was the first to fall as three blades hit him from behind. Persephone didn't see it, but she heard Eres cry his name.

Watching through the doorway that separated the bedroom from the sitting area, Persephone saw Grygor beaten back. The giant made a courageous charge into their ranks, disrupting the assault and clearing a swath, but more filled in the gaps. Valiant as he was, the flood was too great.

Are we all that's left? Persephone wondered. *Is everyone else in the fortress dead?*

Grygor flew backward, and Persephone saw a Fhrey wearing an asica enter the sitting room.

Miralyith.

Moya saw him, too, and fired her next shot at his chest. The arrow evaporated in mid-flight.

The Miralyith fixed her with a terrible glare and thrust out his hands.

"Moya!" Persephone shouted as, like the giant, the Shield to the Keenig was thrown off.

Tesh was surprised to find Sebek alone. The Fhrey convalescing in the little room one floor down from the top of the Kype had no guard watching his door. While it was Sebek's responsibility to protect Nyphron, the Galantian leader apparently felt no need to reciprocate. Not that it would matter. None of them would live through the next few hours. Still, he would have expected Nyphron to join his Shield, but maybe that wasn't the Galantian way.

Sebek sat up in his bed, naked to the waist, his torso wrapped in white bandages. Lightning and Thunder lay on either side of him—a pair of guard dogs that would give pause to anyone who knew the Fhrey. Even as badly wounded as he was, Sebek was dangerous.

The fane's army had found their goal, their prize. They had chased Nyphron up the stairs into the keenig's room, into the Shrine. No one had thought to open this nondescript door—no one except Tesh. He regretted not being with Brin, but there wasn't much he could do for her, or anyone. There was no winning that battle. But there was one victory Tesh could still achieve.

Sebek looked surprised. "What are you doing here?"

"Can't expect enemies to be courteous and only attack when you're prepared. Sometimes they catch you off guard in awkward places where you can't retreat," Tesh told him.

"What are you talking about?"

"Don't you remember saying that on the bridge when you tried to kill me?" Tesh closed the door while Sebek intently watched.

"I did pretty good, didn't I?"

Tesh slid the deadbolt. "I held my own there for a while. I think I surprised you." Tesh offered a grin, then shrugged. "I'm still not as good as you. My wrists aren't as strong, and your speed is superior. You would have beaten me, killed me, if Brin hadn't interfered. But overall, I did surprise you, didn't I? A Rhune like me—just a kid—going toe-to-toe with Sebek." Tesh nodded. "I've learned a lot. Not enough to beat you—not enough to seriously challenge any of the Galantians, let alone the best of them—but eventually . . . well, now we'll never know."

Sebek didn't move, didn't speak, but he watched Tesh's every movement.

"You know, when I first met Raithe, he taught me that the best way to learn how to kill someone is to discover everything you can about how they fight. 'Determine their strengths and weaknesses. Uncover their secrets, and never let them see yours.' That's what he told me. Every night since then I've gone to sleep with those words running through my head. He was right, but I thought I'd have more time, you know?"

"You saw us," Sebek said, his hands clasping the handles of his swords.

"When you and the rest of the Galantians came to my village?" Tesh nodded. "My mother was a wise and intelligent woman. At the first hint of your coming, she sent me into the cellar. We were poor—everyone was—and our storeroom was little more than a hole in the ground bordered by bricks. Didn't even have the wood for a door. My father went out, buying my mother time. She put me in, covered the hole with a rug, and moved the bed over all of it. Then she left to join my dad. From the outside, the cellar was invisible. I removed a brick, and through the tiny gap I watched you kill my father. While she cried over his dead body, you cut my mother's head off." Tesh pointed at the left sword. "With Thunder, I believe. She was a woman, not worthy of Lightning, isn't that right? And, yet, in a way, she'd bested you. You never found what she had hidden."

Sebek struggled to pull himself more upright and winced at the effort.

"You Galantians are such heroes. I could tell that just watching you, the way you slaughtered everyone. All the unarmed men, the women as they clutched their babies, and the children—yes, nothing screams hero quite like butchering an innocent child. I used to think you burned everything just to be thorough, or because your fane ordered it, but he doesn't even know, does he? He never ordered that attack, never ordered any assault. The war with the Fhrey didn't exist until you started it. You murdered everyone in Dureya and Nadak to terrify the rest of the clans. You wanted us to *think* the fane was our enemy, that we had no choice but to fight back. This war was Nyphron's idea, isn't that right?"

Sebek didn't reply, but his eyes were wide. Tesh took that as a sign of confirmation.

"Nyphron wants to be fane, but you can't break the law of your god and still rule in his name, can you? Ferrol forbids Fhrey from killing Fhrey. So, Nyphron needed a Rhune army to do what he couldn't."

Sebek finally spoke. "You're here to kill me."

Tesh was pleased. He wanted to be sure Sebek understood everything. Tesh had waited a long time; he felt he deserved at least that much. "I'd kill you all, if I had the time."

"So why save Nyphron from the raow?"

Tesh smiled as he slowly drew his swords. "*I* wanted to be the one to kill each of you." He sighed. "But Nyphron is probably already dead, so I saved him for nothing. But of the two, I'd rather it be you. Nyphron only gave the order; you were the one who killed my family. Every day for nearly a year, I choked back vomit as I pretended to be your devoted student, waiting until I had the skills."

"You think that because I'm wounded you can take me?"

"Yes."

Sebek gritted his teeth, grabbed his swords, and swung his feet to the floor.

Tesh let him.

Tesh feinted with his left. Sebek met him. In that clash, everything was made clear. Sebek's block was weak, without follow-through.

I'm doing him a favor. He wants me to kill him.

No better death for a warrior than in battle. But Tesh wasn't there to merely kill Sebek. He wanted to hurt the Fhrey, let him know what loss felt like. Roan's iron blade proved to be able to deliver on its promise. He struck Lightning with all his might and was rewarded when the bronze sword was severed at the hilt.

That is for my father.

He could have killed Sebek then, but Tesh wouldn't grant the Fhrey any favors. His next blows weren't aimed at flesh but at Thunder. Acting as giant scissors, Tesh's sword caught Sebek's remaining blade between two strong swings, and it, too, snapped.

That is for my mother.

Sebek staggered backward. He wasn't looking at Tesh. His eyes were focused on the broken hilts, as if his hands had been cut off. Tesh paused to let the full weight of the pain sink in. Tears slipped down Sebek's cheeks.

"Now you know," Tesh said. "Now you understand."

He let Sebek cry. The Fhrey dropped to his knees, and he wept over the broken blades. Tesh gave him a full minute before severing his head from his neck.

To Persephone's surprise and relief, neither Moya nor Grygor were dead. Both got back to their feet, merely knocked down by a strong wind. Shock gave way to puzzlement.

Why are they still alive?

The answer was written all over Moya. After the first battle, she had painted runes on everything she had. But Grygor didn't have any markings, and he didn't wear armor. The Miralyith should have killed the giant at least. But since they couldn't always tell who wore the Orinfar and who didn't, he likely always attacked with air.

Grygor was up again. Recognizing the greatest threat and forsaking all others, he launched himself at the bald figure.

The Miralyith either noticed Grygor didn't have armor, or the fear of a rampaging giant had caused the Fhrey to act out of reflex. In any case, his defense wasn't another blast of air.

A brilliant white light struck the giant.

"Grygor!" Padera yelled. Her voice was louder than Persephone thought possible.

The giant died in an instant.

The Miralyith died a half-second later as Moya, having risen to a knee, held Audrey sideways and launched two arrows before Grygor hit the floor. The first entered the Miralyith's throat; the second got him in the eye.

"In the name of Fane Lothian"—Persephone heard the shout from the other room—*"face your punishment, Nyphron, son of Zephyron!"*

Nyphron pushed Bergin through the threshold, and then he and Tekchin pulled a bleeding Eres into Persephone's bedchamber. This would be their final stand.

Moya leapt up on the bed and resumed firing arrows, but Persephone noticed she was down to only the ones in her hands. Tegan, Bergin, and a blood-covered Harkon took positions around the bed where Brin and Persephone clutched swords and Padera prayed to Mari, rubbing a small polished-stone carving of their god.

Eres got back to his feet and made great use of his spear's long reach. For a time, he forced the fane's invaders to stay back where they were easy targets for Moya's bow. She slew four but had only three arrows left.

Maybe because they finally realized the Galantians weren't willing to kill fellow Fhrey, six invaders rushed forward, forcing their way into the bedroom. Harkon threw himself forward, swinging. A bronze sword entered his chest, and he fell. Bergin killed a Fhrey that Tekchin had distracted with a slash across the face. Moya killed another. Then Bergin went down; Persephone didn't even see the blow that killed him.

Nyphron, Tekchin, Eres, and Tegan were all that remained between the fane's Fhrey and the bed, and the other Fhrey seemed to know that the Galantians were harmless.

A spear slammed into the headboard five inches from Persephone's head, and she screamed. Together, Padera and Brin jerked the spear free, and the old woman took it, aiming the point in defense of the bed.

Four more Fhrey pushed into the room, and Tekchin took a blade thrust to his chest. The stroke landed under his breastplate, and he cried out. Moya's howl was even louder.

"No!" She straddled Persephone and fired her last two arrows one after another into the chests of the newcomers. Each fell, but they were instantly replaced.

Brin pulled Moya down to the mattress as another spear flew. Just missing her, the weapon sparked off the stonework.

"*A curse on you, Lothian,*" Nyphron shouted. "*A curse on you and your entire Tetlin house!*"

Brin raised her dagger as more Fhrey rushed into the bedroom. Persephone gritted her teeth against the pain and raised her blade. She muttered a prayer to Mari.

That's when the roof came off the Kype.

CHAPTER TWENTY-NINE

The Light on Shining Armor

The way Roan described it—the rising sun, the bridge, the beating of her heart—I wish I could have seen it. I wish everyone could have. It was what fairy tales are made of.

—THE BOOK OF BRIN

Roan had watched the entire thing through a wash of tears. She didn't mean to, not the *whole* thing. She had planned to close her eyes before Suri killed him. Didn't seem right to watch that part, but it had happened so fast.

Suri had asked Raithe to lie down. She picked up the sword and Roan expected she would cut off his head, or raise it up and stab him in the chest, maybe cut his throat. Instead, she had laid the sword on his chest. Then she stroked his forehead, whispered something, leaned over, and kissed him on the brow.

That was it. Raithe was dead.

Roan hadn't realized it at first. The only hint was that Suri cried out as if someone had stabbed her. She began to sob, to wail, her body racked with grief, tears spilling down her face. Somehow in her horrific sorrow, Suri managed to sing. Not a nice song, not a song at all really. Nothing rhymed, and the melody was unpleasant. Then the rear wall of the smithy shattered, part of the roof caved in, and the beast appeared. The workshop was simply too small for the Gilarabrywn that was born of that sorrow. The Verenthenon wouldn't have been big enough. Just as Arion had tapped from all of them when they had been in the Agave, Suri had drawn on their combined grief, and what was born from it was impossible to fully comprehend.

The next moment, the Gilarabrywn flew into the night sky. Scale-covered body, massive claws, horned back, barbed tail, and an overabundance of teeth were hoisted by a pair of featherless wings. *Bigger*, Roan thought, wiping tears away. *Much bigger than last time.* The Gilarabrywn gained height, took one circle over the Rhist, then dove on the Kype, claws extended the way Roan had seen birds do on the big lake or the White Oak River. They usually came up with a fish in their talons. The Gilarabrywn came up with the roof.

Definitely bigger.

Suri sat beside Raithe and Arion. She was still rocking and crying.

Malcolm, Tressa, the little men, even Rain—they all cried. Roan had been surprised at that. She didn't know why. The little men just didn't seem the type. They didn't laugh or cry. They yelled quite often—at least Frost and Flood did, usually at each other and occasionally at a hammer.

Time stopped after that. The smithy was gone—most of it—and Roan was looking out at the courtyard where dozens of Fhrey stood. The elves—blood-covered and carrying swords, spears, and shields—had stopped, too, frozen in shock at what they saw. Yet as the Gilarabrywn flew away, time started again.

Beyond the world of the broken smithy, Roan saw a battlefield where a quiet courtyard had been. Fhrey warriors in gold and blue fought men in shining silver. Swords clanged. Shields rang. Blood and fire filled the cracks between. Malcolm valiantly stepped forward, holding his spear. The little men grabbed their hammers from the rack, and even Tressa found a weapon—the iron poker from the forge.

Roan didn't move. Instead, she counted the enemy that came at them: five, three from the left and two from the right. One more looked their way but couldn't make up his mind. She estimated their chance of surviving the next five minutes—those in the smithy at least—to be nonexistent. When Malcolm unexpectedly skewered the first Fhrey with his spear, she revised her estimate to *almost* nonexistent.

Dragging the sword she had laid on Raithe a moment before, Suri began to crawl. She started in the direction of the ruined barracks, but wavered, turning toward the woodpile. Roan was certain the mystic had no idea where she was going. Remembering her state after killing Minna, Roan guessed Suri was dazed and drained and merely moving for the sake of moving.

Then Roan heard a noise to her left and realized one of the Fhrey was looking at her—at the poor girl in the leather apron sitting between the anvil and the worktable. He was strangely barehanded and bareheaded, with a gash across his nose and cheek. Part of his face was also burned, the hair on the left side of his head singed away. And he was covered in blood, not just his clothes, but every part of him as though he'd bathed in a tub. He had a gleeful grin—an insane smile. The same sort Iver had worn. She knew what was coming. She'd watched Iver do it to her mother.

The bloody Fhrey came at her, dodging around Malcolm and the little men, who had their own problems. Tressa took a swipe, but the poker only rang off his armor. Another Fhrey appeared, and Tressa had her own adversary to deal with.

It was just the two of them then: the bloody Iver look-alike and Roan.

Slick hands clutched Roan's throat, and the Fhrey said something she didn't understand. She didn't need to. She'd heard the words before. She'd felt those fingers, too. All of it came back. Roan wasn't in a shattered smithy in an elven fortress; she was in a small roundhouse in Dahl Rhen. But this Iver was wearing armor: a dented, blood-soaked bronze breastplate.

Roan had invented the pocket because she hated not having things within easy reach when she needed them. The panic bag was the next evolutionary step, but upon becoming chief smith of Alon Rhist, neither had been good enough. Out of necessity, Roan had created a tool belt that she wore under her apron. Hanging from it were a small pair of tongs, tinsnips, her gloves, her hammer, and three metal punches. Each had a different purpose. The one she used for detail work was the size of her longest finger. The second was about the size of her hand. The last, which she used to punch holes in iron sheets, was a foot long and sharp as a needle. She'd used these tools every day for almost a year. Each had become an extension of her body, and as with any job that needed doing, Roan's hands found the appropriate tools without having to be told. As darkness began to close in from the edges of her sight, she placed the point of the metal punch on the neat little dent in the Fhrey's breastplate. One strike from Banger the Heavy sent the spike through the armor.

After the first swing, the pressure on her throat eased.

After the second strike, it disappeared altogether.

Suri saw a Fhrey grab Roan and throttle her like a doll, only to collapse, unmoving, a second later. All around, people fought in a blur of movement and muffled sounds. Frost landed a blow with a hammer, shattering a Fhrey leg. Flood was hit and fell beside the forge. Rain put the point of his pick through the back of the Fhrey that had attacked Tressa. Bodies, both human and Fhrey, filled the courtyard, soft twisted lumps of cloth and flesh amidst the broken stone and splintered wood. Farther out, the city burned. Smoke, black and sooty, swirled in gusts, rising toward a pale sky. Morning was creeping in unannounced behind dark clouds.

The big dome had collapsed. The corbel bridge was still there, but the top of the Kype was gone. The Gilarabrywn was digging into it like a bear into a beehive. As she watched, people were tossed out, but these bees didn't have wings, and the bodies plummeted. Suri was too far away to see if the Gilarabrywn was being careful. She had no idea if that rain was human, friendly Fhrey, or enemy elf.

She hadn't given specific orders to it other than to fight in defense of the fortress. She trusted that, like the one born of Minna, this new Gilarabrywn possessed understanding and a good degree of self-determination. The fact that it flew straight to the Kype and Persephone suggested it had that and maybe something more.

A flood of Fhrey spilled out the door at the bottom of the Kype. They retreated across the damaged corbel bridge. The Gilarabrywn dove from its perch on a corner of the Kype's ruined roof and a blast of fire shot from its mouth. The spray of flames created animated torches, some of whom jumped off the bridge, leaving bright streaks of light in their wake.

Like fireflies, she thought.

Suri was still staring in shock when Tressa seized her by the arm and jerked her up. "Get off the damn floor and do something!"

Suri didn't have to do anything. As the Fhrey closed in, she instinctively tugged on the leash. She hadn't realized there was one—a static connection between her and the Gilarabrywn—until that moment. She realized then that she'd performed a similar tug in Neith when the raow had grabbed her. She and her creations were linked, and her need became its concern.

The Gilarabrywn fanned out its great wings and took flight. One *thrump* and it dove.

As it did, Suri closed her eyes and repeated in her head, *Don't kill us all!*

"What in Ferrol's name is that?" the fane asked.

He sat in the big chair they had brought from Estramnadon. Made of gold and velvet, his portable throne was mounted on a wooden base that had been anchored into the ground with spikes to ensure the several-hundred-pound seat didn't tilt.

"Is that . . . is that *a dragon*?" The fane directed his question to the Spiders. The three Fhrey had returned to working in tandem, humming softly and rocking in a synchronized motion. At the question, they stopped just in time to see it breathe fire.

"That's not possible," Onya said. At least Mawyndulë thought that was her name. She'd been just one of the many Miralyith faces seen on the trip, but after the first day's disaster, she had risen in stature.

Up to that point, everything had been going well. The bridges had been completed without incident, and the fane had sent one of the remaining four Spiders across them with Rigarus, Haderas, and half of the remaining Shahdi. This left father and son on the hill in front of the big tent with Sile and Synne, three Spiders, and Taraneh with his twelve ornately dressed members of the Lion Corps. Mawyndulë was certain most positions in the corps were filled according to political favor rather than martial prowess, and he doubted the Lions could be relied on for anything more than staking tents.

After the calamity of the day before, everyone had held their breaths as they watched the invasion. Mawyndulë's father hadn't even looked. He'd stood up and paced. Sile and Synne walked with him. The fane had walked off into the darkness behind the tent twice, only to return and sit back down.

The bridges had held.

The Shahdi had crossed, and the moment they did, the remaining three Spiders, who were freed of their responsibilities to guard the spans, began a barrage of attacks intended to soften the army's path. Progress had been slower than his father had hoped, as evidenced by his constant complaints during the passing hours.

When the servants had dished out a late-night meal of cold meat and day-old bread, he and his father had listened to Taraneh explain that Alon Rhist was designed to make it difficult for an assault. Narrow pathways and plenty of bridges and stairs created choke points and gave defenders the advantage. From their vantage point, Mawyndulë had watched as the Shahdi began by clearing most of the city before scaling the stairs to the fortress. Despite the Spider his father had sent with them, the advancement had taken hours just to reach the upper courtyard.

Mawyndulë had been allowed one small part in the battle. With Jerydd's siphoned power and his father's guidance, he used Avempartha and shook the ground on the far side of the chasm. His part in the weave had been minor. Lothian just used him as a conduit; nevertheless, father and son had shared a rare moment of joy when the dome finally caved in.

"That's more like it," the fane had said while sitting back in his chair.

As morning approached and lightened the sky, his father called for wine. "I think this problem is finally solved."

Then the dragon had appeared.

At first, it was only a dark shadow against the bright fires, and Mawyndulë wasn't certain what he was seeing. All that changed when it breathed its own fire.

"What is it, then?" the fane asked.

Several heartbeats of silence went by. This wasn't unusual for the Spiders. There was always a delay when talking to them.

"We don't know," Onya finally replied.

"What do you mean, you don't know? That's why you're here. That's why you're holding hands and chanting. You're supposed to be monitoring your web. You should be able to tell me everything."

"It's not a creature of blood and bone. It's a light."

"A light?"

"It appears as a terribly bright light. Something none of us has ever seen before."

"What's this *light* doing?"

"It's killing our soldiers."

The fane scowled. "Then destroy it."

"Yes, my fane," Onya said, and the tiny circle of Spiders began to chant. In general, most Miralyith at a certain level preferred storm Art. Mawyndulë, on the other hand, was partial to fire, even though nearly all of his tribe considered it mundane or even childish. He just enjoyed the sense of power, the ease of the draw and release. Storms were more complicated and took far longer to prepare, and he never thought the results were all that impressive.

"My fane." Taraneh pointed to the north at a rider racing across the plain.

The rider was one of the Wolf scouts. He wore no armor, just his wolf helm and blue cape. Lothian set his wine down and stood up. Reaching the encampment, the rider thundered to a stop, dismounted, and ran forward to kneel at the fane's feet.

"What is it?" Lothian asked.

"My fane, a large army approaches from the southeast."

"An . . . an army?" the fane said with a baffled expression, as he looked to those around him for answers.

"The Gula-Rhunes, my fane."

"How many?" Taraneh asked.

"Many thousands, my lord."

"There!" Synne said, pointing with her quick hands.

Revealed by the first light of the brightening dawn, a large host of Rhunes appeared, cresting the distant hill. As the Fhrey watched, the Rhune army split into two groups, half making for Alon Rhist, the others wheeling in their direction. Even divided, the number of Rhunes facing them was overwhelming. There weren't just thousands, but tens of thousands, and they did not walk in rows but in a mass, a jumble like a herd of deer. Even at that distance, Mawyndulë heard their shouts, an awful constant roar as they gleefully charged down the slope.

"You didn't see them?" Lothian asked the Spiders.

"We were concentrating on the battle in the fortress, my fane."

"Blind fools!"

"Do you still wish us to——"

"Forget the dragon, destroy the army!"

Everyone who could run did, including Roan. The Gilarabrywn was supposed to be on their side, but trust wasn't one of Roan's virtues. She'd spent a lifetime learning better ways to hide. Since the beast was three stories tall, had a wingspan of about ninety feet, teeth in excess of a foot long, and the newly revealed ability to breathe fire, Roan didn't need any further incentive. When the Gilarabrywn landed in the courtyard, everyone scattered. She hadn't seen Suri leave, but after all it was her creation.

The foolish had advanced to attack it.

Not foolish, Roan decided. *They're brave. They just don't know what they're doing.*

After getting far enough away for comfort, Roan turned. She'd never seen a Gilarabrywn in daylight. Scales she had remembered as black were more a dark green. They glistened like metal—acted like it, too. Swords and spears did nothing, and Fhrey soldiers died, crushed or devoured. Oblivious and terrified, some of the men attacked as well. The beast ignored them the way a big dog might act with a bratty toddler. There was still danger. The Gilarabrywn was huge and powerful. Every movement brought havoc. A swish of its tail demolished walls, crushing those nearby. The flip of its wings raised a dust storm that blinded and choked.

There were only two exits out of the courtyard—one down a stair through the rubble to the city, and the other up a stair toward the big domed building that led toward the Kype. Roan ran for the safety of the Kype. She had hoped to join Persephone, Brin, and Moya, but the big dome had collapsed, making passage through the rotunda impossible. Now, the only way up was the narrow stairs that led around. Going that way was slow and jammed with people. Those trapped at the base were being slaughtered.

There has to be a better way.

I could hide.

As she looked around for a crevice to crawl into, another Fhrey soldier spotted her alone and in the open. She caught the glint of a smile on his face—that same Iver-smile she'd seen so many times in the past. This one—who still had a helm that was made to look like the head of a bear—was drenched in blood, a lavish splatter that added crimson to the copper-hued armor as it beaded on the surface, running down in tears.

He walked toward her.

She walked away, hoping he wasn't really interested in her.

He started jogging.

She ran.

The stair leading up was a deathtrap, and hiding was no longer possible, so Roan started toward the beast, hoping it would know who she was. But at that moment, the Gilarabrywn flew off. This left only one option—the stairs down to the city. That way was disturbingly empty.

This is not a good idea. This is not a good idea. This is not a good idea.

"Shut up, I'm trying to concentrate!" she yelled at herself. "Can't you see I'm running down steps?"

Reaching the bottom, she found the streets to the city blocked by rubble. Roan had no choice but to follow the path to the lower courtyard, which, like the upper, had been pummeled to pebbles. She had a good start on the Fhrey. He was halfway across the yard when they began the race, and he was slowed by armor, a sword, and shield.

Maybe he's given up and gone after easier prey?

She didn't bother to look, though, didn't need to; Roan heard the clap of shoulder plates behind her.

When she hit the lower courtyard, Roan took advantage of the open field and sprinted hard. Her only hope was distance. Rabbits survived by becoming too much effort to chase, and Roan planned to be one bothersome bunny. For the first time, she regretted her tool belt. The many utensils slowed her down as they flapped and swung.

Bodies were everywhere, human and Fhrey lying side by side. She tried not to look at the faces, didn't want to see someone she knew.

Roan ran past the Speech Rock, heading toward the only open route available—the front gate, or what was left of it. Somewhere in the depths of her desperate mind she saw it as salvation, a finish line, a point of escape, even though there was no door to close, no brace to throw, no wall to hide behind, and the enemy army had its camp on the far side of the gorge. In reality, there were just two big bronze gates lying on the ground beside the residue of a stone wall, but a goal was a goal.

Leaving the fortress is a really, really, really bad idea.

"Shut up!"

Behind her, the Fhrey let out a grunt. He was still after her and closer than ever.

Roan felt her legs growing tired. Worse, she was having trouble breathing. She just couldn't pull in enough air.

I'm going to die.

Roan passed the fallen bronze doors and the collapsed ramparts that had become massive stones of broken architecture. Ahead of her, all that was left was the ford where seven magically made stone bridges stitched the two sides of the chasm together. She was running for the center one, but *running* was an optimistic term for what she was doing. She'd been steadily slowing down, her flight reduced to little more than a jog by the time she could see into the chasm. Despite the dark clouds overhead, there was a gap at the horizon, and the brilliant yellow face of the sun shone through that opening. As she ran due east, the piercing light blinded her to nearly everything that lay ahead. What she did see was an army and the silhouette of a warrior on horseback riding across the center bridge.

I'm trapped.

The race was over. As if to punctuate this, lightning began flashing out of the sky, striking on the far side of the chasm. The turmoil in the heavens, the shouts and cries of men, the cracks and booms all told the same story.

No point in running anymore.

With lungs burning, Roan came to a stop, struggling to breathe and waiting to die. At that moment, a new contest began.

Who will reach me first? The rider crossing the bridge or the Fhrey from behind? Roan managed a miserable smile. *So much effort for the daughter of a slave.*

She didn't care who won, but looking out through bleary eyes at the cliff before her, a new thought popped into her head.

I can always jump.

There was a certain satisfaction in denying both of them the pleasure of her death. *And what if killing me isn't their intent?*

Roan turned off the path to the bridge and aimed for the cliff.

You deserve everything you get. She heard the familiar words, but this time the voice didn't sound like Iver. He was dead. She finally knew that to be true because she'd killed him twice, once with poison and once with a metal punch, with an assist from Banger the Heavy.

Exhausted and unable to run, Roan began to cry as she realized she wouldn't make it to the cliff's edge in time to kill herself. The rider was coming at her, too hard, too fast. She saw the mounted warrior draw his sword. He was a faceless silhouette against the bright morning sun, but she heard it. The ring of that metal coming free of its scabbard, only . . .

That sound was unmistakable. Not bronze—that was *steel*.

As the rider drew closer, she saw the glint of silver. Beneath the helm was a beautiful, misaligned face.

"Gifford!" she cried, sacrificing the last remaining air in her lungs.

He rode at her pursuer, swinging his sword, missing badly. It didn't matter. Whether by intent or accident, the horse trampled the Fhrey.

Having ridden past Roan, Gifford wheeled around. As he did, the full face of the rising sun shone on his armor and upon his white horse. Dazzling and bright, Gifford gleamed like a morning star, wondrous and beautiful. He glowed.

"Woan, I can't get down." Gifford leaned over and extended his arm. "Please, you have to take my hand."

She didn't think, didn't hesitate. Reaching out, she grabbed hold of that offered arm and let Gifford pull her up behind him. Then she hugged him around his waist.

"You're alive! You're alive! You're alive!" she cried, squeezing as hard as she could.

"Woan?" Gifford said. "You know you hugging me? You touching me, Woan."

"I know."

As Gula-Rhunes charged across the bridge and poured into the fortress of Alon Rhist, Roan laid her head on Gifford's back.

Once more, she heard the words: *You deserve everything you get.* The voice wasn't Iver's after all. It was her mother's.

CHAPTER THIRTY

The Dragon

At first I thought it was a dragon, savage and fierce. I wish that had been true. Dragons only kill you; Gilarabrywns break your heart.
                                                        —The Book of Brin

Persephone stared in disbelief.

Above them was open sky.

The roof to the Kype had been ripped off. Most of it was wood, but there had been stone as well, and a dragon had torn it away like a cork from a jug. Then it began to kill.

Persephone assumed the beast was another weapon of the fane.

He has giants, magicians, and storms. Why not a dragon?

She closed her eyes, waiting for death. She cringed, expecting the crush of claws or the bite of teeth.

Nothing happened. Even the screams of the dying fell silent. She heard only the sound of the dragon's breathing, and then Brin's voice. "Mari, mother of us all, protect us. Mari, mother of us all, protect us."

Letting go of her dagger, Persephone reached out and found the girl. She clutched her arm, then found her hand.

"Mari, mother of us all, protect us," Persephone added her voice.

Padera joined in their prayer. A moment later, Moya did, too. Persephone reached out again, found Moya's foot, and held on. The anticipation of the death blow was maddening, but Persephone still held tightly to Brin and Moya. Finally, she chanced a look. The Fhrey that had been the threat only moments before were gone—only Nyphron, Eres, and Tegan were still alive. The dragon was still there, too, perched on the corner of the Kype, anchored by its massive talons. She felt its hot breath and tilted her head higher to see its face. She realized with horror that the dragon, with its two massive eyes and oblong pupils, wasn't merely looking at *them*—it was staring at *her*.

It will kill me now—open its mouth and swallow me whole.

It didn't.

The dragon continued to stare.

Finally, it did open its mouth, but instead of devouring her, the dragon spoke. With a voice more powerful than thunder, deeper than the groan of the rock, it said, "Even now."

The dragon waited a moment more; then, extending its wings, it pushed off, crushing a block of stone the size of a moose.

"Unbuckle his armor," Padera shouted. "Get it off." The old woman was on the floor at the foot of the bed, working on Tekchin, who lay sprawled on his back in a pool of blood. Moya, who was up and moving again, scrambled to him and began jerking the leather straps at the Galantian's shoulder.

"Got him good," Padera said. "Bleeding like a speared boar. Brin, grab the bandages on the table. And get me that belt."

No one else spoke.

A roar erupted a short distance away, but still nothing happened—not to them. Distant screams were followed by a flap of wings. After that, silence.

"How the Tet does this culling armor come off?" Moya shouted as she jerked on the leather straps of Tekchin's plate. Blood spilled from a puncture just below his ribs.

"Just cut it off," Padera told her. "Persephone, give me your blade. Persephone?"

"Here!" Brin tossed down the bandages, followed by one of Roan's daggers.

Rapid footfalls grew louder. Nyphron raised his sword only to lower it again when Anwir rushed in. "What happened?"

"About to ask you the same thing," Nyphron replied. "Where'd the dragon come from, and where is it now?"

"Dragon?" Anwir asked, confused. He looked up. "Where'd the roof go?"

"Forget all that," Padera yelled at them. She pointed at Tekchin, where Moya was desperately trying to saw through the thick leather straps with Brin's dagger, but they were hidden under the shoulder plates and hard to get at. "Your friend is dying."

"He's fine." Nyphron sounded annoyed. "He's had worse and pulled through."

"He's bleeding to death. Any of you killers know how to get this armor off?"

Anwir, who proved adept with straps and ties, bent down and helped Moya.

"Brin, needle and thread," Padera ordered. "Near the basin. Thread it."

"Squeeze," Padera told Moya. They had the breastplate off and had cut Tekchin's shirt away. "Don't be afraid, press hard." Brin came over with the needle. "Now, here, Brin, get the flaps of skin closer together—that's it."

Padera started sewing. When she was done, she sat back and wiped sweat from her brow. "Okay, wrap him," Padera told Moya and Brin. "And don't be timid about it. Pull the strips tight."

"He gonna live?" Eres asked the old woman.

Padera stood up, her hands stained dark. She took a towel and wiped them off, leaving brilliant streaks of red on the pale cloth. "Depends on how much his god likes him. Busted a rib and caught part of a lung sack. He could just as easily drown in his own blood."

Moya sat bent over Tekchin, crying. "Don't you dare die, you son of the Tetlin whore!"

Padera turned toward the bed. "Persephone? You okay? Are you hurt?"

Tesh came through what was left of the door.

"Tesh!" Brin sprinted across the room and hugged the boy, nearly knocking him off his feet. "You're alive!"

"Where've you been?" Tegan asked, then looked at the blood on Tesh's swords. "Finally got to kill some elves, eh?"

Tesh glared at him for a second, then smiled. "Yeah—yeah, I did."

The sound of battle was gone. All around was the sound of wind blowing over the top of the Kype and the flutter of some unseen fabric.

"So, what's all this about a dragon?" Anwir asked again.

A tear slipped down Persephone's cheek, her voice soft and quavering. "It's not a dragon."

What's going on? What are you seeing? Jerydd shouted in his head.

Mawyndulë watched with delight as lightning struck the Gula, killing them. Flash, crackle, drop. Flash, crackle, flame. Over and over the storm delivered an unnatural series of killer bolts that left him seeing after-streaks. These Rhunes did not wear the special armor, and strike after strike, the lightning killed. While dozens of bolts fired at the same time, there were still thousands and thousands of Gula charging at them, big hairy brutes with spears and rough wooden shields. Clearly, the Fhrey could easily kill several hundred but then be slaughtered by the rest.

How can there be so many? They're like rats.

His father realized the danger as well. "Onya, create a firewall."

A firewall? Why? Jerydd asked.

A moment later, as the barbarians threw themselves into a wailing run, a ten-foot wall of flames appeared between the Gula and the last cohort of Shahdi. This flaming fence began in the middle of the field, then rapidly ran out to either side.

Mawyndulë didn't understand why the Spiders didn't just blast the savages with torrents of flame. Their strategy became clearer as the wall began to move. It curled around, driving the Gula west toward the Bern River—toward the cliff.

"Fire the bridges," the fane ordered, and in a few seconds, fire appeared on all seven of them.

Have you become deaf or just stupid? Jerydd asked, his tone an ever-increasing whine of frustration. *Answer me. What are you seeing?*

He'd asked the same question every few minutes since the battle started. At first, Mawyndulë had complied, whispering descriptions, but he grew tired of narrating. He found the process irritating and demeaning. He hadn't invited Jerydd to sit in his head that morning and felt no obligation to relay information like some courier.

"Push them off the cliff," his father said. "Not too fast—a slow and steady creep. I want them to have the opportunity to ponder their fate. Give them time to choose between jumping to their death or burning alive." The fane picked up his wine once more and sat down. He swirled the contents in the cup. "This is the way my mother used to do it. Show them what it means to go to war against the Miralyith," he said, staring out at the thousands beyond the wall of fire that marched unerringly forward. "This is your reward." He gestured to the servant to fill another cup. "Have some wine, Mawyndulë. I don't like to drink alone."

His father was in a dark but generous mood, at least toward him.

Mawyndulë didn't answer. The sight and the anticipation were fascinating. An unrelenting wall of fire drove more people than he'd ever seen in one place toward a sheer drop. A few Rhunes tried to run through. He saw them catch fire and fall. When the wall moved past, he could see their scorched bodies, lumps in a smoking black field. As the wall pressed, those caught inside were squeezed. Those in the rear, row by row, line by line, began to slip into the chasm.

"It's coming," Synne said.

"What is?" the fane asked.

"The light," she said, pointing up at the sky.

Mawyndulë looked toward the fortress and spotted the dark winged creature coming at them. The dragon that had breathed fire was getting larger by the second, and Mawyndulë already thought it was pretty big.

"Synne," his father said. "Use lightning. Kill it."

Lightning crackled and a jagged finger of blue-white light struck the beast. It didn't even dip with the impact, didn't fall. It barely altered its flight. Again and again, Synne jolted the dragon with bolts. The thing kept coming.

Damn you, Mawyndulë! What are you seeing?

"The Art . . ." Synne sounded confused. "The Art has no effect on it."

No effect? Jerydd said in his head. *That doesn't make sense. What does it look like? Scratch that. What does it feel like? Look at it with the eyes of the Art.*

"A bright light. Looks and feels like . . . power," Mawyndulë said softly.

Power?

"Feels like the Art."

Art doesn't affect Art, Mawyndulë. If what you say is true, they are trying to burn a fire, or flood an ocean. It won't work.

"Jerydd says the dragon is the Art, and the Art can't damage itself," Mawyndulë told his father.

The fane glanced at Mawyndulë, his eyes losing confidence. Once more, he set down his wine and stood up.

The beast was crossing the chasm, wings beating in a steady rhythm, tail straight out behind it. Larger and larger it became.

How big is it? Mawyndulë thought. *How can that be the Art?*

The fane took a step forward, cast off his cloak, and with a deep hum and a wave of his arm, the fane sent forth a blast of fire that coursed across the sky, striking the beast in the chest. The flames did nothing, and the monster appeared to swim through the blaze. Then, as if given the idea, the dragon opened its mouth and replied in kind. A blast of fire shot from its mouth at the hill.

Instantly, the flame wall marching toward the Gula vanished when the Miralyith abandoned it in exchange for protection. A defense screen was one of the first things a Miralyith learned. The crossed arms and buzzing sound became as much a reflex as throwing out one's hands in a fall. Mawyndulë put up his own shield; so did his father, and Synne threw up a defense over the fane, but the Spiders, by virtue of their training, reacted differently. They combined their efforts, creating a small dome that capped the hilltop. In doing so, they saved the lives of those few servants lucky enough to be standing close by, including Treya, Taraneh, and his twelve Lions. Everything on the command hill was scorched black, including a dozen tents, a cask of wine, travel packs, linens, tables, torch stands, five soldiers, and two dozen servants who didn't have the time to scream.

When the fire was exhausted, Mawyndulë looked up and saw the dragon was huge, the size of a building—a big building.

"Knock it down!" the fane ordered. "Blow it away! Use the wind. Only wind!"

Onya nodded and the Spiders reconvened their weaving.

"Just channel the natural air, like when combating the Orinfar," his father continued to explain.

The light breeze wafting across the hilltop died. Smoke that had been blowing away hung in the stagnant air as all around them grass continued to smolder. Overhead, a monster, so big it blocked out most of the sky, folded its wings, extended claws the size of swords, and dove.

"Now!" the fane shouted.

A massive roar came from everywhere as an incredible blast of wind hit the beast and set it spinning away. The dragon became a leaf in a hurricane.

Did it work?

Mawyndulë was too scared to be obstinate, too relieved to be vindictive. "Yes, the wind threw it back."

In that brief gap, in that moment left open for taking a breath, Mawyndulë heard the clash of battle. Everyone had forgotten the Gula. With the firewall gone, the horde ran at the Shahdi with a new fury. They shouted and yelled so that their joined voices created a roar similar to the howl of wind the Spiders had harnessed. They charged across the scorched and smoking field and slammed into the remainder of the fane's army. The blue-and-gold warriors were immediately swamped by a sea of Rhunes. There would be no possibility of erecting a new firewall without killing their own soldiers. This wasn't much of a problem; the real concern was the dragon. With the first wind expelled, the Spiders drew another breath. The beast wasted no time flying back toward them.

"Drive it down this time," the fane said. "Slam the dragon to the ground. Crush it."

The beast was fast and only a few hundred yards away when the Spiders struck it from above this time. The dragon hit the ground so hard it bounced and left a long scar in the field, but the fall didn't kill it, didn't faze it, and a moment later the monster was up, this time running toward them.

"Blow it back! Blow it back!" the fane shouted.

The beast was too close. The Spiders couldn't recover in time.

Mawyndulë felt a sudden surge.

Help him! The Spiders are out of power! Help your father!

Mawyndulë didn't have much experience with wind, but it wasn't too difficult, not with the force of Avempartha fueling him. He could have been way off, casting the most inefficient of weaves—which he was certain was the case—and yet the sheer force was capable of sending the beast hurtling backward once more.

Heads turned to look his way, but no one wasted the time to make a comment.

Instead, Onya faced the fane shaking her head. "My fane, we can't kill it."

Taraneh, who up until then had remained silent, turned to Lothian. "My fane, the battle is lost. You must retreat." The leader of the fane's guard waved to the groom to bring horses.

His father exploded. "No! Not again! Not when we are so close."

"My fane," Synne said, and Mawyndulë thought it might have been the first time he'd heard her. "The Shahdi are engulfed by Rhunes, and that beast can't be stopped. You and your son must flee."

"This is my whole army!" his father shouted.

"And they will die so that you can live."

Mawyndulë couldn't help noticing that the dragon was coming back. Once more it had taken flight.

"Mawyndulë," Synne spoke directly to him. "Can you blow it to the ground?"

Say yes.

"Yes."

"Good, do that." Synne faced the fane. "I have an idea that might buy us—might buy *you*—some time."

She meant for his father to escape. Mawyndulë couldn't help but hope he was included in that *you*.

The beast came at them faster this time, more determined than ever.

"Do what she says," his father told him.

Synne looked at Mawyndulë, and in that instant, she spoke a thousand words with her eyes. All of it came down to one simple idea. *Don't miss.*

The surge filled him again. Mawyndulë felt buoyed, rich with strength. He was the Parthaloren Falls. He was a torrent, a great river running in free fall. He was power. On his second try, he tightened his wind weave, made it cleaner, less ugly, and brought the downdraft hard.

The dragon slammed onto the field once more, unfortunately on a section where the fighting was thick. The impact killed a score of Fhrey and Rhunes, but again the beast was unfazed. The moment it hit, however, the grass came alive. Deep, long roots and a million stalks grabbed hold of wings, feet, and tail, looping, swirling, wrapping.

"You've trapped the thing!" the fane cheered. "Synne! You're a genius."

"It won't hold," Onya said. "Spiders, join in!"

"It's only grass," Synne explained, sweat beading on her forehead. "The creature will break free. Open the ground!"

A moment later the plain of rock and soil split apart and the beast fell. Onya clapped her hands and the ground closed, swallowing the beast.

"She's buried it!" Mawyndulë said.

That won't stop it, Jerydd said in his head. *You need to get out of there.*

Down the slope, Mawyndulë saw far fewer Fhrey soldiers defending them than there had been only minutes before.

"My fane," Taraneh spoke loudly, and gestured to a pair of horses being brought over. "You must go."

Lothian looked down the slope at his dying Shahdi, then at the scar left where the dragon had been buried. Then they all felt the tremor under the ground. Something big was digging beneath them.

Taraneh turned to his aide. "Inform the Lion Corps. We are leaving— we are leaving now!"

"You go too, Synne," Onya said. "Protect the fane."

"We can't afford to lose this battle," the fane said softly, already defeated.

"This is but one encounter, my fane," Taraneh said. "It'd be better to fight another day. As long as we have you, the campaign continues."

Mawyndulë saw the resignation in Lothian's eyes. His father had lost so much in that battle. Not just the lives of so many Fhrey, but his belief that the Fhrey were invincible. Mawyndulë feared he would see that look over and over in nightmares and on the faces of many others.

His father, his fane, was not invincible.

CHAPTER THIRTY-ONE

Saying Goodbye

The Battle of Grandford was not only the turning point of the war; it was a watershed for all of mankind. Those three days were our first steps out of darkness and into the light of a new dawn. Beauty and grandeur, the arts and sciences, and peace and civility all grew from seeds watered by the blood spilled on that terrible soil. Alon Rhist remains but a ruin, a bluish stone rising out of a forgotten hill, but it was the beginning of everything else.

—THE BOOK OF BRIN

Victory.

The word was spoken frequently after the Battle of Grandford, but never with the sort of enthusiasm or joy expected with such a term. For Persephone, it was a hollow word, made empty by the many holes cut through her heart. One hole for every life lost, the largest punched out by the death of the man in the grave at her feet.

According to the most recent count, two thousand eight hundred and thirty-three people had died over the course of those three days. The death toll was expected to rise the deeper they dug. One thousand eight hundred and six were human, including Meryl, whom Persephone learned was a slave working in the Kype. The man had taken it upon himself to murder the leaders of what he deemed the enemy. Meryl had avoided capture by hiding in the labyrinth beneath the Verenthenon, only to be killed by the very Fhrey he had sought to aid when they collapsed the great dome.

Two thirds of the defending force of Alon Rhist had perished. Persephone knew the number because she had Brin keep an exact count as the bodies were recovered. In all her dreams, Brin likely never anticipated this would be part of her responsibilities.

By every account, the attacking Fhrey had suffered such a comparatively similar number of casualties that the battle could have been considered a draw. Expectations made all the difference. No one had thought they had a chance. So, by the fact she was still breathing, the world judged Persephone the victor.

Breathing was about all Persephone was doing. Standing between the two graves, she was having a hard time even with that.

Her wounds were still debilitating, so her stomach was wrapped tight, and she'd been carried down from the Kype. Here, she insisted on standing. They had come to say farewell to Raithe and Arion, and one did not sit in the presence of heroes.

Each breath she took hurt. And the pain from her wounds didn't help matters.

She was disappointed by the smaller-than-expected crowd.

Should be thousands, Persephone thought, *given what they've done for us.*

But so many of those who knew of their contributions were also dead and buried on that terrible plain. Raithe had hated that place; Persephone now hated it, too. Someone, maybe Brin, had referred to it as the Field of Heroes. It sounded like her, like something she would put in her book. And while they were heroes, Persephone couldn't help feeling they were also victims—her victims. More so than anyone, she was responsible. This was her *victory*.

Tesh had dug Raithe's grave and placed the Phyre stone, as was fitting for the next of kin. Persephone didn't know who had dug Arion's, but Suri had placed the Phyre stone. Suri stood apart from the others, staring down at the twin mounds of rocks, as if unable to understand what had happened.

Suri had saved them all.

She'd also killed Raithe.

No one had told Persephone this; no one needed to. The moment the dragon spoke, she knew. She knew more than she wanted, and it made standing in that dry wind, trying to breathe, so very difficult.

Gifford made an effort to comfort Suri, putting an arm around her shoulder. She pushed it away. "Don't," she told him. "Don't be nice; bad things happen to people who love me."

As always, Brin stood beside Persephone. She needed to record the event, but she couldn't have seen much through her continual tears. Moya, Tekchin, Padera, Malcolm, Frost, Flood, Rain, Roan, Gifford, Habet—they all showed up to pay respects. Tressa was the surprise. The widow of Konniger usually kept away from crowds.

"I made it extra deep," Tesh said to everyone—or no one. "Then used the biggest, heaviest rocks I could find. Don't want animals digging him up." Tesh wiped his nose and eyes.

Brin moved to his side and, taking his hand, squeezed.

"We should say something," Moya suggested.

To her surprise, Tressa, who held a rock in her hand, stepped forward to place it on the pile.

"Not you," Moya snapped.

"Give it a rest," Tressa responded. "We just finished a battle. Haven't you had enough?"

"Of you, yes."

Tressa sighed and shook her head. "I didn't come here to fight."

"Why are you here?"

She pointed at Raithe's grave. "I wanted to say something to him. Funerals are where people do that, or so I've heard. Do you mind?"

"Yes," Moya said. "Quite a bit actually."

"Good." Tressa grinned.

The Shield took a hurried step toward her.

"Moya," Persephone said, "let her talk." The keenig's voice was soft and weak, but the effect was powerful. Moya stopped abruptly but continued to glare.

Tressa ignored her. "I didn't know you very well," she said to the grave.

"You were Dureyan, a troublemaker. Knew it from the moment you first came to Rhen. Dureyans are nothing but liars, drunks, murderers, and thieves. Everyone knows that."

All of them glared at Tressa, and Moya began rocking on the balls of her feet, glancing over at Persephone, hoping for the leash to be removed.

"Thing is," Tressa went on, "most people don't know Tet. Just think they do. People always think they know everything about a person." She glared at Moya, then stared back down at the pile of rocks at their feet. "You were Dureyan, so you had to be trouble, and maybe you were, but I never seen it. You cut wood for us when everyone else was too scared. Faced the Fhrey when no one else would. Turned down the chance to be the keenig—to rule over everyone. Never saw a man turn down power like that. Konniger wouldn't have. Konniger got himself killed trying to get one tenth of what folks were shoving in your face. Then you"—she wiped her eyes and sniffled—"then you go and do this. Damn lousy Dureyan. Rotten troublemaker. I just wish . . . I wish we had more like you, or that I would have had the chance to know you better. Because people . . . well, I guess people just don't know Tet." Tressa looked up then. She glanced at the rest of them. "That's it. That's all I have to say." She placed her rock on Raithe's pile and turned away.

A long silence followed.

Moya relaxed, her shoulders drooped, her arms unfolded. Finally, she asked, "Tesh? Do you want—?"

He shook his head. "Already spoke the words I wanted while I was piling the rocks."

Moya looked at Persephone, who rapidly shook her head.

"Suri?"

She was looking at the Gilarabrywn. The behemoth was curled up on Wolf's Head, watching the proceedings with casual indifference.

Moya cleared her throat and called her name again. "Suri, do you have anything you want to say?"

The mystic shook her head.

Moya looked to the dwarfs, but they also declined.

"Malcolm?"

The tall, thin man, dressed in clothes Brin's mother had made for him, stood before the pile of stones and raised his head. "This evening has caused me to pause and think." Malcolm tilted his head back and looked up at the slowly darkening sky. "With the passing of Raithe and Arion, *I think* there will be at least two new stars in the sky tonight." He looked at Arion's grave. "And from now on, *I think* the name Arion should be another word for *wise*. For while she was compassionate, intelligent, and giving, more than anything, she displayed wisdom. One might suspect that comes with living so long, but I *think* not. She knew that from arrogance came apathy, from apathy came ignorance, from ignorance came hatred, and from hatred, well . . . nothing good ever came from hatred." He paused to look across the bloody landscape. "She tried to stop this, but I *think* wisdom is rarely ever enough when fighting hatred. Sometimes sacrifices need to be made."

He focused on the other mound of rocks. "I *think* Tesh did a fine job with the stones. Big ones on the bottom, small ones on top. He also put a little one in your hand, Raithe, so you can enter Phyre. You would have approved. I'm sorry I had to mislead you, but then I'm sorry about a lot of things. Be sure to tell your sister and mother that you weren't like your father or brothers. You did something good—something very good. And I *think* your life made a difference. No, that's not true." Malcolm looked up at the sky. "This night has made me think many things, but that is one thing I *know*. Sleep well, my friend. You've earned it."

Then Malcolm lifted his head and sang in an unexpectedly beautiful voice:

> "My love, I give you;
> Into Elan, I send you;
> Forgive me, I beg you;
> Be at peace, I ask you;
> May whatever good is in this universe watch over your journey."

Then Malcolm produced Herkimer's bronze medal, the one Raithe had worn ever since the two of them had met, and he placed it on the grave. He trapped it there with a rock and stepped back.

Then everyone else stepped up, placing their rocks on both of the graves. Grimacing with pain, Persephone placed one on Arion's and then stepped back. She didn't go to Raithe's. This didn't go unnoticed by Moya, who announced that the ceremony was over and urged them to leave.

Moya moved to Persephone's side. "Let's get you back to—"

"No. I'm staying."

"You can barely stand."

"I need a moment alone."

Moya considered this, then nodded. "Fine, but I'll be waiting over there with the litter. Wave if you need me."

Moya moved off, shooing Brin, who asked why Persephone wasn't coming.

"Suri?" Persephone stopped the mystic when she started back.

The girl turned. Her face drawn, eyes tired.

"I want to ask . . ."

Why Raithe? Of all the people, why was it him you sacrificed? Was it because of me? The words caught in her throat, refusing to come out. "Never mind," she said. "I'm sorry."

I know why, and I'd rather not hear it aloud. If you say it, I'll have nothing to hide behind.

"It didn't hurt," Suri said. "It didn't hurt *him*."

Persephone nodded.

"I'll be right over here," Moya reminded. She and Suri walked away, leaving Persephone alone in the light of the setting sun and at the mercy of the harsh wind.

She moved forward only a step. That was all it took. She fell. Caught herself with her hands and knees. The pain ripped through her center, making her cry out. Moya started to come back, but Persephone waved her off.

Then the Keenig of the Ten Clans started to cry. She was stunned that she'd lasted this long. Alone in that horrid place, before that lonely pair of rock mounds, the dam broke—she let it wash over her.

When at last she stopped weeping, the sun had slipped behind the ruins of the Rhist and stars were beginning to appear in the east. From around her neck, Persephone removed the chain that held the chieftain's ring, the one she had let fall the night she said goodbye to Reglan, the one Brin had found. She squeezed it in her hand, feeling the metal cut into her palm.

"I had to do what was best for my people," she told the pile of stones. "I had to . . . I had to . . . I still have to. And I know I hurt you, but dammit, Raithe, you hurt me, too, and this . . . this was just cruel."

She wiped her face with her wrist. "I wish to Mari that Suri had asked me before she asked you. If I had known she was looking for sacrifices, I would have stood in line all night to volunteer. Then *I* could be the hero and you could be the one drowning in guilt and self-loathing. Let me tell you, a painless death at the hands of Suri sounds like a pretty good deal right now. But I won't get to die a hero like you. Women never do. We just get old, then we're forgotten."

She sniffled and shook her head. "Raithe, I wish I could say I was sorry, but I can't. I just can't because . . . because this just hurts too much. You took away my chance, you stole my one hope to make everything right, and honestly, at this moment—I hate you. I hate you so very much . . . almost as much as I hate myself. So take it." She moved to the mound of rocks, lifted one, and set the ring on the pile. "Nyphron gets everything else, but not this. It's yours. I think it always was."

"Seph?" Moya called. It was getting dark, and the Shield was having trouble seeing her keenig.

"I have to go. I have to take care of my people. It's what I do." She waved, and Moya started toward her. "You sacrificed yourself to save us; good for you, but *you* only had to do it once."

CHAPTER THIRTY-TWO

The Message

In my mind's eye, I see this little bird flying past arrows, Miralyith-conjured lightning, and a fire-breathing dragon. What an unlikely hero.

—THE BOOK OF BRIN

Imaly sat sideways in the golden chair in the center of the empty Airenthenon with her legs thrown up on the arm. Most undignified and disrespectful to the sanctity of the chamber, it was also wonderful. At her age, Imaly's feet had a tendency to throb when she stood too long, and she'd just spent hours on them. The weekly meeting of the Aquila had ended, and the assembly had been vicious. Imaly didn't blame them; she was anxious, too. The fane and the army had been gone for weeks without word. Everyone wanted answers. She didn't have them, but that didn't stop the questions.

As Curator of the Aquila, she was acting fane in his absence. This position held no real authority. The martial powers bestowed on the fane by Ferrol did not transfer. She also had no authority to set policy. All she could do was oversee the appointment of a new fane should the old one die and, as was the case just then, fail miserably at answering questions about Lothian's progress.

Some of the questions, like the one posed by Minister Metis, were legitimate concerns for the fane's well-being. More, like Volhoric's inquiries, were politically motivated. Like many, he saw a rare opportunity. Fane and heir were both at war. War was dangerous. Should something happen to them both, the field of options would be wide. The Aquila, and most especially Imaly herself, would have the power to direct the future of Erivan. If they allowed only non-Miralyith to blow the Horn of Gylindora, the Fhrey would have a new ruling tribe, one with the power to castrate the growing supremacy of the magic class. The course of history might be forever changed should the fane and his son die. Volhoric was probing, seeing where her intent lay. He would, of course, want to endorse an Umalyn for fane. He said as much when he stated that the Fhrey were in need of strong religious leadership to help return to Ferrol's Fold.

As self-satisfying as it might be to deflate the egos of the Miralyith, who had indeed become too full of themselves, doing so was dangerous. The riot of the year before had proved that the Miralyith might not dutifully accept a place at the back of the line. Handled poorly—no, even if handled well—Erivan could explode into civil war. She considered going to the Garden to think, but she'd avoided the bench across from the Door since her unexpected encounter with the unseemly stranger who announced he'd be watching her. As far as she could tell, he hadn't been. She'd asked around and discovered nothing. Imaly had gone so far as to send people to walk by that bench to determine if he was still there. He was. She found this both unsettling and reassuring. Yes, he was still around, but obviously not stalking her. Her initial thought that he might be a threat had faded over time. Now she wondered if she should have gone back. The fellow on the bench was an enigma that haunted her, but he was also a potential source of information. He appeared to know more than he ought to.

Imaly had been on her feet far past the usual two hours, and they were screaming at her because of it. Lifting them up helped drain the swelling. She'd take a soak when she got home in the hope that they would be recovered for the next week's assembly.

She heard the echoing clack of shoes on the marble floor and jerked her legs off the arm with an unhappy grunt. She didn't need Volhoric or Kabbayn to see her lounging on the sacred chair. Little things like that had the ability to become big things when said in the right way to the wrong people. Only it wasn't Volhoric or Kabbayn, nor any of the councilors. She was most certainly the last person Imaly expected, and seeing that familiar face, Imaly was both stunned and terrified.

With hands clasped before her, Makareta entered the Airenthenon. The Miralyith, who had seduced Mawyndulë into unwittingly aiding a revolt against his own father, walked across the marble floor.

This is how these things happen, in empty, hallowed chambers when no one is looking. I wonder if she's in league with the fellow on the bench. Both of them lying in wait. Both remarkably patient.

Imaly was reminded of the broken leg and sprained arm Makareta had given her as a result of a magical toss across the chamber. It still hurt, still ached on rainy days. Yet Imaly wouldn't give the child the satisfaction of showing fear.

She sat up, brushed the folds from her asica, and smiled. "What brings you out of hiding?" she said as casually and good-naturedly as possible.

"I need help," the girl replied.

Only then did Imaly notice the filthy state of Makareta's asica. Stained and torn in places, it looked more like a rag. And she had hair. Not just a bit of stubble, the result of lazy neglect, but locks that covered both ears and the back of her neck.

She's been in hiding. By the look of her clothes, she did most of it in a hole.

"I suppose you do, but why come to me?"

"You're the only one who might listen."

"Why would I help? It's not like I have fond memories of our time together."

"Because you're wise and compassionate."

Imaly laughed despite—and possibly because of—her fear. Terror had a way of making her overreact. The Miralyith standing in front of her wasn't only incredibly powerful, but given that she'd already killed Fhrey, Makareta was no longer bound by Ferrol's Law. She was a wanted fugitive, desperate and unchecked, and in her eyes, Imaly saw her own death. Having revealed herself, she couldn't allow Imaly to live past the end of their conversation, whatever that might be.

"You have me confused with Mawyndulë. Flattery won't work."

The girl smirked. "I'm not flattering you. Those aren't compliments; they're facts. I've watched you under this dome for years. You listen. You hear. You're fair, and you have the best interests of your fellow Fhrey at heart. You are the only non-Miralyith I respect."

Imaly clutched her arm. "Was it respect that caused you to fling me across this room?"

"Yes," Makareta said. She pointed at a marble statue of Fane Ghika. With a snap of her fingers, the statue burst into powder.

Imaly hated herself for it, but she flinched at the loud crack, magnified by the echoing dome. The point was clear. Looking at the dust and rubble that had once been a very fine depiction of Ghika, Imaly took her life in her hands and said, "I'm sorry, but I can't help you. I don't have the power, and I wouldn't even if I did. What you did and what you tried to do were unforgivable—incomprehensible. We only just repaired the scars you left in this building and the square outside. Our whole society is based on the principle that Fhrey don't kill Fhrey, and most of all that we revere the fane."

"Do you think Lothian is a good fane?"

"Good or bad, he *is* fane. There is nothing anyone can do about that. Besides, you would prefer a world where Miralyith were gods and those like me your slaves. I hope you can see that it's not in my best interest to bring about such a transition."

"Right now, I'd settle for a non-Miralyith fane, if that fane didn't want me dead." Makareta looked at her own feet. "Aiden, Rinald, Inga, Flynn, Orlene, Tandur—they were all killed or executed without hope of an afterlife. Flynn was kept alive by the Art as his skin was melted from his body."

Imaly nodded. The fane had decreed that all Fhrey in the capital had to witness the executions. Imaly had defied Lothian's edict, claiming illness. Having seen how he killed Zephyron of the Instarya during the challenge in the arena had been enough for her. Still, she had heard the stories. Dozens of people in the audience had become physically ill, and several had suffered nightmares for weeks afterward.

"You're the Curator of the Aquila. You have influence."

Imaly noticed fear in Makareta's eyes. What stood before Imaly wasn't a rabid dog; she was a frightened child, an orphan on Imaly's doorstep. Makareta's face was pale, her eyes outlined by dark circles. She was thinner, too. The Makareta might be able to explode a marble statue, but she was wasting away.

Where have you been hiding? What life have you led for the past year that finally drove you to me?

"I'll do whatever you want—whatever you ask. I'm actually a very skilled Miralyith." She looked at the pile of rubble that had been the statue, and with a few words and a flip of her fingers, the powder reassembled back into the likeness of Ghika, as if nothing had ever happened. "A Miralyith without a tribe, without a friend. I thought such a thing might be of value to a Nilyndd Curator of the Aquila. And, you owe me your life, sort of."

"What exactly do you want from me?"

"Right now?" Makareta licked chapped lips. "Food and a safe place to sleep. Later, maybe you could make a case for leniency? Or, perhaps convince the fane to stop looking and let me go somewhere far away where I can try to live. It's so hard to constantly block the searches. I can't even shave my head. It's disgusting." A tear slipped down the girl's cheek. "I'm—I'm only a hundred and sixteen. I'm—" She sucked in a sharp breath and squeezed her lips tight, then wiped her eyes. "I don't want my life to be over before I've had a chance to do anything. I made a mistake. I know that, and I'm sorry. We were all so swept up; it was all so—I'm sorry. I'm sorry."

She sobbed then.

Imaly let her. The girl was a manipulator, but then Imaly had spent nearly three thousand years dealing with far more savvy ones than Makareta. She got up, walked the distance between them, and put her arms around the girl, hugging back while she cried into the curator's chest.

"I'm so scared."

"You should be," Imaly said.

The sound of footfalls came from the outside steps. Makareta looked up, pleading.

"Hide behind the pillar."

The girl sprinted out of sight.

What am I doing? Harboring a fugitive—a traitor to the fane, no less!

She was still shaking her head when the Fhrey who made the noises came into view. Imaly knew him only vaguely, a face seen on occasion. She couldn't remember the name, but the uniform said everything she needed to know. He was a courier from the Talwara. In his hand, he held a dispatch.

"A message," he told her with a modest bow of his head.

"Message? From where?"

"Bird from Alon Rhist. Usually, we would let it sit, waiting for the fane's return. But it's possible the fane sent it from there, and if that is the case, it would be meant for your eyes."

She took the sealed wooden tube encased in wax and cracked it open.

The palace servant waited.

"You can go," she told him.

He obviously wanted to know what was in the message, and so he gave a look of disappointment before he pivoted and walked out.

Listening to his fading footfalls, Imaly drew forth the small bit of parchment and unrolled it. She read it three times before Makareta emerged from the shadow of the pillar and approached.

"What does it say?" the girl asked with a hopeful tone.

"It doesn't say the fane is dead," Imaly assured her. "In fact, this isn't from our forces at all. This appears to be from the enemy holding Alon Rhist."

Makareta appeared disappointed. "What *does* it say?" she repeated.

Imaly crushed the paper in her hand and smiled at the girl. "It says I could benefit from the services of an outlawed Miralyith who is willing to do whatever she's told."

Afterword

And there you have it. We've concluded another installment, and I hope you've enjoyed the tale. My name is Robin, and I'm Michael's wife. I asked him if I could write the afterword for this book, and he agreed, so here I am! Michael says I tend to proclaim *my favorite book* to be whichever novel I just finished reading. He's probably right. As we were finalizing the edits for *Age of War,* I recall I used the word *favorite* several times.

Don't get me wrong; I love *Age of Swords* (my previously self-proclaimed favorite book of the series). One of the reasons was learning more about the characters of Roan, Moya, and Gifford. I cried at the heartbreaking sacrifice of Suri, and I cheered that Persephone went off and accomplished the impossible while men in power sat around, trying to advance their ambitions. Ah, it makes me smile just thinking about those things now.

Okay, so let me bring the focus back to *this* book. What did I like so much? I'd say the number one factor is how often it pulled at my heart. I cried when Suri once more had to kill someone she loved to serve the greater good. Had she not, I'm sure it wouldn't have been possible for the Rhunes of Alon Rhist to survive. I loved Suri at the opening of *Age of Myth*, but her growth from caterpillar to butterfly is a remarkable transformation. In many ways, I can't help but see corollaries between her and Myron from the Riyria books, and as much as I loved him in *Theft of Swords*, he was even more incredible in *Heir of Novron*. But I've digressed once more.

What else . . . oh, Gifford. He's been one of my favorites since we first met. Michael writes about unlikely heroes, and no one better illustrates that point than this incredibly talented cripple. I loved that Padera's mistreatment of him paid off after all, and I was thrilled Tura's prophecy came true. But even better than those events is the moment when he finally felt Roan's embrace. How great was that?

But for me, the most significant emotional impact of the book revolved around Persephone and Raithe. Having read The Riyria Revelations, I was aware of Novron's marriage to Persephone. But I also knew that there were lies in the historical records, and I hoped history got the identity of her husband wrong. When I first read *Age of War*, I begged Michael to give Persephone and Raithe one last scene together. I wanted her to be able to confess that she did love him. It tore at my heart that he would die not knowing the truth, and she would be forever burdened with regret. Having them reunite was one piece of advice my husband didn't implement. Damn you, Michael! Instead, he added the scene at the grave, which stomped on the heart he'd already ripped from my chest. That man can be so cruel sometimes. I'm sure you feel the same way about his sadistic tendencies. Remembering it now is still difficult. I'll have to take a moment. I'll be right back.

Okay, I'm better now. So how about other things I liked. What about the revelations! I always knew that Nyphron was using the Rhunes to do his dirty work, but I never suspected that *he* orchestrated the war by an unauthorized attack on Dureya and Nadak—sneaky bastard. And then there was Malcolm! Since the ending of *Age of Myth*, we knew there was more to him than met the eye, but whether he is "good" or "evil" is a determination that eluded me. Ultimately, we still don't know at this point in the book, but it was great seeing him reveal himself (somewhat), and I loved being present while he smacked Nyphron around, taking him down a peg or two.

Well, those were my favorite moments from *Age of War.* I hope you had some as well. As Michael mentioned in his author's note, he genuinely enjoys receiving email, so if you want to drop a line with some of your favorite aspects (or things that didn't work for you), then, by all means, send an email to michael@michaelsullivan-author.com. Oh, and leaving a few comments on sites like Amazon, Goodreads, and Audible.com is always graciously appreciated. It's third-party validation like that that helps to give others the confidence to give the books a try.

In conclusion, I'd like to express that Michael and I are forever grateful for all the support you've given the books. Did you know we are coming up on Michael's tenth anniversary? Yep, *The Crown Conspiracy* was first published by Aspirations Media Incorporated in October 2008. Back then we never thought the books would earn any "real money," but the joy Michael received by writing was more than enough reward for us. Still, people have spread the word, and the Riyria books have sprouted incredible legs, and the readership for that series keeps growing. It's your continued support that makes it possible for me to forgo a day job, and that means I can help Michael get more stories out into the world. It's a rare thing to be able to do the one activity you love the most for a living, but Michael is one of those people who has become that fortunate, and it's because of you. We both thank you from the bottoms of our hearts.

Glossary of Terms and Names

Agave: The prison of the Old One, which is deep in the heart of Elan and was discovered by the dwarfs when excavating Neith. During Persephone's trek to find and destroy Balgargarath, the Agave was rediscovered.

Agave Tablets: Written by the Old One, these tablets detail the creation of the world, the secrets of various metallurgy (such as bronze and iron), and the weaves (spells) to manifest the Art into immortal creatures to do the summoner's bidding.

Aiden (Fhrey, Miralyith): One of the leaders of the Gray Cloaks, a secret Miralyith society that tried to kill the fane and raise the Miralyith's position above all other Fhrey tribes.

Airenthenon: The domed and pillared structure where the Aquila holds meetings. Although the Forest Throne and the Door predate it, the Airenthenon is the oldest *building* in Estramnadon. It was nearly destroyed during the Gray Cloak Rebellion, saved only by the efforts of Prince Mawyndulë.

Alon Rhist: The chief outpost on the border between Rhulyn and Avrlyn. Staffed by the Instarya, the fortress acts as a bulwark preventing the Rhunes from crossing into the Fhrey lands. It was named after the fourth fane of the Fhrey, who died during the Dherg War. After the death of Zephyron, rule of the Rhist was granted to Petragar.

Alward (Rhune, Nadak): The new chieftain of Nadak, one of the two clans destroyed by the Fhrey.

Alysin: One of the three realms of the afterlife. A paradise where brave warriors go after death.

Amphora: A delicate storage vessel with an oval body that tapers near its base. It has two handles near its top.

Anwir (Fhrey, Asendwayr): Quiet and reserved, he is the only non-Instarya Fhrey member of Nyphron's Galantians. He has a penchant for knots and uses a sling for a weapon.

Anyval (Fhrey, Umalyn): Healer of Alon Rhist.

Aquila: Literally "the place of choosing." Originally created as a formalization and public recognition of the group of Fhrey who had been assisting Gylindora Fane for more than a century. Leaders of each tribe act as general counsels, making suggestions and assisting in the overall administration of the empire. Senior council members are elected by their tribes or appointed by the fane. Junior members are chosen by the senior. The Aquila holds no direct power, as the fane's authority is as absolute as Ferrol Himself. However, the Aquila does wield great influence over the succession of power. It is the Curator and Conservator who determine who has access to the Horn of Gylindora.

Aria (Rhune, Rhen): Mother of Gifford who died when giving birth to the cripple.

Ariface: A rare and vicious creature.

Arion (Fhrey, Miralyith): Also known as Cenzlyor. The former tutor to Prince Mawyndulë and onetime student of Fenelyus. Arion was sent to Rhulyn to bring the outlaw Nyphron to justice and was injured when a Rhune named Malcolm hit her on the head with a rock. After partially recovering from her wounds, she fought Gryndal, a fellow Miralyith, when he threatened to destroy Dahl Rhen and kill all its residents. She now resides with the Rhunes and hopes to find a peaceful end to the conflict between Rhunes and Fhrey. During Persephone's trek to Neith, Arion was critically injured and returned to Tirre in a comatose, near death, state.

Art, the: Magic that allows the caster to tap the forces of nature. In Fhrey society, it's practiced by members of the Miralyith tribe. Goblins who wield this power are referred to as oberdaza. The only known Rhune to possess any Artistic ability is the mystic known as Suri.

Artist: A practitioner of the Art.

Arwal: Location of one of the Galantian's greatest battles. Tekchin was severely wounded there.

Asendwayr: The Fhrey tribe whose members specialize in hunting. A few are stationed on the frontier to provide meat for the Instarya.

Asica: A long Fhrey garment similar to a robe. Its numerous wraps and ties allow it to be worn in a number of configurations.

Audrey: Moya's bow, named after her mother.

Avempartha: The Fhrey tower created by Fenelyus atop a great waterfall on the Nidwalden River. It can tap the force of rushing water to amplify the use of the Art.

Avrlyn: "Land of Green," the Fhrey frontier bordered on the north by Hentlyn and by Belgreig to the south. Avrlyn is separated from Rhulyn by the east and south branches of the Bern River.

Bakrakar: Patron god of Clan Nadak. A giant stag that ensures fortunate hunting.

Balgargarath: A creature created by the Old One in retribution for his mistreatment by the elves. It rendered Neith, the homeland of the dwarfs, uninhabitable. Created by an incredibly powerful weave, it is the Art manifested into corporeal form and as such it can't be harmed by any use of magic. It was destroyed by Persephone's party by unraveling its spell after penetration of a weapon that contains its name.

Battle of Grandford: The first official battle in the war between Rhunes and Fhrey.

Battle of Mador: During the Belgric War, the battle between the Fhrey and Dherg when Fenelyus first used the Art, crushing the Tenth and Twelfth Dherg legions under a pile of rock that subsequently formed Mount Mador. The battle turned the tide of the war by stopping the Dherg advance.

Belgreig: The continent to the far south of Elan where the Dherg people reside.

Belgric War: A war between the Fhrey and Dherg. Also referred to as the Dherg War and the War of Elven Aggression.

Belgriclungreians: The term Dherg use to refer to themselves and their kind in the years after settling in Belgreig.

Bern: A river that runs north-south and delineates the border between Rhulyn and Avrlyn. Rhunes are forbidden from crossing to the west side of this river.

Black bronze: A metal alloy whose recipe—known only to the Dherg—utilizes gold, silver, and copper. It's especially important in the making of sculptures.

Book of Brin: The first known written work chronicling the history of the Rhunes. It dates back to the time of the first war between Rhunes and Fhrey.

Brazier: A shallow metal container raised off the ground that holds combustible material. Braziers are constantly tended to ensure they have a burning flame that is used as the source of cook fires by all members of a Rhune village.

Breckon mor: The feminine version of the leigh mor. A versatile piece of patterned cloth that can be wrapped in a number of ways.

Brin (Rhune, Rhen): Keeper of Ways for Dahl Rhen and author of the famed *Book of Brin*. During the giant attack on Dahl Rhen, Brin's parents, Sarah and Delwin, were killed.

Carfreign Arena: A large open-air field in Estramnadon where contests and spectacles are held. It was there that Lothian defeated Zephyron in a particularly gruesome Uli Vermar challenge.

Cenzlyor: In the Fhrey language, the term means "swift of mind." A title of endearment bestowed by Fane Fenelyus onto Arion, indicating her proficiency in the Art.

Chieftain: The leader of a given clan of Rhunes. Since the appointment of the keenig, their positions of power were decreased as the keenig rules over all Rhunic people.

Clempton: A small village of Dureya, home of Raithe (the God Killer).

Conservator of the Aquila: The keeper of the Horn of Gylindora and, along with the Curator, one of the two Fhrey most responsible for administering the process of succession. The Conservator is also responsible for picking a new Curator when needed. The current Conservator is the Umalyn high priest, Volhoric.

Council of Tirre: A coalition of Rhulyn clan leaders convened to appoint a keenig to rule over all the Rhunes and lead the battle against the Fhrey.

Crescent Forest: A large forest that forms a half circle around Dahl Rhen.

Crimbal: A fairy creature that lives in the land of Nog. Crimbals travel to the world of Elan through doors in the trunks of trees. They are known to steal children.

Curator: The vice fane who presides over the six councilors of the Aquila, elected by a vote of senior members. The Curator leads meetings of the Aquila in the absence of the fane, and chairs the Challenge Council, which decides who has the right to blow the Horn of Gylindora. Together, the Conservator and the Curator are the Fhrey most responsible for determining the succession of power and administering the Uli Vermar challenge process. The current Curator is Imaly.

Dahl (hill or mound): A Rhune settlement that is the capital city of a given clan and is characterized by its position on top of a man-made hill. Dahls are usually surrounded by some form of wall or fortification. Each has a central lodge where the clan's chieftain lives, along with a series of roundhouses that provide shelter for the other villagers. Originally there were seven Rhulyn-Rhune dahls, but two (Nadak and Duryea) were destroyed by the Fhrey and one (Rhen) was destroyed by giants.

Delwin (Rhune, Rhen): A sheep farmer who was the husband of Sarah and father of Brin. He was killed by the giant attack that destroyed Dahl Rhen.

Dherg: One of the five humanoid races of Elan. Skilled craftsmen, they have been all but banned from most places except Belgreig. They are exceptional builders and weaponsmiths. The name is a pejorative Fhrey word meaning "vile mole." The Dherg refer to themselves as Belgriclungreians.

Didan (Rhune, Dureya): One of Raithe's brothers.

Dome Mountain: Raised peak above the city of Neith, brought down by Suri and sealing the entrance to the dwarven homeland.

Door, the: A portal in the Garden of Estramnadon that legend holds is the gateway to where the First Tree grows.

Downriver Tower: One of two towers near the front of Alon Rhist, so named as it is the southernmost tower and the Bern River flows north to south.

Drome: The god of the Dherg.

Drumindor: A Dherg-built fortress located on an active volcano at the entrance to a large strategic bay on the Blue Sea. Two massive towers provide protection from any invasion from the water.

Dunn: One of the three Gula-Rhune clans. The other two are Strom and Erling.

Dureya: A barren highland in the north of Rhulyn, home to the Rhune clan of the same name. The entire region and all the clan members were destroyed by Fhrey Instarya. Before their destruction, they were the most powerful warrior clan of the Rhulyn-Rhunes. Only two Dureyans are known to survive: Raithe and Tesh.

Duryngon: A prison under the Verenthenon at Alon Rhist used to house prisoners and exotic animals that are studied to determine how best to fight them.

Dwarf: Any flora or fauna of diminutive stature (as in *dwarf wheat* or *dwarf rabbits*). Also, the name Persephone gives to the residents of Belgreig, that is easier to pronounce than Belgriclungreians and not as insulting as *Dherg*.

East Puddle: The less affluent area of the Rhen settlement in Tirre.

Eilywin: Fhrey architects and craftsmen who design and create buildings.

Elan: The Grand Mother of All. God of the land.

Elf: Mispronunciation of the Fhrey word *Ylfe,* meaning "nightmare," and a derogatory term used by the Dherg to insult the Fhrey people.

Elysan (Fhrey, Instarya): Close friend and adviser to Zephyron.

Erdo (Rhune, Erling): Chieftain of Clan Erling who took over after the former chieftain, Udgar, died in a challenge battle with Moya.

Erebus: Father of all gods as discovered by Brin in the Agave Tablets.

Eres (Fhrey, Instarya): A member of Nyphron's Galantians. His main prowess is with spears and javelins.

Erivan: Homeland of the Fhrey.

Erling: One of the three Gula-Rhune clans. The other two are Dunn and Strom.

Ervanon: One of the four Fhrey outposts manned by the Instarya to protect the frontier. It is the one farthest north.

Estramnadon: The capital city of the Fhrey, located in the forests of Erivan.

Estramnadon Academy: Also known as the Academy of the Art. The school where Miralyith are trained in the ways of magic. Entrance to it requires passage of the Sharhasa, an aptitude test.

Fane: The ruler of the Fhrey, whose term of office extends to death or until three thousand years after ascension, whichever comes first.

Fenelyus (Fhrey, Miralyith): The fifth fane of the Fhrey and first of the Miralyith. She saved the Fhrey from annihilation during the Belgric War.

Ferrol: The god of the Fhrey.

Ferrol's Law: Also known as Law of Ferrol, it's the irrefutable prohibition against Fhrey killing other Fhrey. In extreme situations, a fane can make an exception for cause, or can designate a person as exempt. Breaking Ferrol's Law will eject a Fhrey from society and bar the perpetrator from the afterlife. Since it is the Fhrey's god that will pass judgment, no one can circumvent Ferrol's Law by committing murder in secret or without witnesses.

Fhrey: One of the five major races of Elan. Fhrey are long-lived, technologically advanced, and organized into tribes based on profession.

Fhreyhyndia: The literal translation of *killer of Fhrey.* It is the name Tesh of Duryea wanted to be known by, but Raithe prohibited the boy from adopting that name.

First Chair and *Second Chair:* Honorific for the chieftain of a dahl and their spouse. Its origin comes from actual chairs that are placed on a dais in a dahl's lodge.

First Minister: The third most important person in Fhrey society (following the fane and the Curator). The primary role is the day-to-day administration of the Talwara. The present First Minister, Kabbayn, replaced Gryndal upon his death.

First Tree: Fruit from this tree is believed to grant immortality, and it's rumored to lie behind The Door in Estramnadon. The Belgric War was fought largely due to the dwarfs' belief that this treasure was being kept from them.

Five major races of Elan: Rhunes, Fhrey, Dherg, Ghazel, and Grenmorians.

Flood (Dherg): A builder, Frost's brother, and one of three Dherg responsible for unleashing Balgargarath from a complex series of noise-creating traps. To save him from execution, Persephone takes the three dwarves back to Tirre after Gronbach's broken promises.

Florella Plaza: A large public square with an elaborate fountain outside the Airenthenon in Estramnadon.

Forest Throne: The seat of the fane, located in the Talwara in the capital city of Estramnadon. Created by Caratacus, who intertwined six trees as symbols of the (then) six tribes of the Fhrey.

Forks, the: Place where the North Branch and the High Spear portions of the Bern River converge and the burial place of Herkimer, Raithe's father.

Frost (Dherg): A builder, Flood's brother, and one of three Dherg responsible for unleashing Balgargarath from a complex series of noise-creating traps. To save him from execution, Persephone takes the three dwarves back to Tirre after Gronbach's broken promises.

Frozen Tower: One of two towers near the front of Alon Rhist, so named as it is farther north and as such catches the brunt of the cold winter winds. Also, it lacks a fireplace to provide warmth.

Furgenrok (Grenmorian): Leader of the Grenmorians, the giants of Elan. He was employed by the Fhrey to attack Dahl Rhen. While many were killed, and the dahl destroyed, the ultimate goal of killing Raithe, Arion, and Nyphron failed.

Galantians: The Instarya party led by Nyphron and famed for legendary exploits of valor and bravery. Exiled from Alon Rhist for disobeying orders to destroy Rhune villages, they have joined with the Rhunes to oppose the fane.

Garden, the: One of the most sacred places in Fhrey society, used for meditation and reflection. The Garden is in the center of Estramnadon and surrounds the Door, the Fhrey's most sacred relic.

Gath (Rhune): The first keenig, who united all the human clans during the Great Flood.

Gavin Killian (Rhune, Rhen): The new Chieftain of Clan Rhen, who takes over after Persephone is appointed as the keenig.

Gelston (Rhune, Rhen): The shepherd who was hit by lightning during the giant attack on Dahl Rhen; uncle to Brin.

Gifford (Rhune, Rhen): The incredibly talented potter of Dahl Rhen, whose mother died during his birth. Due to extensive deformities, he wasn't expected to live more than a few years.

Gilarabrywn: A dragonlike creature created by Suri by sacrificing her best friend, Minna. It was created using the same spell that made Balgargarath, and as such it is the Art in corporeal form. It was crucial to the survival of Persephone's party and ultimately destroyed by Suri when it was discovered it couldn't leave the confines of Neith.

Goblins: A grotesque race feared and shunned by all in Elan, known to be fierce warriors. The most dangerous of their kind are oberdaza, who can harness the power of elements through magic. In the Dherg language, they are known as:

Ba Ran Ghazel (Forgotten Ones of the Sea)
Fen Ran Ghazel (Forgotten Ones of the Swamps)
Fir Ran Ghazel (Forgotten Ones of the Forest)
Durat Ran Ghazel (Forgotten Ones of the Mountains)

God Killer: A moniker given to Raithe of Dureya, who was the first known Rhune to kill a Fhrey (Shegon of the Asendwayr tribe). While staying in Dahl Rhen, he killed another Fhrey (Gryndal of the Miralyith).

Grand Mother of All: Another name for the goddess Elan (the world).

Grandford: The location of a great bridge that allows crossing of the Bern river. It marks the boundary between the Fhrey-held fortress of Alon Rhist and the Rhune plains of Dureya.

Gray Cloaks: A secret society of Miralyith who attempted to overthrow Fane Lothian because he wasn't doing enough to elevate the position of Miralyith over other tribes in the Fhrey society. Principal members include Aiden, its leader, and Makareta, who manipulated Mawyndulë to help them discover weaknesses in the fane's defenses.

Great War: The first war between the Fhrey people and the Rhunes.

Grenmorian: The race of giants who live in Hentlyn in northern Elan.

Grin the Brown: A ferocious bear who was responsible for the deaths of many residents of Dahl Rhen, including Mahn, Persephone and Reglan's eldest son; Konniger, former chieftain; and Maeve, the dahl's Keeper of Ways. The beast was eventually killed by Persephone.

Gronbach (Dherg): The mayor of Caric and Master Crafter of that city. He deceived and tricked Persephone into ridding Neith of Balgargarath and failed to uphold his promise to provide weapons to the Rhunes to fight the Fhrey. His treachery led to the eventual destruction of Neith by Suri. Brin's outrage with the dwarf makes him a central villain in her famed *Book of Brin*.

Grygor (Grenmorian): A member of Nyphron's famed Galantians, and the only giant of the group. Known for his love of cooking and use of spices. This fondness for the culinary arts has fostered a friendship between him and Padera, Dahl Rhen's oldest member.

Gryndal (Fhrey, Miralyith): The former First Minister to Fane Lothian. Respected as one of the most skilled practitioners of the Art, Gryndal was killed in Dahl Rhen by Raithe when the Miralyith attempted to extract retribution for the dahl harboring Nyphron and Malcolm's attack on Arion.

Gula-Rhunes: A northern alliance of three Rhune clans (Dunn, Strom, and

Erling) that have a long-standing feud with the seven southern Rhulyn-
Rhune clans. Historically the Fhrey have pitted these two sides against
each other and fostered their mutual animosity. As conflict with the
Fhrey intensified, the Gula and Rhulyn Rhunes joined forces, all serving Keenig Persephone.

Gwydry: One of the seven tribes of Fhrey. This one is for the farmers and
laborers who are responsible for raising crops and livestock.

Gylindora Fane (Fhrey, Nilyndd): The first leader of the Fhrey. Her name
became synonymous with *ruler.*

Habet (Rhune, Rhen): The keeper of the Eternal Flame, responsible for
ensuring that the braziers and the lodge's fire pit remain lit.

Haderas (Fhrey, Asendwayr): Leader of the Bear Legion, a fighting force
made up of Asendwayr and Gwydry, who were tasked with stamping
out the Rhunes.

Harkon (Rhune, Melen): Chieftain of Clan Melen.

Hawthorn Glen: Home to Suri and Tura.

Hentlyn (land of mountains): An area to the north of Avrlyn, generally
inhabited by Grenmorians.

Herkimer (Rhune, Dureya): The father of Raithe and a skilled warrior
known as Coppersword. He was killed by Shegon.

High Spear Valley: Grassy plain just south of the High Spear Branch of the
Bern River. Home of the three clans of the Gula-Rhunes.

Hopeless House: Alon Rhist residence of Gifford, Habet, Mathias, and
Gelston. So named because it housed the most unworthy of Rhen's remaining people. While not a resident (due to being female), Tressa
spends much of her time there as an honorary member.

Horn of Gylindora: A ceremonial horn kept by the Conservator that was
originally bestowed on Gylindora Fane by the legendary Caratacus.
The horn is used to challenge for leadership of the Fhrey. It can only be
blown during an Uli Vermar (upon the death of a fane or every three
thousand years). When blown at the death of a fane, it's the fane's heir
who is challenged. If the fane has no heir or if it is blown after three
thousand years of reign, the horn can be blown twice, providing for two
contestants.

Huhana Hill: Also known as Little Rhen. It is an area of Alon Rhist largely populated with former residents of Dahl Rhen. The houses there were largely abandoned after Rhunes took over the fortress.

Imaly (Fhrey, Nilyndd): A descendant of Gylindora Fane, leader of the Nilyndd tribe, and Curator of the Aquila.

Instarya: One of the seven tribes of the Fhrey. Instarya are the warriors who have been stationed on the frontier in outposts along the Avrlyn border since the Belgreig War.

Iver (Rhune, Rhen): A woodcarver and abusive slave owner; the former master of Roan and her mother, Reanna.

Jerydd (Fhrey, Miralyith): The kel of Avempartha. He led the attack on Dahl Rhen, which destroyed the village but failed to kill Arion, Nyphron, or Raithe.

Kabbayn (Fhrey, Eilywin): The current First Minister, who replaced Gryndal after his death.

Karol: The room in the Kype where the ruler of Alon Rhist hears grievances and makes judgments on those accused of crimes.

Kasimer (Fhrey, Miralyith): Leader of the newly reformed Spider Corp, a group of Artists who can combine their power for coordinated attacks.

Keenig: A single person who rules over the united Rhune clans in times of trouble. Until the appointment of Persephone during the Fhrey war, there hadn't been one appointed since the days of Gath, who saved mankind during the Great Flood.

Keenig's Council: A body of advisers to Persephone consisting of the ten chieftains of the Rhune clans.

Keeper of Ways: The person who learns the customs, traditions, and general memories of a community and is the authority in such matters. Keepers pass down their knowledge through oral tradition. The most famous Keeper is Brin from Dahl Rhen, who created the famed *Book of Brin*.

Kel: The administrator of a prestigious institution such as Jerydd, the kel of Avempartha.

Knots: Known to disrupt the natural flow of the Art, knots often create difficulty in communication and prevent consensus building. Once a knot is unraveled, so, too, are arguments unknotted, leading to eventual agreement. The knot that holds together a being created from the Art (such as Balgargarath or the Gilarabrywn) is loosed by piercing the creature with its true name.

Konniger (Rhune, Rhen): Shield to Chieftain Reglan of Dahl Rhen and husband of Tressa. Konniger ruled Rhen for a short period of time between the reigns of Reglan and Persephone after assassinating the former. He also tried to kill Persephone and was inadvertently killed by Grin the Brown.

Krugen (Rhune, Menahan): Chieftain of Clan Menahan, the richest of the seven Rhulyn clans.

Kype: The most secure building of Alon Rhist. It is used as living quarters and meeting space by Persephone, Nyphron, Suri, and Arion.

Language of creation: The root language of the gods and every living thing in Elan. The chords plucked while performing Artistic weaves taps into the language of creation, the building blocks of all living things.

Leigh mor: Great cloak. A versatile piece of fabric used by Rhune men that can be draped in a number of ways, usually belted. A leigh mor can also be used as a sling to carry items or as a blanket. Usually, they're woven with the pattern of a particular clan. The female version, known as a breckon mor, is longer, with an angled cut.

Linden Lott: The chief Dherg city after the fall of Neith. It holds an annual contest to determine the best in various endeavors valued by the Dherg people, such as building, forging weapons, and digging.

Lion Corps: Personal bodyguards to the fane.

Lipit (Rhune, Tirre): The chieftain of Dahl Tirre.

Little Rhen: The area of Alon Rhist that mainly houses Rhunes displaced from the destroyed Dahl of Rhen. The original Fhrey inhabitants left that area of Huhana Hill after the Rhunes took over the fortress.

Lothian, Fane (Fhrey, Miralyith): The supreme ruler of the Fhrey, father to Mawyndulë, son of Fenelyus. He came into power after an unusually gruesome challenge in which he defeated Zephyron of the Instarya in a humiliating and cruel display of power.

Maeve (Rhune, Rhen): The former Keeper of Ways for Dahl Rhen and mother of Suri; she was killed by Grin the Brown.

Magda: The oldest tree in the Crescent Forest; an ancient oak known to offer sage advice, including information that was instrumental in saving the village of Dahl Rhen when it was targeted by First Minister Gryndal of the Miralyith. She was killed during the Grenmorian attack on Dahl Rhen.

Mahn (Rhune, Rhen): The son of Persephone and Reglan. He was killed by a ferocious bear known as The Brown.

Makareta (Fhrey, Miralyith): A member of the Gray Cloaks and the object of Mawyndulë's first romantic crush. After the rebellion, she (nor her body) were never seen again.

Malcolm (Rhune): The ex-slave of Zephyron, former resident of Alon Rhist, and best friend of Raithe. He's attacked two Fhrey with rocks: Shegon and Arion.

Mari: The patron god of Dahl Rhen.

Master of Secrets: The adviser to the fane who is responsible for Talwara security. Vasek is the current holder of that title.

Mawyndulë (Fhrey, Miralyith): Prince of the Fhrey realm; the son of Lothian, grandson of Fenelyus, and former student of Arion and Gryndal. He was present at Dahl Rhen when Raithe killed Gryndal. For a short time, he represented the Miralyith in the Aquila as the junior councilor and later as the senior. He was duped by the Gray Cloaks into providing them aid, but was not involved in the rebellion. His action to save himself ended up saving the life of Imaly and several other Fhrey when he held the Airenthenon together.

Medak: A Galantian who was killed by Gryndal during Gryndal's attack on Alon Rhist. Younger brother to Eres.

Melen: A Rhulyn clan known for its poets and musicians, ruled by Chieftain Harkon.

Melvin (Rhune, Rehn): Deceased husband of Padera.

Menahan: The richest of the seven Rhulyn clans. Known for its wool and great sheep flocks. It's ruled by Krugen.

Merredydd: One of the four Fhrey outposts manned by the Instarya to protect the frontier. It is the one farthest south.

Meryl (Rhune): A former slave of Shegon and roommate of Malcolm.

Metis, Minister (Fhrey, Nilyndd): Highest ranking member of the Nilyndd tribe, responsible for creating weapons and armor.

Minna: A wolf and the best friend of Suri, who dubbed the animal the wisest wolf in the world. Minna was sacrificed by Suri and turned into the Gilarabrywn that fought Balgargarath.

Miralyith: The Fhrey tribe of Artists—people who use the Art to channel natural forces to work magic. Their tribe is currently in power, and due to their skill with the Art that is not likely to change in the coming future. Many of this tribe have begun to think of themselves as gods, or at least at a higher level than other Fhrey tribes, as evidenced by the recent Gray Cloak uprising.

Mirtrelyn: A building where Fhrey go to socialize, consume alcoholic beverages, sing, and tell tales. Its Rhunic translation is Land of Mirth.

Misery Rock: A large pillar of stone that rises above the Dureyan plain. A small path makes it scalable. It is an excellent spot for observing the Grandford Bridge and the entrance to Alon Rhist.

Mount Mador: A mountain conjured by Fane Fenelyus during the Belgreig War that killed tens of thousands of Dherg.

Moya (Rhune, Rhen): Shield to Keenig Persephone, who killed Udgar (Chieftain of Gula-Rhune Clan Erling). She's the first person to use bows and arrows and was the one who shot and destroyed Balgargarath. She is romantically linked to Tekchin, one of the Fhrey Galantians.

Muriel: Daughter of Erebus as discovered by Brin in the Agave Tablets.

Mynogan: The three gods of war worshipped by the Dureyans and other warrior tribes. They represent Battle, Honor, and Death.

Mystic: An individual capable of tapping into the essence of the natural world and understanding the will of gods and spirits. Both Tura and Suri are mystics from the Hawthorn Glen.

Nadak: A region in the north of Rhulyn that is home to the Rhune clan of the same name. It was destroyed by the Fhrey Instarya, and most of its residents were slaughtered.

Naraspur: The horse that Arion rode from Estramnadon to Alon Rhist. She left it at the fortress after a fall during her debut trip.

Narsirabad: A large spear from the lodge of Dahl Rhen used by Malcolm. Its name is Fhrey for "pointy."

Neith: The original home of the Dherg in Belgreig. It was an underground city and the most revered place in the Dherg culture. For thousands of years the Dherg were denied use of Neith by the Old One, who in revenge created Balgargarath to kill any who entered the city. Neith was later destroyed, buried by Suri during an emotional outburst.

Nidwalden: A mighty river that separates Erivan (the land of the Fhrey) from Rhulyn (the land of the Rhunes).

Nifrel: Below Rel. The most dismal and unpleasant of the three regions of the afterlife.

Nilyndd: The Fhrey tribe of craftsmen.

Nyphron (Fhrey, Instarya): The son of Zephyron and leader of the famed Galantians. After attacking the new leader of Alon Rhist, he was declared an outlaw. He and his Galantians found refuge in the Rhune village of Dahl Rhen. His bid to become the Rhune keenig failed since only humans can rise to that position.

Old One: Also known as "The Three." A being whom the Dherg claimed predates the gods of Elan. He was found locked deep underground in the Agave, where he wrote a number of tablets about his existence and the origin of Elan.

Orinfar: Ancient Dherg runes that can prevent the use of the Art.

Padera (Rhune, Rhen): A farmer's wife and the oldest resident of Dahl Rhen, she is known for her excellent cooking ability and for being the best healer in the dahl.

Parthaloren Falls: The massive set of waterfalls that Avempartha resides on. The rushing water provides an enormous power source to channel the Art.

Persephone, Keenig (Rhune, Rhen): Ruler of all Rhunes, former chieftain of Dahl Rhen, and widow of Reglan. She killed Grin the Brown and led a party to Neith to kill Balgargarath. When Gronbach failed to provide promised iron weapons, she tricked him into revealing the manufacturing process to Roan, who took this knowledge to the Rhune people.

Petragar (Fhrey, Instarya): The lord of the Rhist, appointed by Fane Lothian after the death of Zephyron.

Phyre: The afterlife, which is divided into three sections: Rel, Nifrel, and Alysin.

Plymerath (Fhrey, Instarya): The gate guard who was on duty the night the fane's army arrived at the outskirts of Alon Rhist.

Poric (Fhrey, Instarya): Main gatekeeper of the Kype.

Pyridian (Fhrey, Miralyith): First son of Lothian, brother to Mawyndulë, and founder of the Estramnadon Academy of the Art, now deceased.

Rain (Dherg): Perhaps the best digger of his people, he is one of three Dherg responsible for unleashing Balgargarath from a complex series of noise-creating traps. To save him from execution, Persephone takes the three dwarfs back to Tirre after Gronbach's broken promises. He is a grand-prize winner at the Linden Lott competition.

Raithe (Rhune, Dureya): The son of Herkimer; also known as the God Killer. He killed Shegon (a Fhrey Asendwayr) in retribution for his father's death, and Gryndal (a Fhrey Miralyith) when he threatened the people of Dahl Rhen. He refused the position of keenig because he felt war with the Fhrey was impossible. He is in love with Persephone, but she does not reciprocate. He was the first person to train Tesh in combat skills.

Raow: A feared predator that eats its prey starting with the face. Raow sleeps on a bed of bones and must add another set before going to sleep. A single raow can decimate an entire region.

Rapnagar (Grenmorian): The leader of a raiding party sent by the Fhrey to destroy Dahl Rhen and kill Arion, Nyphron, and Raithe.

Reanna (Rhune, Erling): Deceased mother of Roan and slave of Iver.

Reglan (Rhune, Rhen): The former chieftain of Dahl Rhen and husband to Persephone. Killed by Konniger in an attempt to usurp his power.

Rel: One of the three regions in the afterlife. The place where most people who are neither heroes or villains go when they die.

Rhen: A wooded region in the west of Rhulyn that is home to the Rhune clan of the same name. It was formerly ruled by Reglan and later his wife, Persephone. Dahl Rhen was destroyed by a Grenmorian attack initiated by Fane Lothian for harboring Nyphron of the Instarya and killing First Minister Gryndal.

Rhist: A shortened name for Alon Rhist the Frey outpost.

Rhulyn: The "Land of the Rhunes," bordered by the Frey's native Erivan to the east and the Frey outposts in Avrlyn to the west.

Rhulyn-Rhunes: The southern clans of Rhunes: Nadak, Dureya, Rhen, Warric, Tirre, Melen, and Menahan. The Rhulyn-Rhunes have been in constant conflict with the northern tribes of the Gula-Rhunes.

Rhune: One of the five major races of Elan, the race of humans. The word is Frey for "primitive," and for some, it is seen as derogatory. This race is technologically challenged, superstitious, and polytheistic. They live in clusters of small villages, and each clan is governed by a chieftain. There are two major groups of Rhunes, the Gula-Rhune from the north and the southern Rhulyn-Rhunes. The two factions have warred for centuries.

Rhunic: The language spoken by the humans who live in Rhulyn.

Rigarus (Frey, Asendwayr): Leader of the Wolf Legion, a fighting force made up of Asendwayr and Gwydry, who focus on scouting.

Roan (Rhune, Rhen): An ex-slave of Iver the Carver. An incredibly talented, emotionally scarred inventor. With the help of the Dherg, she perfected wheels and carts. She adapted the javelin and the device used to start fires to invent the bow and arrow. Thanks to Persephone, she was able to observe the Dherg process of making iron swords.

Rol: A small Dherg fortification. Rols were created throughout the frontier to provide shelter during the Belgreig War. Most have a hidden door that opens and shuts via a series of pulleys and gears and are lined with Orinfar runes to protect those inside from magical attacks.

Roundhouse: A typical Rhune dwelling consisting of a single circular room with a cone-shaped roof, usually covered in thatch.

Ryeteen: The Fhrey term for a simplistic system of markings carried over great distances by birds for limited communication. Ryeteen is also used for the keeping of itemized lists.

Sarah (Rhune, Rhen): Mother of Brin, wife of Delwin, best friend of Persephone, widely known as the best weaver in Dahl Rhen. She was killed by the giant attack that destroyed Dahl Rhen.

Sebek (Fhrey, Instarya): The best warrior of the Galantians. He uses two cleve blades named Thunder and Lightning.

Shahdi: The non-Instarya military group charged with maintaining order in Greater Erivan.

Shegon (Fhrey, Asendwayr): A hunter stationed at Alon Rhist to provide the warrior tribe with fresh meat. He was killed by Raithe after the Fhrey killed Herkimer (Raithe's father).

Shield: Also known as shield to the chieftain or chieftain's shield. The chieftain's personal bodyguard, and generally the finest warrior of a given clan.

Shrine, the: The previous living quarters of Fane Alon Rhist when he was stationed at the fort. After his death, the room remained unoccupied and has been memorialized as tribute to him.

Siegel (Rhune, Dunn): The chieftain of Clan Dunn.

Sikar (Fhrey, Instarya): An officer and patrol leader in the Instarya tribe stationed at Alon Rhist and also a former friend of Nyphron before the Galantian's desertion.

Sile (Fhrey, Asendwayr): Employed after the Gray Cloak Rebellion, he is one of two bodyguards who never leave the side of Fane Lothian. His size indicates he may have Grenmorian blood.

Speech Rock: A large stone in the lower courtyard of Alon Rhist that is generally used to give orders to soldiers before going into battle.

Spider Corps: A group of Miralyith specially trained in coordinated attacks where one Artist directs the combined power of the others in the group.

Spyrok: The tallest tower in Alon Rhist. It lies across a bridge on the far side of the Kype.

Strom: One of the three Gula-Rhune clans. The other two are Dunn and Erling.

Suri (Rhune, Rhen): The illegitimate child of Reglan, who had an affair with Maeve (Dahl Rhen's Keeper of Ways). She was left to die in the forest but was saved and raised by a mystic named Tura. She may be the only Rhune known to possess the ability to use the Art. Her best friend, a white wolf named Minna, was turned into the Gilarabrywn in the Agave of Neith. Later, Suri destroyed the entrance of Neith during an emotional outburst. Arion of the Miralyith believes Suri is the key to peace between Fhrey and Rhunes.

Synne (Fhrey, Miralyith): Employed after the Gray Cloak Rebellion, she is one of two bodyguards who never leave the side of Fane Lothian. Renowned for her quick reflexes.

Talwara: The official name of the Fhrey's palace, where the fane resides and rules.

Tegan (Rhune, Warric): The chieftain of Clan Warric.

Tekchin (Fhrey, Instarya): One of Nyphron's band of outlaw Galantians, Tekchin is a rough, outspoken warrior whose preferred weapon is a thin, narrow-bladed sword. He is romantically linked to Moya, Shield of Persephone.

Ten Clans: The entirety of the Rhune nation, comprising seven Rhulyn clans and three Gula clans.

Tesh: The orphan boy who, along with Raithe, is all that remains of the Dureyan clan. His hatred of the Fhrey has driven his intensive training.

Tet: A curse word derived from *Tetlin Witch*.

Tetlin Witch: The universally hated immortal being thought to be the source of all disease, pestilence, and evil in the world.

Tirre: Clan of Rhulyn-Rhunes. Its dahl is Located in the south of Rhulyn on the Blue Sea. They are known for salt production and trade with the Dherg. Their chieftain is Lipit.

Tirreans: Members of clan Tirre.

Torc: A rigid circular necklace that is open in the front. In Rhune society, it is a mark of leadership. The Dherg often bestow a torc as a reward for a great accomplishment.

Traitor, The: The moniker Mawyndulë bestowed on Arion for her part in First Minister Gryndal's death while aiding the Rhunes of Dahl Rhen.

Tressa (Rhune, Rhen): Widow of Konniger who was the ex-chieftain of Dahl Rhen. She is generally despised and shunned by those who know her.

Treya (Fhrey, Gwydry): Personal servant of Prince Mawyndulë.

Trilos (Fhrey, unknown tribal affiliation): A mysterious person obsessed with the Door in the Garden.

Tura (Rhune, no clan affiliation): Mentor to Suri and an ancient mystic who lived in the Hawthorn Glen near Dahl Rhen. She was most noted for her ability to predict the future.

Uberlin: Mythical source of all wickedness in Elan, believed to be the father of the Tetlin Witch.

Udgar: The former chieftain of Clan Erling of the Gula who challenged Persephone for the position of the keenig. He was defeated in one-on-one combat by Moya.

Uli Vermar (the reign of a fane): An event that occurs three thousand years after the crowning of a fane or upon his death, when other Fhrey can challenge to rule. This is done by petitioning the Aquila and being presented with the Horn of Gylindora.

Umalyn: The Fhrey tribe of priests and priestesses who concern themselves with spiritual matters and the worship of Ferrol.

Urum River: A north-south Avrlyn river west of the Bern, and the place where Raithe would like to make a new start.

Vasek (Fhrey, Asendwayr): The Master of Secrets.

Vellum: Fine parchment perfected by the Dherg for drawing maps, made from the skins of young animals.

Verenthenon: The huge domed meeting room of Alon Rhist that sits across the corbel bridge from the Kype and is used for official meetings and dissemination of orders from the leader of Alon Rhist.

Vertumus (Fhrey, Instarya): The personal assistant to Petragar.

Vidar (Fhrey, Miralyith): The senior councillor of the Aquila representing the Miralyith tribe who made Prince Mawyndulë the junior councilor. He was framed by the Gray Cloaks and removed from his position by Fane Lothian.

Volhoric (Fhrey, Umalyn): The senior councillor of the Aquila representing the Umalyn tribe. He also holds the position of Conservator of the Aquila.

Vorath (Fhrey, Instarya): A member of Nyphron's Galantians. He has taken to the Rhune custom of wearing a beard. His weapon of choice is a pair of spiked-balled maces.

Warric: One of the seven Rhulyn-Rhune clans, ruled by Chieftain Tegan.

Wolf Legion: Fhrey military, light infantry/cavalry.

Wortman (Rhune, Strom): Chieftain of Clan Strom.

Yolanda Hill: A particularly nice area of Alon Rhist populated with supporting Fhrey, such as Asendwayr, who provide game for the Instarya. There is a house there that was the former residence of Malcom and is now the current living quarters for Meryl.

Zephyron (Fhrey, Instarya): The father of Nyphron, killed by Lothian during the challenge for fane upon Fenelyus's death. Zephyron died in an unusually gruesome fashion to make a point about Miralyith superiority and the folly of challenging their rule.

Acknowledgments

I feel as if I'm starting to sound like a broken record with regard to my acknowledgments, but when you have a team of people as good as mine, why wouldn't you continue to use them? In *Age of Swords,* I dedicated the book to Tim Gerard Reynolds (the narrator for all my Riyria and Legends tales), this time I'm tipping my hat to Marc Simonetti, artist extraordinaire. Marc's covers have graced many of my books, including the French editions of *The Crown Conspiracy, Avempartha,* and *Nyphron Rising.* For the US English market, he's created covers for *Age of Myth, Age of Swords, Age of War, Hollow World, The Death of Dulgath,* and *The Disappearance of Winter's Daughter.* At the writing of this acknowledgment I've seen the new cover for *Age of Legend,* and, of course, it's as excellent as always. Marc is a master and has worked on virtually every major fantasy franchise, including the works of George R. R. Martin, Terry Pratchett, Brandon Sanderson, Patrick Rothfuss, and dozens more. Words cannot express my gratitude for his incredible contributions.

Speaking of people I've been working with for a long time, Linda Branam returns to add her copyediting talents to this book. I'm starting to lose track of how many of my books she has edited, but it's at least six and maybe seven. The great thing about Linda is that she knows how I think and, more important, knows the mistakes I commonly make. As always, she saves me from looking like a fool, and I'm grateful for that.

Once more I had a wonderful group of beta readers, both old and new. My thanks go out to Michael Jay Brunt, Jeffrey Carr, Beverly Collie, Buffy Curtis, Louise Faering, Cathy Fox, Sheri L. Gestring, Chris Haught, Craig T. Jackson, Toby Johnson, Marty Kagan, Evelyn Keeley, Nathaniel and Sarah Kidd, Amy Lesniak Briggs, Richard Martin, Jamie McCullough, Elizabeth Ocskay, Christina Pilkington, Beth Rosser, Melanie Sanderson, Jeff Schwarz, Sarah Webb, and Dick Wilkin. I'm one hundred percent positive I have THE BEST beta team on the planet, and your hard work has made the book so much better than I could have done on my own.

And this time we added something new: gamma readers! These are people with eagle eyes that looked over the book after copyediting but before it went to press. Their job was to find any last-minute typos or errors that slipped through the cracks. After so many years in the business, I'm convinced that no book is completely error free, but the gamma readers helped to get it as close to that goal as possible. I thank them for their dedication and hard work. In particular, I'd like to mention the following gamma readers by name for their outstanding contributions: Audrey Hammer, Chris McGrath, Christopher Griffin, Alex Makar, Michael DePalatis, Sarah Webb, Julian Portillo, Jennifer Strohschein, Steve Kafkas, Beverly Collie, Mark Larsen, and Brittany Hay. Audrey, Chris, and Christopher were exceptionally helpful, and I hope I haven't forgotten anyone. If I have, I'm extending my sincerest apologies.

And, of course, no acknowledgment section would be complete without mentioning Robin, whose tireless efforts have more impact on the book than anyone else's. Even as we were reading the copyedited version, she was finding some little tweaks that if made would significantly improve the book, so I bit the bullet and made the adjustments. We had tremendous "discussions" (of course I won't call them fights) over the layout of Alon Rhist, and through those talks, many errors were corrected because the town had morphed while writing the book and Robin caught the discrepancies when changes weren't incorporated throughout. An interesting side note, I built the entire citadel of Alon Rhist in Minecraft (which is about as geeky of a thing as I've ever done). If you don't know what that is, it's kind of like Legos on computers. The great thing is you get unlimited pieces. If anyone wants to see Alon Rhist, drop me an email, and I'll share a video that shows off my little creation. Okay, back to Robin. Besides all the alpha feedback, organizing the beta readers and summarizing their feedback, and the tireless help she provided during the copyediting, she also should receive the award for most improved Book of Brin entry. She was the one who wrote: *Dragons only kill you; Gilarabrywns break your heart.* Maybe for her birthday, I'll get her an engraved plaque with that line on it.

And as before, I want to thank the people at the publishers for all their help in making this book so professional. In particular, I'd like to thank Tricia Narwani, my editor; Sarah Peed, who also provided some editorial assistance; Scott Shannon, Del Rey's senior vice president and publisher; Ryan Kearney, Tricia's assistant; and Nancy Delia, the book's production editor. On the audiobook side of things, I'd like to thank Troy Juliar, who purchased the books; Andy Paris, who organized the production (and is responsible for pairing me with Tim Gerard Reynolds in the first place); Brian Sweeny, who is always a helpful hand with logistics; and Howard Bernstein, who did a fabulous job as the book's recording engineer. And, of course, Tim Gerard Reynolds, the voice of Elan. Not only does he do an incredible job with the narration but he's a genuine fan, and I think that shows in his work. Thank you, Tim, through your enthusiasm I feel as if I wrote something that touches people. I appreciate the encouragement.

With all that said, there is still one last person I want to thank, and that is you, kind reader. Thank you for buying the books, recommending them to loved ones, and writing reviews that warm my heart. I even want to thank those who have written negative comments because I've learned a lot from what you've said (probably even more than from the ones that sing my praises). I don't write books for love of money or fame. I write to tell stories that are near and dear to my heart, and while that is indeed its own reward, the satisfaction is even greater when shared with others. Thank you for making a good thing even better.

ABOUT THE AUTHOR

MICHAEL J. SULLIVAN opened the first door to his imagination with typewriter keys found in a friend's basement when he was just eight years old. Today he uses computer keys, writing classic fantasy with unlikely heroes, including the bestselling Riyria novels and his latest epic, the Legends of the First Empire.

riyria.com
Facebook.com/author.michael.sullivan
Twitter: @author_sullivan

ABOUT THE TYPE

This book was set in Fournier, a typeface named for Pierre-Simon Fournier (1712–68), the youngest son of a French printing family. He started out engraving woodblocks and large capitals, then moved on to fonts of type. In 1736 he began his own foundry and made several important contributions in the field of type design; he is said to have cut 147 alphabets of his own creation. Fournier is probably best remembered as the designer of St. Augustine Ordinaire, a face that served as the model for the Monotype Corporation's Fournier, which was released in 1925.